Harvest Moon Misfortune

Copyright © 2023 by London Lovett

All rights reserved.

No part of this book may be reproduced in any form or by any electronic or mechanical means, including information storage and retrieval systems, without written permission from the author, except for the use of brief quotations in a book review.

ISBN: 9798863497358

Imprint: Independently published

HARVEST MOON MISFORTUNE

FROSTFALL ISLAND
COZY MYSTERY SERIES

LONDON LOVETT

one

A SPRINKLE of sun on the horizon provided the perfect light for my painting. My hand flew back and forth across the paper like a broom whisking along a dusty floor. My model, a personal favorite, was a 40-foot-tall silky sassafras tree. How could anyone not love a tree named *silky sassafras*? There was fun in every syllable. My timing was perfect. The tree's distinctive three-lobed leaves were in the middle of their color change from banana yellow to crimson red. As was always the case in my nature-bound art studio, I was racing against the light. Once the sun lifted higher, the shadows, the colors and the groggy state of the tree would change entirely.

    I plunged my brush into the cup of water, pressed it into the tray of watercolors and picked up a good amount of red and brown. The result was perfectly blended smears of rust for the tips of the leaves. A dab more brown and I could add the dimension I needed to the craggy trunk.

Huck's bark echoed off Calico Peak. We'd traveled especially far for our morning walk, all the way to the top of Calico Trail and on to North Pond where the tree had sat for probably 40-plus years. The sassafras tree was an old friend and regular model. He never seemed to mind sitting for long periods of time while I caught all the different colors and lines of his handsome silhouette. I made a point of painting his portrait at least once during each of the four seasons. His fall sitting was always my favorite.

Huck barked again. I glanced around and found him staring out toward the landscape at nothing in particular. At least, that's what I thought until his tail began gyrating like a helicopter blade and his single, loud bark became a series of excited yelps. He only chirped like a puppy for one person. A little spark of joy shot through me. I started to clean up my paints. Nate had gone for a run around the island. He knew I was hiking up to the old sassafras tree.

I poured out the brush water and snapped shut the tray of paints, then dropped everything into my bag. A breeze pushed a ghostly whistle through the leaves of the sassafras. It pushed a strand of hair across my face. As I flicked it back, something made me pause. A shiver ran up my spine, but it wasn't from the cold. I pushed back the sleeve of my sweater. Goosebumps. I shook myself to get rid of the creepy feeling. I was still out of sorts by the time Nate and Huck reached me, but seeing both of their enthusiastic smiles made me feel instantly better. Nate hadn't missed the few seconds before though. He must have been an excellent detective because he never missed anything. He scrutinized me with a look of concern.

"What's wrong, Anna?"

I forced a smile. "Nothing. Sorry. It's just a breeze kicked up, and I thought it messed up my picture, but all is good." I was a terrible liar. And darn if his detective instincts didn't also make him an expert at detecting lies.

He stepped closer, as usual, disarming me with his navy blue gaze. "You are the worst liar on the planet."

I wriggled a little and added a chin lift. "How do you know? Have you met all the liars on the planet?"

"And now, you're trying to change the subject with your overall cuteness." He splashed on a smile that, for a second, made me forget the rest of the world existed.

I smiled back and moved closer. "How dare you accuse of me of weaponizing my cuteness, sir."

He laughed and leaned over to kiss me. My "moving closer" maneuver worked.

Huck barked again, something he did whenever he wanted to be included. Only this time, he'd trotted off toward the trail. The big dog, a chaotic mix of shepherd and wolfhound, stared into the surrounding landscape. The hair stood up on his nape, and his ears and tail were at attention. The creepy feeling returned. An involuntary shiver followed.

Nate's face snapped my direction. "See, something is bothering you." Nate gave me *the* look, the one that said *out with it, Anna.*

"It's ridiculous and it will sound silly."

"Anna—" he prodded.

"Fine. I was painting, and, for a second, it felt like someone was watching me. See, it's silly."

Nate looked back at Huck. The dog barked once more, then wagged his tail and spun back in our direction. I nudged him with my bag of art supplies. "Let's head back. I need to make breakfast. Hash browns and eggs today." Nate had joined my family of boarders at the Moon River Boarding House a little more than a year ago. Since then, we'd grown *extremely* fond of each other.

Nate dropped the subject. The topic of food always helped. He patted his stomach. "That run made me hungry."

We reached Calico Trail. The vibrant colors of fall were always the last splashes of nature on the island before the frosty white mantle of winter swept in to shut everything down with a layer of snow. Knowing that winter was around the corner always made me appreciate autumn more. (Not that there wasn't already a lot to appreciate with its snappy, scented breezes and flurry of fiery colors.) Knowing the entire island would soon be shrouded in an icy blanket made me want to savor and enjoy every fall day.

"As a kid, this was my favorite time of year," Nate said.

"Let me guess—" I turned slightly his direction as we walked. "Halloween."

"Jeez, I forgot about Halloween. I was thinking about jumping my BMX bike into piles of freshly raked leaves and getting kites stuck in trees. But you're right—Halloween. Boy, I loved to put together scary costumes. The gorier the better. I once showed up to the school parade as a zombie. I was holding a plastic arm that I covered in fake blood. I asked people to shake my hand and then I'd let go of the arm. I thought it was the coolest thing ever. The school principal, not so much. He made me put the arm in my backpack. Got fake blood all over my lunch."

"I'll bet you were quite the rascal back in those days."

"Rascal was one way to put it. Let's just say, the school principal and I had lots of conversations. Far more than either of us wanted. Hey, did I tell you? Arlo called me last night."

Nate's friend, Arlo, had come to stay at the boarding house a few days before he started his training for the FBI. Nate and Arlo had worked together on the police force. I was sure Arlo's move to the big league, the Feds, would spark Nate's desire to join him. It was always a worry for me that Nate would get bored of living on an island and return to the mainland to get back to his original career. He'd been a little forlorn after Arlo's departure, and while he never said it out loud, I knew he was thinking about all the action and adventure he was missing. For now though, Nate seemed perfectly content on Frostfall Island. He had a good job working on the restoration of the island's two lighthouses, and he was happy living at the boarding house. It was all I could ask for.

"What did he have to say?" I asked.

Nate stooped and picked up a stick, which he promptly threw for Huck. Huck ran after it but got sidetracked by a squirrel. "That dog is the worst fetcher in the world, and before you ask, I haven't met all the fetchers in the world. But I still stand by my assessment." Huck helped punctuate the opinion by literally running over the stick to go after the squirrel. Nate smiled smugly at me.

"Well, if you were a dog, you'd choose the furry, squirmy little thing over a dead stick every time. How is Arlo doing?" I hoped he'd say terrible and that he hated it, but it wasn't to be.

"He loves it," Nate said. "Guess bootcamp was a soul-crushing experience. His words, not mine, but then Arlo tends to exaggerate."

"Considering that is coming from a man who easily tossed about *worst on the planet* and *in the world* comparisons, I'll assume Arlo is a tall tale expert."

Nate laughed. "Jeesh, you use a little exaggeration and you're branded a sensationalist for life."

"That's even more exaggeration," I added. "So, Arlo likes it, eh?"

"He hasn't done anything too exciting yet. It's like when you first join the force. Or any job, for that matter. If you're at the bottom of the ladder, the people on the higher rungs don't let you forget it, and they're happy to step on your head to put you in your place. But he's loving it." For a second, Nate gazed out toward the ocean. I wondered if he was putting himself in Arlo's place.

I'd been working hard to shore up my emotions, reminding myself every day that Nate might pack up and kiss me goodbye forever. It was hard. I assumed I was extra sensitive because of losing my husband, Michael, all those years back. Michael sailed out on his fishing boat one morning and never returned. You'd think I'd have learned my lesson.

Instead, I allowed myself to fall head-over-heels for the man walking next to me. Now, I'd have to live with the consequences of giving away my heart, yet again. As I thought it, Nate took hold of my hand. I'd grown to love his firm, callused grip. For now, I wasn't going to let "what-ifs" ruin my mood. A gorgeous fall had settled on the island, and the overall spirit on Frostfall and in the Moon River Boarding House was pleasant and peaceful. With any luck, it would stay that way.

two

A BUTTERY AROMA rose from the pan as I flipped a chunk of golden brown hash browns over. Nate had gone up to shower and get ready for work. Tobias hadn't returned from his morning swim yet. Opal was pacing around in her room. (It was directly above the kitchen.) My sister, Cora, was taking her usual 30-minute bath, and Winston was in the laundry room, our makeshift home for a seagull that had been battered by a storm at sea. The smell of the bird's raw fish breakfast overtook the smell of hash browns until Winston walked out and closed the laundry room door. I must have been making a crinkly, raw-fish-smell face.

"Sorry about that, Anna. I'll be taking the gull with me this morning. We finally made room for him at the sanctuary. Not that he'll need the room long. He's already improved." Winston had a mop of yellow, wavy hair and brown eyes that always sparkled with energy and youth. He was especially happy now that he was dating his longtime crush, Alyssa.

She ran the Frostfall Wildlife Rescue where Winston worked. From what I could tell, things were getting serious. And since they were both dedicated to the rescue and to the animals they helped, neither of them had to worry about the other getting bored of island life. Boy, my pity party was going overtime this morning. I needed to shut it down.

Winston went upstairs to wash. The kitchen door opened, and brisk air followed Tobias inside. His face was red from the cold ocean swim. "It's great out there today," he said.

I laughed. "I'll have to take your word for it, Toby, because I can't imagine ever jumping into that ocean in October."

"It's the most invigorating thing you'll ever experience." Tobias sniffed the air. "Hmm, hash browns. I'll be right back down. Worked up an appetite."

Opal passed him as he left the kitchen. She walked straight to the coffeepot. "How does that man do it?" she asked. "I find it hard to step into a hot shower in the morning. I can't imagine jumping into the ice cold Atlantic... at any time of day, for that matter."

"I'm with you," I said. "But then, the man is in his fifties and has the physique of a 20-year-old."

"Good point." She sighed as she sat down with her coffee. "What I wouldn't give to be my gorgeous, 20-year-old self again."

Nate stepped into the kitchen as she said it. He squeezed her shoulders affectionately. "You're still gorgeous, Opal." He'd come so far since he first arrived at the island, a depressed, broken man drowning in the knowledge that he'd failed to catch a serial killer. The same killer, nicknamed the

Pillow Talk Killer because he covered his victims' heads with a pillowcase and left messages in lipstick on their mirrors, was still menacing the mainland. Several months ago, he claimed another victim. It nearly sent Nate back into his broken shell. And once again, in his usual pattern, the notorious killer had gone silent afterward. No new murders (thankfully), only it left the investigators standing at the start of a cold dead end. It was brilliant and diabolical. Each brutal murder was followed by complete silence.

The buttery aroma drifting through the old house brought everyone down to the kitchen in record time. Winston was usually in a hurry to get to work and to Alyssa, but he stuck around a little longer this morning to eat eggs and hash browns. I handed Tobias his special plate where the eggs and hash browns didn't touch. He set to work oversalting everything. At first, I was insulted by his salt habit, deciding it was a reflection on my cooking. But I came to realize it was just one of his various quirks. He insisted once, when we all watched in awe as he salted a soup that I had already oversalted (In my defense, Nate had come into the kitchen and kissed my neck while I was in the middle of pouring in the salt and well... enough said.) that he had burned off his taste buds as a kid and that was why he always had to salt everything heavily. It was an understatement to be sure. I had to keep big containers of salt in my pantry just to keep up with his salt habit. Surprisingly, it never seemed to affect his blood pressure. I figured those vigorous morning swims counteracted the sodium intake.

My sister was extra shiny this morning in a white angora

sweater that was adorned with thousands of tiny white pearls. She'd let me know that I was not to give her a plate with greasy hash browns and eggs. She insisted on one hard-boiled egg with a plain piece of toast. She was now staring at everyone else's plates piled high with crispy potatoes and butter drenched biscuits.

"Are you sure I can't at least get you a biscuit?" I asked as I sat down to my own plate.

She was shaking her platinum hair before I could finish. "Nope. I'm planning to wear my black leather pants to the harvest moon celebration on the wharf." Every three years, Frostfall hosted an event to celebrate the harvest moon. For some unexplained reason, the celebration had become a "can't miss" event for wealthy boaters on the east coast. It was far from a lavish event, but they flocked here in their high-dollar pleasure boats to join in the celebration. "There are already numerous expensive boats arriving in the marina. I'm looking forward to meeting all the visitors." Cora picked up the dry slice of toast and broke off a small piece. Cora had been married twice, both times to billionaires who were literally taking some of their last breaths (one even had an oxygen tank painted black to go with his wedding tux.) Both marriages ended exactly as one would expect, with the new, beautiful bride weeping crocodile tears at her groom's funeral before being hastily shooed off the estate by the groom's previous family.

"You mean the *rich* visitors," Opal teased as she added a spoonful of honey to her biscuit.

"I didn't say that, but if the visitor happens to be captain of a 50-foot yacht, then I'm certainly not going to ignore him, am I?"

"I like her philosophy," Nate mused. "Anna, these potatoes really hit the spot. By the way, I don't remember this harvest moon event last year."

Tobias cleared his throat, signaling he would explain the matter. He loved to dole out information when it was something he knew a great deal about. "A harvest moon is the full moon closest to the autumnal equinox. It usually occurs in September, but every three years it lands in October, like this year. About 15 years ago, Frostfall became the unofficial meeting place for boaters to gather during the harvest moon. Naturally, we took advantage of it by turning it into a celebration of sorts, complete with a dance, good food and all-around revelry."

"And that is why I'm taking my leather pants out of hibernation," Cora stated as she picked up the dry piece of toast. "And since there are no decent tailors on the island to—well—to make them fit better, I'm avoiding potatoes and butter and—"

"Everyone, I'm making a chocolate cake for Toby's birthday," I interjected. Everyone but Cora cheered. Sometimes, I still enjoyed being the bratty little sister. Growing up, I'd lived through so many of Cora's nutty, restrictive diets, they became a source of entertainment for me. Things hadn't changed much, it seemed.

"You're doing that just to be mean," Cora said with a haughty little wriggle that caused all the shiny beads on her sweater to shimmy.

"You're right," I said. "I'm sorry, Tobias. You'll need to change the date of your birthday so it lines up better with Cora's black leather pants."

Everyone laughed.

"Sure, make fun, all of you. When one of those yacht owners falls madly in love with me and my leather pants, I won't invite any of you to the wedding."

Opal was smiling into her plate of food. "Well, darn."

"Guess if there's going to be a dance at this thing, I'd better pull out my dancing shoes." Nate winked at me over his forkful of eggs. "But I have to warn you"—he was talking directly to me—"I don't come with a yacht. Or a boat of any kind."

Everyone laughed. I loved these meals when everyone was around the table, enjoying the food and the conversation. Even Cora didn't mind the teasing, but that was because she was solely focused on meeting a rich man this weekend. And knowing my sister, she'd do exactly that. My only worry was that she'd marry again and leave the island. I was getting used to having my sister around. I hated the thought of her leaving. And there I was again, worried about my wonderful little Moon River family finding their way out into the world. I needed to shake the worry for good. It was going to be a big, busy weekend on the island, and I didn't want to miss any of it.

three

SERA BUTTERPOND'S WONDERFUL SHOP, Tea, Tarts and Tittle-tattle (better known as the 3Ts), was the purest definition of fall this morning. Pumpkin spices, heavy with clove and nutmeg, punctuated the air with an energetic zip. Sera had replaced the silk rose garlands that were normally draped around the shop with silk autumn leaf garlands. A cluster of mini pumpkins, orange, white and gold sat in the center of each table. She'd even ordered special full moon napkins for the upcoming celebration.

I'd eaten far too much breakfast at home but managed to nibble down one of her freshly baked pumpkin tarts. It was topped with a brown sugar crumble and a dollop of fresh whipped cream.

"Seconds?" Sera asked as she stepped out of the kitchen with a new tray of tarts.

"My mind and heart are saying yes, but my stomach says don't even try it. But I will take one and walk it over to

Tobias's office. He loves your pumpkin tarts and it's his birthday."

"I'll box one up for him." Sera's gaze shot to the door. She leaned over the counter to lower her voice. "There are some fancy boats this year. Word is really getting around in wealthy social circles."

I glanced over my shoulder without turning on the stool. A man and a woman in expensive matching attire—periwinkle blue coats with brass buttons and pristine white slacks—headed to one of the back tables. He was carrying his captain's hat in his hand, and she had a Gucci handbag that was decorated with silver anchors.

I turned back to Sera. "Do not expect my sister to be on top of her game this weekend. She sees men in yachting attire and suddenly dollar signs cloud her eyes and wedding bells plug her ears."

Sera nodded along. "She already warned me not to give her too many tasks because she was going to be busy with a task of her own, landing her next billionaire. I warned her there might only be millionaires out there in the marina. I can't imagine billionaires spend much time at these quaint events."

"They *are* at a whole different level of living, aren't they? I can't imagine having a million, let alone a billion, but I know my sister. She will not lower the bar. Although, if someone's fortune is in the hundreds of millions and they're willing to shower her with diamonds and new cars, she'd probably consider it."

We had a good laugh. "Speaking of Cora, where is she this

morning? We're starting to get busy."

"If I know my sister, and, trust me, I do, she's taking the very long way to work by circling the marina first to check out the boats and their respective captains."

Sera shook her head as she handed me the box with the pumpkin tart.

"Excuse me, excuse me, we'd like some service, please." It was the matching periwinkle blue customers.

"Rich people," Sera muttered as she walked past me.

I finished my tea, picked up the tart box, waved to Sera and headed out the door. It was a fabulous fall day, and the weather app on my phone promised more of the same. It would have been disappointing to have clouds or fog block out the harvest moon. It was always a majestic and other-worldly sight to see in a clear night sky.

I headed toward Molly's produce stand to pick up some potatoes for Tobias's birthday dinner. He loved my scalloped potatoes, and since we'd adopted a vegetarian lifestyle at the house due to Winston's various needy critters visiting from time to time, I'd fill in the rest of the meal with a hearty chopped salad, roasted carrots and fresh baked rolls. Molly was helping a man in a white chef's coat and pants. I sensed by the scowl she was wearing that the man was being extra picky about the produce. He was actually weighing carrots on his palm and turning them over several times. Even then, he put two back and picked up two more. If there was one thing Molly hated it was someone handling the produce and then putting it back. As her frequent customer, I was not a fan of it either. It was obvious the man was a personal chef on one of the big boats. I waited for him to finish his finicky produce purchase. I certainly didn't want to get in the way of perfection or be the cause of a snooty yacht owner ending up with mismatched carrots on his plate. Molly kept shooting me secret eye rolls.

I glanced out at the harbor. It was filled with anchored boats. The bigger luxury boats were mostly moored in slips. Boat owners who usually kept their vessels in the marina, including some of our local fishermen, had anchored offshore. They'd rented their slips out for exorbitant prices for the weekend. Aside from the posh boats, everyday pleasure boats and their far less snooty owners had also arrived for the event. Massive, elegant luxury yachts, some over 40 feet long with upper decks and lower decks and all the amenities in-between, filled the marina. It was a sea of sparkling white fiberglass and glossy brown teak. I was certain if I looked close enough I'd see my sister strutting around, catching her $2,000 heels between the planks of the pier.

After a great deal of scrutiny, the chef managed to pick a dozen carrots and four large onions. It was a lot of work for two vegetables. I could only imagine the time and effort that went into picking out lobster or salmon.

The chef walked away, and I joined Molly under her umbrella. She'd replaced her usual rainbow-colored umbrella with one that had witches flying past a bright yellow moon. "Can you believe that?" she asked. "How do these people get through their day if each carrot has to be perfect? By the way,

I saw your sister scurry toward the marina. I suppose she's hoping to meet one of the persnickety yacht owners."

"I'm sure she's already picking her wedding colors and dress. Cora has one motto in life—if he doesn't come with a yacht, then he's not worth knowing."

Molly laughed. "You've got to admire a woman who sticks to her guns and knows exactly what she wants. Unlike that silly chef and his vegetables. He put back one of those carrots and then picked it back up, not even realizing it was the same one he'd just put down. Somehow, it was better on the second round. They're all so fake and ridiculous. I love this event, but each time, it brings in a more pretentious crowd."

Frannie Bueller's tugboat ferry was already parked at the dock as I reached the produce stand. Fran walked over to join the conversation. "I've never seen so many multi-million-dollar vessels in one location. My humble little *Salty Bottom* looks like a relic from a tin can factory next to those sleek white yachts."

"And we love *Salty Bottom* for her humbleness," I said. "She provides a service. Those fancy boats probably only leave their slips once or twice a year to cruise the Caribbean or float aimlessly around the Mediterranean."

"I'll remind her of that. I could swear she was chugging along sluggishly after she caught sight of those modern beauties. Sure would love to take one of those 50-footers around the harbor. I'll bet they float like they're riding over soft cream."

"I noticed they were getting the decorations up on the wharf," Molly said. "And they're setting up the dance floor and speakers. The weather is going to cooperate too. It'll be a touch brisk, but not a cloud in the sky. That harvest moon is going to shine down on the whole harbor." Molly winked and smiled. "Will you be bringing your fine gentleman friend to the dance, Anna?"

I laughed. "Fine gentleman friend? It sounds like you just stepped off the movie set of *Gone with the Wind*. That said, Nate did mention something about pulling out his dancing shoes. I think we might make an appearance."

"Well, count me out," Frannie said. "I'm married to a man with two left feet who is under some strange illusion that he's Fred Astaire. He insists on dancing, only he spends so much of the dance stomping on my feet, I end up having to soak 'em in a tub of ice. Not worth the pain."

"But you should come out anyhow," Molly said. "There's going to be a lot of tasty food, and Sera said she was making apple and pumpkin pies to sell on the wharf." Molly wiggled her nose. "In fact, I think she might be baking them right now. I smell cloves and nutmeg."

I lifted the box I was holding. "That's a pumpkin tart. I'm going to walk it over to Toby's office. These are his favorite."

"Is he going to salt them?" Frannie asked, and both women snickered. They'd each been to dinner at my house enough to have witnessed Tobias's salting event.

"He doesn't usually salt his desserts. I guess I'll see both of you soon. If you see my sister sailing off on a yacht without so much as a farewell, send me a text. That way I won't call out a search party." It sounded like I was joking, but it wasn't that farfetched when it came to Cora.

I didn't get two feet before I got a text from Sera. "Are you still near the marina? Can you please find your sister? It's getting crowded, and I need her to serve."

"I'm near the marina. I'll go look for her, but if she's already found her million-dollar target, you're on your own."

four

MY SISTER HAD a special laugh when it came to men. It was fluttery and flirtatious, a sound that made it seem as if she was laughing for the very first time in her life at something he said. She had a magical way of making any man caught in her viewfinder feel special. And most men ate it up like a hot fudge sundae, or, in this case, buttered lobster and French wine.

Cora's special laugh and the sparkly sweater made it easy to find her. She was standing at the bow of a shiny white, chrome and glass pleasure boat that was at least 30 feet long. It was a sleek, new model with a low profile for swift movement across the sea. It was not even nine in the morning, but she was holding a fluted champagne glass in her long fingers. Her pearly pink nails glistened in the sunlight bouncing off the shiny boat. The man, who was already completely taken in by the gorgeous woman standing on his boat, looked to be 40-something with curly hair that he kept smoothing down. A thick gold chain hung around his neck, and an equally thick gold watch was fastened around his wrist. A ring with a big blue stone was jammed on his stubby pinky finger. The clothes he had on made it seem as if he was trying very hard to look like old money but doing a terrible job of it. The periwinkle blue couple in the tea shop oozed old money, but this guy was new to the realm of the rich. The oversized jewelry was a dead giveaway. Fortunately, Cora didn't care if the money was old or new as long as it was there and readily available to keep her closet filled with designer clothes and shoes.

The stinker side of me wanted to yell up to her, reminding her she needed to get to work slinging tarts at the tea shop. She was dressed to the nines, and her watch was more bejeweled than King Tut's sarcophagus. Chances were, the new money man didn't have well-oiled radar to let him know he was flirting with a gold digger and not some rich-since-birth debutante. Most men couldn't see past the blinding glare of my sister's beauty and the charm she could turn on with the velocity of a fire hose. They were generally rendered senseless within 10 minutes after meeting her, and from the way the man grinned at her and laughed at everything she said, I'd say that this guy was already smitten.

An overdone bout of laughter that resulted in Cora accidentally spilling champagne on her angora sweater gave me an opening. The man hurried into the cabin to get a napkin.

I cleared my throat loudly. Cora heard it but couldn't see me down on the dock. "Cora," I finally called up to the boat.

She came to the side and peered down. She just as quickly

glanced back to make sure the man was still below in the cabin. "What are you doing here?" she hissed.

"I'm here to remind you that a certain boss would like her employee to join her at the tea house." I spoke just loudly enough for her to hear me without broadcasting it all over the marina.

"I'm having such a good time. He's so nice. His name is Ansel Dell. Isn't that a great name?"

"He's working the 'I'm a rich man' angle pretty hard with all that jewelry."

Cora waved her hand angrily. "Shh, he'll hear you." I heard his deep voice up on deck.

Cora pulled away from the railing. I could still hear their conversation. "Oh, don't worry about this ole thing," Cora said. I could only assume she was talking about the sweater. "You know, Ansel, honey, I would love to stick around longer, but I promised to meet a friend for coffee. Are we still on for later?"

"You bet, honey. Just stop by the boat, and we'll take it from there."

I didn't want to be caught standing around, so I moved back toward the boardwalk. Cora's heels clicked behind me as she caught up to me. "He's so nice. Did I tell you his name is Ansel Dell?" Her hair was windblown, and her cheeks were pink from the champagne.

"You mentioned it. Is he related to the Dell computer family? Actually, is there a Dell family?"

"No idea." Cora picked up her pace, now realizing Sera

was going to be plenty angry about her being so late to work. I hurried to keep up with her clickety-clack heels.

"So, what does Ansel Dell do?" I asked.

She shrugged. "I think he said investments or something like that."

"Vague but then it doesn't matter, does it? As long as he's rich."

Cora clucked her tongue. "Here you go again with that nonsense."

I stopped and looked at her. She paused, too, and parted her heavily glossed lips in question. "You literally only like men who are rich. Or did I miss, somewhere in your dating history, the guy who lived in a small rustic cabin and sold pottery out of his back shed?"

She smiled and kept walking. "Specific but there was no such cabin dwelling potter. It just so happens I end up meeting guys who have money."

I laughed so hard it caught people's attention.

"Laugh all you want. Ansel could be the one."

"The third one, you mean. Isn't he a little, you know, how shall I put it—a little too alive? You prefer them to be on walkers and oxygen tanks. Ansel might even be younger than you."

It was her turn to laugh, only it was done with much more finesse, something she learned while sitting through dull, staid luncheons with other billionaires' wives. "I'm sure he's not younger." She looked over at me. "Do you think he is?"

"Possibly and he's also not old money."

"I noticed that too." She wriggled with excitement, causing all the beads on her sweater to vibrate. "That means no massive family in his history waiting to kick me out of the estate with just the clothes on my back."

I shook my head. "You really have this all figured out already. You're ready to leave your little sister just like that. Off into the sunset with Ansel and his new money without looking back."

This time she stopped. "Aw, you're upset I'll leave. That's so cute."

"Who else will I tease and play pranks on if you're gone? But maybe we're getting ahead of ourselves. I wouldn't order that dress quite yet. So far, you've only had a short conversation with the man. What if he doesn't even own the yacht? Maybe his boss let him borrow it for a weekend," I suggested.

Cora walked along with her chin lifted. "I'm not going to let you spoil this. I haven't been this excited about a new acquaintance in a long time. And I haven't ordered any dress. Although, I do have one in mind. It's got mother-of-pearl sequins on the bodice and a tiny row of real diamonds running along the décolletage. I saw it online at a shop in Paris."

"Whatever you say, Princess Cora, but for now, you'd better pull on that linen apron so you can serve tea and tarts. By the way, you're late, and it's crowded in the shop."

Cora paused and bit her lip. "Sera's going to be mad, isn't she?"

"I doubt she'll be giving you a hug and a round of applause."

Cora looked distraught for about two seconds before she shrugged. "Oh well, I have a good excuse for being late. And if this works out with Ansel, then I'll be turning in my two-week notice."

"Again, Cora, don't order that dress yet. Ansel could turn out to be a toad that, even when kissed, still stays a toad."

"You're so cynical, Anna. Besides, I can't order the dress. It costs 50 thousand dollars."

"Maybe you'll get some really good tips today," I called to her.

She waved without looking back. The pumpkin tart had been on quite a journey already. I needed to deliver it to Tobias and get home to bake his cake. I had a good laugh about my eccentric sister all the way to Toby's office. Of course, crazier things had happened. Especially when they revolved around Cora.

five

TOBIAS LIKED HIS CAKE EXTRA-CHOCOLATY. Maybe he really did have muted taste buds. I had a canister of specially processed Dutch cocoa that made any cake or brownie that much richer. It had been some time since I used it. In the meantime, the can had gotten pushed to the back of the top pantry shelf. I carried the stepladder out from the laundry room. It was still in disarray from our winged visitor, but Winston would clean it up when he got home. I shut the door and carried the stepladder to the pantry cupboard.

Even on the stepladder, I had to get on tiptoes and reach blindly around, stretching my fingers as far as they could go. My fingertips hit cold, smooth metal. With some concentration and a lot of fingertip dexterity, I managed to slide the can forward. I grabbed hold of it and carried it down from the shelf. It wasn't the cocoa can. It was an old coffee can, Uncle Joe's dark roast, Michael's favorite brand. It had an incredibly rich aroma, and Michael would brew it extra strong. I couldn't drink it. I joked once that it was as close to drinking tar as I'd ever come. Still, that was the way he liked it. I took the can down. The contents shook. It wasn't coffee though.

I walked to the counter and set the can down. After our first newlywed's quarrel, some silly argument over whether or not to paint the porch, I cleaned the empty can. I told Michael every time one of us was grumpy with the other, the *grump* would have to put a five-dollar bill in the can. Once it was full, we'd buy something special with the money. I opened the lid.

There was still a smidgen of coffee aroma left behind even though I'd cleaned the can out. The can was empty except for three quarters and a folded piece of paper.

My hands trembled for a second. I balled my fingers into fists and then opened them. I lifted out the note and opened it. My heart instantly skipped a beat when I saw Michael's familiar handwriting. It was surprisingly neat and academic looking. "I'm sorry, Anna" was all it said. We'd had plenty of grumpy moments in our short time together. By my calculations there should have been at least $100 inside the can. I'd never touched it. I'd forgotten all about the can and the money until now when I snatched it off the top shelf.

The kitchen door opened. Salty sea air rushed in ahead of a salty-looking lighthouse builder. Nate had pulled on a cap, but his thick hair was sticking out in every direction. His tanned skin was covered with a light-coating of sand. Huck jumped up and raced across the floor to greet him.

I stuck the note in my apron pocket and pushed aside the empty coffee can. "You're home."

"That I am." Nate was on one knee rubbing Huck behind the ears. "We were working up high on scaffolding when a very insistent, harsh, onshore wind kicked up. It didn't seem to be stopping anytime soon, so they gave us the rest of the day off." He lifted up his tin lunch pail. "I've still got lunch, but I'm going to shower first." He glanced at the counter and all the cake ingredients. "Think you'll have time to walk down to the marina and look at the boats? I don't get many afternoons off."

"Sure, after I get the cake baked. It has to cool before I can frost it."

"Yum, frosting," he muttered as he left the kitchen.

I was glad he left to shower. I needed a few minutes to collect myself. I pulled the note out again. When was it written? Why didn't he tell me he was short on cash? For months the catches weren't great. It was another source of tension between us. I wanted to go back to work to help out. I even suggested getting the boarding house started again, but he was adamantly against it. He didn't want strangers in the house, and he hated the notion of me traveling to the mainland every day. I didn't love the idea either, but he was stressed about finances, and I had an easy fix. Before we got married, I'd made good money in the financial world, and I could have easily found a job. But Michael fought against it, so I gave up on the idea, leaving our financial burdens for him to shoulder alone. Had it really gotten so bad that he needed to take our special grumpiness stash? For so long, I'd mourned his loss and the tragic end to what I considered a blissful marriage. But slowly, as some of the grief was peeled away by time, I was able to look back with a clearer head. Michael's coldness for the last months before he disappeared had been easy to push out of the way. Now, those last months were back with crystal clarity. Then, there was the wedding photo. A woman from his distant past had somehow ended up at our reception. I'd been dancing on clouds of happiness all day, and I never noticed the intruder. Why was she there? I would probably never know the answer. That was frustrating but probably for the best.

The shower turned on upstairs. Nate was counting on a trip to the marina for his afternoon off. I needed to get to work on the cake. I returned to the stepladder and hopped onto my toes once more to retrieve the cocoa.

The soft tapping sound of bedroom slippers let me know Opal had walked into the kitchen.

My fingers made contact with another metal canister. I pulled it forward. This time it was the cocoa.

"Uncle Joe's Coffee," Opal said from behind.

The stepladder wiggled a little. I grabbed the edge of the cupboard door to steady myself.

"Oops, didn't mean to startle you. It's just I haven't seen a can of Uncle Joe's in years. I think they went belly up once those fancier coffee brands hit the market."

I carried the Dutch cocoa to the counter. "It used to be the only brand Michael drank." I picked up the empty can, considered keeping it for all of a second and then dropped it in the recycling bin. I was going to stop dwelling on the past.

I wanted Tobias's cake to be perfect. He was looking forward to it, and he deserved a nice treat.

Opal reheated some of the morning's coffee in the microwave and sat at the table. "Cora was sure dazzling this morning. I guess she's hoping to catch the eye of one of those yacht owners."

"She's already checked that off the list. His name is Ansel Dell or something like that, and he likes showy jewelry."

"Sounds like a match made in heaven." Opal chuckled. "It won't be the same without her around here." There was a touch of sadness in her tone.

I spun around holding an egg. "She's not gone yet. Right now, she doesn't know anything about the guy. She was up on that boat pretending to be rich and pompous with her diamond watch and angora sweater, but we both know her wealth doesn't go beyond her closet. This guy might be pulling the same shenanigans."

"Never thought of that. But don't worry, Anna. No matter who else leaves, you'll still have me." She smiled and toasted the air with her coffee cup before taking a drink.

"That's good to know, Opal." I spun back to the mixing bowl and cracked in the egg. The note crinkled in my apron pocket. I pulled it out, crumpled it up and tossed it in the trash. I had to put it all behind me for good.

I whipped up the batter and slid the cake pans into the oven. Then, I reheated myself a cup of coffee. Opal was wearing a bright blue and white striped muumuu dress. It was a particularly bold print, but Opal always pulled off *bold* well.

Opal breathed in deeply. "Smells good. Can't wait to taste it. Was that Nate in the shower?"

"Yes, the workday was cut short by the wind." As if on cue, a strong gust circled the house. Wind always made the old bones of my treasured Victorian lady creak.

"What was in the can?" Opal asked.

My face shot up from my coffee cup. "What can?"

"The old coffee can. You threw it away like you were trying to throw away a bad memory." Opal spent most of her time watching black and white movies, but still, nothing escaped her notice.

I shook my head. "It was stupid. I started the can after the first fight Michael and I had. I made a rule that if either of us was grumpy, we had to put a five-dollar bill in the can. I was hoping to save up for something fun like a trip to Hawaii. It was silly."

"That doesn't sound so silly. Did you and Michael fight a lot?"

I put my cup down and fiddled with the handle. "You know, if you asked me that five or six years ago, closer to Michael's disappearance, I'd have said no, but now—"

"Now, time has removed those rose-colored glasses," Opal said astutely.

"Yes, I guess so."

Nate walked into the kitchen. His long, thick hair was wet and brushed back off his face. I didn't need rose-colored glasses with Nate. So far, he was everything I could wish for and more.

six

EVEN MORE BOATS—EVERYDAY pleasure boats and extravagant cabin cruisers—pretty much every vessel you could think of had floated into Bayberry Harbor. Nate was like a kid in a toy store looking right and left and back again at all the shiny toys. In this case, some of the *toys* were worth 10 million dollars.

"Look at that." Nate stopped and pulled out his phone. He lifted it and took a picture of a huge yacht with its own smaller powerboat sitting on a specially lifted deck at the stern. "I'd be thrilled just to have the powerboat in the back, let alone the massive yacht where it's parked." He wrote a text and sent off the picture. "Arlo will get a kick out of it."

I laughed as I took hold of his hand. "I never pictured you as the yachting type."

"I doubt I'd be welcomed with open arms to any yacht club, but it'd be pretty sweet to sail around the world on a luxury yacht." He finally pulled his focus from the rows of fancy boats. "You'd be my first mate."

"In that case, which one should we order? I hear you can customize everything right down to 14-karat toilets."

"I'll just tuck away a little from my check each month, and by the time I'm 300-years old I should have enough…" He grinned at me. "For the gold toilet. You know what I *can* afford though?" He reached into his pocket and pulled out a five-dollar bill. "I can buy my sweetheart one of those hot apple ciders they're selling on the wharf."

"And see how lucky you are. I'm perfectly content, in fact, I'm thrilled about drinking a hot apple cider."

We turned back around and headed toward the food and drinks on the wharf. Sera had already set up her special table near the bicycle rentals for her apple and pumpkin pies. The hot cider kiosk was right across the way. In addition to offering hot cider, they were deep-frying mini cinnamon and sugar donuts. It was one of the first food booths to open, so the line was long. A chilly wind was keeping the sky clear of clouds and fog, but it was also making for a choppy bay. The boats, even the big ones, bobbed up and down in an almost synchronized dance. Most of the owners had come ashore to avoid the wild ride and getting seasick.

It was easy to surmise that the couple in front of us were yacht people. For one, the man hopped up on his toes and glanced around muttering something about how they shouldn't have to wait in a regular line. Apparently, he was used to having separate special lines, like the first-class passengers who always boarded first and never had to fraternize with those of us in coach. His wife looked angry about it too. She was 50-something with such a heavy layer of hairspray on her teased hair that it didn't move in the wind. Her long red nails fidgeted with her gold-trimmed sunglasses. She had a tiny button nose that looked as if it might have come from a surgeon's knife instead of nature. She was wearing the old-school yacht attire with a heavily pleated, knee-length, navy-blue skirt, white blouse and matching blue blazer.

The woman spun the platinum watch on her wrist to check the time. "Sanford, it's already past noon," she snapped as if it was his fault time had moved forward.

Sanford was also 50-something with side parted hair that looked an unnatural brown underneath his blue captain's hat. He flinched at the sound of her voice. "Well, Roberta, dear, we can forget the cider and head back to the yacht. I'm sure we have something comparable in the pantry."

"There is only apple Schnapps. I would like a hot, spiced cider." She said it in a way that seemed to be telling Sanford that he needed to get her the cider and all without waiting in the long line. "I've told you I don't like this event. Why, Louise and Virginia practically laughed in my face when I told them you insisted on taking the yacht to this ridiculous island to look at some stupid moon. It's the same moon as the one we see at home."

Sanford was ignoring her as he checked his wallet for cash. It seemed he was planning a little bribe for the hot cider people. He only seemed to have hundreds. He pushed them back into his wallet. "Why don't you head back to the yacht. I'll wait for the cider."

Roberta was getting her way, but she still marched off like a spoiled brat.

Nate leaned close to my ear. "She seems sweet."

I burst out with a laugh and quickly covered my mouth.

"Anna!" someone called from the other end of the wharf. It was Fran. She waved at me.

Nate shrugged. "Let's have hot cider another time. Looks like Fran needs to talk to you."

We left the slow-moving line. Sanford was probably just as happy to stick it out because it meant less time on deck with Roberta.

We reached Fran. She was sticking close to the ferry dock because passengers were getting on board. "Glad I spotted you," Fran said. She glanced back at her boat.

Nate motioned with his head. "We can walk with you back to the ferry."

"Thanks. There are a lot of people boarding. About an hour ago, Anna, a man came up to me. He asked if I knew where he could find Anna St. James. I'd never seen him before, so I told him you lived on the island, but I couldn't give out your address." She covered her mouth in worry. "Maybe I shouldn't have told him you lived on the island."

"That's all right, Fran. What did he look like? You're sure you've never seen him before?"

"Nope. I think he was around 40, big guy with the leathery look of a fisherman. He was wearing old cargo pants and a sweatshirt. He didn't come over on the ferry, so he must have gotten here on his own boat."

"Did he say why he needed to see Anna?" Nate asked.

Fran shook her head. "I asked but he was evasive. He just said he needed to talk to Anna. I'll keep an eye out for him and text you if I see him. Are you going to be out on the wharf much longer?"

"We've been checking out the boats," I said. "What color was the sweatshirt? Maybe I can spot him first, and the mystery will be solved."

Fran rubbed her chin in thought. "Green, olive-green. The cargo pants too. Sorry I'm not more help. You don't think it has anything to do with Michael, do you?"

It hadn't crossed my mind, but the question threw me.

Fran must have noticed. "Sorry, no, of course not. I don't know why I asked that," she said quickly. "I guess he just seemed like a fisherman, but what do I know? You two go and have a nice walk. Maybe he's already gone."

I touched her hand. "Don't worry about it, Fran. We'll keep an eye out for a guy in olive-green."

Nate and I left the ferry dock and headed back toward the marina. I was curious about the stranger, and, at the same time, I was feeling uneasy about the whole thing. Fran's question had come out of nowhere, but as soon as she said it, the breath caught in my chest. I still hadn't recovered from it, but I blamed that more on the recent escapade with the empty coffee can.

Nate reached over and took my hand, and I instantly felt

better. "You're quiet, Anna. Maybe we need to find this guy, so I can have a chat with him."

I smiled over at him. "My protector."

He shrugged. "At your service, madam."

"Ew, no 'madam,' please. Milady works better."

"Yes, milady." He leaned over and kissed my cheek, and all my troubles fell away. At least for now.

seven

SOME OF THE BOAT OWNERS, even the snootier ones, had started decorating their boats with leafy garlands, lights and even some beautifully carved pumpkins. It was a celebration of the harvest moon, but it was also October and October always brought with it a celebration of everyone's favorite orange gourd.

While Nate gushed over the beautiful boats, I kept my eyes peeled for a man in olive-green cargo pants. Something told me he wasn't going to be standing around sipping cocktails with the yachting set. If he was around, and, at this point, it was hard to know, then he was either on the wharf or out on one of the boats anchored in the harbor. There were so many people coming and going and milling about Bayberry Harbor, it would be hard to find someone I knew, let alone a stranger. I pushed the whole thing aside for now. Like Nate said, he rarely had an afternoon off, and we almost never had a few hours to ourselves. Not that we were by ourselves out on the busy marina, but since we were usually surrounded by our housemates, it was as close to being by ourselves as we could get.

A harsh, scolding tone pulled our attention up to the railing on one of the more magnificent boats in the marina. It was named *Grand Dame*. While it didn't have a motorboat attached, it did have a hot tub on the rear deck. The woman who'd just finished scolding her husband was none other than Roberta. Her shellacked hair still hadn't moved an inch. It sat on her head like a helmet, ready to protect her from any falling debris. I hadn't seen that much hairspray since I was a kid. I still remembered the cloud of hairspray my mom created as she lacquered her newly curled hair.

"Figures she'd have a boat like that," Nate said with a head shake. "Some people get what they deserve, and others get what they absolutely don't deserve." He chuckled. "Boy, that was profound, eh? I should write a book titled *Important Nonsense from Nathanial Maddon*."

I wrapped my arms around his. Everything about him was so solid. I always felt grounded when I was with him, like he was my anchor. "Well, I think that was profound but then I might be biased because I have a very big crush on the author. But I know exactly what you mean. That woman, Roberta, seems like the kind of woman who tips the wait staff at an expensive restaurant with a handful of quarters. She also seems miserable, so I'd say that's proof that money doesn't buy happiness."

Nate glanced back at the elegant boat. "I'd say her husband is the miserable one in that pairing. Roberta probably enjoys scolding and complaining. I'd also like to add that money can't buy happiness, but it can buy a very big boat that could, in turn, provide happiness."

I leaned out and looked at him. "You are certainly in a Cora-style mood today, and I mean that in the best possible way."

"You mean I look like a movie star?"

I squeezed his arm. "I could see you on the big screen, but I was speaking more about the shallow, money-is-everything side of my sister."

"Guess I'm having a little moment of yacht-envy. But that's only because we're surrounded by people who drip gold from their wallets. It's funny, but when you don't see the ultra-rich, you kind of forget they exist. I prefer it that way."

"I agree. Whenever Cora married into a super wealthy family, I found it hard to visit her. Not because I was envious but because I felt sorry for her. I couldn't see anything in her posh lifestyle that would make me happy. It was all so fake. Even their parties are the opposite of fun. They're staged and extravagant and everyone acts the way they think they're supposed to act. It's pathetic, really."

"I never thought about it, but you're right. It would be hard to enjoy yourself at a party like that."

"And yet, my sister is chasing down that same lifestyle again. Just when I think she's finally settled into life at the boarding house, she gets the *catch a billionaire* bug and off she goes. The sight of dozens of gleaming yachts set off a chain reaction. I wouldn't be surprised if she sails off into the sunset on one of these boats this weekend."

Nate looked at me. "You're kidding?"

"I'm not. Cora isn't terribly discerning when it comes to men with money. She's already picked out her target." I looked around to see if I could recognize Ansel Dell's boat. "I'd point him out, but I can't remember what his boat looks like."

We continued to the end of the marina. After you'd seen one big, splashy boat, you'd seen them all. Without voicing our plans, we headed toward the boardwalk in front of the Frostfall Hotel where you could see all of Bayberry Harbor.

Motorboats, sailboats and even some fishing boats filled the harbor. Some were anchored together in clusters with boating friends. Music blasted over the water and plenty of beers were being passed from coolers to waiting hands. There was laughter and yelling and general merriment.

"I see what you meant about terrible parties," Nate said. "When we walked between the boats, all we heard was Roberta scolding her husband and a few quiet conversations. The people out here are having a blast in comparison."

"See, it's like being royal. You've got everything at your fingertips, but you've got to dress and act a certain way to fit with your station in life. No letting your hair down."

As I said it, a sudden gust pushed a strand of my hair across my face. Nate's callused fingertips warmed my cheek as he pushed the strand off my face and behind my ear.

I hugged him. His arms wrapped around me. "Well, I'll have to push rogue strands of hair aside more often if this is the usual payment."

I tightened my arms around him. It seemed I was feeling

rather needy after the morning of empty coffee cans and strangers in cargo pants. I rested my chin on his shoulder, and my gaze swept around the harbor. Then, I caught sight of something that caused the ground beneath me to give way.

Nate sensed that my knees had buckled before I barely moved. He tightened his arms. "Hey, what's wrong? Are you all right?"

The breath had been swept from me, so I couldn't answer. I held him tighter for a second until I regained the strength in my legs. By the time I peeled myself away from him, my head felt dizzy and I could barely catch my breath.

Nate held my arms. "Anna? What's wrong? I think you should sit down."

I shook my head and swallowed to relieve the sudden dryness in my throat. I looked out at the harbor again to make sure I wasn't imagining it. I wasn't. Michael's fishing boat, *Wild Rose*, was bobbing up and down next to the other boats.

Nate looked so worried, he'd lost some color from his face.

"I'm sorry, Nate. I'm fine. It's just that I see Michael's boat anchored out in the harbor."

Nate turned toward the water.

"It's anchored next to the blue catamaran, the fishing trawler with the white and black wheelhouse and the maroon stripe on its hull. After the Coast Guard found Michael's boat, they towed it here. It sat in the marina for several months. I avoided walking down here because it hurt too much to see it. Frannie's husband knew someone who ran boat auctions. The boarding house was just getting started, and I needed the money. I sold the *Wild Rose*." My throat tightened around the words. "I felt guilty, but it was costing money to keep it in the marina and it was going to rot away to rust without anyone taking care of it. And I hated seeing it. It was the boat that carried Michael away from me for good."

"Do you know who bought it?" Nate asked.

"No idea." I shook my head and had to grab his arm to steady myself. I was shocked at how much seeing the boat had bothered me.

"We need to get you back to the house," Nate said.

"Yes, I need to finish the cake."

"You need to sit with your feet up. You've had a shock."

"I'll be fine. The walk will help. But yes, it was a shock. I don't know why. It's been so long, and I knew the *Wild Rose* was still out there. I just didn't expect it to show up here."

Once my feet started moving and the sea breezed cooled my head, I felt more myself. Nate kept tight hold on my arm. It was sweet.

"Do you think that man who was asking Fran about you is the new owner?" Nate asked.

I paused and looked at him. "I hadn't thought of that. You're right. I wonder why he wanted to see me."

"Maybe he just wanted to thank you for selling him the boat," Nate suggested.

"Maybe," I said. I took a deep breath and scooted closer to Nate. "Now, all I want to do is get home. I'll need a frosting taste tester if you happen to know someone interested in the position." I was working to shake him out of his state of concern. The mention of frosting helped.

"It's a sacrifice, but I'll do it."

I leaned over and kissed his cheek. "Thank you, Nate."

"Well, I haven't given my critique on the frosting yet."

I laughed softly. "Not that. Thank you for being my anchor. Sometimes I need it more than I realize."

eight

THE BRISK WALK home had me feeling loads better. I was silently chastising myself for falling utterly apart at the sight of the *Wild Rose*. It was, after all, just a boat. We reached the path leading up to the boarding house. Nate took my hand and scooted me protectively behind him. I'd been lost in my thoughts and hadn't noticed the man standing on the front porch.

"Can we help you?" Nate asked tersely.

I spotted the olive-green cargo pants as soon as he stepped out to the edge of the porch. He was a 40-something man, or possibly older. Just as Fran had noted, he had the leathery look of someone who'd spent a great deal of time out on the ocean. His smile seemed friendly enough. "Are you Anna St. James?" he asked as he walked down the steps.

Nate stayed in front of me. "Who wants to know?"

I leaned to the side to get a better look at the man. I'd never seen him before.

The man grinned politely. "I'm Carlson Grant." He stuck his hand out for Nate to shake. "I'm sorry if I startled you guys."

Nate seemed to sense that Mr. Grant was not a threat. His shoulders and posture relaxed as he shook the man's hand. "Nate. Why are you looking for Anna?"

I stepped forward and shook his hand. "You bought the *Wild Rose*."

He had one gold tooth front and center in his smile. "I did and I can tell you we've bonded well. I can't imagine fishing in any other boat." His expression grew somber. "I've heard the history behind the boat, and I'm very sorry for your loss."

"Thank you. I'm glad you're putting her to good use." I assumed that the man had just stopped by to meet the previous owner of the *Wild Rose*, but he reached into his pocket and pulled out a photo.

"I was in the harbor for the harvest moon celebration, and I figured it was the perfect opportunity to meet and thank you and give you this." He handed over the photo. "I found it in a side compartment in the wheelhouse and thought you might want it back." He glanced out at the yard. "Are the twins around? I'd love to meet them."

His question confused me, and then I looked down at the picture in my hand. A woman was holding a baby in each arm. They were dressed identically in blue-and-white striped t-shirts and tiny jeans. One had a little more hair than the other, but it was easy to see they were identical. The woman, the mother I presumed, was photographed from the neck down. Only her arms and hands showed. The babies were the focal point of the photograph.

"I don't have twins," I said absently. So much was racing through my head, I wasn't even sure I said it out loud.

I must have because Carlson looked embarrassed and fidgety. "I'm sorry, I just assumed…"

I turned the picture over. The message was even more startling than the photos. "Mikey, we need to talk." It was written in red ink, and the letters were curly and feminine.

This time I wasn't weak-kneed. This time it felt as if a cannon ball had been shot straight into me. Nate sensed I was processing this with a great deal of anguish. He maneuvered between Carlson and me and slowly, without being rude, turned the man in the direction of the path. "We'd love to have you in for coffee, but we're in the midst of getting ready for a birthday party."

"Right. No problem. I'm off to try some of those meat and corn hand pies they're selling on the wharf." He glanced back over his shoulder at me, then turned back around. "Hope I didn't upset her," he said quietly to Nate.

"Not at all. Well, have fun this weekend. And thanks for dropping by."

Carlson left looking a little worried and confused. In his mind, he was dropping off a cherished picture of my twins. After all, why would Michael have a photo of someone else's babies in his wheelhouse? Why indeed?

Nate reached me and didn't say a word. He knew. We didn't need to say any of it out loud. We walked in stunned silence up to the house. I was thankful that no one else was around. Opal was upstairs, probably sleeping with a book open on her chest. She had a predictable routine.

Nate led the way to the kitchen. Huck met us in the hallway. He walked straight to the kitchen door to be let out. The dog bounded down the back steps and trotted enthusiastically toward the river where he would spend the next half hour menacing the ducks.

More than anything, I needed to sit down. It didn't take much for Nate to read my mind. He pulled out a chair and walked straight to the cupboard for a glass. He filled it with cold water, carried it over and pulled out a chair next to me.

"I'm here if you want to talk. If you don't want to talk, then I'm here for that, too," Nate said.

I drank the water down in a few gulps. He hopped up, refilled it and sat back down.

The water helped clear my head. I took a deep breath. "They have to be his. If a friend had sent him the photo of her twins, he wouldn't have hidden it in his wheelhouse. He knew I never went in there. It was his personal sanctuary. Besides, we didn't have that many friends, and certainly, I would have known if one of them gave birth to identical twins." I finally looked up at Nate. "My gosh, it seems Michael had a secret life." I hadn't looked at the photo again, but I pulled it out now and turned it over. "'Mikey.' I don't know of anyone who called him Mikey." I laughed but there was no humor in it. "He didn't even like to be called Mike." And then it struck, a place where I'd seen the nickname Mikey being used. "Hang on."

I hopped up and raced to my bedroom. It took me less

time to dig out Michael's yearbook because I'd looked at it fairly recently. The woman who'd intruded on our wedding reception was in the yearbook. Denise Fengarten had been Michael's high school sweetheart, but he broke things off with her, deciding she was too clingy. Somehow, she'd ended up at our wedding reception, possibly proving Michael's point. But now, it seemed, there was far more to it than a clingy ex-girlfriend crashing an ex-boyfriend's wedding.

I carried the yearbook downstairs. Earlier, I'd felt weak, nauseous and like I'd lost control of my life. Now, I was angry. I needed answers. Was Michael leading a double life? Had he gone out to sea that day to end the complex mess he'd found himself in?

Nate was still at the table when I returned. Just seeing him gave me the fortitude I needed to investigate. Michael was gone. It would have been easy enough to just leave it alone and move on. But now I needed to know. I placed the book on the table. Nate scooted his chair closer.

"Remember my mom's visit?" I rolled my eyes. "Of course, you do. She's not an easy person to forget. She had the photo album with my wedding pictures."

"Right and you'd noticed a strange woman in one of the photos," Nate added.

"Yes, her name is Denise Fengarten. Michael dated her in high school." I shuffled through the book as I spoke. "Here she is." I pointed hard at her picture. I wanted to poke a hole right through her senior portrait. Next to it was her sweet note to Michael in the same curly writing. Interestingly, she'd used red ink in the yearbook too. I'd mostly ignored it the first time I looked through the book.

"Mikey, I can't wait to spend a wonderful summer with you. Romantic trips to the beach are first on my list. Love, your DeeDee."

"She called him Mikey," I said. "Just like on the picture with the twins." Some heavy stuff was landing on my shoulders. I was determined not to fall apart, but it was hard.

"You don't know what it is she wanted to talk to him about," Nate said. "Maybe they weren't his twins."

I looked at him with a raised brow.

"Yeah, I guess that's kind of a stretch. The easiest thing to do, if you want to know the truth and it seems like you do, is contact this woman and ask her point blank."

"I tried to call her, but the only number I found for Denise Fengarten was disconnected." I took a deep breath. "You know what? I've got an important cake to frost. I've been looking forward to this weekend, and I'm going to toss all this unwanted noise out of my head for now and concentrate on making a nice birthday dinner for Toby."

Nate pushed up a smile. "I think that sounds like a good plan."

nine

BRAVE BUT SOMEWHAT HOLLOW resolve helped me finish a delightful meal and cake for Tobias's birthday. I'd plastered on a smile and joined in the festivities. The photo kept poking its way into my thoughts, but I pushed it back.

Tobias sat behind his pile of gifts, grinning ear-to-ear like a kid. We'd sung a rousing rendition of *Happy Birthday,* and Tobias blew out the candles. I was sure I'd noticed a tear in his eyes as we piled the gifts in front of him.

I cut slabs of double-layered chocolate cake, thick with a Nate-approved buttercream frosting. Opal passed them out. Tobias took a big bite and moaned appreciatively. "You know, Anna, I think this is the best cake I've ever eaten." He said the same thing every year, but I was just as happy to hear it each time.

"Made with butter and love, Toby. Go on, open your gifts."

Tobias wiped his hands on his napkin. He'd always been fairly guarded compared to the rest of the people at the table.

Even Winston, when we had some time alone, would tell me about his parents, both teachers. By all accounts, he had a wonderful childhood with lots of love and support. He'd turned out to be a well-rounded young man because of it, one who'd dedicated his life to helping animals. It was admirable, and I was sure his parents were proud. But Tobias only shared little snippets of his boyhood. From what I gathered, both his parents had little time for their son. His father was a lawyer, and his mother was very social. She spent more time with her clubs and friends than with her only child. Tobias was left with nannies and sitters. Several birthdays ago, he told me his parents left on a trip the day before his tenth birthday. They'd forgotten it entirely. That year, I put a big waxy *ten* candle on his cake. He'd gotten so emotional, he could barely talk.

A cheer went up when Tobias pulled a shiny, new pair of swimming goggles out of the gift bag. "Thank you so much, Winston. My old ones are so stretched out, they barely stay on my head. Very thoughtful, Winston."

"Milk!" I said and hopped up. "How did I forget the milk?" I busied myself pouring glasses of cold milk. (What was chocolate cake without a milk chaser?)

"Oh, Cora, it's just magnificent." I turned around with cups of milk. Tobias was holding up a dark gray sweater.

Cora was beaming. "I thought it would suit your complexion."

I winked at my sister as I handed her a glass of milk. Sometimes, I wanted to shake her and remind her that what she had here at the boarding house was special. It was far more valuable than a loveless marriage filled with diamonds and platinum.

Tobias reached into a plain brown bag. I didn't need to see the gift tag to know it came from Nathaniel. He was sitting forward anxiously, waiting for Tobias to pull out the gift. He'd mentioned to me more than once that he'd found something *cool* for Tobias.

Tobias pulled out a sculpture of two dolphins swimming side-by-side. They were carved out of wood with beautiful layers of grain. Each dolphin was intricate. They looked so real you could almost see the sculpture in motion, the two animals flying through the waves. Tobias was always excited after his swim if he'd spotted dolphins. He'd even joked more than once that one day he might just follow them and never return.

The room grew quiet as Tobias held up the sculpture and turned it around in his hands to get a better look at it. When Nate first arrived, Tobias and Nate had gotten off on the wrong foot, mostly due to Nate's sour mood. Nate had arrived at the island sad and angry and broken. But he'd come full circle. He'd been making an effort with Tobias to make up for the rough start. I was sure he'd clinched the deal with this gift. Tobias was nothing short of speechless.

"That is beautiful," Opal said.

Tobias still hadn't commented. Nate looked disappointed, but I knew Tobias better. He was taking in the meaning of the gift. He swallowed hard and looked at Nate. "I'll keep it in my office, so I can look at it every day." His voice cracked a little. Without looking around I knew everyone, me included, had gotten teary eyed.

Nate nodded. "A friend at work knew a carver. I sent him a photo, and he recreated it. I'm glad you like it, Toby." He'd really put thought into the gift, which made it extra wonderful.

"It's perfect, Nate. Thank you."

The room had tightened some with emotion, but Cora managed to break through it. "So, who wants to hear about my date with Ansel Dell, financier? He floated in on *Blue Diamond*, a sleek, shiny pleasure boat." The last part wasn't necessary, but Cora preferred to punctuate her stories with yachts and all things extravagant.

"How did you manage to get a date with him already?" I asked. "You only met the man this morning and then you had to go to work."

"We slipped in a little cocktail hour on his boat after I got off work. Ansel came here alone. He's divorced." A smile followed. I could almost see those dollar signs in her green eyes. "Anyhow, there is plenty of drama in the yachting set, apparently. I asked him about the two biggest yachts in the marina. Ansel said one was owned by a man named Sanford Graves. He's in shipping or something." She waved her long nails. "It doesn't matter because he's married." This time a frown followed. "Anyhow, apparently, Sanford arrived at the marina aboard his yacht *Grand Dame* only to discover that his brother, Gerard Graves, owner of the magnificent 50-foot yacht, *Gemstone*, was moored there too. Gerard is newly divorced," she added unnecessarily for those of us at the table but an important detail for Cora.

"We saw those boats today," Nate said. "Sanford and Roberta. Now we know their last name too. What's so dramatic about two brothers coming to port at the same time?"

Cora wriggled and sat forward. Her eyes glittered as she realized she was in her favorite place—the center of attention. "There has been a long, ongoing dispute over the Graves' family fortune. Apparently, their father, Martin Graves, passed away a year ago. He was 96." It was amazing how many details my sister could pick up and retain when it pertained to rich men.

"I'm sorry," I said.

Cora looked at me confused. "Why? He wasn't my father."

"No, I'm sorry you didn't get to meet and marry Martin Graves before he—you know—kicked the billionaire bucket." There were a few chuckles at the table. Admittedly, I was in an ornery mood, but sometimes, Cora was such an easy target.

Cora rolled her eyes. She was used to my teasing, so it rolled off of her easily. "Anyhow, I guess there's a real Hatfield-and-McCoy-style feud going on between the brothers, and Ansel's yacht is anchored between them."

"Vanderbilt and Rockefellers," Opal said.

We all turned her direction. Up until now she'd been rather quiet. She shrugged. "I was just trying to think of two wealthy families that might have a feud. Hatfield and McCoy doesn't really work for rich people." She filled her fork with a piece of cake. "I thought it was clever, but carry on."

I winked her direction. Like me, Opal adored Cora, but sometimes my sister could be a touch ridiculous.

"Actually, Vanderbilt and Rockefeller does work better. From what Ansel said, Martin left behind billions. I'm meeting him later for martinis," she added casually.

"You're meeting a dead man for martinis?" Nate asked.

Another round of chuckles.

"No, silly. Of course not," Cora said.

"She's meeting the newly-divorced brother," I explained. It didn't take my investigative skills to decipher her meaning. Martin would have been her first choice, but since he was already dead, she opted for the next best thing—his newly-divorced son.

"That's right. Gerard seemed very nice when I accidentally slipped and twisted my ankle on those nasty old planks on the docks. He came right down from his boat to help me."

"Ah, the damsel-in-distress move," I said. "Well played. More cake anyone?" I asked. It was time to move on from the *Cora Marries a Billionaire* show. It had been a long, emotional day, and I was looking forward to a hot bath, a book and, with any luck, sleep.

ten

I SLEPT SOUNDLY despite all the chaos in my head. I did, however, skip my morning painting session. There just weren't enough creative sparks to work up the enthusiasm. After breakfast, everyone left for work. Cora dolled herself up like she was meeting royalty. Her ears dripped with diamonds, and an equally dazzling pearl choker topped off a green silk blouse and black pencil skirt. She wore her fanciest pair of heels with rhinestone crusted ankle straps. It was a bit much for a morning serving tea and tarts. Nate was back off to work. He'd hugged me extra long, knowing I was going through some turmoil. Opal seemed to sense something was up but then she was generally more in tune with my feelings than everyone else.

I got busy packing up leftovers to take to my friend, Olive Everheart. Olive left her house less and less, and I worried that she was growing too thin. It was going to be a long, brittle winter in her small cottage. The house was located at the top of the Thousand Step Beach on the east side of the island, so if a harsh wind blew, it hit Olive's place extra hard. I figured scalloped potatoes, rolls and chocolate cake would put some meat on her bones to help her through the glacial months.

Opal was pouring herself another cup of coffee to carry up to her room. "I assume you'll talk about it with Olive," she said, sounding a little hurt.

I spun around. "I'm worried she's not eating enough," I said and then looked down, a little embarrassed. "And yes, I've got some stuff to talk about with Olive. But you know how it is. She's a friend who is not part of this family." Her face brightened some when I used the word family. Opal's husband left her for another teacher, a coworker. She'd decided then never to remarry, and with no children and her parents long gone, we were definitely her family. I felt the same about everyone in the house. "You know how sometimes you need to lean on that shoulder outside of the family? But I promise, when I get all this together in my head, I'll be coming straight to you to talk about it."

Opal smiled. "All right. You know this shoulder is always here." She yawned. "I think I'll go back to bed for a bit. I watched a long Cary Grant marathon last night. And Cary Grant is like a good potato chip. One just isn't enough."

"I'll see you later then. Have a good nap." Huck had seen that I was filling the basket. He was already at the door waiting to head out to Olive's house.

It was another beautiful, albeit brisk, day on the island. I cherished each one, knowing winter was around the bend. I was especially grateful for the terrific fall weather this week since so much had been thrown my way to make it gloomy.

The walk pepped me up more. Huck reached Olive's door first. She answered with a treat in her hand. Huck carried it inside to enjoy in his favorite spot in front of the fireplace. Olive was nearing 60. She usually wore her long gray hair in braids or a bun, but today it flowed over her shoulders. "Anna," she said cheerily. "I thought I might see you today." Olive's intuition was unmatched. She always seemed to know when I was going to visit just like she always sensed when I had something heavy on my mind. Today, I must have been showing it like a neon sign.

As I stepped through her garden gate, her smile faded and she waved me urgently inside. "Anna, what's wrong?" she asked. "Here, come sit in the kitchen. I made some pumpkin spice tea knowing you'd be visiting." Her small kitchen was filled with the scent of cloves, ginger and nutmeg.

"You're the best, Olive." I set the basket on her counter and pulled out the potatoes. I put them in her tiny refrigerator. "I brought leftover cake from Toby's birthday."

"How exciting. I can't wait to try it." Olive set the teacups down on the table and pointed to a chair. "Sit and tell me what's on your mind."

Johnny, her rock-and-roll singing scarlet macaw, trotted in to join us. He flew up to the back of my chair. "Awk! Anna, baby!" he squawked, signaling he wanted me to rub his chest, which I was glad to do.

"All right, off with you, you spoiled bird. I need to talk to Anna."

Johnny squawked and raised his wings a second as if to tell her he wasn't finished yet. Then, he hopped down and trotted out of the kitchen. Olive reached over and took my hand. Her fingernails always had paint beneath them, and her skin was chapped from her art. "Now, what's happened? Is it Nathaniel?"

I shook my head. "No, he's been wonderful. This has to do with Michael."

She sat back a little stunned. "Michael?" She sat forward quickly. "Have you heard something? Has he been found?"

"No, nothing like that. Let me show you." I pulled the photo out of my pocket and handed it to Olive. She stared at it and turned it over to read the back. She looked up at me, confused. "Very pretty babies. Who do they belong to?"

I sighed. "That's the million-dollar question, Olive. Yesterday afternoon, a man showed up at the boarding house. It turns out he's the man who bought Michael's boat at auction. He's on the island for the harvest moon celebration. He found this picture tucked into a compartment in the wheelhouse and thought I'd want it back." Olive looked at the photo again. The whole thing seemed to be coming together in her head.

"Oh, Anna, do you think these are Michael's children?"

"I think they might be. Remember when I told you Michael's high school sweetheart had somehow ended up at our wedding reception?"

"Yes, shocking to say the least." Olive handed back the photo and sipped her tea.

"Well, I looked her up in his yearbook, and she wrote him

a little love note next to her senior portrait. The note is in red ink with curly writing, and she calls him Mikey. Just like on the back of the photo."

"Do you think she's the one holding the babies in the photo?"

"Seems like too many coincidences, don't you think?"

"I do."

We both paused to savor the fragrant tea while it was still steaming hot.

"Have you tried to call the woman?" Olive asked. "It seems like you have every right to ask her if Michael fathered her children."

"I've tried to reach her, but she doesn't seem to exist."

"Maybe she changed her name. Of course, that doesn't help you much. Oh, how frustrating this is, Anna."

"You're telling me. I almost wish there'd be a murder on the island just so I'd have something to take my mind off of it."

We both laughed about that macabre wish.

"Actually, I take that back," I said. "The last thing I need is to see Detective Buckston Norwich with his spitty toothpick and ugly scowl." I rested back against the chair. "I don't know what to do, Olive."

She smiled kindly. "Aside from this little obstacle, are you happy? With your life? With Nathaniel?"

"So much so I worry that something will come along to ruin it."

"Well, stop doing that and live in the moment. Worrying never helps anyone, and that is coming from someone who allows worry to keep her from leaving the house. It can get out of control, and then where will you be? Like me. A shut-in."

I realized I was always spending our time together talking about my problems. "Olive, what if we spent part of today's visit on a short walk? We could just walk up to the bend. It's a beautiful day."

Olive stared down at her teacup. "I don't know. Maybe not today, Anna." She looked up at me, letting me know she wasn't ready.

"I sprang this on you too fast. Let's make a plan. On Monday morning, I'll drop by, and we'll both walk to the bend. Then, we'll turn right around and head back home. Little steps." Maybe this was the distraction I needed. I could help Olive take small steps toward getting out of the house again.

"I suppose we could do that," she said.

My eyes rounded. "Great. It's a plan then. This way, you'll have a little time to get the idea in your head. Do your meditation, and while you're relaxing, try to imagine yourself out on the trail, looking at the water. It'll be a short walk, and Huck and I will be by your side."

"I'll look forward to it, Anna. In the meantime, remember what I told you. Live in the moment. Whatever went on all those years—that's in the past. It's behind you now."

I reached over and placed my hand on her arm. "I'm so glad I came to visit today, Olive."

"Me, too."

eleven

MOST EVERYONE PLANNED to eat on the wharf tonight. There were many options like fish tacos, clam chowder and pumpkin chili. Opal insisted I didn't need to worry about her and that she'd fix herself a sandwich. Not having to prep for dinner freed up a few hours of time. Once I got back home from my visit with Olive, I threw myself into household chores, vacuuming, dusting and laundry. But the work didn't help relieve the anxiety I was feeling, so I decided a brisk bike ride around the island would be the best medicine.

I put on my sneakers and grabbed my sunglasses. "Huck, do you want to trot along for a bike ride?"

He stared at me with big, brown eyes, his tail swishing back and forth (only Nate got the full helicopter spin) then he turned around, walked to his pillow and plopped down. I had my answer. I scribbled a quick note for Opal that I'd gone on a ride, then I headed out the back door.

A few stray clouds had floated in, but it seemed we were still destined for a beautiful, mostly clear day on the island. With the ambers, reds and yellows fluttering over the entire landscape and the spicy bite in the air, it was the truest example of a fantastic fall day. I was thankful for that. It helped improve my mood. This whole thing would weigh much heavier on me if the island had been socked in by a dreary mist.

I climbed on my bike and headed toward Beach Plum Trail. The beach plums for which the trail was named had lost their lush summer green. The leaves had turned to a fiery rust color. Soon, the plants would be bare.

A breeze blew against me, so I lowered my body and pedaled hard. My heart rate was up and my blood was pumping by the time I reached the path leading down to the Southern Lady Lighthouse where Nate was working. I hadn't really planned it as a destination on my bike ride, but I'd never gotten a chance to tell Nate that his gift was absolutely perfect. Plus, if I was really being honest with myself, I was feeling unusually vulnerable. Seeing Nate always made me feel better.

The Southern Lady, one of two lighthouses on the island, had a prim and proper Georgian look to her. A two-and-a-half story brick house, with two gabled rooflines to give it character, was attached to a squat lighthouse tower. The octagonal tower was draped in black cast iron, including the cap on top. The old lighthouse had the best view on the island, but she also had little protection from the elements. When a storm blew in from the ocean, she stood stoically in place, battered by wind, rain and whatever else blew in with the storm.

Nate had gotten a position on the construction crew in charge of restoring both of the island's lighthouses. He'd grown very fond of the Old Man of the North lighthouse during the eight months they worked to bring the old guy's exterior and interior up to code. Now, Nate was finding the same love for the Southern Lady. I couldn't blame him. I loved both of the lighthouses. Frostfall wouldn't be the same without its tall, historical bookends.

Scaffolding had been erected around the entire tower. Several workers were on the top level. It was easy to see why they were let off work early yesterday. Strong gusts and tall scaffolding didn't mix well. I got lucky enough to catch Nate on a coffee break. He was standing with a few other men, sipping from a paper cup.

Orange plastic fencing had been placed around the entire site to keep nosy people from wandering around the construction area. I stood on my bicycle just above the fence line and waited to see if Nate would notice me. The men laughed about something, and as Nate turned, his gaze swept past me, then it snapped back. He waved, said something to his coworkers and walked toward me.

"Didn't expect to see you," he said cheerily, then his expression changed. "Everything all right?" he asked when he reached me. I hated that I was in the kind of mood where everyone had to ask me if I was all right. I didn't like trouble or drama or concern being cast my direction. I was trying my hardest to hide the way I felt, but, obviously, I was doing a terrible job.

I pushed up a smile. "I'm just out for a bike ride. I don't have to make dinner tonight, so I have a little spare time, and I thought some rigorous exercise might do the trick." It was a poor choice of words.

His dark brows bunched together. "Do the trick? You're still thinking about that picture."

"No." I shook my head to add weight to it, but he knew. "Well, yes, but I'm determined to get past it. Just give me a little time."

"Take all the time you need."

"Nate, I wanted to tell you—what you did—for Toby's birthday—" I rarely had trouble voicing what I thought, but my frazzled nerves and the emotion on Toby's face was still fresh, so my words stumbled out in little meaningless bits. But Nate knew what I was trying to say.

He raked his hair back with his fingers. "I needed to make up for being such a jerk to him when I moved into the house. I hoped it would help mend some of the rift."

"I think we can put the term 'rift' out of its misery. I know Toby, and he was overwhelmed with how thoughtful it was. Thank you. It means a lot to me too."

Nate glanced back toward the work site before leaning in for a quick kiss. "My break is up, but I'll see you tonight. The guys told me I had to try the pumpkin chili."

"That would be my choice, too. I'm looking forward to it."

He took my hand for a second and stared at me. The navy blue of his eyes matched the ocean behind him. "And put all that junk in the past, Anna. He's gone and you're living a whole new life."

I smiled. "Have you and Olive been talking?"

"You mean Olive stole my talking points?"

"It was like you both wrote the script together." This time, I leaned forward and kissed him. "Get back to work. I don't want you to get in trouble."

"Too late. Trouble is my middle name." He laughed as he spun around on his work boots to head back.

I climbed on the bike and pedaled up to the trailhead. I stopped and gazed out at the water from the fateful spot where I last saw Michael as he left for a day of fishing. His disappearance and the shock of losing him had kept me from digging deeper into our relationship. It had been pure bliss for the first eight or nine months of our marriage, but then there were small changes, and they were all coming from him. He was grouchier and quicker to get angry. He was short with Huck, and the dog started to avoid him. More importantly, he was short with me, and I'd started to avoid him too. That thought took the breath from me. I stood there for a long moment absorbing that bitter truth. For the first nine months, I waited anxiously for Michael to return from his day on the boat. I'd have a snack ready, and I'd stand on the front porch waiting to see him walk up the path, salty and bedraggled and weatherworn from his day. Near the end, I started fretting, and my whole body would tense when I heard his boots on the front steps. How had I pushed all that aside? Why had he changed so drastically? I'd told myself it was because the catches weren't great, and he worried about money. Now, I wasn't sure that was the case. Finding out you had twins would definitely change a person's mood.

"Argh, Anna, you're supposed to be putting this behind you." I got on the bike and pedaled hard. A good sprint around the island was exactly what I needed.

twelve

THE RIDE from the top of Island Drive down to the harbor was mostly downhill. My legs were grateful for the rest. After my unsettling few moments thinking about Michael and the steady decline in our relationship that I'd somehow blocked out, I rode my bike fast and hard up to the northernmost point on the island. I rested a few minutes, even getting off my bike to rest my legs and bottom before climbing back on for the trip toward town. The exercise had helped. I was feeling less on edge. That might have been due to exhaustion, but, with any luck, the reprieve would last.

The harbor, and especially the marina, looked filled to capacity. The festivities were already in full swing. The mix of food aromas was so rich and, frankly, so pungent, it masked the smell that hundreds of boats and their gas engines had brought with them.

The *Salty Bottom* was halfway across the harbor heading back to the island. The boat was heavy with passengers. Its bow dipped low and popped back up, only to dip again into the choppy chaos created by the heavy boat traffic in the harbor. I could see Frannie in the wheelhouse with a bright orange knit scarf wrapped around her neck.

I slowed as I passed the 3Ts. The morning and early afternoon rush was over, and there was a bright yellow sign on the door that said *closed at twelve today*. Sera and Samuel would be selling pies out on the wharf this afternoon. One couple sat at an outside table with empty plates and teacups. They each stared at their phone. I couldn't see Sera or her husband, Samuel. They were most likely in the kitchen getting ready for the pie sale. Cora didn't seem to be inside the shop either. Sera was very good to my sister. Cora probably pleaded and gave her one of those sweet smiles she was so good at, and Sera probably gave her the afternoon off. That way Cora could spend the next several hours getting ready to wow the yachting set.

My legs were starting to feel a little rubbery. I got off the bike and locked it to one of the racks on the boardwalk. I walked toward the produce stand, but Molly was busy with customers, so I headed up to the wharf. Ansel Dell was leaning against the railing, drinking a smoothie and thumbing through his phone. This afternoon he was in full yachting attire: a pair of dark blue dress slacks and pale-yellow polo shirt, his captain's hat and an additional gold chain joining the duo around his neck. My sister was nowhere in sight, confirming my theory that she had begun the long, labor-intensive task of getting ready for this evening.

The smoothie actually looked tasty and more refreshing than chowder or buttery corn on the cob after the long ride. The smoothie kiosk also had the shortest line. I ordered a mango-strawberry smoothie and stepped off to the side to wait for it. Below me, on the dock leading to the marina, two men were having a loud, angry discussion. Curiosity urged me to look over the railing and find out what was going on.

A 50-something man with a big gold watch around his tanned wrist was holding a martini in his hand. The contents sloshed over the side as he scooted forward toward his opponent in a brisk, agitated manner. His loafers were so shiny they looked brand new. The man on the other side of the splashing martini was none other than Sanford Graves. His wife, Roberta, was not with him.

"Next time, give a man a warning if you're going to show up in your rusty eyesore," Sanford snarled.

"You weren't here when I moored, which means I got here first. So, why don't you take your overpriced spectacle of a boat right back to the hole you came from."

The argument had, of course, gotten the attention of fellow boaters. But most couldn't be bothered to leave their glossy teak decks to get a better view. Instead, they leaned with their own martinis against the railings of their yachts. A few more brazen people had brought out binoculars to get a closer look at the argument.

"Paul Thornton is the one on the left with the martini, and the man he's yelling at is Sanford Graves." I smiled up at Ansel Dell. He'd joined me at the railing to see what was happening on the dock. His aftershave was a little overwhelming, but, up close, he had a nice, polished smile.

"I gather they aren't friends," I said.

"You could say that."

Sanford was the first to stomp away from the scene. It seemed he'd noticed they were getting too much unwanted attention. It did seem beneath a rich man like Sanford to stand out on a dock and have a yelling match. Paul tossed the rest of his martini toward Sanford but missed hitting him with it.

"What was all that about?" I asked.

The woman in the smoothie kiosk was nice enough to carry my smoothie out. "Thanks so much." She returned to her kiosk, and Ansel and I returned to our conversation.

"It's just one of those things, you know. They've always been enemies. From what I've heard, and this is just a story whipping around the rumor mill, Graves had Thornton kicked out of the Mariner's Yacht Club. Paul had supposedly started a relationship with one of the servers in the club restaurant. Sanford considered it inappropriate. At the time, he was one of the board members, so he got Paul's membership revoked."

"I guess that would put a thorn in the relationship."

Ansel stuck out his hand. "Ansel, nice to meet you."

"Anna, and likewise. I think you know my sister."

He looked baffled for a second, then his eyes rounded. "Cora is your sister?"

"Yes." I realized then that I was bound to secrecy on everything I knew about my sister. I had no idea how much she'd shared with Ansel, but I was sure she'd never mentioned living in her sister's boarding house during their conversations.

"Cora is a jewel. I haven't seen her today. You don't happen to know where I can find her?" Before I could offer my theory that Cora was getting ready for this evening's activities, he surveyed the dock and the boats and froze in place. "Never mind, I see her."

I followed his sightline down to the dock. Cora was standing at the bow of one of the bigger yachts in the marina. A tall man with a thick head of gray hair and an impressively wide shoulder span leaned against the railing, facing her direction. Their laughter could be heard over the clamor on the wharf.

"I don't know how I missed seeing her," Ansel said more to himself. "My boat is right next to Gerard's."

I perked up at the name. "Gerard Graves?" I asked.

"That's him. He's the brother of Sanford Graves, the man who was arguing with Paul. Both of the Graves brothers are expert at getting everything they want." His jaw was tight as he spoke.

"Ansel, my sister is extremely friendly. Don't take it personally."

He nodded. "Sort of knew she was too good for me anyhow."

"Not at all. She just loves to meet people."

"Yeah, I can see that." He forced a smile. "Well, it was nice meeting you, Anna." He walked away dejectedly and tossed the remainder of his smoothie in the trash.

I turned back toward the dock. The smoothie was cold, delicious and just what I needed for the ride home. Cora was still having a laugh with Gerard. She said she'd be getting to know Gerard Graves, and she'd followed through on it. It explained this morning's fancy attire. I had to admit, she looked as if she fit in perfectly with the yachting group. No one was more elegant and charming and beautiful than my sister when she was working to impress people.

thirteen

SERA and Samuel were wheeling a rolling cart and dolly, both stacked with pie-shaped boxes, across the wharf as I finished my smoothie. The argument down below was over. Cora was still standing at the bow of Gerard's massive yacht. She was in her element, and if I knew my sister (and I did) she had visions of her next wedding floating through her head.

I waved and hurried to catch up to Sera and Samuel. "Anna, didn't expect to see you," Sera said. She looked past me. "Is Cora with you?"

"My sister is working on her next husband."

Sera shook her head. "She talked of nothing else all morning. I suppose having an entire set of future husband prospects float almost literally up to your door would make for an exciting weekend. She promised to help set up the pie booth."

"I've got some spare time. What can I do to help?"

"You're a doll. Samuel is going to bring the rest of the pies. If you could help me set up the table, that would be great. I've had people asking about pies, so I think customers will be swarming the table soon."

"Should I bring all of them?" Samuel asked. Sera had landed herself an absolute gem of a husband. Samuel was so caring, and he worked hard alongside her. He'd also become one of Nate's good friends. I was thankful for that because Nate had come to the island alone. He'd left behind everyone he knew to live in the middle of the Atlantic, and I was sure those connections would eventually pull him back toward the mainland. Instead, he started making new connections here on Frostfall.

Sera contemplated the question for a second. She surveyed what they'd brought with them. It looked like an enormous load of pies already but then Sera's tarts were an island favorite. I was sure people would, as she put it, swarm the table for her pies.

"Actually, Sam, just bring another 12. I don't think I have room on the table for more."

"Not only that," I noted, "you'll need some for tomorrow."

Sera laughed. "I'm only doing this for one day. I don't have time to make more pies."

"I can't believe you made this many," I said. "I mean you're a marvel with a pie crust, but, my gosh, this must have taken hours."

Samuel covered a yawn as I said it. "We only got two hours sleep last night."

"Yes, and I told you to go home and take a nap after this."

Sera turned to me. "He gets very cranky when he hasn't had enough sleep."

We set to work unloading the cart and dolly. The scent of cinnamon and cloves fluttered around us in a fragrant cloud. "I can't imagine Samuel ever getting grumpy," I said.

"Thank you, Anna. By the way, did Nate tell you we're heading across to the mainland in the morning to go mountain biking?"

"He might have mentioned it," I said. I was flipping back through my memory Rolodex to find that conversation. I was sure it was there, but it was lost in the clutter. A love for mountain biking had sealed Samuel and Nate's friendship. Unfortunately, the single trail on Calico Peak was not enough to keep them on the island for a day of fun. There were much better trails across the harbor.

"That's another reason I'm not selling pies tomorrow. I'll be running the shop alone," Sera said.

"Do you want me to stay?" Samuel asked half-heartedly.

"No, because your mopey mood is even less pleasant than your grumpy mood." She stepped toward him and gave him a kiss. "You go and have fun with Nate. I don't expect many customers tomorrow. I mean, look at all these food kiosks."

We all took a moment to look around. The last harvest moon event had only half the vendors. By comparison, the food vending area looked almost like a carnival. Aside from the fall-inspired, cozy foods like pumpkin chili and clam chowder, there was blue and pink cotton candy and rainbow-colored snow cones. One couple was even offering deep fried pickles.

"I think I might be the only local out here," Sera said. "Frannie said *Salty Bottom* has been packed to the gills for every trip across but almost empty going the other direction."

I placed the last two apple pies on the table. "It looks like it's going to be a massive event."

"All right, so I'll go get 12 more?" Samuel said it as a question to be sure.

Sera nodded. "Then, you can head home and rest."

Samuel lumbered off, the empty dolly bouncing behind him. "I'm glad he's getting out with Nate tomorrow." Sera paused the conversation. "Apple on the right and pumpkin on the left, and don't stack them more than two high or the boxes collapse." We set to work. I hadn't anticipated this diversion, but it always helped to keep busy, especially when something was bothering me. "Lately, Sam has been getting island fever," Sera said. "He's even mentioned moving our tea shop across the harbor."

I stopped and looked at her to see if she was serious. It seemed she was. "I don't know what I'd do if you left the island, Sera." I hadn't meant to let any emotions spill, but what she said had fluffed my feathers enough that they came out anyway.

Sera put down the apple pie she was holding. "We're not going anywhere, Anna. Like I said, Sam just has a touch of island fever. After a day on the mainland, sitting on a crowded bus, fighting for right-of-way on the busy trails and waiting in a long line to buy a burger and greasy fries, he'll come back to Frostfall ready to kiss the ground. I'm sure

Nate will feel the same." Sera scrutinized my face. "Something else is wrong. What is it, Anna?"

I rolled in my lips, unsure of whether I should mention the picture. But Sera had been my strongest shoulder after Michael's disappearance. I could use that same shoulder now. "The man who bought the *Wild Rose* is here on Frostfall this weekend. He came to the house to return a picture he'd found tucked in a compartment in the wheelhouse." I took a deep breath. "The photo was of twin babies, only a few months old. I can't see who is holding the babies, but I'm almost certain it is a woman named Denise, Michael's high school sweetheart."

Sera's eyes rounded. "You don't think—"

"I'm not sure, but the back of the note said, 'Mikey, we need to talk.' I matched the handwriting to a note Denise wrote in Michael's yearbook. She called him Mikey."

"Is the pie booth open?" a woman asked.

"Come back in 10 minutes," Sera said somewhat sharply. I'd stunned her with my news. I felt a little stunned all over again just talking about it. The woman walked away looking insulted.

"We can talk about this another time, Sera. You've worked hard for this pie sale. I don't want to get in the way."

"You're not in the way. I'm worried about you, Anna. I can see this whole thing has you upset, and I don't blame you. What on earth was Michael up to?"

"I'm not sure I'll ever find out. I tried to contact the woman, but her number was disconnected. I can't find anything about her. It's like she vanished." As I said it, a new layer of shock hit me. "Sera, what if Michael's disappearance was staged? What if he left to be with Denise and her twins?"

Sera hugged me. "Stop. Relax. There are a lot of unanswered questions, but coming up with unsupported theories is not going to help. You look tired. Why don't you go home and get some rest. Come out tonight and have fun and put all this behind you."

I nodded in agreement. She handed me a box with an apple pie. "And while you're resting, treat yourself to some pie. I think I really outdid myself on these."

"They smell wonderful. Oh, and Sera, I haven't mentioned the picture to Cora or Opal. Only Nate and Olive know about it, so if you could keep this between us."

"Absolutely. And remember, Anna, you're happy now. The past is the past."

"Heard that a lot lately. Thanks, Sera. See you later."

I left the wharf. It was becoming more crowded by the minute. I was almost tempted to sit out tonight's activities and stay home. I was sure Nate would be disappointed.

I placed the pie box in the basket on my bicycle. My legs weren't thrilled that they were expected to pedal again, but we were almost home. After the long ride and all the unsettling thoughts, rest with a piece of pie was just what I needed.

fourteen

I WAS TRYING to decide if having a night off from cooking dinner was a good or bad thing. Normally, it would have been well-received. I loved cooking for the group, but having a night off from cooking and cleaning usually gave me a tiny spark of joy, like when you were young and the teacher announced there'd be no homework for the night. It was a sweet treat, indeed, but this afternoon, I needed something to occupy myself. I took Huck out for a walk along the river but realized I'd spent all my leg energy on the bike ride. Nate was looking forward to tomorrow night's dance, and I didn't want to disappoint him or myself by missing it. So, much to Huck's chagrin, we headed back to the house.

After downing a large piece of pie (delicious as expected) I sat on the couch in the front sitting room, thumbing through some fashion magazines Cora had left there, but I bored of that quickly. My sister might like spending her day in designer duds, but I was just as happy in my soft jeans and well-worn sweaters.

My next attempt at distraction came when I pulled out all the ingredients for some banana bread only to find that I was lacking the very important bananas. I put everything away, and now, I was stuck at my kitchen table sipping the same cup of coffee for so long, it had grown cold. And since I had nothing else to think about except the cold coffee, my mind started playing its dirty, rotten tricks on me. As hard as I tried not to think about the picture, I kept seeing those chubby, little babies.

A new idea, one that was entirely counterproductive and one that went against all the good advice from my dear friends, sent me upstairs to my closet. After a bit of frantic digging, I found a box with Michael's childhood photos. For the longest time, I had a hard time looking at his pictures, but time had helped me get over that, and with all the distressing theories messing with my head, it was even easier. It almost felt like I was looking at a stranger because that was how I was starting to feel about the man I married.

I sifted through his school photos and the ones where he was on a fishing boat or on a soccer field until I found one of him as a baby. I pulled it out and carried it downstairs. I'd shoved the twin baby photo into the desk drawer in the kitchen. The desk, which sat in its own nook, was where I kept my laptop and my paints and anything else I needed a place for. I plucked the photo from the drawer and carried it to the window to compare to Michael's baby picture. I moved the photo up and down to find the best light and angle.

There was some resemblance, but that might have been because all babies tended to look like each other with their sort of deer-in-headlights expressions, round cheeks and dimpled chins.

The back door opened. I'd gotten so caught up in the ridiculous photo comparison I hadn't seen Cora return home. I shoved the pictures into my pockets so fast and clumsily, Cora laughed.

"Why do I feel like I'm twelve again, and you're trying to find a place to stash the spelling test you failed so Mom won't see it?"

"No spelling test," was all I said. I didn't have the energy or the stamina to tell the whole thing to Cora. I quickly changed the topic. "I should probably let you know—Ansel saw you on Gerard's boat earlier. He was quite heartbroken."

Cora did her best to put on a sympathetic pout. "Poor Ansel. Gerard says he tries very hard to be part of the yachting set, but he's only leasing that boat. He's wealthy by most standards, but not in Gerard's circle." One day with the ultra-wealthy and Cora had already taken on a snooty sounding tone.

I had no choice but to mimic her. "You're so right, dahling. Poor little Ansel should stick with Gretel and gingerbread houses. He's not ready for the real world where diamonds are used as paperweights, and Rolex watches are changed as often as socks."

"Oh, shut up. Besides, you're the one who brought up Ansel. And really—Gretel?" she asked.

"It sounded right. He's very nice, by the way. Ansel, not

Hansel. He was explaining to me why a man named Paul Thornton was having a loud argument with Gerard's brother, Sanford."

"Estranged brother," she corrected quickly as if she was already an integral part of the family's inner circle. Cora slipped off her fancy shoes and padded barefoot around the table to the pie. "Is this one of Sera's pies? Never mind. Of course, it is." She continued to the cupboard to pull down a plate.

"Did you see the argument from Gerard's yacht?" I asked.

"Everyone saw it. Apparently, those two have been enemies a long time." She cut herself a slice and sat down with it. "Gerard told me Sanford has a lot of enemies. And he has a big gambling addiction, which is why Gerard has been fighting to keep control of the family fortune. He has every intention of sharing it with Sanford, but he says Sanford has to have it doled out to him conservatively, or he'll wipe out seven figures on a horse race. Gerard said their father and grandfather worked too hard to build up the fortune, and he's not about to let it slip away from this generation because of Sanford's gambling."

"Or by way of a marriage," I added. "Sounds like Gerard would definitely be a prenuptial kind of groom."

Cora had a mouthful of pie as she grinned smugly at me. She swallowed and realized she needed some milk to go with the pie. I held up a hand to let her know I'd fetch the milk.

"He's very nice and quite charming," she said that with some degree of surprise. "A lot of rich people are lacking that. He's even more humble than most."

"Maybe he was trying to convince you of that?" I handed her the milk.

She held off drinking it and, instead, took the time to frown up at me. "Why do you have to rain on my parade? I'm having a lot of fun, and frankly, it's nice hanging out with people that fit more to the life I'm used to."

I laughed. "Excuse me? I'm pretty sure you were the sister who had to pack up her little pink Hello Kitty suitcase every other weekend, so we could be transported across town to our dad's apartment. You were married to elderly billionaires, both who died very shortly after the nuptials and both who left you, almost literally, with only the clothes on your back."

She lifted the milk and stared at me as she drank it. She smacked it down on the table like a drunk sitting at a bar and wanting the attention of the bartender. "Someone is in a terrible mood. Did something happen? Nate and you have an argument?"

I turned to the sink and busied myself with the few dishes that had piled up. "No, we didn't argue, and nothing has happened. I just think you waste a lot of time looking for a rich husband when you should just be happy with what you have."

She laughed. "Oh, you mean my single room and shared bathroom?"

I slammed down the spoon I'd been holding and turned around. "Well, if it's so awful here, then why don't you pack up your Louis Vuitton luggage and join Gerard on his boat?" There it was again, that waver in my tone that was totally uncharacteristic. Darn Michael and his secrets.

Cora should have looked angry. Instead, she looked worried. She got up from the table and walked over. "What's wrong, Anna? This can't be about me hanging out with rich men. Besides, I do love it here. It's the most fun I've ever had." She hugged me. "I'm sorry if I hurt your feelings. You know I like it here. But, you also know I like to have nice things. It's shallow and silly and I should be ashamed of myself, but it's who I am."

"I know and I want you to be happy, Cora. I'm sorry I snapped. I guess I was feeling a little hurt because it sounded like you were unhappy here." I was relieved to have something else to blame my distress on.

"I really do enjoy living here. I get to see my baby sister all the time. I love the island, even if it lacks a Saks Fifth Avenue—a Fifth Avenue altogether, in fact." We both laughed. "Please don't be upset with me for always wanting more. It's just the way I was programmed. I love diamonds and expensive cars and French perfumes, but I also love the Moon River Boarding House. I even love my job." She gasped and covered her mouth. "Oh no, I promised Sera I'd help her at the pie table. I forgot all about it."

"I helped out a bit, but she could probably use your help this afternoon," I said.

Her eyes rounded. "But I need to get ready, and what if Gerard was to see me selling pies?"

I rolled my eyes. "Never mind. For a second there, I thought your feet had landed back on earth. Carry on, o shallow one."

fifteen

NATE ENDED up working later than expected. I assured him we could skip the festivities this evening and join them tomorrow night. Saturday night was a bigger deal with a few bands and dancing, but he insisted he wanted to go.

I made Opal a sandwich while I waited for Nate to shower and get dressed. "Sure you don't want to go along tonight, Opal? I hear the pumpkin chili is delicious."

She laughed. "No thanks. I've got a silent movie marathon lined up. I'm starring in two of them. Although, I'm always very critical of myself on the silver screen. I'm overacting in some of the scenes, and, in others, I look bored. I remember always getting tired when we had multiple scenes to shoot. It's not like today's movie stars with their unions making sure they are treated right. Back then, they'd have us on set for hours without a break." Opal was convinced she'd been the famous movie star Rudolph Valentino in a previous life. None of us ever debated it. There was no reason to. She was sure of it, and we certainly had no way to disprove it. Occasionally, like now, when she spoke about her previous life, she showed a lot of expertise about life back then. Sure, a lot of it could be learned and known through research, but she spoke very confidently, enough so that it was easy to believe she had actually been Valentino.

I handed Opal her sandwich, and she carried it upstairs to eat. Nate's heavy footsteps drummed the stairs seconds later. His wet hair was brushed back off his face, and he'd shaved off the dark stubble. He held out his arms. "Better?"

"Hmm." I tapped my chin. "I rather liked the dusty, bearded guy who walked in fifteen minutes ago."

"Sorry, I'm not sure how to get the dust and, more importantly, the stubble back."

I plucked my coat off the hook. It was a clear, brisk night, and the temperature was always lower on the wharf. "Speaking of dust, Samuel reminded me you're going mountain biking across the harbor tomorrow."

Nate came over to help me with my coat. "Yeah, I'd almost forgotten that we had those plans." He spun me around and straightened the collar on the coat. "Hope that's all right. I know you're kind of in the middle of something right now. I could always cancel."

"Of course, you should go. You boys deserve a little break from island life. Island fever is a real thing. Sometimes this island feels small. I know—I've experienced the fever a few times."

He zipped up his coat. "I get it every once in a while, but a day on the mainland reminds me how much more crowded and hectic it is across the harbor. It always makes me happy to get back to Frostfall."

I smiled to myself. It was exactly what Sera had said. I was lucky to be surrounded by so many wise friends. People on the island had somehow picked me as the person to go to when there was trouble or a murder, but what they didn't realize was their island problem-solver relied on a lot of supportive friends, especially when one of my own problems popped up.

We headed out into the chilly night. As always, the harvest moon did not disappoint. The massive orb was filled with swirls of tangerine, amber, rust and bronze, a veritable painter's palette of warm colors.

"Star of the party," Nate said. "It's really showing off tonight."

"It seems to know it's being celebrated." The pathway to the boardwalk and eventually the harbor had been lit with pumpkin shaped solar lights. We followed the lights toward the music and voices. "I think this is going to be our biggest turnout."

"That's social media." Nate took my hand. I loved that he was a hand-holder. Michael never was, and I realized now what I was missing. "Word gets around and next thing you know, you've got a million people flocking to Frostfall Island for the pumpkin chili and apples pies. Samuel told me he'd pack up slices of Sera's pie to take along with us tomorrow. Looking forward to it." He patted his stomach with his free hand. "Oh wow, did you hear that? Hollow."

"You poor man. We need to get you fed. I just hope the

million people on the wharf haven't bought out all the goodies."

"All right, million might be an exaggeration, but I've seen perfectly quiet biking trails turn into circus-style free-for-alls because someone posted about it online. It's so stupid. If you find a cool place to ride or live," he said pointedly, "why broadcast it to the masses? Keep it to yourself."

"So, you're saying greedy and selfish is the way to go." I laughed.

"Exactly. And that's not being greedy. If you find a cool place to hang out, it's no longer cool once everyone else knows about it. You're just practicing conservation."

"You need food in that belly. You're talking a bit of nonsense at the moment." I squeezed his hand and swung our arms back and forth. I felt so much better just being with him. "Are we starting with the chili?"

"Yep. I've also heard there's a hot dog stand. I'm thinking that could be a good combo."

I smiled at him. "Sounds like you've been giving this some thought."

The bands didn't play until tomorrow, but speakers had been set up around the wharf. The music was working hard to be heard over all the voices and laughter. There was always something about a crystal clear night. It allowed voices to carry over the entire island. I was sure if I stood on Calico Peak, I'd be able to hear distinct conversations.

It was as I expected—a party-like atmosphere with a lot of noise, an incredible amount of food and even some impromptu dancing. Nate and I made our way toward the pumpkin chili kiosk. It was hard to determine which of the many treats on offer lent more to the aroma on the wharf, but the chili was a top contender. It was doing an admirable job, considering the fish and chips booth was just across the way.

Nate hopped into the line, and I scooted off to a clearing (there weren't many) and scoured the crowd for familiar faces. Tobias's was the first one picked up on my radar. He'd joined a few of his friends at the tables. They were all leaned over bowls of cracker-laden clam chowder. The friends were people he knew mostly through his work. He seemed to be enjoying himself. Naturally, there was a pile of small salt packages in front of his bowl.

Cora had left the house early, dressed in a shiny gold pair of pants, a cashmere sweater and one of her fur-trimmed coats. She had a date with Gerard. My sister worked fast. I didn't see them on the wharf and could only assume they decided to stay on the yacht. I couldn't blame them. It was crowded.

Most of the boats in the harbor were lit up. Some were decorated with strings of lights. Even the yachts had put on their decorative finery with twinkling lights and colorful leaf garlands. It was quite a sight to see.

"Roberta, I think you've had enough," a voice said from behind. I looked over my shoulder. Roberta Graves was trying her hardest to keep steady on a pair of high heels. They weren't the most practical shoes for a walk on the wharf, but her unsteadiness seemed to come more from alcohol. The impractical shoes only made her gait less steady.

Sanford Graves was reaching for a silver flask that Roberta had gripped in her hand. She yanked her arm back to keep him from grabbing it. The movement pitched her backward. She hit the railing.

"See what you've done. I'm going to have a bruise on my back. I'll tell everyone you gave it to me." Her words were definitely stretched longer than normal. That didn't stop her from twisting off the top of the flask and taking another drink.

Sanford scowled in disgust. "People are watching." His gaze flicked my direction.

I turned away quickly, feeling a little embarrassed that I'd been caught. Nate found me in my small, anti-social clearing. "There you are. There's about a 10-minute wait. They'll call my name. Should we find a table?"

"Looks like we might be out of luck on that. I know, let's carry the food down to the marina. We can sit on one of the benches."

"Good idea. Boy, never expected this kind of crowd," Nate said glancing around. "I'm not entirely sure I want to stay long."

They were words I was hoping to hear. "I've still got some of Sera's apple pie at home. We could eat our chili and then head home to the quiet, to enjoy some pie. I think I even have some vanilla ice cream to put on top."

"You don't have to ask me twice."

sixteen

IT WAS an odd dream where several women stood on the bows of boats screaming at each other, but the words weren't coherent and the screams were high-pitched—high-pitched enough that they pulled me from a deep sleep. I squinted into the darkness. It took me a second to realize that it wasn't women screaming. It was sirens. I reached for my phone. It was one in the morning. By the time I got out of bed, there was a knock on my door.

"Anna, it's me," Nate said through the crack. "Sounds like something is going on at the harbor."

I pulled on my robe and opened the door. Nate had already gotten dressed in his jeans and a coat. "I'm going to head down there and see what's going on."

"Wait for me. I'll only be a second." I'd shaken off the grogginess, and I was in full adrenaline mode. We had one ambulance, and a medic team was on the island for the busy weekend, but sirens had to be coming from the Coast Guard.

I pushed aside the curtains. Red lights glowed and spun around wildly in the distance. Between the red lights, I noticed a thick plume of milky-gray smoke. Something was on fire.

Huck was still curled up on the foot of the bed. He'd even pulled his nose in tighter to assure me he wanted nothing to do with our nighttime adventure. I pulled on pants, a sweater, a beanie and gloves. The evening had been brisk. The middle of the night would be downright cold. As I stepped into the hallway, a frightening thought struck me. What if Cora was still on Gerald's yacht? I tiptoed down the hallway and quietly opened Cora's door. Relief washed over me. She was fast asleep.

Nate was downstairs with a pair of flashlights. He'd pulled on a beanie and gloves as well. "I stepped outside a second and realized I could see my breath, so I grabbed my heavier coat. I smelled smoke when I was out there."

"I could see a plume of it when I looked out the window." We walked out the front door and shut it gently so as not to wake the others. The moon was still giving the island a nice glow, but the flashlights would come in handy. "If the Coast Guard was called, I assume one of the boats caught fire."

"Your sister?" Nate asked urgently.

"I checked. She's in bed." We hurried along the trail toward the activity, only this time it was a different kind of activity than we'd seen earlier. The music, laughter and food had been shut down for the night.

"Looks like it's one of the boats in the marina," Nate noted as we got closer to the smoke. The sirens had been turned off, but red lights still lit up the marina and surrounding harbor. A long spray of water and whatever they used to put out a boat fire arced through the air, landing on one of the boats below.

"Not a great night to have the harbor and marina filled to capacity," I said.

"I'll say. But it looks like they're handling it. The smoke is already turning white. That's usually a sign that the flames are under control, if not extinguished."

Two Coast Guard boats and an accompanying fire boat were anchored in the marina. Most of the boat owners had been jostled from their beds. There were a lot of robes and coats over pajamas out on the decks.

"Thank goodness, they've got it out," I heard a man say as we passed one of the yachts. As we got closer, it was easy to see which boat was on fire. It was Sanford Grave's 50-foot yacht, the *Grand Dame*. There was no sign of the boat owner. I gasped as we neared it. The fire had been centered mostly around the cabin area.

Nate was thinking the same thing as me. "That doesn't look good. If they were below deck, fast asleep—"

"Let's hurry."

The Coast Guard had put up a gangplank to easily enter and leave the yacht. Firemen climbed onto deck to make sure they'd smothered the fire completely. With so many gasoline-filled vessels parked in the marina and adjacent harbor, it seemed they'd averted a terrible disaster.

"Let's go on board," I said. "We might get asked to leave,

but I've found that the Coast Guard officers are not as strict and pushy as the police."

Nate raised a brow.

"Well, I mean one policeman in particular. I'm sure you were a perfectly polite policeman."

"That's better." Nate took my hand and led me up the gangplank.

Several of the firemen were prying open the door to the cabin. Nate and I stood back and waited for them to get the door open. Smoke flowed out through the opening. The team wore respirators as they entered the smoky cabin. Less than five minutes later, one emerged. He was on the radio and speaking loud enough that we could hear him.

"This is Fire Team 2, over."

A muffled response was returned.

"We have a lone female, deceased. We're going to need a coroner and law enforcement at Bayberry Harbor. Over."

I looked at Nate. "Roberta Sanford. She was quite drunk last night when I saw her on the wharf."

"She might have passed out and slept through the commotion. It was probably smoke inhalation that killed her."

It was a tragedy, but I was somewhat relieved it was an accident. However, I had a few outstanding questions. How did the boat catch fire in the first place? And where was Roberta's husband, Sanford Graves? As I thought it, there was a shocked moan behind us.

We both turned toward the sound. Sanford Graves was

standing in a coat, but he was wearing pajamas and loafers. "So it's true," he said weakly to no one in particular. "I saw the smoke and worried it was my boat." He teetered unsteadily on his feet.

Nate and I moved toward him. Nate took his arm. "Let's get you a seat." We walked him to one of the lounges on the front deck. Sanford plopped down hard, then sat forward. "Where's Roberta?" he asked. He stood back up, still unsteady. "Where's my wife?" He looked at us, confused. "Are you with the Coast Guard? Where's Roberta? I need to see my wife."

Nate and I exchanged strained looks. We weren't with the officials, and it wasn't our place to tell him. And, it seemed, we weren't going to have to.

"Which one of you is Sanford Graves, the owner of the vessel?" one of the firemen asked.

Sanford stepped forward, hesitantly. "I'm Sanford Graves. Where's my wife? Where is Roberta?"

I didn't envy the man tasked with breaking the news. "Can you come with me, Mr. Graves? The fire is out, but there's been a casualty."

Sanford paused. Nate noticed it before anyone else. He lunged forward to keep Sanford from crumbling to his knees. He caught the man under the arms and steadied him. Sanford remained in place for a second, trying to get his bearings. There was enough choppiness in the marina to make it even harder. The fireman stepped forward to lend Sanford a hand, and they headed toward the damage. Nate and I watched from the deck as they carried the stretcher with the fire victim out from the cabin area. Sanford cried and moaned and sank to his knees as he realized his wife, Roberta, was dead.

"I don't understand," Nate said after some of the shock subsided. "If Sanford is in his pajamas, that means he was sleeping. Which makes sense given the hour."

"Then, why was he not in the cabin with Roberta?" I asked finishing his thought.

"Exactly."

"If he had been inside, he might have prevented this. When I saw them, only Roberta was inebriated. Sanford would have been woken by the smoke or, at the very least, the alarm. I'm sure these expensive yachts have extensive alarm and security systems."

"Do millionaires sleepwalk?" Nate asked facetiously.

"They wouldn't dare," I said with a posh accent. It was the middle of the night, and we'd both been woken from deep sleeps, so the tiredness sillies were taking over. "I suppose there will be a lot of questions for Mr. Graves to answer once the smoke has cleared… literally."

seventeen

IT WAS NEVER easy getting officials out to the island, especially in the middle of the night. The *Salty Bottom* didn't run at night, so it was up to the Coast Guard to get the coroner and his team to the marina. I was sure a fire inspector would be called as well. They needed to find out the source of fire on the boat. The task of bringing mainland officials to the island was made harder by the fact that the harbor was packed with boats. The whole scene was chaotic for at least an hour after the fire. Curious spectators stood on decks and the wharf and docks. Eventually though, yawns started to make their way around the crowd, and people began to peel off a few at a time to go back to bed. The medics had been called to take Sanford to first aid. He was in a terrible state of shock. Roberta Graves was still on the stretcher, under a metallic sheet, at the bow of the boat. The coroner would need some space to do his work.

After some insistence on my part, Nate had returned

home. He was supposed to be up in three hours to go mountain biking, and I didn't want him to be tired for his day of riding. I stayed behind, wanting to make sure this was, indeed, a tragic accident. A young Coast Guard officer stood amidships on the deck of the *Grand Dame* as the rest of the crew rode off toward the mainland to wait for the coroner. I didn't have an official badge, but in these kinds of circumstances, I felt I had some authority.

I strode purposefully toward the young officer. "Evening." I smiled. "I mean *morning*. You're new to the crew, aren't you? I haven't seen you before."

"Just transferred here from South Carolina," he said proudly.

"Oh wow, welcome—"

"Lieutenant Brunswick," he replied.

"Welcome to Frostfall Island, Lieutenant Brunswick. I'm Anna St. James."

His eyes rounded. "You're Miss St. James?" he asked excitedly. "Commander Carlisle was talking about you. He saw you earlier and mentioned that you are the stand-in detective because the island doesn't have law enforcement."

It was always hard not to smile when someone had heard of me, especially when it was someone outside the small, permanent population of Frostfall.

"That's kind of your commander to say. I'm wondering if I could take a look around. I won't move anything, and"—I held up my gloved hand—"I've got gloves just in case."

"Well, it's probably against orders." He seemed to give it some thought. "But since Commander Carlisle made special mention of you, I suppose it's all right. It was an accident, right?"

"It sure looks that way. Terribly sad," I added. "I'll just be a few minutes."

He nodded reluctantly. The *Grand Dame* was eerily dark and quiet and wounded. It was hard to tell if the boat could still be saved. I still had the flashlight from the walk to the harbor. I pulled it out of my pocket and turned it on. The glossy teak door to the living quarters was singed black. Even the shiny brass door handle on the outside was smudged with ash. I pulled it carefully open and pointed the light inside. The haze and pungent smell of smoke was still strong enough to make my eyes water. The elegant galley kitchen and dining nook were charred, but the cabinets and the white marble countertops were still intact. Even the peach-colored cushions in the dining nook were still whole, although they'd been ruined by smoke and water. The fire had been mostly outside, but smoke and heat had penetrated the living quarters enough to cause severe damage and, more importantly, death.

I swept the light around. There was a bedroom on one side of the cabin and what looked to be a bathroom on the other. Most everything was singed and wet, but I could still see some of the shiny brass embellishments and polished wood that I'd expect to see in a luxury yacht.

I swept the beam of light around and along the floor. Smoke and ash had settled in puddles over a lot of the polished wood floor, but one large swath was mostly free of debris. Several small orange cones had been placed around the area. My stomach knotted as I realized the clean spot was in the shape of a body. The Coast Guard had entered the cabin after the fire, and one of the men came back out quickly to call in the death. That made sense now. It seemed Roberta Graves had died on the galley floor and not in her bed. I processed that revelation for a moment. Roberta Graves was not asleep in bed. She was awake. It was still a theory, but it seemed she was trying to escape the smoke and heat. Had she collapsed from smoke inhalation just 10 feet from the door? And where was Sanford during the fire? That was a big, puzzling question. He'd been in no shape to answer questions after he learned his wife had died, but we sure needed some answers.

    I stepped out of the rancid, smoky air. My flashlight beam swept over the outside of the door. That was when I spotted something odd. Directly beneath the brass door handle was another one of those clean spots, just like the one on the kitchen floor. This one was a straight line, about twelve-inches long and three-inches wide. I stared at the mark trying to figure out what would leave that kind of void. It had to be something pressed against the door while the fire was happening. Minor soot was smeared along the mark, but it had definitely avoided the brunt of the damage.

    I walked along the deck, looking for something that might have fit the mark on the door. I headed along the starboard side to the stern. The yacht was neat as a pin except for two black balls on the railing of the stern. I walked over to them and leaned down to get a better look. The black ends were holding onto what boaters called a Jacob's ladder, a soft rope ladder that allowed you to climb down into a smaller vessel or raft or even into the water. It seemed odd that the ladder was hanging down while the boat was moored in the marina. Had someone used it to come onboard and start a fire?

I moved across the stern and walked along the port side. It wasn't until I reached the bow again, where Roberta Graves lay waiting for the coroner, that I spotted a deck chair that wasn't sitting with the other chairs. The squat, ladder-back chair had a straight top edge that was about the same size as the mark on the door. Lieutenant Brunswick was staring at his phone. I lifted the chair. It was heavier than I expected, but I managed to get it up to the cabin door. I leaned the chair so that the top rung landed in the clean spot on the door. It was a perfect match. For the top rung to hit the door in that exact spot, it needed to be tipped onto its back legs. It was as I thought. The chair had been used to jam shut the cabin door. A person on the other side of the door would be trapped because the chair was holding it shut.

Across the way, I heard a motor. One of the Coast Guard boats was returning. It looked like the boat was filled with passengers. It was the coroner's team arriving to examine the body. It seemed obvious enough how Roberta died. Smoke inhalation was fast and deadly. But had someone helped her along to her death? It sure seemed that way.

The scenario bouncing around my head was that someone came on deck, lit a fire and pushed a chair up to the door to make sure Roberta couldn't escape the smoke. The culprit stuck around long enough to make sure she was dead, then they moved the chair, climbed down the ladder and sped off in another boat. They might have swum away. It would be easy enough to do in a marina. If my theory was right, that meant Roberta's death was murder. Of course, I already knew what Norwich would say once he was called to the scene. He'd call it an accident and shut the case before Roberta was laid to rest. Now, it was up to me to decide whether or not to point out the chair and the ladder or stand back and wait for Norwich to discover it on his own.

That thought made me laugh out loud. Norwich's face popped into view as he boarded the gangplank. I sealed my lips shut and flashed him a smile. I needed to get home and catch a few winks. I'd been hoping for a distraction, and it seemed I'd found it. I had a murder case to solve.

eighteen

I HAD to pull myself out of bed at seven to start breakfast. My body and head begged for a few more hours, but there was a meal to cook and, after that, a murder to investigate. I wondered how many other boarding house managers had that same agenda on a Saturday morning. Because I was a little groggy and, at the same time, in a hurry, I put off the blueberry pancakes I had planned and made scrambled eggs and toast.

Nate had left earlier to go on his mountain bike ride. I felt guilty that I hadn't gotten up in time to make him a sandwich. I just couldn't pry my eyes open at that time because I'd only just gotten back in bed an hour before. Winston took a scrambled egg sandwich to go. He was on feeding duty at the wildlife rescue, and he didn't want to be late. Opal had slept in. She'd left a note on the refrigerator that she would skip breakfast to catch an extra hour of sleep, and Cora had taken a piece of dry toast with her coffee. She had to get to the tea shop early. I mentioned that business might be slower than expected, but she never asked why. She was in a hurry, and I was in no state to rehash the night's events. I was too tired. Besides, she'd hear about it soon enough. It did alert me to the fact that, with the exception of Nate and me, our housemates were heavy sleepers. The rest of the house had slept through the whole thing.

Tobias was at the table, showering his eggs with salt. He was the only person truly disappointed by the lack of blueberry pancakes. He also had no idea what I'd been up to all night.

"It's strange but I could have sworn when I went for my swim this morning, I saw a lot of smoke lingering in the air." Tobias had finally decided he'd had enough salt. "And I'm sure I spotted that ridiculous Detective Norwich on the wharf. He's so easy to see with that oversized, wrinkled coat."

I carried my plate to the table. "Yes, there was an incident in the marina. One of the yacht owners died when their boat caught fire."

Tobias lowered his fork and looked at me in shock. "My goodness. When did this happen?"

"In the middle of the night."

"I can't believe I slept through it. Were you there? Of course, you were. Was it foul play?"

"I think so, only it could easily be considered an accident if certain evidence is ignored."

Tobias grinned. "And we all know how easily Norwich overlooks evidence."

"He's better at overlooking it than finding it." Suddenly, it seemed more urgent that I got to the *Grand Dame*. If Norwich was on the island, then he was, no doubt, already working hard to close the case as an accident. I pushed in two bites of egg. "I need to get over there, Toby. If you want more toast, the bread is in the bread box. I'll see you later."

"Oh, well, yes, all right. We'll see you later, and I expect we might be sitting around the corkboards tonight, eh?"

"You might be right." I pulled on my coat. "If you see Opal, tell her I put some eggs in a container. She can just pop it in the microwave. You stay, Huck." The dog was at the door. He'd missed his morning walk, and I felt guilty having to leave him behind again.

"I'll take Huck out for a walk," Tobias said. "I don't have anything pressing this morning, and he looks like he needs it."

"Thank you so much, Toby." I headed out the door.

The sun was shining, but its brilliant light was being filtered through some wispy clouds. A breeze picked up as I crossed the boardwalk and reached the entrance to the marina. The people who'd made the trip for the celebration had gone right on with those plans. The food kiosks were up and running and sending an aroma-filled smoke over the entire harbor. There was plenty of activity on the boats, as well. Boats in the harbor were clustered together, so friends could hop from boat to boat and enjoy each other's company.

Activity on the yachts had not been slowed by the shocking incident. Although, on second thought, the mood was more somber. And, it seemed, when it came to yachters, every hour was martini hour, no matter what the clock said.

The coroner's team was already done, and Roberta's body had been removed. I heard the grating sound of Norwich's voice up on deck. It was going to take all my fortitude (and I didn't have much this weekend) to talk to the man. He'd just scoff, tell me to mind my own business and shoo me away before I could show him all the evidence.

A gangplank was still in place for easy access to the *Grand Dame*. At the same time, cones had been set up with a sign that read 'officials only beyond this point.' I would ignore it, of course. In fact, I felt more official than the actual toothpick-chewing official on deck.

Before I could take my first step past the Keep Out sign, a figure appeared at the top of the plank. It was Sanford Graves, and his name fit his expression. His face was pale, and there were dark rings under his eyes. His shoulders were hunched as if he was in physical pain, but I was sure the grim posture was more due to emotional distress. He'd changed into a pair of trousers and a sweater, but he was wearing the same loafers. They slipped back and forth on his feet as he plodded with heavy steps down the ramp.

This would be my opportunity to get some very crucial questions answered. He still looked entirely bereft, but hopefully, the shock had worn off enough that he could answer questions. I just had to be delicate about it.

"Mr. Graves," I said loudly enough to catch his attention but quietly enough not to startle him out of his somber state.

His eyes were red, which could have been from crying or from being up most of the night. "Yes," he said hoarsely.

"I'm Anna St. James. I was on your boat this morning with a friend."

"Yes, the man who helped me to the chair. Please, thank him." He kept walking.

"Mr. Graves, I know this is unusual, but I investigate crimes here on the island. You see, we don't have any law enforcement on Frostfall."

"No, but there should be. Obviously, someone sabotaged my boat. That's what the fire inspector said. An accelerant was used. All it took was a match, and the cabin caught fire." He pressed his fist to his mouth to stifle a sob. "And my lovely wife Roberta is dead."

I was learning something new. "I see. So, this will be considered a murder?"

"That's what I don't understand," Sanford said. "The detective on the boat said her death was an accident, but the damage to the boat was sabotage. He said he'd be handing the case off to the unit that handles vandalism."

I took a deep breath to give myself a second to wrap my mind around the convoluted logic of Detective Norwich. "I believe that will change soon enough," I said without divulging what I knew. After all, Sanford was a suspect. Spouses always rose to the top of the list. However, he seemed to be in a great deal of genuine despair. "Mr. Graves, I must ask. I noticed you were in pajamas this morning when they found your wife. Were you sleeping out on deck?"

He shook his head sadly. "No, I was supposed to be in the cabin. You see, I snore. Roberta has a hard time sleeping. At home we have separate bedrooms. She reserved a suite at the hotel, but she came back to the boat and—well—she'd had a little too much to drink. She fell asleep in the bed. I didn't want to bother her with my snoring, so I took the hotel key and went to the suite. My room looked over the harbor. I heard the sirens and saw the lights. It looked like there was smoke close to where the yacht was moored, so I pulled on my coat and shoes. As I hurried toward the marina, I heard people saying it was the *Grand Dame*. I still can't believe this has happened." His face lost more color, and he swayed on his feet.

"I'll let you go, Mr. Graves."

"Yes, I'm going back to the hotel to rest."

"I'm so sorry this happened. We'll get to the bottom of it soon enough."

"Not putting much faith in that detective up on deck," he muttered as he shuffled away.

"You and me both," I said to myself.

nineteen

AS I WALKED up the gangplank, I could hear Norwich on deck telling the uniformed officer who'd been unlucky enough to get paired with the detective for the morning that this was an open-and-shut accident case. Norwich had radar when it came to me. His sharp, mean scowl shot my direction before I'd even placed one foot on the deck.

"St. James," he barked, "you're not needed here. Go home."

I ignored his order and headed straight toward him.

His signature toothpick moved up and down like a lever between his teeth. "Is your hearing all right, St. James?"

I stopped in front of him with the straightest posture I could muster. "My hearing is just fine. I was here last night when the fire was being extinguished—"

"I'm not surprised," he snarled. "Awfully strange how whenever something bad happens on this island, I can always count on you being in the midst of it." He said it in his usual accusatory tone.

"While I was on the yacht, I spotted some things that looked suspicious."

He laughed around the teeth clenched over his toothpick. "Suspicious? No kidding. Some vandals set a boat on fire. I'd say that's suspicious. Now that we've had your unwanted opinion, please leave this vessel, or I'll have you forcibly removed."

"Mrs. Graves was trying to escape from the smoke." I had to speak fast to keep his attention. I had no doubt he'd make good on his threat to remove me from the yacht.

His snarling laughter was toe-curling. "But she didn't make it to the door in time. People die in fires every day, St. James. This was an accident."

"Seems to me the vandals should be charged with murder," I said.

The accompanying officer looked up from the notes he'd been writing. "That is what I've mentioned, sir. Even if they'd only intended on vandalizing the boat, their act resulted in a woman's death."

"Officer Miller, when I need your opinion, I'll ask for it."

The young officer glanced quickly at me and then returned to his notepad. I wondered how many conversations about Norwich took place in the lunchroom at the precinct. I'd love to be privy to those chats.

"What if the vandal who lit the boat on fire *had* meant to kill the occupants of that cabin?" I moved toward the fire damage. It was surrounded by yellow tape, most of which had come loose in the constant sea breeze. "This door has a clear mark on it." I had Officer Miller's attention, but Norwich pretended to be looking at something on his phone. As if anyone would ever send him a text.

Officer Miller was young, probably a rookie because those were the officers who always ended up with the unenviable task of assisting Norwich on his excursions to the island. He was different than the others. He joined me at the door, even though he knew Norwich would scold him for it later. Most of the other officers did as they were told.

I pointed out the light spot on the otherwise blackened door. "Do you see this mark? I found a deck chair that matches this clear spot perfectly."

Miller crouched down to get a better look at it. "So, someone leaned the chair against the door to lock Mrs. Graves inside. There was no mention of a chair on the fire report."

"That's because the killer removed the chair before the firemen got here."

Miller had an intelligent, inquisitive sparkle in his eyes. "Killer? I suppose that fits if they purposefully jammed shut the door." He took a picture of the mark on the door.

"Miller!" Norwich yelled. "We're done here."

Officer Miller flinched and then sighed dejectedly before turning back. "Yes, sir." Never had I ever heard so much derision in the word *sir*.

"Actually, sir," Miller added confidently, "I think you should look at this."

Norwich's angry scowl darkened even more, and he

turned his wrath my direction. "Officer Miller, I order you to escort Miss St. James off of this boat right now."

"But, sir," Miller was persistent. I liked him.

"That's an order, Miller."

"It's all right," I said quietly behind the officer. "But let's take the long way around. I'll show you the chair, and there's one more thing I need to point out."

Miller gave a slight nod. "Let's go, Miss St. James," he said in an authoritative tone. "I need to see you off this boat."

Norwich's evil grin made its debut whenever he was certain he'd got the best of me. He could grin all he wanted. I was going to solve this case without him. I led the way toward the port side of the boat and the rope ladder. I had no idea if it was significant or not, but it seemed odd to have the ladder in place, ready for use while the boat was docked.

Norwich was making a call. He hadn't noticed that we'd taken the long way around. "This is the chair," I said as we reached the deck chair. "This top rung fits perfectly into the clean mark on the door. I tried it myself by leaning it into place. Someone had positioned it there to keep the door shut." Miller took out his phone for another photo.

"Miller, you're going the wrong way," Norwich snapped. "Of course, if you throw her overboard, I won't say a word." His grating laugh floated around the entire marina. Some of the nearby seagulls took off, flapping their wings fast to get away from the sound.

We reached the stern and the black knobs that held the ladder in place. "I noticed the yacht had its ladder down." I leaned over the side. Miller did too. The ladder had been rolled up. It was no longer hanging down to the water. "It was open this morning. I saw it." I was angry at myself for not taking a picture, but it had been the middle of the night. I was tired, and there had been so much on my mind. Still, it was a mistake, and now, that piece of evidence was gone without proof.

I looked at Miller. "I assure you, it was hanging down when I was on the boat this morning. I assumed whoever did this used the ladder to make his or her getaway."

Miller opened his notebook and wrote it all down. So, this was what it was like to have law enforcement work with you instead of against you. He shut the notebook and nodded in the direction of the gangplank. "I guess I should see you off the boat before he blows a gasket."

I laughed. "Would that be so bad? Thank you for listening to me, Officer Miller." I turned and led the way toward the exit ramp.

"It's an honor," Miller said. "Your name is quite well-known at the precinct. Anna St. James is as famous as Detective Norwich is infamous. Everyone knows that Norwich tries to avoid Frostfall Island. He doesn't think it should fall under our jurisdiction."

"It's all right. I think we manage better without him." We reached the gangplank. Norwich had already exited the boat. He was standing farther down the dock admiring the boats.

"Miller, what took you so long? Hurry up. The ferry is leaving soon, and I don't want to stay on this lump of sand any longer than I have to."

Miller smiled graciously at me and hurried to catch up to

the detective. It was aggravating to think a man like Norwich outranked a man like Miller, but unfortunately, that was the way of it sometimes. Life very rarely made sense, and I knew that better than anyone at the moment. But I wasn't going to get dragged back into the dark thoughts that had cluttered my mind this weekend. I had a murder to solve, and, as was always the case, the local detective was going to be no help at all.

twenty

I'D FELT a twinge of guilt after replacing blueberry pancakes with scrambled eggs and toast, so I decided to make up for it at lunch. There was enough chill in the air for hot tomato soup and grilled cheese. I usually loved walks on brisk fall days, but the long night and the few minutes with the most annoying person in the world had drained me. I was happy to reach the boarding house.

Tobias often worked on Saturdays to catch up on things, but he'd taken the day off. He and Huck had just returned from a long walk when I got back to the boarding house. Huck looked more exhausted than Tobias. His big head hung low, and his giant paws thumped the ground as if they each weighed five pounds. Tobias, on the other hand, smiled and practically skipped to the back door. Maybe those morning swims were the answer to everlasting youth.

"Were you at the marina?" Tobias asked as he held the door for me and Huck.

"Yes." We both shuffled inside. Huck went straight to his water bowl, and I went straight to the cupboard for two glasses. I filled them with cold water and handed one to Tobias. We sat at the table to drink the water.

Tobias's cheeks were pink from the long walk. He'd pulled on one of his floppy brimmed hats, but the wind managed to chap his skin anyhow. "What's happening with the murder case?"

"First of all, if I was on a shipwreck and I managed to survive and make it to a beautiful tropical island and the only other person to survive with me was Buckston Norwich, I would walk back into the ocean to take my chances with the sharks."

Tobias covered his mouth to avoid spitting out the water. "I take it that means Norwich was his usual cantankerous self."

"That word doesn't even do his foul personality justice. And, of course, he's already written the death off as accidental. The fire inspector has confirmed that the fire was intentional."

"Then, whoever set the fire would also be responsible for the death. That's at least manslaughter." Tobias got up to refill his glass.

"See, you're an accountant, and you know law enforcement far better than Norwich."

"Everyone knows more about the law than Norwich." Tobias reached into Huck's treat jar and pulled out a bone-shaped cookie before returning to the table. Huck had already settled on his pillow. He stared longingly at the cookie with big dark eyes and a drip of drool on his chin. "I guess you're not coming to get this." He tossed the treat over to Huck.

"I found evidence that this whole thing was far more nefarious than vandalizing a yacht. Someone had pushed a chair against the door to lock Roberta in the cabin."

Tobias's chin dropped. "First-degree murder?"

"Exactly." And then, something occurred to me, something very significant and stunning. "Oh my gosh, I can't believe I didn't think of this before."

"What is it?"

"I spoke to Sanford Graves. He was in a terrible state of grief and shock, but he answered a few questions. He said he was supposed to be sleeping in the cabin alone because Roberta had reserved a room at the hotel. Apparently, Sanford snores and Roberta has a hard time sleeping in the same room with him. But Roberta drank too much. I witnessed her state of inebriation when I saw the couple on the wharf. She had her own shiny silver flask. She fell asleep on the boat, so Sanford took the hotel key and went to the hotel room. He said he didn't want to wake her."

Tobias figured out where I was headed with this. "So, Sanford Graves was the intended victim."

"I think so. And he has more than a few enemies." I went to the closet. I pulled out the corkboards and carried them to their respective hooks on the kitchen wall.

Opal walked in right then. "We've got a new murder?"

"We sure do, and it's a doozy," Tobias replied. "We think this one is a case of mistaken identity."

Opal looked at me for clarification.

"It's possible the wrong person died." I pulled my colorful index cards from the box on my desk.

Opal heated herself some coffee and sat at the table. "What have we got?"

It was another thing I loved about my Moon River family. They were always keen to jump in and add their two cents on a murder case. It was always greatly appreciated and often came in handy.

Before we could get started, the front door opened and shut. It was Cora. She preferred the front door because it meant less trekking over soft ground in high heels. She was wearing a pink puffy coat and tight black pants, an interesting combo for serving tea. I was sure she'd spruced up in case her newest conquest Gerard Graves came into the shop. That thought reminded me that I hadn't seen Gerard once in all this chaos. Yes, they were estranged, but you'd think he'd have at least dropped by to see if there was anything he could do for Sanford. They were, after all, brothers. Instead, he'd been conspicuously absent.

Cora spotted the corkboards and rolled her eyes. "Not the corkboards again," she muttered. Well, *most* of the Moon River family liked to join in on the investigation. It was hit or miss with Cora, and today was obviously a miss. But my first suspect would probably catch her attention. I focused on my captive audience of two and ignored the pink and black sideshow with the attitude.

"Last night, a yacht called the *Grand Dame* caught fire in

the marina. The owner's wife, Roberta Graves, died from smoke inhalation."

Opal straightened. "How do we know Roberta wasn't the owner? We always assume the man owns expensive things like yachts, but maybe it was her family money."

"Good point, Opal, and you're right. It's far too easy to jump to the conclusion that the man has the wealth and the woman is along for the ride." I looked pointedly at my sister, who leaned against the kitchen counter eating an apple. I returned my attention to Opal and Tobias. "In this case, I happen to know that Sanford Graves is from a very wealthy family. I don't know much about Roberta except she liked to complain and get angry at her husband, and she, apparently, enjoyed a drink or two." Things had gone off on a long tangent, all stemming from Opal's comment. "What I've learned is that Sanford Graves was supposed to be sleeping on the boat, and Roberta was supposed to be sleeping in a suite at the hotel. From there, it's easy to conclude that the culprit killed the wrong person. With that in mind, we're looking at people who might have had motive to kill Sanford Graves."

"I know where this is going," Cora said. "Well, it wasn't Gerard. I'll tell you that right now."

"Do you have any proof to back that up?" Suddenly, it was a sibling argument, and the rest of the group didn't know why.

"Wait," Opal said sharply. "Who is Gerard, and why is he a suspect?"

"Gerard Graves is Sanford's brother. There's been an

ongoing battle between the brothers over the family fortune," I explained.

"Gerard is not a killer," Cora said emphatically.

"You've known him less than a day," I reminded her. I picked up an index card and wrote down the name Gerard Graves along with the family fortune as motive. It was easy to assume that if Sanford died, the fight over the family fortune would end, and the bulk of it would end up in Gerard's lap.

Cora lifted her chin and shrugged. "You're wasting your time." She clacked out of the room on her heels.

Opal and Tobias returned their attention to me.

"I take it Gerard is the rich man Cora has set her sights on," Opal said. Tobias would never join in on a catty conversation, but Opal had no problem jumping on board.

"She's already got the wedding dress picked out," I added. "Now, to get back to the important stuff." I pinned Gerard's green card (green for money) to the board. "Aside from his brother, I personally witnessed Sanford Graves, the intended victim as I'm now calling him, in a loud argument with a man named Paul Thornton. The two men were standing on the dock between the boats, and the conversation was anything but congenial. I learned from a man standing nearby that Sanford had Mr. Thornton thrown out of the yacht club. There was something about an inappropriate relationship with one of the staff members." I wrote the name Paul Thornton on a card and added his motive. I stuck it on the board and stood back. "This has to be the saddest looking murder case board we've ever had."

"Is there anything else you can add about the intended victim?" Tobias asked. "His wife died, so I guess we can count her out. What about neighboring yacht owners?"

"I only witnessed the argument with Paul." I snapped my fingers. "Cora told me that Gerard mentioned Sanford had a gambling problem."

"Oh my, that might open a whole other can of worms," Tobias said grimly. "Some of those bookies are downright ruthless. Maybe this was a hit job. You have to admit, it was a pretty elaborate scheme for murder."

I wrote down "gambling problem" on a card. It wasn't a suspect, but it could easily be connected. Tobias was right. You didn't want to get on the wrong side of a bookie.

"I think that's all I've got for now, but I'll keep at it." I smiled. "How does tomato soup and grilled cheese sound for my co-investigators?"

Tobias nodded enthusiastically. "I was just thinking soup and sandwich. You must have read my mind."

twenty-one

AFTER A HEARTY LUNCH I was ready to get back to the marina. The beautiful fall weather was holding. I put on a light coat and scarf and set out toward the harbor. Blush-colored apples were growing on some of the island's wild apple trees. The fruit they produced was tart and too mealy for baking, but the animals and birds loved them. For me, they were the last great show of fall before winter settled in. The entire island vibrated with color, and the sky was a clear blue. Even without a murder to investigate, it was a great day for a walk. I'd found that the less I thought about the mysterious photo and the missing coffee can money, the better I felt. The initial shock had left me feeling beside myself. My limbs felt strangely heavy, and a knot had formed in my stomach, but this afternoon my steps felt lighter. All my dear friends had given me the same advice. Push away the past and get on with living. That was great advice.

The wharf was packed with an afternoon crowd, and the smell of savory sizzling food wafted over the whole boardwalk. I was still full from the soup and grilled cheese, but a cherry snow cone sounded refreshing. I stopped to buy one and noticed Ansel Dell was in his usual spot with a hot dog on a stick. He was still decked out in clunky gold jewelry. He was smiling smugly and looking quite happy about something. Glancing around, I realized Roberta's death had not caused even a ripple in the festivities.

I bought my cherry snow cone and stepped away from the kiosk. The first bite was cold and sweet. I spotted Paul Thornton, the man who'd argued with Sanford and one of the two suspects on my corkboard. He joined Ansel at the railing with a cup of hot cider. There was no reason why I couldn't also enjoy my cherry treat at the railing. I positioned myself not so close as to look as if I was eavesdropping but close enough that I could, indeed, eavesdrop.

They were in the middle of a conversation and, not surprisingly, the topic was the fire and resulting death. "Graves is probably doing a little happy dance," Paul said between sips of cider. "That woman was always complaining and whining. She had everything, but it was never enough."

"Still, it's a tragedy," Ansel said, proving himself more human than his acquaintance. "Do you think they'll be able to save the *Grand Dame*? It was such a nice boat."

"Nah. I'm sure they'll salvage her for parts. Sanford can use the insurance to build another."

It was an interesting conversation. A woman had died. A

man had lost his wife. Even if she wasn't the most pleasant person, I'd witnessed Sanford in a terrible state of grief. He was not doing a happy dance. But Ansel and Paul were focused on the yacht's fate and the prospect of building a whole new one. It was those shallow bits of reality that made me glad I was just a pauper with an old boarding house and little else to my name. I never wanted to be like them.

The two men went their separate ways. I didn't hear anything in the conversation that would have put the spotlight on Paul Thornton as the killer. This case was particularly confusing because it seemed the wrong person was locked in the smoky sleeping quarters. Was someone trying to kill Sanford? If that was the case, then Paul was still a viable suspect. Was Roberta the true victim? Then, I had work to do to come up with a list of possible suspects. Sanford would be on the list, even though he seemed in a genuine state of grief.

I was in luck. The gangplank was still in place on the *Grand Dame*. The cones and yellow tape were still up, and the sign warning everyone to keep out remained. I stepped over the yellow tape and headed up the ramp. Damp soot made the whole boat smell like a campfire. It was sad to see such an elegant vessel, one that used to ride the waves in glossy glory, be reduced to a broken-down yacht that would be salvaged for parts. Paul had brought up the insurance on the boat. I was sure the insurance company wasn't going to be pleased to hear about the calamity. The *Grand Dame* had to be worth a few million.

The cabin door was hanging slightly open. I pushed it wider and stepped into the cabin. The smell of wet smoke was even stronger inside. It was still acrid enough to make my eyes water.

I moved cautiously around the cabin, not wanting to disturb anything. In my eyes, it was a crime scene, even if Norwich didn't think so. A half-empty bottle of wine sat on the blackened galley counter. An empty wine glass covered with soot stood next to it. Had Roberta fixed herself one more nightcap before falling asleep? Aside from being covered in soot, ash and moisture, the galley was clean. I walked over to the upholstered dining nook and spotted a light green linen napkin on the cushion. Small black anchors were printed around the border of the napkin. It looked like a custom linen. I took a picture of it. I wasn't going to make the same mistake I'd made with the rope ladder. Something told me I'd missed a key piece of evidence by not taking a photo of it.

It felt wrong but since I was the only person trying to get justice for Roberta, I headed into the bedroom. The bed, also covered with soggy soot, was open. The quilt had been pushed haphazardly aside, which lined up with my theory that Roberta had smelled the smoke and tried to escape. If the chair hadn't been jammed against the door, she very likely would have survived. Her purse, a lavender Chanel clutch, was sitting open on the dresser. It was unlatched and looked as if someone had gone through it. A linen handkerchief with the initials RG embroidered into a cluster of purple violets was draped over the side of the purse, and her lipstick and mascara were sitting outside the clutch. It made sense if Sanford had decided to go to the hotel room. The key might have been in her bag. That was when I noticed the corner of something sticking out from underneath the purse. I moved the purse aside. It was one of the folded envelopes the Frostfall Hotel gave out with key cards for the rooms. One of the cards for Suite 505 was missing. Sanford obviously took it to get into the room.

It seemed I wasn't going to learn much from the crime scene. I'd already discovered the biggest piece of evidence, though it wasn't really physical evidence, just a clean spot on the door.

The smoky odor was getting to me. It seemed there wasn't much evidence inside, but that made sense since the victim was alone in the cabin. I gulped in some of the fresh sea air as I walked around the outside of the cabin area. It was easy to find where the fire had started. It was on the port side of the yacht. Most of the damage was located around the cabin area. Parts of the fiberglass structure on the outside had collapsed. My foot kicked a chunk of debris. It moved enough to expose the end of a stick. It was bigger than a toothpick, so I knew it hadn't been dropped by Norwich. I pushed the debris aside farther. It was a used matchstick.

After standing in the same spot for a few seconds, the breeze kicked up another scent, one that was far more chemical than the melted fiberglass. It was gasoline. I took in another whiff. Definitely gasoline. I hadn't been privy to the fire inspector's report, but it seemed gasoline was the accelerant, and a simple matchstick was the starter. It was astounding to think that Norwich had stuck his head in the sand on this one. Nothing about the case said accident.

I'd spent enough time at the crime scene. It was time to talk to some of the suspects. And Paul Thornton, the man who'd argued with Sanford Graves, seemed like a good place to start.

twenty-two

I KNEW little about my first suspect, Paul Thornton, except that he drank martinis, he wore pressed trousers and shiny shoes, and he didn't like Sanford Graves. I hadn't seen him on any of the boats, but I spotted Ansel Dell sunning himself on the bow of his leased yacht. It was a much smaller vessel, not nearly as elegant on closer inspection, and it was sandwiched between the two Graves brothers' yachts.

"Excuse me," I called up to him. It took me a few tries to get his attention.

He lifted his sunglasses and sat forward. "Yes?"

I shielded my eyes. "I wonder if you could tell me where I might find Paul Thornton."

"Thornton?" he repeated. "Of course, he's on the Majesty 70, third slip from the wharf. It's called *Sea Glass*."

"Thanks so much."

"Did I see you coming off the *Grand Dame*?" he asked before I could walk away.

"Uh, yes. Guess I was just being nosy." Occasionally, I took the time to explain myself, but I was in a hurry. The harvest moon celebration would be over tomorrow, and all the boats would be heading back to their home marinas. I needed to find the killer before everyone floated off into the wild blue yonder.

Ansel found my "being nosy" comment amusing. My answer seemed to satisfy him. He lowered his sunglasses, rested back in his chair and picked up the drink next to him. I headed off toward Thornton's yacht.

The *Sea Glass* had beautiful clear green stained-glass embellishments at the bow of the boat. It was a nice change from the mostly white fiberglass in the marina. Like Ansel, Paul and a woman were sitting on deck chairs enjoying the lovely weather. If not for a chill in the air, it could almost be mistaken for a summer day.

I needed to be bold. Time was not on my side. Most of the vessels had their gangplanks lowered so people could visit between boats. I headed up the ramp and then, not knowing the protocol, I awkwardly knocked on the railing to get their attention. "Hello, permission to come on board," I said cheerily. Oddly enough, a pair of white deck shoes was sitting on top of the railing. As I turned my head in the direction of the shoes, I caught a whiff of gasoline. Certainly not what I was expecting.

Paul stood up to greet me. "Please, permission granted," he said with a laugh. "How can I help you?"

Since I was not a member of his social circle, my best route was to tell him the truth. "I'm Anna St. James. I'm an island-appointed investigator. Whenever something particularly significant happens, like a death on the island, I get to the bottom of it."

Paul took his time to look me up and down first. He grinned smugly. "Well, isn't that quaint."

I had to hold back a scowl. "I suppose that's one way to put it. Anyhow, I've got a few questions, if you don't mind."

Paul crossed his arms—casually, not defensively—and tilted his head. He was showing me that he didn't take any of this seriously, which was fine. He didn't know my track record. If he did, and, if he was the killer, then he might be a little less flippant.

"I witnessed an argument between you and Sanford Graves. It was quite public."

Paul's head straightened. "That's right. I'm not embarrassed about it. What do you want to know?"

"What started the fight?"

He squinted at me. "What's this about?" Now, his eyes rounded. "Was someone trying to kill Sanford Graves when they lit the boat on fire? I thought it was awfully lucky of him to be across the way in the hotel last night."

"I can't confirm that. As I said—I'm just trying to get all the facts together. We take safety and security very seriously here on Frostfall."

His grin was annoyingly smug. "Then, you should get some security out on this marina because a multi-million-dollar yacht just got charred like a piece of toast."

"We don't normally have yachts parked in our marina," I

noted. "What was the argument about?" I asked curtly. I needed to get to the point because the man was irritating.

"Not sure if it's your business," he said, then shrugged. "Sanford is a cranky old man with too much money and power. He didn't like me, so he got me kicked out of the yacht club. I found a better one, more suited to my lifestyle, so he actually did me a favor. We're not friends. Never were. But if you're snooping around here trying to find out if I tried to kill the man because I didn't like him, you're wasting your time. Jennifer and I"—he glanced back at the woman sitting on deck—"we went to bed at 10. The sirens woke us. I didn't have anything to do with the fire. If you think it was Sanford that was supposed to die—"

"I didn't say that. I'm just covering all aspects of the case."

"Well, Sanford Graves is not a well-liked man. Last I heard, he was having some problems with gambling debt. He used to bet big on the horses, sports—you name it, the guy was laying down money."

"But would killing the man help repay the debts he owed?" I asked. I wasn't fully convinced it was angry bookies plotting to kill Sanford. It didn't make much sense.

Paul looked down and flicked a gnat off his blue polo shirt. "I think if you anger someone enough, they'll resort to drastic measures."

"But he never angered you enough?" I asked.

He shook his head. "I couldn't care less about Sanford Graves. As long as he stays out of my way, I can just as easily pretend he doesn't exist."

The woman, Jennifer, decided to find out what we were

talking about. She was attractive with a slim figure and long brunette hair. She looked about ten years younger than Paul. She laced her arm around his when she reached us. "What's this about, Paulie?"

"This woman is some kind of an investigator." He was starting to annoy me more. Maybe it was just the rich, snobby tone that was irritating, especially coupled with the phrase *some kind*. There was no way to take that phrase as anything but insulting.

"Jen, can you give Miss St. James the rundown of our evening last night?"

Jen pressed a long red fingernail against her chin. "Well, we went to dinner at the hotel restaurant. We had white wine with the meal, and it gave me a headache. It happens a lot when I drink wine. Then, we took a short walk on the wharf, but it was horribly crowded and that made my headache worse. At about nine we came back to the *Sea Glass*. I took some sleep tablets, and we went to bed."

"Sleep tablets?" I asked.

"Yes, I opted for sleeping tablets instead of aspirin. We'd eaten spicy food, and I knew the aspirin would give me heartburn."

"I guess you slept pretty tightly then," I noted.

She laughed but Paul's jaw tightened. He knew what I was getting at. Jennifer jumped right back in. "Paul woke me to let me know there was a fire on one of the boats. This morning, when I woke up, I thought I'd just dreamt the whole thing. Then, I saw that poor pretty boat, and I realized it had happened."

"I can assure you, I was right next to her all night," Paul added.

"Of course. I won't take up any more of your time." I turned, then noticed the white deck shoes again. I looked back. "Odd place to keep your shoes."

"I'm airing them out," Paul said. "I spilled gasoline on them. The pump wasn't working right." He rolled his eyes. "I guess I should have expected it from a place with an island-appointed investigator."

I forced a smile. "Have a nice day." I headed toward the gangplank. I didn't like the guy at all, but he had that spilled gas story ready to go. Was that because he needed to have a story ready in case someone asked or because it was exactly what'd happened? It did seem odd that he'd put the shoes out in plain view if they were evidence.

I was just as glad to be off the *Sea Glass*. The sun was starting to get low in the sky. I could hear musicians warming up their instruments on the wharf. All the activities were going on as usual. It seemed odd, but then the official detective on the case had already declared it an accident. If he'd labeled it a murder, it might have made some people think twice about staying for the second night of fun. I supposed, in that respect, I had Norwich to thank for everyone sticking around.

I still had one major suspect to talk to—Cora's new friend and Sanford's estranged brother, Gerard Graves. I hoped he'd be more congenial than Mr. Thornton.

twenty-three

VOICES and quiet music drifted off the deck of Gerard Graves' *Gemstone*. The tone of the conversations and music was somewhat sedate. I wasn't surprised to see Cora sitting amongst the small group gathered around a table drinking cocktails. My sister was the first to spot me, and she didn't look too pleased. Gerard looked up next. He said something to Cora, which I partially lip read as "is that your sister?" She nodded *yes* with little enthusiasm. However, he hopped right up, smoothed back his graying hair and headed toward me with a welcoming smile. Just like with Cora and me, the difference between the brothers was remarkable. Sanford was small and slender and dressed impeccably with a sharply-pressed shirt and trousers. Gerard was a big, burly man with an impressive, almost menacing, shoulder span. The white cotton shirt he was wearing was noticeably wrinkled, and he wore faded jeans. He almost bordered on slovenly. Cora normally preferred impeccably dressed men, but I supposed, as long as Gerard had a bursting-at-the-seams bank account, Cora could overlook a wrinkled shirt.

Gerard put out his hand. "Welcome aboard. May I call you Anna?"

"Absolutely."

"I'm Gerard. What can I get you? A whiskey sour? A vodka and orange juice?"

"No, I'm fine, thanks."

Cora meandered over, most likely to make sure her sister didn't do anything to ruin her latest *project*. "Anna, what brings you here?" Of course, Cora knew the reason for my visit.

"It's about Roberta's death, isn't it?" Gerard asked me. "Cora told me you investigate murders on the island. I'm impressed. I've always thought if I hadn't been stuck in the family business, I would have become a private investigator." Gerard was a credit to wealthy people. It seemed you could be both extremely rich and charming. He was rare for his species.

"I was with Gerard last night until 10," Cora blurted. "You know that, Anna."

Gerard seemed to find it sweet that she was sticking up for him with a very flimsy and mostly meaningless alibi. The fire didn't start until well past midnight. Gerard winked at her for the effort.

"I understand that you think Roberta's death was intentional. While I wasn't close with my sister-in-law, I've never had ill-will toward her. She used to throw lovely holiday parties, and she was always a gracious host." It was the first nice thing I'd heard anyone say about Roberta.

"That's good to hear," I said. "I think this is a little more complicated and somewhat shocking."

Gerard's brows lifted. His face and features were big like the rest of him. "Is that so?" He glanced over at his guests. They were involved in a conversation that seemed to be centered on the stock market. "Let's go inside, so we can talk about this in private. Cora, sweetums, why don't you join the others."

Cora's small chin hung down. When she recovered, her lips formed a frown. Gerard leaned over and kissed her forehead. That seemed to placate her. She flashed me one of her sisterly scowls and spun around on her heels.

"My friends are already utterly besotted with your sister. She's like no one I've ever met."

"Yes, besotted-ness kind of follows her around." It seemed that my sister's magic hadn't lessened with age. She was still stunning, and she still held a captive audience wherever she went. Maybe I'd be losing her soon. I hoped not, but at the same time, I wanted her to be happy.

We stepped into the cabin area. It was simpler with far less marble and brass than on Sanford's boat. It wasn't neat and tidy either. There were dishes in the galley sink, and a carton of milk had been left out. Several dirty napkins were bunched up on a plate that was covered with ketchup. It sat on the dining table. Still, it was a magnificent boat.

"Are you sure I can't get you something?" he asked again.

"No, I'm fine, thanks."

He motioned to the table and then hastily picked up the ketchup covered plate. He carried it to the sink. "You'll have to excuse the mess. I didn't bring my crew with me because it was just going to be for a weekend. I tend to be somewhat of a slob." It was a nice save. The mention of his crew was putting him back on that shiny, rich man pedestal, but he added in a nice, warm touch with a little self-deprecation. I was sure not many men of his status would admit that about themselves. Maybe this time Cora was heading the right direction with her choice. He even looked fit and healthy and, more notably, decades younger than the last two.

We sat at the table. I was always far less comfortable inside a cabin than out on deck. I rarely stepped into Michael's wheelhouse or cargo hold because I tended to get seasick. There was just enough wind in the harbor to cause the boat to bob up and down. I'd have to make it a quick interview. I'd hate to embarrass myself, acting as the all-important investigator one minute and hanging sick over the railing the next.

"What's all this about, Anna?"

"I haven't spoken to Sanford about this yet. The few times I saw him he was still deep in a state of shock."

Gerard's face twitched a little. I couldn't be certain, but it seemed he didn't believe his brother's state of grief. I decided to let it go. After all, they were estranged, so it would be a biased opinion either way. "I see," he said. "Is he a suspect?"

I didn't expect the abrupt turn. "Actually, I think he might have been the intended victim. Roberta was supposed to be staying at the hotel last night. But she fell asleep, so Sanford took the key and used the hotel room. Apparently, he has a snoring problem."

Gerard laughed. "That he does. I used to hear him down the hallway. He sounded like a bear. He broke his nose playing polo when we were teens."

"This might be the first time I've met anyone who played polo as a teenager. Anyhow, if my theory is correct, and the person who started the fire intended for Sanford to be asleep on the boat—"

"Sanford hasn't spoken to me, but I've heard others talking about it. The detective who came to the island said the death was accidental. Although, if the boat was vandalized, I suppose that would make the vandal a killer. But you think the death was intentional?" He seemed genuinely surprised by that revelation. That was because Norwich had already put everyone's mind to rest that all of this was just a boat fire and that Roberta's death was one of the unfortunate consequences. Of all the detectives in the world, how on earth did Frostfall end up with such a clown?

"I've found evidence that points to possible murder." I was being vague on purpose. I'd found in my short career as an investigator that keeping all the cards "close to my chest" was the best way to go. "I think there's a good chance your brother, Sanford, was the target."

Gerard rubbed his chin between his fingers. "I suppose that makes sense if Roberta was supposed to be staying at the hotel." He shook his head. "Maybe my brother is deeper into his gambling problem than I thought."

"I've heard about his gambling debts. I'm just not sure

how his death would help the people he owed. Mr. Graves, Gerard, I'd like to ask a question, but it's just that—a question. Please, don't let it have any bearing on your new friendship with my sister. Otherwise, she'll never talk to me again."

"The inheritance would all come to me," he said before I could ask. "That's what you wanted to know, right? Like I said, I often fantasized about being a private investigator, and I know money is always a big motive for murder. I'll lay the cards on the table, Anna. If Sanford had died in that fire, my inheritance fight would be over, and the entire fortune would go to me. I'm not in this legal battle because I want it all. I just want to protect the fortune my grandfather and father built from Sanford's gambling addiction. If I kept control of the money, I could keep control of his spending."

"That makes sense, and it seems like a good way to help your brother, but I'm sure he doesn't see it that way."

"No, and because of this legal battle, we're both cash poor at the moment. I know that sounds impossible, but everything is tied up in assets and stocks. The accounts are frozen until we get this sorted. That's why he's struggling to pay his gambling debt. To be honest, I've drawn this fight out longer in hopes that he'd learn his lesson and change his ways. But now, with this boat incident, I'm not sure he's changed at all. There are obviously people out to get him."

"That's only if my theory is correct," I added quickly. "Well, I won't keep you from your guests any longer." I stood from the table and was looking up to admire some beautiful hand-blown glass light fixtures when Gerard's hand shot out to keep me from falling headlong over a basket of laundry.

"I'm so sorry. Are you all right?" he asked.

"I'm fine. It was my fault for getting distracted by the pretty light fixtures." I glanced down at the basket. It was overflowing with clothes, mostly casual things like shorts and t-shirts. There was even a sweatshirt on the heap.

"Thank you. I bought those in Italy. The light fixtures, not the laundry. I have plans to walk over to the marina laundry room. Like I said—I'm a slob."

"I must say—you're different than your brother." I smiled. "But then, you've probably noticed that I'm different than my sister."

"I think you're both outstanding in your own ways. I find it incredible that you're out here trying to solve a murder on your own."

"Thank you." Being inside and on a boat was starting to get to me. I was anxious to get into the fresh air. Gerard walked me to the gangplank. I shot a wink at my sister to let her know I heartily approved. Although, if the very kind Gerard turned out to be a killer, then all bets were off. I sure hoped that wasn't the case. He was impressively down to earth ... for a rich man.

twenty-four

I NEEDED SOME REFRESHMENT. Interviewing suspects had left me parched. It had also left me feeling like I was no closer to solving the case. Both men had to remain on the suspect list for now, but my whole theory of Sanford being the intended victim was starting to fray. What if this had just been an act of vandalism with the unfortunate consequence of someone dying? That could broaden the suspect pool to include someone who was merely out to do some damage. Maybe one of the boaters in the harbor was jealous of the fancy yachts and decided to light one on fire. It wasn't all that farfetched an idea. I walked along the dock between the big boats. Rich people sure did like to chat over cocktails.

I glanced to the right to admire a line of illuminated glass pumpkins sitting on the railing of a yacht when I spotted movement from the corner of my eye. I looked over my shoulder, but no one was there. I must have seen something else, like a pigeon or seagull. I continued walking, only this time I heard footsteps behind me. Unless the Frostfall gulls had taken to wearing shoes, I had to dismiss the earlier bird explanation.

I slowed my pace and kept an ear turned back toward the footsteps. I noticed they slowed too. I picked up the pace, and the footsteps sped up. There was still plenty of daylight, and I was far from alone in the busy marina. I stopped abruptly and spun around. The man was small and slightly hunched and dressed in a drab green coat. He looked around quickly for a hiding place, but there weren't any.

I walked toward him. For a second, it seemed he might make a run for it. Nothing about the man looked dangerous. In fact, he looked nervous, almost paranoid. He glanced quickly around again.

"No need to hide. I've seen you. Why are you following me?"

His dark eyes shifted from side to side, and he ducked lower so that the collar of his coat shielded his face. "Shh, not here. Follow me, but try not to look like you're following me." With those confusing, cryptic instructions, he took off toward the wharf. I had to pick up my pace to keep up with him and, at the same time, try and make it look as if I had nothing to do with him. He disappeared behind one of the fish cleaning stations. Not exactly a prime location for a covert discussion. There weren't any fish cleaners this afternoon. Why go fishing when you could get a bowl of clam chowder or a basket of fried fish from one of the kiosks. Besides that, the crowded harbor made fishing difficult. There was too much water traffic for the fish and too many boats and people to get in the way of a fishing line.

I hesitated for a moment before joining him behind the cement wall at the back of the cleaning station. He was a complete stranger, a stranger who was acting very oddly. Then again, what if he knew something about the murder? Besides that, the wharf was packed with people. I could easily make a run for it and be perfectly safe.

I walked around to the back of the station. The man nodded anxiously. "Did you make sure no one saw you?" he asked.

I really hadn't. "People are very busy with their food and the music. I don't think anyone saw me. What's this about, Mr.—"

He shook his head and pulled a handkerchief out of his pocket. "I'll keep my name to myself, if you don't mind." His hands were rough and chapped as he wiped sweat from his forehead. "The important thing is—I know who you are."

Admittedly, I was starting to feel uncomfortable with the whole thing. But curiosity was beating out caution. "I don't understand," I said.

"You're Anna St. James, and you solve crimes. I come to Frostfall to fish. I live just across the harbor. I have a few acquaintances here on the island." He shook his head again. "I won't tell you their names either." He wiped his forehead again. "You'll have to excuse me, I've never done this before."

"Done what before?" I asked.

"Been an informant, an eyewitness. They can remain

anonymous, right? I wouldn't want anyone to know that I told you what I'm about to tell you."

The man did like to talk in circles.

I leaned forward and was instantly assured that he was, indeed, a fisherman. "You know something about the fire this morning?"

He nodded emphatically and finally put away the handkerchief. "I was out on my fishing boat at around midnight. It's just a little tin can with an outboard motor really, but it gets me where I need to go." He paused to smile about his boat. "I puttered toward the marina. The water was less choppy around the yachts, and I tossed in my line for a midnight catch. The harbor is too crowded right now. A man can't even toss his line without hooking it into someone's beer can or bag of chips." He was lightening up considerably from a few minutes earlier when he skulked through the wharf as if he was carrying the nuclear codes in his pocket.

"Did you see something?" I hoped this was going somewhere because I really needed a push on the investigation.

He nodded. "I did. I saw a small dinghy like mine. It had a red number on it, so I think it was one of Kent's rental dinghies." Kent Strong rented fishing boats from a small dock near the swim beach. "I thought, well, that guy had the same idea as me. I thought it might be one of my buddies. There's a group of us who like to fish under the moon, and the moon is sure something this weekend." His teeth were tobacco stained, and the lines on his face were like the ground in a drought-stricken desert, but his smile was warm.

"Was it a friend?" I asked.

"Nope, never got to see the person's face. He was bent over, moving the rudder, and he was wearing a sweatshirt. I think it was dark gray or black. The hood was pulled up over his head, so I couldn't get a good look at him. He didn't notice me either. He headed right toward the yachts, then turned off the motor and pulled out a paddle. Rowed right over to the boat that caught fire. I didn't think anything about it, and I went on with my fishing. Had my headphones on listening to music and sipping from the thermos of hot coffee I'd brought along. I even closed my eyes for a while. Next thing I know, I smell smoke and flames are lapping up over the top of the yacht."

"Did you see the little boat leave?"

"Must have missed him when I had my eyes closed." He grinned. "Did I help? My friends here on Frostfall say you do a real good job catching killers."

"That's nice of them to say. And, yes, you've helped. Thank you so much for taking the time to talk to me. Is there anything else?"

He thought about it for a second. "Only, I hope you catch 'em. Can't have people like that giving us fishermen bad names."

"And may your next midnight catch be a good one. I'll go out first so no one sees us together." I doubted he was in much danger, but if it made him feel better, I was all for keeping the covert operation in place.

"Much appreciated."

"Bye and thanks again." I walked out from our secret hiding place. As I predicted, no one noticed me. I had my next move, and it might be the end to Cora's new romance. Moments before, I nearly tripped over a laundry basket, and there just happened to be a dark gray sweatshirt sitting in the middle of the dirty clothes. I needed to find Gerard Graves.

twenty-five

I HAD to ignore the possibility of a big, loud sister fight. Cora was not going to be happy that I was pursuing Gerard as my number one suspect, but I had a job to do. As soon as that thought crossed my mind, I stopped dead in my tracks. Why *was* this my job? After all, it wasn't as if I was going to get a paycheck for, once again, bringing another killer to justice. This time, my involvement could cause a major rift with my sister, and that didn't seem fair. This was Detective Norwich's job. I hadn't seen him on the island since early this morning, but maybe, just maybe, he'd rethought the whole thing. Maybe he'd open this back up as a murder case. Officer Miller, his assistant, agreed with me that, at the very least, the arsonist who started the fire should be held responsible for Roberta's death. What if he'd gone over Norwich's head to make his concerns known? It wouldn't be the first time Norwich got called out on his insufficient (code word for lazy) investigation.

The music was loud, but the voices on the wharf were louder because they were competing with two large speakers. I headed back to the marina and toward Gerard's boat. It was quieter along the wall of gleaming fiberglass hulls, so I paused to give my friend, Mindy, a call. Mindy used to live on the island, but she moved to the mainland to be closer to her job at the police station. She worked behind a desk, typing and filing reports and keeping the precinct running smoothly. She also knew, mostly from living on Frostfall, that Norwich was a terrible detective. He particularly loathed working on the island. That was why he was always so quick to wrap up cases here, even if it meant arresting the wrong person or calling an obvious murder an accidental death. This time he'd taken the accident shortcut, which was always a little less alarming than the false arrest shortcut.

Mindy answered after three rings. "Hello, Anna, haven't heard from you in ages. I guess that means the island's been murder-free for a few months."

I laughed. "Maybe I should make one of those signs like they have in industrial workplaces where they keep count of the number of days without an accident. Only ours will be for murders. And now, the poster would be back to zero. The winning streak is over."

"But I thought this last death was an accident?" I could hear Mindy shuffling through some papers. "Yep, have it right here signed off by our highly esteemed (sarcasm noted) Detective Buckston Norwich. I was typing it up, and, I thought, why on earth wouldn't the person who set fire to the boat be charged with manslaughter? But then, I'm just a lowly paper shuffler so I can't add in my two cents."

"First of all, 'lowly?' I think not. We both know that precinct would tangle itself into a legal knot if you weren't there keeping things in order. And, as for your two cents—wouldn't it be a kick if you could type a little addendum on each of Norwich's reports citing what he did wrong."

It was her turn to laugh. "That would take me far too much time. So, what's up? Are you looking for the arsonist?"

"I am but arson is the wrong label. This was murder, pure and simple. I found evidence that a deck chair had been pushed against the cabin door, trapping Mrs. Graves inside. She was trying to get out. She was on the floor in front of the door."

"Interesting." Paper rattled through the phone. "It says here that Mrs. Graves had passed out from drinking, this was according to her husband. The husband wasn't on the boat at that hour? That seems strange."

"Apparently, he snores, so Roberta, the victim, had a hotel room reserved. Only, she fell asleep on the boat, so the husband, Sanford, took the hotel room."

"It sounds like he was the intended victim," Mindy said.

"Yes, thank you. See, it's all so clear cut, but Norwich couldn't get out of here fast enough. Not that I'm complaining. I'm always pleased to see the back of him. In this case, I was hoping he'd changed his mind. Officer Miller accompanied him, and he could see how this was, at the very least, manslaughter. I guess I hoped Norwich had reflected further on the case and reopened it as a murder investigation."

"Uh oh, sounds like Frostfall's finest isn't too keen on solving this one on her own," Mindy said.

"This one might be a little stickier than usual."

A phone rang in the background. "Darn, that's the captain. I'll have to hear more about this later, but, as far as I can see, this case is closed on Norwich's end."

"That's what I figured. Talk to you later, Mindy."

I continued on toward Gerard's boat and was almost relieved when I found no one on board. Gerard had mentioned he was going to do his wash at the marina laundry. That basket of dirty clothes was my main focus. I continued on toward the end of the marina where a boat supply shop, a mini market, a laundry room and the gas pump were located.

I could hear the industrial-sized washing machine spinning all the way down the dock. The marina laundry room had two massive washers and dryers, all coin-operated. Anyone could use it, but it was mostly there for the convenience of boaters visiting the island.

I opened the door to the laundry room. It was warm and humid and smelled of detergent. The empty basket in front of the spinning washer matched the basket I'd nearly tripped over. Gerard had, obviously, started his laundry and then took off. I was sure if I walked out to the wharf I'd find him with Cora, either dancing or enjoying some of the food.

The washing machine had a glass front. I stood in front of it for a second, watching as the wet and soapy clothes circled around. After a few turns, the sweatshirt had its moment at the glass. A gray hooded sweatshirt was such a common piece of clothing. I had one somewhere in my closet. But was it a common piece of clothing for a billionaire yachter? Gerard was definitely dressed more casually than most of the other yacht owners, so a gray sweatshirt didn't seem too farfetched. Was he the man my secret informant saw on the fishing dinghy?

I walked out of the laundry area. Sunlight was fading, and soon, the wharf would be even more crowded as people gathered for dancing and an evening under the harvest moon. I needed to talk to Gerard, but I didn't want to waste time searching for him in the crowds. I had a new piece of evidence that might very well lead to the killer. My informant brilliantly noticed that the fishing dinghy the hooded stranger was riding in had big red numbers on the side. It was one of Kent's fishing boat rentals. Whoever rented the boat had to leave a name and credit card.

I headed back the way I came. Kent's rentals were past the harbor near the swimming beach. He ran the whole thing from a small hut on the sand. I was feeling more hopeful now, thanks to my secret informant.

twenty-six

KENT WAS A RETIRED FISHERMAN. He knew Michael. They weren't close, but he came to the memorial and his wife, Joan, brought me several casseroles after Michael's disappearance. Kent had gotten a little rounder in the middle and grayer on top since the last time I saw him. He was standing next to a double kayak showing a young couple how to hold and move the paddles. Kent rented kayaks and boogie boards along with a half dozen fishing dinghies. In the summer, you had to get to the hut early to grab one of his rentals. He usually closed up shop mid-September, but he'd opened up for the special weekend event.

While he gave the slightly nervous future kayakers the rundown on safety and the best places to paddle to, I used the time to check out the dinghies. All six of his *fleet* had been dragged up on the sand. At least two had enough wet sand stuck to their hulls to indicate that they'd been in the water recently. The dinghy used for the crime would've had time to dry.

I wasn't exactly sure what I was looking for, but it seemed Kent would be a few minutes because the couple had a lot of questions. I started with the wettest boats. There was some tangled up fishing line in the bottom of the first one. It was knotted into an angry ball, as if the person started with a slight tangle only to work the whole darn thing into something that was never going to straighten out, so they just twisted it into a ball. The next dinghy was empty except for some wet sand.

I continued my visual inspection. The third boat was free of debris and sand... and a motor, I realized. It probably hadn't been out on the water in a long time. A candy wrapper fluttered underneath one of the paddles in the fourth boat. The fifth boat was my golden ticket. I wouldn't have noticed the matchstick if I hadn't accidentally moved the end of the paddle with my knee. It was a lone matchstick, and it matched the one I saw on the boat. I crouched down and took a picture of it. Then, I backed up and took a picture of the red numbers on the side of the dinghy.

"Is that you, Anna?" Kent called as he trudged toward me through the sand. A big smile deepened the creases around his mouth and across his forehead. He'd always had the look of a salty old fisherman. Retirement hadn't taken away that wonderfully weathered appearance. One thing was certain, he'd slowed down in the last year. The sand wasn't that deep, but he was hiking across it like he was wearing cement boots, instead of the sneakers on his feet.

Kent was breathing hard after the short walk. "What brings you out here, Anna? Don't tell me you're thinking of doing some fishing?" As he said it, he seemed to realize it was a bad taste joke considering my past. His mouth turned down at the edges. "I'm sorry. That was a terrible thing to say given that—well—because—you know." His cheeks reddened under the windburn.

"Please, Kent, don't worry about it. It's been many years. You don't have to tiptoe around me anymore."

"Of course. What brings you out here?" His thick brows hopped up. "Does this have something to do with the yacht fire? I understand someone died. Terrible news."

"Yes, it was very tragic. This does have to do with the boat fire. Come closer to this dinghy. I found something that might be evidence."

Kent walked around to my side of the boat.

"Do you see that matchstick?"

Kent took his glasses out of his shirt pocket. He propped them on his nose and leaned down. "Ah yes, there it is." He reached for it.

"Wait, Kent, is it possible to leave it in place? I took a photo too."

Kent straightened and smiled. "You mean my fishing boat might be part of the crime scene? Well, I'll be. I have a no-smoking rule on my boats." He waved toward the square plastic fuel tank connected to the outboard motor. "It's dangerous to be puffing on a cigar with five gallons of gasoline sitting a few feet away. Still, I know these guys get out there, cast their lines and then think 'Gee, a smoke'd be great right now.' That match might have been dropped by someone breaking that rule." He said it sympathetically, not wanting to be the person to burst my investigator's bubble.

"This match is the same kind I found on the destroyed boat. I have a witness who saw one of your dinghies in the harbor just after midnight last night."

Kent looked stunned. "But I don't rent boats out at night."

"That's what I was afraid of."

"That said, I do rent them out for multiple days, and when they take them out is not really my concern. However, I do warn against going out on the water at night."

I perked up. "How about this one? Was it rented recently?"

"We'll have to look. I was off for two days." He scrunched up his face. "Had to go to the dentist in the city. I've got this one molar"—he shook his head—"You don't want to hear about that. My nephew, Terrence, was running the rental booth." I followed him to his hut. He pulled out his ledger and flipped it open. He squinted out toward the boat to check the number. Then his thick finger ran down a few lines. "Woohee," he said on a puff of breath.

"Did you find out who rented it?" I asked, anxiously. I could have this solved by sunset. I could also ruin my sister's whole day with news that she'd attached herself to a rich, charming killer.

"No, there was hardly any activity at all these past two days. Almost makes me wonder if Terrence even opened the hut or if he just sat in here with the closed sign hanging out front. That kid plays video games like his life depends upon it. I rented those first two boats, the ones closest to the shore, this morning. They were only out for an hour each. The renters both came back angry because there was too much activity in the harbor for a good fishing day. I tried to tell 'em," he added. "That boat with the match hasn't been used at all this weekend."

"How else would the match have gotten inside of it?"

He shrugged. "Could have gotten blown in by the wind." Kent didn't look convinced that anyone had used the boat, but I wasn't so sure.

"What about the fuel tank?" I asked. "Would you be able to tell if it somehow got used without permission?"

"Gosh, Anna, I hadn't thought about that. We usually rope them all together on the sand once we close up, but now that you mention it, I arrived this morning, and Terrence hadn't roped them together. That kid." He shook his head again. Something told me Terrence was going to get an earful. "The tank should be full since it hasn't been out in the water." We headed back across to the small boat. Kent threw a leg inside the dinghy. He pulled in the other leg, slowly. "This darn knee of mine. It's at bone-on-bone. At least, that's what the doctor tells me."

I winced. "Ouch. Bone-on-bone does not sound good."

"Nope, not good at all." He unscrewed the cap on the tank and stuck his eye over the opening. "Well, I'll be darned." He pulled his eye away and put the cap back on. "Someone's used this boat. It's a few good inches below the fill line. You're a heck of a detective, Anna. And, I've got to have a long chat with my nephew."

"Don't be too hard on him," I said. "Thanks so much for your time with this, Kent. I have one more favor."

"Don't let anyone rent that boat in case it's evidence," he said.

"Exactly."

Kent laughed. "And Joan tells me I watch too many of those crime shows. Maybe I'll join ya on the next one." He lifted his bad leg over the side of the boat. "But first, I'm going to need that new knee. It won't be a problem keeping that boat on land. Most of the visitors this weekend came on their own boats, and the few that didn't prefer the kayaks. That is, until they get halfway across the swim beach and then realize they have to paddle all the way back."

"I've been in that predicament myself. Thanks for your help, Kent. I'll let you know what's going on, so we can free that boat up again soon."

"No hurry. After this weekend, everything goes into storage for winter."

"That's right. The weather's been so nice, and there are so many people on the island, I forgot this isn't summer."

I waved and headed back toward the wharf area. I'd put it off long enough. I needed to confront Gerard Graves about his gray sweatshirt.

twenty-seven

MY MAIN SUSPECT'S giant build made him easy to spot, even in a thick crowd. Unfortunately, my sister was still attached to his side. Cora had to really work her pointy heels to avoid the spaces between the planks on the wharf, all while keeping up with Gerard's long stride. Together, they were a striking couple, her elegant beauty and that Grace Kelly profile peering out from the fur-trimmed hood of her coat and Gerard's six-foot-plus, broad-shouldered physique topped off by a thick head of silver fox hair. They were headed toward the end of the marina. I assumed Gerard was picking up his laundry.

That was exactly what I hoped for (except, in my perfect scenario, Cora was at home). The food aromas on the wharf made my mouth water. I was getting a hollow ache in my stomach. Investigating was hard work… when it was done right.

Cora's laugh floated out of the laundry room. I paused. I didn't want to walk in on a kiss or flirty moment. She laughed again. It was flirty, but there was conversation along with it, so I assumed they weren't in the middle of a smooch. Just in case, I knocked lightly on the slightly ajar door. Cora pulled it open. Her big, shiny smile drooped to a disappointed frown. "Oh, it's you."

"Love you, too, sis," I said cheerily. I was going to have to ignore Cora's attachment to my top suspect. If he caused Roberta's death, he needed to pay for it with some serious prison time.

Cora stood in the center of the doorway with her plush, oversized coat. I sidled past and shot her a wink. Gerard was far less happy to see me this time. He did his best to sound polite.

"Anna, didn't expect to see you in the laundry room. I'm all done if you need the machine."

The basket of freshly washed clothes sat at his feet. There was a cloud of warm, fragrant air around them. He'd just pulled them out of the dryer.

"Actually, Gerard, I need to ask you about an article of clothing in your basket."

His first reaction was to laugh. "Wait, you're serious? Well, this is a first." He laughed again. "My wardrobe is rarely of interest to anyone." He waved a hand to remind me of the faded jeans and slightly wrinkled shirt he was wearing. If Cora had found any fault with her newest catch, it would be his sense of fashion. Cora fancied impeccably dressed men. I preferred the ensemble in front of me.

I pointed to the basket. The sleeve of the gray sweatshirt was only partially visible beneath a pair of jeans. "I'm interested in that gray sweatshirt."

"Seriously, Anna," Cora said angrily. Of course, she had no idea where this was heading, so I ignored her.

Gerard looked puzzled. "Gray sweatshirt? I don't think I have a gray sweatshirt." He leaned down to the basket and pulled on the gray sleeve. The rest of the hooded sweatshirt followed. "Well, what do you know? I seem to have a gray sweatshirt. Only, it's not mine."

"But it's in your laundry," I noted.

"That it is. Just not sure how it got there." He smiled. "But I can prove to you this isn't mine." As he pushed his first massive arm into the sweatshirt, it became instantly and comically clear that the sweatshirt did not belong to Gerard. Cora giggled behind me, thrilled to see her sister humiliated in this endeavor. The sleeve was stretched to the limit on Gerard's big arm, and the end of the sleeve came halfway up his forearm. "I can keep going, but as you see, it's not exactly my size."

"Yes, I see that. Why was it in your basket?" I asked.

"That's a good question." Gerard held up the sweatshirt and checked the pockets. They were empty. "Now that I think about it, I'd set the basket out near the gangplank as a reminder that I needed to take a trip to the laundry. Then, people were stopping by to visit and share their condolences, so I pushed the basket back inside. Remember, you almost tripped over it."

"Right. And I saw that sweatshirt in the basket of clothes when I stumbled over it."

"I didn't notice it. The last thing I expected was someone adding clothes to my laundry basket. Why is the sweatshirt important? Does it have something to do with the fire and Roberta's death?"

Cora circled around and stood next to Gerard to let me know she was standing by her man. She even wrapped a hand possessively around his arm. Her annoying, smug smile followed. It did seem that Gerard had dropped to the bottom of the suspect list.

"A witness saw someone in a rented fishing dinghy motoring around the marina and the *Grande Dame* just before the fire. The person in the boat was wearing a dark sweatshirt with the hood pulled up over their head."

"Wow, someone really planned this," Gerard said. "I was sure it had been a random act of arson that went terribly wrong. I'm afraid you're wasting your time with me, Anna. I'm not your guy. You can take this if you need it."

I took hold of the sweatshirt. It didn't do me much good without the owner attached. It was obvious someone had ditched the sweatshirt to get rid of evidence. That meant the suspect knew he or she was seen. Gerard's basket happened to be out sitting in the sunshine, so they dropped it in. What if the basket being outside was more than convenient? I looked up at Gerard.

"Do you think someone was trying to frame you for this?" I asked point blank. It seemed that unsettling thought hadn't occurred to him.

"I don't know." He looked stunned. "This is getting very worrisome. Listen, Anna, do you still think that Sanford was the intended victim?"

"It's a theory. By the way, is your brother staying at the hotel? I haven't seen him all day."

"Yes, he's there trying to make arrangements. I'm sure he's also dealing with the insurance side of this. Frankly, this whole thing has him in a terrible state of distress. I called him earlier. I didn't expect him to be friendly, given what's going on between us, but he could barely form complete sentences. This has really destroyed him."

"I'm sure this has been difficult. This case is especially hard because I don't know if I'm looking for motive to kill Roberta or to kill Sanford."

Gerard straightened. "I asked you about your theory again because I might have a lead. I heard from friends this afternoon that Sanford is even deeper into debt than I realized. There's a man here this weekend. His boat is called *Blue Maiden*. The owner's name is Jim Griffith. Apparently, Sanford owes Griffith ten grand from a poker game. Now, I haven't spoken to Griffith, but I intend to get the debt paid. I can talk to the lawyers. They'll free up some assets to take care of the problem. I know Griffith pretty well. He's a bit of a hothead. I've seen him hurl a golf club clear across the green in a temper tantrum over a lost golf game. He's a big gambler like my brother. Most of Griffith's money is from a massive inheritance, but he's built it up with good investing and a lot of risky bets that paid off. Now, I'm not saying Griffith did this. I just want to help out with the information I know. I'm regretting that Sanford and I fell so far apart in our relationship. It seems he needed me more than I realized. It's hard when siblings grow into adulthood. I'm only three years older than Sanford, but I watched over him growing up. He was always slight in his build, and I was a teenage tank. He'd get bullied, and I'd step in to terrorize the mean kids. I liked that I could take care of my little brother. We grew up in a 30-room mansion with nannies and staff. Our parents hardly had time to say hello, let alone show us the attention kids need."

I smiled briefly at Cora. We'd definitely had our differences, only we were already worlds apart as children. It actually made our relationship more fun, like a vaudeville act. As children of divorce, we were each other's best and most secure family member.

Cora had softened her angry stance. She was relieved that the ill-fitting sweatshirt had basically cleared Gerard from the suspect list. Now, it seemed, I had a new suspect on my list. I wondered how many other names should be on it. The weekend was rushing by too fast, and there were far too many people on the island to narrow it down to an important few.

"Well, Gerard, thank you for indulging me by trying on the sweatshirt. I let my suspicions get ahead of me. My informant didn't mention anything about the person in the boat being bigger than average."

Gerard's laugh boomed off the walls of the small room. "That's one way to put it. Please, if you talk to Jim Griffith, don't mention the information came from me. I play golf with him occasionally."

I smiled. "Not sure if I'd play golf with a man who hurled his club across the green."

Gerard shrugged his wide shoulders. "He's pleasant enough when he's in a good mood. And we both like the same golf course. That's why I've got to square things with him on Sanford's debt. I doubt Jim's your man either, but I thought you should know just how deep my brother's problems run." His brow furrowed. "Couldn't they call the detective back to the island? This seems like something he should be handling."

Cora hugged his arm. "Remember what I told you, darling?" The word darling was being tossed about. This was getting serious fast. "Norwich hates coming to the island, so he writes everything off as an accident. That's why Anna has to cover for him."

"That's a shame. Still, I envy you getting do a little sleuthing on the side." Gerard picked up his basket. I balled up the sweatshirt and tucked it under my arm. I had to keep my eyes out for a much slighter suspect.

We stepped outside. The celebration was in full swing on the wharf. Music thrummed over the harbor, and a mix of savory and sweet smells swirled through the air. The sun was clinging to its last hour of power before a rosy dusk streaked the sky. There were a few wispy clouds on the horizon, but it seemed the star of the party, the harvest moon, was still going to loom large and unobstructed over the event.

"I'll see you both later. Thanks again for your help." I had another lead, and with the way things were going, I was happy to have it. First, I needed some sustenance. I was losing energy fast. A smoothie was the perfect choice.

twenty-eight

I'D SEEN Jim Griffith's *Blue Maiden* during one of my many hikes along the boat slips. It was a remarkably pretty boat, pearl white with periwinkle blue trim. The yacht was moored about halfway down the marina. Gerard and Cora had taken off with his basket of laundry. I heard them make plans— Cora would head home to shower and change for dinner at the hotel and then dancing on the wharf. My sister was smiling and giggling like a teenager when they parted ways. It was hard to gauge just how serious this thing between them was. After all, they'd known each other less than a day, and for a big portion of that time, the man was my main suspect for murder. I was firmly on the other side of that fence now. Gerard had nothing to do with his sister-in-law's death. I was sure of it.

A strawberry and mango smoothie put the pep back in my step. I walked, yet again, toward the marina. I was starting to memorize the order of the yachts. Ansel Dell's leased vessel was easy to spot because he was sandwiched between the Graves brothers. Sanford's charred yacht looked sad and lonely. There was no sign of the owner. Ansel, however, leaned against the railing of his boat taking pictures of the harbor.

"Afternoon," I called up to him. "Mind if I come aboard?" It occurred to me as I walked by his boat for the millionth time that he had the best vantage point to have seen something suspicious.

"Sure, come on up? Is your sister with you?" he asked, hopefully.

"I'm afraid it's just me." I tried not to be too insulted by his utter disappointment. After all, it had happened to me constantly when I was a kid. I headed up the ramp and joined him up near the bow of the boat.

"There was so much activity in the harbor, I decided to take a few videos to remind myself of this weekend," Ansel explained as I reached him. "Not that I'll need much reminding after all that's happened," he added grimly.

"Have you seen Sanford Graves?" I asked. "I've been all over the wharf and marina, and I haven't seen him."

"I saw him this morning but not since then. It's not like he can hang out on his boat." He glanced in the direction of the wrecked yacht and clucked his tongue. "Such a shame." He turned back to me. "I'm sure he's taking care of insurance claims and, of course, there are calls to make to family." He shook his head. "Again, such a shame. So, is she with Graves?" he asked suddenly.

"Who?" I was confused.

"Cora. Is she with Graves? Oh, he puts on a good act, always charming and friendly." This new topic had my interest. If Gerard did have an ugly side, I wanted to know about it for Cora's sake.

"Are you saying he's not usually friendly? Is there a dark side to Gerard Graves?" Maybe deep down I was hoping it was true, so I could warn Cora and talk her into staying on the island. But would she believe me? Would she listen? Probably not.

"Well, I don't know him that well," Ansel admitted. "He's always smiling and laughing and wearing those wrinkled clothes to show how down-to-earth he is. But with that fortune, how could he possibly be?"

It was clear that this whole topic was driven solely by jealousy. Ansel didn't have any specifics to prove that Gerard wasn't who he purported to be. I was probably more relieved than disappointed. I didn't relish having to tell Cora that Gerard wasn't the man for her.

"I'm sure there are plenty of rich people who are earthier like us regular folk," I said. I had to work hard to hide my amusement. It seemed that Ansel worked his entire life to be the opposite of earthy. "Mr. Dell, I was wondering, given your proximity to Sanford's yacht, did you hear or see anything last night? One witness mentioned they saw a small, rented dinghy in the water near the *Grand Dame* just before the fire."

I certainly didn't expect the reaction I got from the simple question. Ansel fidgeted with the edge of his jacket. He was no longer smiling or looking me in the eye. "Uh, no, I'm a heavy sleeper. Didn't hear or see a thing," he said.

I waited a second to see if he wanted to amend his statement with one that sounded far more honest. Instead, he turned his attention back to the harbor. "With so many boats out here, I don't see how anyone could have seen a dinghy. Maybe the person was mistaken."

"Yes, that's possible. So, you didn't hear a motor? Those little boats produce a loud buzz."

"Nope, nothing." His head was shaking emphatically. It was overkill, actually. He wanted me to know that he saw and heard nothing, which led me to believe that he did see or hear something. Or was he the culprit?

Ansel had a slight enough build to fit the sweatshirt tucked under my arm. I considered, briefly, asking him to try it on, but I didn't want to scare him off. Did he have motive? It seemed like he had more motive to harm Gerard than Sanford. Since I conveniently had the sweatshirt, I had an idea. I unfurled it. "I found this nice gray sweatshirt sitting on one of the marina benches." I gave it a little shake and even held it up near him. "Looks like your size. Are you missing a sweatshirt?"

Ansel laughed. "I assure you I don't have any hooded sweatshirts in my wardrobe." The snooty implication could not be missed. He didn't have the same fidgety reaction when I held up the sweatshirt, which led me to believe he was not the killer.

"I suppose you're not the sweatshirt type. I was hoping to find the owner. You didn't happen to see anyone wearing it out here on the marina?"

He laughed. "It's hardly a clothing item worth notice."

Ansel forced a grin. "Well, I've got some calls to make. It was nice of you to drop by and say hello." To go along with his earlier caginess, I was being brusquely dismissed. Ansel walked me personally to the exit. He was certainly acting oddly. I tucked this whole interaction away for now. "Thanks for letting me stop by. Will you be at the dance tonight?" I asked.

"I doubt it. Too much of a crowd. I suppose Cora will be there with Graves," he said grumpily. Poor guy, one or two quick dates with my sister, and he was fully smitten.

"I don't know what her plans are. I'll see you later, Mr. Dell." I left his boat and turned in the direction of Jim Griffith's *Blue Maiden*.

twenty-nine

I'D REACHED Jim Griffith's boat. A member of his crew was hosing off the hull. The yacht was pretty spectacular with its bright blue accents, shiny chrome railings and teak trimmed deck. It had a long, low profile, which made it look sleek and far more modern than most of the vessels moored around it. Before I could ask the crewmate if Griffith was on board, my phone vibrated with a call. I'd been out and about all day and hadn't spoken to anyone but Cora. I was sure Opal was getting concerned, but the call was from Nate.

"Hey, what's up? Did you solve the crime?" he asked first.

"Not quite. In fact, I'm sort of back at the start because my main suspect, Sanford's brother, was too big to fit in my main piece of evidence."

"Hmm, sounds like a lot to unpack there. I'll have to hear all about it."

"How was the ride?" I could hear talking and music and the distinct sound of beer mugs clinking in the background.

"It was great, but we're both beat. We stopped to have a beer with a few of my old friends."

I should have been happy that he was meeting old friends, but I always worried that those same friends would lure him back to the mainland, back to his old life. "Friends from work?" I asked and immediately wanted to kick myself for being nosy.

"Yeah, my friends are mostly from work." He sounded disappointed that I asked, and now, I double wanted to kick myself. "I'll be back in time to shower, so we can go to the dance."

"The dance," I said. "I forgot all about it. I've been out on the wharf all day doing the work of the local detective."

"Yeah, that's not right, Anna." Someone called his name in the background.

"I don't want to keep you from your friends, and I've got a suspect to interview."

"I know you're great at this, and you know what you're doing, but be careful."

"How dangerous can a multi-millionaire with a blue-trimmed yacht be?" I decided not to mention that Griffith was considered a hothead who hurled golf clubs when angry.

"We'll be back soon. Love ya." He hung up with that sweet sentiment, which helped counter the worry I had that he was back on the mainland having a great time with his friends.

Opal called before I could put the phone away.

"Hey, Opal, I'm still out on the wharf," I said before she could ask.

"I was starting to wonder. Tobias went to meet friends for

a day hike on Calico Peak, so Huck and I have had the whole day to ourselves. He decided to join me for a Gregory Peck marathon, but he got bored and fell asleep halfway through *Roman Holiday*. You must be exhausted, Anna."

"Now that you mention it—I am. I think it might just be eggs and potatoes for dinner."

"Don't worry about dinner. Cora came home a while ago and went straight in for a bath. I'm sure everyone is planning to go to the dance. I'll make myself some toast and tea."

"Thanks, Opal, but I'm hoping to get home soon. I've got sourdough bread in the breadbox. I'll hard boil some eggs and make egg salad. I've got one more stop to make and then I'm tossing in the towel for now. I'll see you soon."

"All right. Hope this next stop is the winner," she said.

I sighed. "Me too."

I didn't need to ask the man hosing off the hull if Griffith was on board. A wealthy-looking man, about 50 and with a big Rolex watch, was just disembarking from the *Blue Maiden* as I hung up the call. I was tired, hungry and getting nowhere fast. I decided to get straight to it.

"Mr. Griffith," I said, "may I have a word?"

He had thinning hair that was greased down, and his blue shirt matched the trim on his boat. "Who are you?" he asked. There was enough condescension in his tone to assure me he was *that* kind of rich person. It made me think that if Cora could land Gerard Graves, then I'd be all for it. So far, he was the only yacht owner I'd met without *attitude*. It would be a wonderful and rare catch to snatch up one of the charming ones.

"My name is Anna St. James," I said sharply. "I'm investigating the murder of Roberta Graves." Like I said—I was too tired to run circles anymore.

His trimmed gray brow lifted. "You're law enforcement?"

I supposed it was a reasonable question. "Not exactly."

"I think you have the wrong person." He tried to sweep past me.

"Is it true Sanford Graves owed you money?" I blurted.

He paused his pristine blue deck shoes and turned back around. "How on earth did you know that?"

"Look, I know this seems odd, but I'm investigating the death of Roberta Graves. Her death wasn't accidental."

"That's not what I heard," he said. He was less abrupt. It seemed the mention of money and, possibly, morbid curiosity had reeled him back in. "The local detective said it was exactly that."

"An accelerant was used to spread the fire. Does that sound accidental?"

He had the thinnest gray moustache that rocked up and down as he considered the question. "Well, no, I hadn't heard anything about an accelerant. But what does this have to do with the money Sanford owed me? You don't think I had anything to do with it. Besides, he told me he had the money to repay me." He glanced around. "Speaking of which, I haven't seen Sanford all day."

"I think he's at the hotel recuperating from the shock and taking care of arrangements."

"Yes, that makes sense. Quite stunning what happened.

Even more so if it was all intentional. But why would anyone want to kill Roberta Graves?"

"I'm not sure Roberta was the intended victim."

My meaning was becoming clearer to Mr. Griffith. "You think someone tried to kill Sanford, and you think that I had something to do with it and all for a paltry sum of 10 thousand dollars. I didn't even care if he paid it back. It's just the principal of the thing. Sanford has a gambling problem and making sure he pays off his debts will show him he needs to take care of it."

Griffith wasn't giving off any guilty vibes. After an abrasive start, he wasn't even giving off hothead vibes, but then we weren't on a golf course. He could have easily taken great offense to me asking about the debt, threatening to call his lawyer and all that stuff rich people liked to say.

"My wife, Hannah, and I decided to rent a suite in the hotel last night. We just finished a tour in the Greek Isles, and we were exhausted. I didn't want to come to this event, but Hannah was looking forward to it. It was so noisy out here on the harbor, we decided we could get better sleep in the hotel. We weren't even out here last night. In fact, we slept through most of the chaos and woke to the news." He snapped his fingers. "Come to think of it—when we were leaving the hotel restaurant, we spotted Sanford in the lobby. It was quite late, possibly eleven. I called to him, but he didn't hear me. I thought it was strange because the lobby was mostly empty. I figured he was avoiding me because of the debt. But earlier yesterday, he'd texted me that he had the money. Never saw even one dollar. I wondered why he was in the hotel and not on the boat."

"Roberta had reserved the room. She didn't want to sleep on the boat, but she ended up falling asleep, so Sanford took the room." The more times I repeated that explanation, the sillier it sounded.

Griffith nodded. "I see, so Sanford should have been in the cabin. All of this is quite stunning. Should the rest of us be worried?"

Of course, I didn't know anything for certain. "I don't think this was random. I'm just trying to get to the bottom of it."

"I'm confused. How did you end up with the task?"

I smiled. "It's a long story. Thank you for your time, Mr. Griffith, and enjoy the rest of your stay on the island."

That was it. I'd reached the end of the line with leads. Ansel's nervous behavior had me wondering if he should be placed on the list or if he just knew more than he was letting on. All I knew was I needed a break from the busy wharf area. It was time to head home, sweet home.

thirty

A HOT SHOWER, an hour of rest and an egg salad sandwich recharged my energy. Seeing Nate helped, too. He came home just in time to shower and eat a sandwich. I gave him an out, telling him we could admire the harvest moon from the front steps, but he insisted he was up for a night of dancing. We arrived just in time for a slow dance, my kind of dance after a long day. There wasn't much dancing involved. It was mostly the two of us wrapped neatly in each other's arms while the band sang "My Girl" from the Temptations.

No one had expected such a massive crowd, and people kept coming. Frannie's husband, Joe, was keeping the ferry running until 10 to provide travel back to the mainland. After that, visitors were on their own for transportation. Most of the kiosks had run out of food by the time the moon made its appearance. I was just as happy to have some of the smoky, pungent aromas that had clouded the wharf and my head all day take a much needed break. Some of the natural scent of the sea was returning. It was far less obtrusive.

I rested my cheek against Nate's shoulder and lost myself in the feel of his strong, protective arms and that wonderful soapy smell that always clung to his skin after a shower. He hadn't talked about the case, and I was glad to leave it behind for now so I could enjoy the evening.

"This is my kind of dancing," Nate said as we both shuffled our feet around, barely moving out of the same four-foot circle. "I don't have to do anything but hold my favorite person and move my feet a few inches here and there."

"I think it's my favorite too." I lifted my head. He kissed me lightly. "How long did you and Sam ride for? I can't believe you had the energy to come out here tonight. Samuel is conspicuously absent."

"Ah, that's because he twisted his ankle on one of the downhills."

"Ouch, poor Samuel."

"Nah, he was fine after a beer or two. But dancing was off the list. He said Sera was too tired to come out tonight. They're looking forward to a much slower week."

"Pretty soon, everything will come to a standstill," I said. "After this weekend, I look forward to it." The music ended. Everyone clapped as the band put down their instruments to take a break. Cora and Gerard had stuck around for a dance, then they decided to take a walk on the swim beach. Winston and Alyssa had been given a sickly seal pup just before dusk, so they had to stay at the wildlife rescue, and Tobias had decided to skip the festivities altogether.

"Want to take a walk?" Nate asked.

"Only if you buy me a bag of hot chestnuts first."

"I think I can swing that."

The chestnuts came in a brown paper bag, and the steam seeping from the top assured us they were still hot. After a rather trying day, the evening under the golden moon was wonderful.

The chestnuts were tender and buttery.

"Hmm, these are close to perfect," I noted. "And that's not easy with chestnuts."

"I told the girl I wanted the perfect ones," Nate teased. "What's going on with the case? Or would you rather not talk about it."

"I suppose it wouldn't hurt to hash it out while I have an expert's ear."

Nate shook his head sadly. "No expert on murder, that's for sure. A few of my partners from the precinct were at the bar having beers. They're no closer to catching the PTK." The Pillow Talk Killer, a serial killer with the creepy habits of covering his victims' heads with pillowcases and writing notes in lipstick on mirrors, had been the case that pushed Nate to leave behind his detective's badge and move to Frostfall Island. In an odd, mostly macabre way, I had a serial killer to thank for sending me Nate. The murders had been stretched out over eight years. The victims were all women. PTK broke into their homes and stabbed them in their beds. Nate had been on the team dedicated to tracking him down, but there'd been no break in the case. After a few hours of getting nowhere on the Roberta Graves case, I was very frustrated. I couldn't imagine how hard it would be to chase an elusive serial killer. One of the things that made it so hard was that PTK struck only once every six months or so, leaving behind no evidence or DNA. The killer's latest murder had thrown Nate into a tailspin. He'd finally found his groove on the island with a good job and friends, but news of another brutal attack had reopened old wounds. He rarely talked about it with me, but I knew whenever he went to the mainland and saw his friends, it all came back to the surface again.

"I can't believe how meticulous PTK is. No evidence, no DNA," I said.

"Going dark for months at a time doesn't help either. This is too nice of a night for this topic," Nate said. He put his arm around my shoulder as we walked between the moored yachts. "Where's your sister? Has she bagged herself a billionaire yet?"

"I think she might have," I said. We just happened to be passing Gerard's boat as I said it. A string of gold twinkling lights was wrapped around the railing. Otherwise, the boat looked dark. They were still on their walk.

Nate laughed. "I was kidding, but clearly, you're not."

"That beauty, the *Gemstone*, belongs to Gerard Graves. He's the estranged brother of Sanford Graves, the man who lost his wife in the fire. Gerard seems likable, for a rich man."

Nate laughed and pulled me closer to kiss my cheek. "See, that's what I like about you. You prefer us penniless chaps to the wealthy blokes. And don't ask me where all the British slang just came from. It seemed appropriate for the situation."

"I like it. Feel free to go all Brit like that anytime."

Ansel Dell's boat had a few lights on, but it was quiet on deck. His gangplank was lowered. He might have gone to the wharf, or maybe he was expecting guests. My interaction with Ansel was the only part of the day that still stuck out as strange.

I folded up the bag with chestnuts. I'd eaten four. They were the kind of treat that could sit heavy in your stomach if you overindulged. I stuck the bag in my coat pocket. "I have to say, for the first time, I'm really annoyed that Norwich was able to close this case with hardly a second thought. Now, I'm stuck trying to untangle what happened."

"You could always just let the accident label stand. But," he said briskly before I protested. "I know you won't because it's important to get justice for Roberta Graves."

"Exactly. And, if I'm being honest about it, I always love to put Norwich in his place by pointing out how spectacularly wrong he is. But I can't seem to get a grip on this one. I think I'm feeling unsure of all of it because I'm not entirely sure who was supposed to die. My intuition tells me Sanford was the target, but a string of events led to Roberta's death instead. It would sure be easier if I knew for certain whom the killer was after. There was one person I interviewed today, Ansel Dell. He got fidgety when I asked if he'd seen or heard anything. His boat is right next to the one that burned."

The farther we got from the wharf, the quieter it got. The

moon sat up above, practically casting a daylight magnitude glow on the water. It was truly a magical scene—a magical, romantic scene that was instantly interrupted by a terrified scream.

Nate and I turned back and walked quickly in the direction of the scream. Two women in high heels and shiny pants were hurrying down the gangplank of Ansel Dell's boat. Other boat owners and their guests had moved to the railings on their yachts to find out what was happening.

One of the women spotted Nate and me heading toward them. Her face had a look of shock. "Hurry, I think he's dead. Hurry, please."

Nate and I raced up the gangplank. I could see a pair of shiny loafers in the doorway to the cabin. Ansel Dell was lying motionless on the floor. A piece of rope was wrapped around his neck.

Nate jumped ahead of me and untied the rope, but it was too late. Ansel was dead. Nate looked up. "This wasn't a suicide. There's no hook on the ceiling. Anna, you'd better call the police. Looks like there's been another murder."

"This is the guy," I said as I pulled out my phone. "The one who acted funny when I asked him if he saw or heard anything."

Nate looked down at Ansel. "Maybe he had seen something, and the killer came back to take care of witnesses."

I nodded as I dialed emergency. "Norwich isn't going to be happy about this."

thirty-one

"THEY'VE CALLED the Coast Guard to check out the scene first," I told Nate. He was standing in the small galley area surveying everything without touching a thing. "I guess they didn't trust our opinion that the man was dead."

"Or dispatch was hesitant to pull Norwich out of bed without confirmation," Nate suggested.

"Yep, probably that too." I couldn't hold back a smile. "As much as it gives me no pleasure to see Detective Norwich, it gives me great pleasure to know that he'll be yanked from his bed for another late night visit to the island." I glanced around too. Smooth, gold-specked granite covered the kitchen counter and a small cooking island. Three fluted wine glasses sat next to a tray of cheese and crackers and a bowl of mixed nuts. A bottle of chardonnay was chilling in an ice bucket. A corkscrew sat nearby, waiting to yank the cork from the chardonnay.

"Looks like he was going to have an intimate party," I

noted. "I wonder if those women are still on the dock. I think I'll go talk to them while you wait for the Coast Guard."

"Good idea. See what you can find out from the women. I'll glance around the deck for evidence." Nate had a touch of an investigator's sparkle in his eyes as he said it.

It made me smile, but it was bittersweet. It was cute to see him excited about investigating a murder, something he'd done for a living. At the same time, he was excited about investigating a murder. It made me wonder if he missed his former job.

I didn't have time to dwell on all my usual insecurities. Word must have gotten out about Ansel's death. People were starting to gather on decks, looking stunned and worried. Two deaths in a short weekend didn't bode well.

Fortunately, the women who'd discovered the body were easy to spot because of their shiny pants. One had on silver, reminding me of aluminum foil, and the other woman was wearing shiny hot-pink pants that were so tight they looked painted on. It was easy to figure out how news of the death had spread so quickly. They were talking fast and anxiously to some of the people who had gathered on the dock.

"Excuse me," I said to the woman in the silver pants. She was the one who'd told us Ansel was dead. She turned around, reluctant to leave her captive audience. "Yes, it's true, I did discover the dead body," she said and then turned back to the larger crowd. It seemed she'd gotten over her initial terror and shock quickly, and now, she was using the incident for her 15 minutes of fame.

"Excuse me again," I said sternly. She turned around with

an irritated sigh. She was quite young, possibly mid-twenties. "I need to ask you some questions. The Coast Guard is on their way, and they'll want to know details."

Her blue eyes rounded. "The Coast Guard is coming here? I suppose they'll need to talk to me."

"That's possible. How well did you know Mr. Dell?" I asked.

"Mr. Dell?" she looked baffled. "Oh, you mean Ansel. Not well." I'd gathered that when she had no idea his last name was Dell. "We met him on the wharf this afternoon, and he invited us onto his yacht for some wine."

"Did you hear or see anyone as you and your friend climbed on board?"

"Gosh no. Ivy and I were a little freaked out because the boat was super quiet and dark as we stepped on deck. She spotted his shoes first." She fanned herself. "I'm going to have nightmares about this for weeks. Boy, do I have some stuff to talk about with my therapist on Monday."

"That's good you'll have someone to talk to about this. The two of you stepped on board. Ivy saw his shoes, and—"

"She froze in fear, but I thought—what if he needed our help? What if he was choking or he'd had a heart attack? So, I walked over to him. When I saw the rope around his neck, I knew he was dead. Did he hang himself?"

"Not sure yet. Thanks for your help. Your friend's name is Ivy, and you are—?"

"I'm Megan. Will the Coast Guard be here soon?" She rummaged through her bag and pulled out a compact and lipstick. "I suppose I should stick around to give them my side of the story."

"That's a good idea. Thanks for your time, Megan." She turned immediately back to her newly-attained fans.

I returned to the boat. In the distance, past the swim beach and the northern tip of the island, two bright lights appeared on the dark water. It was the Coast Guard. Megan was going to be thrilled to see not one, but two Coast Guard boats.

Nate stepped out from the shadows on the starboard side, giving me a bit of a startle. "Oops, sorry, didn't mean to lurk around in the darkness. Deck looks clean. I'd say the perpetrator walked on deck, went straight to the cabin where Ansel was getting ready for his guests, came up from behind with a rope and that was that. His body is still fairly warm and pliable, so this happened in the last hour or so."

"I wonder if the two murders are connected," I said.

"It'd be an awfully big coincidence otherwise. You mentioned that Dell was acting strangely when you asked if he'd seen anything."

"Yes, he fidgeted. I left the boat thinking something was up with him."

"What if he was blackmailing the killer?" Nate asked.

"Could be, but what evidence do we have? Blackmail would be hard to prove."

Nate waved for me to follow him back inside the cabin. We both stepped carefully around the body. "I saw this folded napkin sitting on the dresser in the bedroom. It seemed to be holding something. I used my shirt to lift the edge of it back." He led me into the sleeping quarters, a small, oak-paneled bedroom with a double bed between two matching nightstands. The dresser Nate mentioned was sleek and mid-century. A mirror in the shape of a ship's wheel hung over the dresser. A light green linen napkin lay open on the top of the dresser next to a hairbrush and bottle of cologne. A stack of crisp $100 bills sat in the center of the unfolded napkin.

"Wow, I figured rich people kept a lot of petty cash around, but that's a big stack," I noted.

"Yeah, probably more than a casual stack of petty cash. I'd say it's three or four grand. Not entirely sure because I've never had that many hundreds at once."

"Do you think it's a payoff of sorts?" I asked as I took a few pictures.

"Not entirely sure but it seems like a nice chunk of change to leave in a napkin," Nate said.

"Wait a second, I recognize this napkin." I pulled my sleeve down to cover my fingers and folded the napkin over. "Light green linen with tiny black anchors around the border. I saw the same napkin on Sanford's boat. At the time, I didn't think much of it. I figured they were custom made for Sanford's boat. I wonder..." I walked out to the kitchen. With my fingers still under my sleeve, I pulled open some of the kitchen drawers. After a few tries, I found a drawer with folded linen napkins. They were navy blue with white trim. "That napkin did not come from this boat." I held up a napkin to prove my point.

"Which makes it a pretty sure bet that it came from Sanford's yacht," Nate said.

The Coast Guard boats were getting closer. Lights were flashing, but there were no sirens this time. No vessels were on fire.

"I guess we should greet them," I said. "Boy oh boy, I wouldn't want to be the one to get Norwich out of bed. His usual state is grumpy. Can't imagine what he's like without enough sleep." I laughed. It was late. I was tired, and that generally meant I'd laugh at anything.

Nate smiled. "What's got you so tickled?"

"I'm just wondering how many pretzel knots Norwich will twist to declare this case an accident."

thirty-two

IT HADN'T TAKEN the Coast Guard more than five minutes to confirm that there was yet another dead body on a vessel in Bayberry Harbor. They had other emergencies to attend to, so they called local law enforcement and then took off. Nate and I were left behind to secure the crime scene while we waited for Detective Norwich to arrive. If he hurried, which wasn't usually the case, he could catch the last ferry over to the island.

    Nate was sitting on one of the deck chairs, staring up at the moon. He'd stared at it long enough that he'd drifted off to sleep. He looked extremely cute snoozing in the deck chair. He'd left the house this morning before dawn, spent a long, exercise-filled day on the mainland and then returned for the dance. He had to be utterly exhausted. I was, and I hadn't engaged in nearly as much physical activity. I took a tiptoe-style walk around the boat with only my phone for light. Nate had already walked the deck. I had to agree, there wasn't anything that seemed out of place.

The crowd of onlookers had gotten bored and mostly dispersed. Cora and Gerard had returned from a long walk on the beach. Cora looked disheveled enough to assure me there was a little more to the adventure than a stroll on the sand. My sister had worn a pair of designer jeans and a plush pink sweater for her date. She'd even put on semi-practical ankle boots. (They had rhinestone covered buckles.)

Gerard spotted me up on Ansel's deck first. He waved. "What's going on? We saw the Coast Guard go past."

I walked over to the gangplank and met them at the bottom. "Ansel Dell has been murdered," I said bluntly. Gerard's reaction was what I expected, stunned, baffled.

"What on earth is going on around here?" he asked, and rightly so.

"Oh, didn't I tell you?" Cora asked. "Frostfall Island is a magnet for murderers. That's why Anna is always busy solving a case. Opal insists the island is cursed."

"I wouldn't say a magnet for murders," I interjected briskly. "And Opal spends a lot of time watching Vincent Price and Bela Lugosi movies. There is no curse," I spoke pointedly toward my sister.

"Are you certain it was murder?" Gerard asked.

"Yes, I'm certain," I said.

"Let's get on board your yacht," Cora said as she squeezed Gerard's arm. "It's getting cold out here."

Gerard nodded to me before leading Cora to his boat.

Detective Norwich's snarls could be heard all the way down the dock. The music had stopped for the night and things had quieted down considerably in the harbor. The detective was accompanied by an officer, but it wasn't Miller. I'd hoped to see him again.

I supposed Norwich was too groggy from leaving his bed to remember his signature toothpick.

"Detective Norwich," I said as he reached the bottom of the gangplank. "Almost didn't recognize you without your toothpick."

"Easy to recognize you, St. James, because you are always in the way. I hear you have another corpse."

"It's not my personal corpse, but if you'd like to see him, right this way." The young officer he'd brought along to assist seemed confused by our wry exchange. As I headed up the gangplank, I spotted Paul Thornton, the man Sanford had kicked out of the yacht club, on the dock. He seemed to be waving at me.

"Right through there, and I'll leave it to the professionals," I said with a simpering smile.

"About time you did that," Norwich muttered.

I turned back. "By the way, the rope, the murder weapon, was wrapped around his neck, but we removed it in case there was a chance to save the victim."

He paused when he saw Ansel with the rope next to his head. "And that's the problem with having an amateur mucking up the crime scene before I can get to it."

"I moved the rope," Nate said curtly from behind.

Norwich spun around. "Maddon, you're an amateur, too. You gave up your badge, remember?" As much as Norwich hated me, he loathed Nate more.

"I saw a victim with a rope cutting off his air passages, so I loosened the rope in case there was a chance he was still alive," Nate explained. He turned his groggy expression in my direction. "Are you ready to head home?"

"Yes, get her off the boat before she compromises the investigation more," Norwich snarled.

"It was compromised the second you arrived," Nate replied. He motioned for me to follow him. It was for the best. Norwich wouldn't bother to ask me for any background on the victim, and frankly, I didn't feel like filling him in. I wondered if he'd even notice the stack of money in the bedroom. Most likely he'd write it off as typical cash for rich people.

I caught up to Nate. Paul was still standing on the dock. He was definitely waving me over. "I'm going to talk to Mr. Thornton for a second. I'll catch up to you."

Nate stopped and gave Mr. Thornton a scrutinizing look. "I'll be just over here, waiting."

"All right. I don't think it'll take long." I walked over to Paul Thornton. He glanced around, apparently to see if there were any familiar faces or people watching our conversation, but the dock was mostly empty. Even the boaters had gone to bed.

"I heard Ansel Dell was murdered," Thornton said.

"It appears so. Did you see or hear something?"

"Well, it might not mean anything, but this afternoon, I saw Sanford Graves standing on Ansel's deck. They were having a heated discussion about something, but I couldn't make out what it was about. The funny part is that I didn't realize they were even acquainted. At the risk of sounding snobbish, Ansel is kind of a wannabe. He does all right, I think. He works in the insurance industry, but most of what you see is show. I've met him a few times at different parties. Nice enough guy but instead of enjoying what he has, he is always looking for more."

"It's kind of the American way, isn't it?"

"It is. Anyhow, their unusual interaction came back to me when I heard that Ansel was dead. I'm sure it had nothing to do with Ansel's death. I suppose the best thing would be for all of us to lift anchor and sail out of here in the morning. Seems like there's a killer out here on this marina."

I hated the idea that a lot of people were going to leave with a terrible opinion of Frostfall Island. It was especially unfair if the yachters had brought the murderer with them.

"Frostfall is a lovely place, and it's perfectly safe. If the two deaths are connected, which I suspect they are, then the killer is amongst the people moored at this dock. The local detective is on the scene now. He'll find out what's going on." It was hard not to laugh out loud at my own statement. Still, Thornton didn't need to know that local law enforcement was worthless.

"Oh, should I talk to him? Should I tell him about Sanford and Ansel having words?" Thornton asked.

"Sure, he's always receptive to witness statements." Again, I had to stifle a laugh. I was sure Norwich wouldn't even write it down. In fact, he was probably up on the boat trying to find a way that rope could have accidentally wrapped itself around Ansel's neck.

"Maybe you could tell him," Thornton suggested. "I've got a few guests on my boat. I need to get back to them."

"No, it'll be better coming from the actual witness. I've got to head home. Detective Norwich is still on board waiting for the coroner. I'm sure he'll be happy to take your statement." I was really cracking myself up tonight. It showed just how tired I was.

Nate had sat down on a nearby bench. He'd watched the entire conversation. He got up as I headed toward him. "What was that about?" he asked.

"Paul Thornton, one of my original suspects in the Graves murder, said that he saw Sanford arguing with Ansel earlier in the day. Maybe Sanford is connected to that money after all."

"Or maybe this guy, Thornton, is trying to cast the blame elsewhere because he's guilty," Nate suggested.

I looked over at him. "You're good at this even when you're sleepy."

"Yeah, I'm a regular Sherlock Holmes," he said grumpily. "Why was Thornton a suspect in the Graves case?"

"He had a loud, very public argument with Sanford Graves the morning before Roberta's death. But I spoke to him, and I didn't get any feeling that he was guilty."

Nate covered a long yawn.

I wrapped my arm around his. "Let's get you home, sleepy head. I'm too tired to think about murder right now. We'll let the professional handle it." I was a regular standup comedian this evening.

thirty-three

AFTER THE LONG DAY, I surprised (and delighted) myself by getting up just before dawn to walk Huck. I left my paints behind. I needed to concentrate on the case and not the landscape. (Though I much preferred the landscape.) The chill in the air seemed to whisper "winter is coming." I always loved the onset of winter, where plants turned down their colors and seemed to show us humans "this is how you take time off." Animals were vanishing, getting their burrows, nests and holes ready for the coming frost. Most of the birds had already taken off for their winter homes far from the island.

Even though we could still count on a few more spectacular moonlit nights, the harvest moon celebration was officially over. Once the sun was up, vendors would pack away their kiosks and boaters would set sail back to their home harbors. This morning there was a particularly eerie quiet on the island. The silence was in stark contrast to the boisterous noise of the last two days. I looked forward to having my island back to its serene, peaceful self again.

This had been a trying weekend all around. The murders had helped take my mind off the photo of the twins and the secrets that lay behind the picture. It was possible, one day, those secrets would shake loose and turn the past upside down. It was also entirely possible that I'd never find out what the photo meant. That was all right too. In fact, as much as curiosity had always been my thing, I was more at ease with the latter. Knowing the truth was not always a good thing. Besides, I had no time to think about it. I had a double murder on my hands. I was sure that Norwich hadn't gotten anywhere last night.

The case had taken a significant and dark turn with the murder of Ansel Dell. Two important details emerged last night after the grim discovery. Ansel had a hefty stack of hundred-dollar bills in his sleeping quarters. It was wrapped in a linen napkin that matched one I saw on Sanford's boat. Paul Thornton had witnessed Sanford and Ansel having an argument earlier in the day. Unless, like Nate suggested, Thornton was trying to frame Sanford for a crime he committed, I had no reason to doubt Thornton's story. There was also the small matter of motive. What motive did Paul Thornton have to kill Ansel Dell? Did Ansel lie when I asked if he'd heard or seen anything? If Ansel had seen the killer, that would make him a target. It would also give him some major leverage for a blackmailing scheme.

Was it Thornton? My intuition was telling me no. It was

hard to admit, but I might have been on the wrong track the whole time. I blamed the mysterious photo for my ineptitude. However, I'd made a reasonable conclusion. Sanford was supposed to be in the boat that night. Therefore, it made sense that he was the original target. But what if Roberta had been the intended victim? What if Sanford plotted to kill his wife? I'd witnessed her griping and sniping at Sanford. He'd seemed mild-mannered about the whole thing. Of course, even mild-mannered people could snap. If you're constantly berated and griped at, you can only absorb so much of it before you've had enough. But was that enough motive? After all, divorce was a much easier, less risky option. Or was it? If there was no prenuptial agreement, then Sanford stood to lose half of his fortune, a fortune that was tied up in the courts. And then there was his gambling addiction. What if his obsession with gambling had gotten so out of hand, he'd found himself in deep financial trouble?

"Lots to think about, Huck," I said. The dog pulled his nose out from a bush and looked at me. His tail wagged. "Let's go home and start breakfast, buddy."

Huck knew the word *home* almost as well as he knew the word *cookie*. He tore off toward the boarding house.

I planned to make pancakes to make up for the lack of decent meals this weekend. I had some tart apples that I could turn into a caramel-coated topping with a little brown sugar and butter. I picked up my pace. To the east of me, the sun was starting to make an appearance. There were enough clouds in the sky to signal it would be a gloomy day on the island. We'd gotten lucky that the sky had been clear for the harvest moon. I'd hardly had time to enjoy any of it, bogged down as I was with the case.

Nate was already up. He'd made the coffee, and the smell of it lured me right over to the pot for a cup.

"How is the world's hottest sleuth doing this morning?" he asked before sipping his coffee.

"First, your compliment is accepted. I've been going through it, turning ideas over in my head, and I think I've been wrong this whole time."

"Really? How's that?"

I sipped some coffee, set the cup down and tied on my apron. "What if Roberta was the intended victim all along?"

"That's entirely possible. Seems like that would narrow down your suspect list to the usual culprit—the spouse."

"Exactly." I pulled out my mixing bowl and the pancake mix. Then, I walked to the refrigerator for milk and eggs.

Tobias came in the back door. He'd pulled his winter coat on over his wet swim trunks. The new goggles were propped on his head.

"Morning, Toby. Pancakes in thirty," I said.

"Hmm, pancakes. Wonderful news."

"Maybe Sanford was being blackmailed by Ansel Dell," Nate said, continuing our conversation.

The comment made Tobias pause in the doorway. He turned back around. "Sanford Graves?" he asked. "Is he a murder suspect now?"

"He has jumped to the top of the list," I said.

Tobias's expression turned grim.

"What is it, Toby?" I asked.

"I'm meeting with Sanford Graves in my office this morning. He called me yesterday. I'm the accountant for several of the yacht owners, and he got my number from one of them. I was surprised to hear he needed a financial advisor and accountant. A man like that had a financial advisor long before he was born. He said he needed to separate some of his finances out because of the lawsuit with his brother. It seemed plausible to me. He mentioned he had to stay on Frostfall until the insurance company came out to look at the boat. The part of our phone call that gave me pause was the multiple life insurance policies on his wife."

I nearly dropped the egg I was holding. I placed it carefully on the counter to avoid a mess. "Did you say multiple policies?" I asked.

Nate had put down his coffee. He listened with interest and that detective gleam in his eye.

"Three separate policies for a million dollars each," Tobias said. "I'm sorry, Anna. I should've brought this up sooner. I wasn't thinking."

"Nonsense, Toby, you couldn't have known what was happening with the case. Frankly, up until this morning, I was still convinced that Sanford was meant to die in the fire."

"Life insurance policies with hefty payouts are always a great motive for murder," Nate said. He'd returned to his coffee. His suntan had deepened after a day mountain biking, and it made his eyes look cobalt blue.

"My goodness." Tobias looked as if the wind had gone out of him. "I should cancel the appointment."

"Actually, Toby"—I pulled out a chair because the poor man needed to sit, and I needed him sitting for what I was about to ask—"could you keep the appointment?"

Tobias looked from me to Nate and back again. "You're serious." Then, a sliver of a grin appeared. "Am I going to be part of the team to trap the killer?"

"You are," I said.

Nate sat by, without comment, and let me spell out the plan. He probably knew exactly where I was going with it, but he didn't interfere. He knew this was my case, so he left it entirely to me. I appreciated his confidence in my ability to solve a murder.

"I'm game." Tobias rubbed his swim-chapped hands together. "What should I do? As long as it isn't too dangerous," he added.

"Not at all. Just continue with your meeting and proceed exactly as you would if you hadn't heard that Sanford was a suspect in a murder. It'll give me time to check out Sanford's hotel suite."

"How will you get in?" Tobias asked.

"I might know where to find the spare key." I looked at Nate. "What do you say? Up for some gumshoe work today? Or do you have plans?"

"I'm available. My only plans, so far, are to eat an obscene number of pancakes."

"Then, I guess I should get the batter started." I turned

back to the mixing bowl before looking back over my shoulder. "Exactly how many is an obscene number of pancakes?"

Nate raised his palm parallel to the tabletop to show me the stack he hoped to get.

"Right. Gonna need more eggs."

thirty-four

"ALL RIGHT. I think, possibly, an obscene number of pancakes is a few too many," Nate said as we walked the trail toward the boardwalk. He patted his flat stomach. "But every bite was perfection," he added.

"I think I could have stopped a few pancakes short myself. I feel like I'm plodding at a snail's pace."

"You already walked this morning," Nate reminded me.

"Yes, but I walk every morning, and I usually still have pep in my step until at least five in the evening. It's barely 10, and I'm ready for a nap."

Tobias's meeting with Sanford was set for 10 o'clock. My plan required Tobias's help. He said he could easily stretch the meeting until 11 with paperwork. That was enough time for us to go to the boat, get the key card and head over to the hotel for a quick room search. I had no idea if we'd find anything of worth in the suite, but I was running out of options. If Sanford was the killer, he needed to be stopped before more people ended up dead. I assumed he never had any plan to kill Ansel Dell, but if Ansel had seen Sanford set fire to his own boat, then it was in Sanford's best interest to get rid of the witness. And, if that witness was bold and, frankly, ignorant enough to use the information to extort money out of Sanford, then there was a double motive. Blackmail schemes forced people into a corner—pay or have your reputation ruined. Arson and murder were definitely reputation destroyers. A long jail sentence wasn't great either. It would be quite a life change for a man who grew up in a 30-room mansion.

"After you wrap this thing up," Nate said with more confidence than I was feeling, "how about we spend the rest of the day crashed in front of the television."

"Not exactly the romantic scenario I thought you'd suggest, but I can crash in front of the television as well as the next gal."

Nate took hold of my hand. "We could kiss during the boring parts."

I nodded. "I like that plan even better."

We reached the wharf. Most of the activity and noise was coming from the gulls as they hovered and dove toward morsels left behind by humans. Tables, booths and kiosks had been deconstructed and removed. A cleanup crew had emptied trash cans (much to the chagrin of the same gulls), and most of the permanent shops were closed for the day. Overhead, a carpet of gray clouds seemed to be signaling a change in weather.

"Looks like we might get a thunderstorm this afternoon," I said.

"Then, let's get this guy cuffed and in the paddy wagon, so we can be tucked on the couch before the rain falls."

We reached the dock. About half the yachts had cleared out. Gerard's *Gemstone* was still moored in its slip. Cora had texted that she was too tired to come home last night. She didn't join us for pancakes, so I could only assume things were moving along quickly in her new romance. It seemed crazy to think that she might sail away with Gerard. She hardly knew the man. Unfortunately, Cora had done much crazier things in her life.

Ansel's boat had been taped off, but there was no sign of Norwich. Past the newest crime scene sat the charred wreckage of the *Grand Dame*. The yellow caution tape fluttered in the wind as we ducked beneath it. Nothing on the boat had been touched. The deck chair that I was sure had been used to trap Roberta in the smoky cabin was still sitting on its own, away from the rest of the set. I hoped everything inside was untouched, as well. It was entirely possible that Sanford had returned for some of his belongings and, in the process, took the second hotel key. I hadn't seen him at the marina the day before, but according to Paul Thornton, he was there having an argument with Ansel Dell.

We pulled open the cabin door. "Phew," I said as I waved my hand in front of my face. It was a mix of stale smoke and the moisture left behind by the firefighters. Together, it had created a pungent mix of odors. We were in luck. The inside of the cabin had remained exactly as it was. The outline of

Roberta's body was still clear on the soot covered floor. Most importantly, her purse was still sitting on the counter. The key card was jammed beneath it. "Looks like our murderer never returned to the crime scene."

"Some do. Some avoid it altogether." Nate spotted the incriminating napkin on the seat cushion of the dining nook. "Looks like Norwich did his usual thorough job."

"Remember, according to him, this was not a murder scene. He was planning to hand the case off to the arson division. Most of that evidence is outside the cabin."

Nate shook his head. "Can't believe they keep that guy on payroll. And with a detective's badge, no less."

I picked up the envelope with the key card and stuck it in my pocket. "Why do they keep him on?"

"Not exactly sure. From what I've heard, his uncle or some relative is on the city council. Lots of palm greasing to keep Norwich in his job. At least, that's what people say. No one knows for sure."

"I've got the key. Let's get over to the hotel and look around."

The Frostfall Hotel looked nearly vacant as we stepped inside the lobby. The activity of the weekend was over, and Sunday morning checkout was all but complete. There were people in the restaurant enjoying brunch. The hotel put on quite a spread every weekend.

Nate and I walked to the elevators and got on to ride up to the luxury suites on the fifth floor. Tobias was on standby. He was supposed to text us if Sanford left his office early. It was the perfect setup. We'd have plenty of time to vacate the room if Sanford was heading back.

We stepped out onto the fifth floor. You could instantly feel the difference on the suite floor. The hallway was wider, and there was a lot of space between doors to accommodate for the size of the rooms. Room service trays sat outside two of the rooms, including suite 505, Sanford's room.

I knocked to make sure we had the right room and that no one was inside. There was no answer, so I passed the key over the digital reader. It flashed green. I opened the door and we stepped inside. The suite had a small kitchenette, a living room complete with widescreen television, and a small dining area. A crystal chandelier glittered in the light coming through the balcony doors. Below the balcony was an unobstructed view of the harbor. Most of the smaller boats, including the *Wild Rose*, had left the harbor. Gulls dotted the rippled tops of the waves as they did their own version of cleanup.

"Well, this is fancy-schmancy," Nate said.

I handed him a pair of latex gloves and pulled mine on too. "We're looking for something, anything that could—"

"Implicate our suspect in the crime?" he asked facetiously.

My face warmed with embarrassment. "Right. Sometimes I forget that you kind of know your way around a crime scene."

"Yes, but I've never had such an adorable partner. In fact, the cutest one I had was a guy named Morty who ate far too much garlic and always had a coffee stain on his shirt."

"But he was cute?" I asked with a laugh.

"Compared to the others, yes."

I laughed again as I walked around the living room area. An empty bottle of wine and one glass sat on the shiny coffee table in front of the sofa. "He was here alone, it seems."

Nate walked into the bedroom.

I glanced at the kitchenette. Other than a used coffee cup, it looked untouched. That lined up with the breakfast tray outside the door. Sanford was a tidy man. His coat was hung in the closet and two pairs of shoes sat beneath the coat. It looked as if he'd used a ruler to make sure the toes were lined up perfectly. I went to shut the closet door, but my attention was pulled back to the coat. It was a nice wool coat with wooden buttons and big cuffs. It wasn't the coat that had my interest though. It was the white corner sticking out of one of the pockets.

I pulled the paper free. It was a crumpled note written by hand in black ink.

"Three thousand dollars today or I tell the police." The message couldn't have been clearer. Sanford was being blackmailed. "I found the smoking gun, Nate."

He came out of the bedroom. "There aren't many clothes in the drawers. Seems like he packed up." Nate walked across to read the note. He smiled at me. "You are a top-notch detective, Anna St. James."

thirty-five

NATE and I had just left Sanford Graves' hotel room when I got a call from Tobias. "The rat must have left the trap. It's Toby."

I could sense he was frantic even before he spoke. "Toby?"

"Anna, thank goodness. Sanford left the office abruptly." He paused to take a deep breath. "I shouldn't have asked, but I got all caught up in solving the case, and his hands were so red and raw—I didn't realize it had something to do with murder."

"All right, Toby. Catch your breath. First of all, we're already out of the room. Do you think he's coming back to the hotel right now?" We stepped into an empty elevator and headed down to the lobby.

"That I couldn't tell you. He was carrying a small duffle bag. He was sure in a hurry to get out of here. He must be guilty." Tobias paused and took another deep breath. "Woo,

I'm not used to this kind of adventure. It's exhilarating, but I don't think I'm entirely cut out for it."

"It takes some getting used to, Toby. You really helped out the case because we found crucial evidence in his hotel room."

The elevator doors slid open and we stepped out. The lobby was mostly empty except for staff. No sign of our suspect.

I put the phone on speaker as we walked outside. "Nate is here with me. What did you say about his hands?"

"Oh, didn't I tell you? No, I suppose I was so busy blathering on like a silly fool I forgot. The palms of both his hands had red marks. It looked like rope burn. When I asked him what'd happened to his hands, he got very defensive. Told me it was none of my business. Then, he softened his tone and said it happened on his boat. After that, he told me he'd look over the paperwork and get back to me. He'd been ready to start a new account. He picked up his duffle and hurried out the door. He turned in the direction of the harbor. That was when I picked up the phone to call you."

"More good detective work, Toby," Nate chimed in. "Those rope burns are more evidence."

"Thanks, Nate." I could almost see Tobias's big grin through the phone. "Glad I could help, and let me know if there's anything else I can do. As long as it's not too dangerous," he added.

"Right. We'll let you know. Bye." The second I hung up, another call came through from a number I didn't recognize.

My phone didn't warn me it was a scam number, so I answered.

"Hello."

"Hello, is this Anna?" a deep voice asked. I still couldn't place it.

"Yes, this is Anna."

"Hello, Anna, this is Kent Strong from Kent's Rentals. I hope you don't mind—Sera gave me your number."

"No, that's fine. How can I help you, Kent?" I still had it on speaker, so we walked to a quiet place near the boardwalk.

"Remember that dinghy with the matchstick, the one you told me to leave untouched?"

"Yes, I do. I think that evidence will be needed, after all," I added.

"Well, I never touched the matchstick. Unfortunately, someone stole the boat again. The boats were tied together with rope. I came out this morning planning to start packing things up for winter, and I saw that the boat was missing. The rope was cut. In fact, I think whoever took the boat took a big piece of the rope along with it."

Nate and I looked at each other. We'd found the source for the murder weapon.

"The fuel tank doesn't hold much on those small boats," Kent continued.

"But it's enough gas to get someone to the mainland, right?" I asked.

"Oh yeah, no problem. Long, slow trip in that dinghy, though."

"Where are you right now, Kent?" I asked.

"I'm putting the rest of the boats in storage so they don't get stolen too. I didn't see any sign of the stolen dinghy on the swim beach, but you know there's that strip of sand south of the hotel. A lot of people pull boats and kayaks up there to eat lunch or buy some more bait."

Nate tapped my arm lightly. I followed his line of sight. It was Sanford Graves and his duffle bag heading in exactly the direction of the strip of sand Kent was talking about.

"A friend and I are on the boardwalk in front of the hotel. We're going to check out that strip of sand right now."

"Thanks, Anna. I'll head that way just as soon as I lock up here."

Nate and I took off at a run. If Sanford *did* have a boat waiting for him, we needed to hurry. Once he got out in the harbor, all he needed was to get across to the mainland. Then, he'd be much harder to catch.

"Regretting that stack of pancakes now," Nate said. Even laden down with pancakes, I couldn't keep up with his pace.

"Go, I'll catch up. Do you know where you're going?" I asked.

"Yep. Starting to know this place pretty well." Nate ran most days when the weather permitted. I knew he was holding back and using the pancakes as an excuse. He took off like the roadrunner, and I was Wile E. Coyote with my feet moving and going nowhere. At least I wasn't hovering off the edge of a cliff. But I could have definitely used one of those ACME rockets right about now.

Sanford had a good head start. He had no idea we were following him. Obviously, Tobias's question about his hands caused him great anxiety, but he still had no idea that we'd zeroed in on him as the killer.

I walked and biked and hiked all the time, but I was still winded by the time I reached the small strip of sand. Sanford reached it before me and somehow, Mr. Roadrunner had passed our suspect. He even had time to start the boat and take it 50 feet offshore. He was teasing Sanford as he went around in small circles in the water.

Sanford was waving his fist at him. "Thief. That's my boat!"

Nate pointed at the boat. "This boat?" he called.

"Yes, bring it back right now, or I'll call the police."

I snickered at that hollow threat. So many people came to our tiny island and expected it to have all the amenities of an island like Oahu.

"No, this isn't your boat," Nate said. "You've got that big boat. The one that you charred like a piece of toast."

Sanford's shoulders sank. "You don't know what you're talking about," he said with a little less forcefulness. "You're a thief. Bring me back my boat."

"Uh, I think that's my boat," Kent said from behind.

"See, it's his boat," Nate called.

Sanford spun around with a look of horror on his face. He looked at Kent, then at me.

"It's over, Sanford," I said. "We know you killed your wife for the insurance money and Ansel because he was blackmailing you."

Kent looked at me with round eyes. "Really?" he asked.

"Yep."

Sanford took off at a run. Nate raced the small boat back to shore. We both took off after the suspect. I didn't relish another long sprint, but apparently, it was all part of the job. No wonder Norwich wanted nothing to do with these cases.

Again, Nate took off running. It seemed our chase was heading toward the marina. By the time I caught up to the men, Nate had Sanford's arms behind his back. They were standing at the bottom of the gangplank to Gerard's *Gemstone*.

Gerard was at the top. There was no sign of Cora.

"What have you done, Sanford?" Gerard asked.

I reached the gangplank and worked hard not to show that I was breathing like a woman in labor. Nate nodded toward Gerard. "He's all yours. I'll call the police." Nate stepped away from the scene to make the call.

"Yes, Sanford," I said, "why don't you tell your brother what you've been up to."

Sanford's fight-or-flight mode had ended. His posture crumpled, and he covered his face with his hands.

"Sanford, my brother." Gerard sounded a little choked up as he walked down to Sanford. It would be shocking to learn that your sibling had killed two people. "How did you let it get this far?" Gerard lifted a hand and put it on his brother's shoulder to comfort him, but Sanford wasn't having it.

He pushed Gerard's hand away. Sanford's face was red. "This is your fault, Gerard. If you'd let me have my half of the inheritance, it would never have come to this."

Gerard seemed to reflect on that for a second. "I was

trying to protect you from yourself. I just didn't realize how bad things got. But, my lord, Sanford—you killed your wife."

"Don't pretend you liked her," Sanford snarled. "No one liked her. She was a horrid woman, and the world is better without her." He was going full confession now, just letting all his feelings hang out there. "Then, that weasel, Dell, thought he could blackmail me. Told me he had pictures of me climbing onto the *Grand Dame* to set her on fire. If not for him, this would have been over. The detective called it an accident. I would have gotten the insurance money for Roberta and the boat. Dell deserved to die, too," he said through gritted teeth.

Gerard looked gripped with grief as he looked at me. "I should never have fought to keep control of the money. I worried he'd gamble it all away."

"Seems like you might have been right about that."

Sanford sat down at the bottom of the gangplank and rested his head in his hands.

"My sister?" I asked Gerard.

"She went home about an hour ago. I was about to shove off too. Guess I better get on the phone and call the family lawyer."

"That's probably a good idea. Gerard, I'm sorry that this turned out so badly for your family."

thirty-six

NATE and I had made good on our plans to crash in front of the television. I made buttery popcorn, and we pulled one of my winter throw blankets out of the closet. After what seemed like an eternity of channel surfing we'd finally settled on a *James Bond* movie. After the morning we'd had, we were both feeling a little Bond-ish.

I rested my head against Nate's shoulder. "This was a perfect way to end a rather chaotic weekend."

"I agree." Nate dug his hand into the popcorn bowl.

Cora stepped into the den. She was napping when we got home, so I hadn't spoken to her all day. "Oh, sorry, didn't mean to interrupt your snuggle session. I was just looking for my fashion magazine."

I pointed it out on the end table.

"Right. I'll just grab it and then you two can get back to whatever it was you were doing." She picked up the magazine. "Gerard called me. He told me what happened. I can't believe it. He's really broken up about it."

I sat up straighter. "What about you and Gerard? I half expected you to pack your things and sail away with your newest love interest."

Cora smiled dreamily. "I really do like Gerard. He asked me to sail around the world with him, and I was this close to saying yes." She pinched together her two long, pink nails.

"What happened?" I asked.

Cora lifted her shoulders in a shrug. "After hanging out with all those wealthy people again, I realized they're really boring. You guys are way more fun."

"I agree," Nate said.

"Anyhow, I doubt Gerard will be going on that trip now," Cora said. "He's got to take care of this new legal problem. He's worried about the damage to the family legacy. Still, we're going to keep in touch. I really liked him." With that, she flounced out of the room on her feathery slippers.

"What do you know," Nate said. "We're more fun than a bunch of stuffy millionaires."

I snuggled against him. "I'm glad she's staying," I said.

"I know you are."

"I like my new family just the way they are," I said. Opal and Olive were right. Leave the past in the past.

FROSTFALL ISLAND
COZY MYSTERY SERIES

CANDLELIT CALAMITY

LONDON LOVETT

Frostfall Island Cozy Mystery #6

about the author

London Lovett is author of the Port Danby, Starfire, Firefly Junction, Scottie Ramone and Frostfall Island Cozy Mystery series. She loves getting caught up in a good mystery and baking delicious, new treats!

Learn more at:
www.londonlovett.com

Printed in Great Britain
by Amazon

Unsafe: Book 1

Christopher Artinian

CHRISTOPHER ARTINIAN

UNSAFE: BOOK 1

Copyright © 2025

Christopher Artinian

All rights reserved.

ISBN: 9798310870253

CHRISTOPHER ARTINIAN

DEDICATION

To Daisy. We could not have asked to share our lives with a sweeter soul. She will remain in our hearts forever.

CHRISTOPHER ARTINIAN

ACKNOWLEDGEMENTS

Tina is always there for me. She has proved that more than ever in the last few days. I will never be able to thank her enough for her support.

Thanks so much to the gang across in the fan club. You never let me down.

Thanks to the amazing Christian Bentulan for another great cover. And a huge thank you to my editor, Ken. A great guy and a great editor.

And finally, a big thank you to you for buying this book.

PROLOGUE

BD didn't have the best luck in the world. One could say this began soon after being born. His having worked tirelessly since middle school to become known as BD and not Bert, Bertie or Bertram, as it was recorded in the register of births, was a testament to this fact.

His prospective name had been a matter of debate between his parents for some time. Eventually, his father had entered the office of births, marriages and deaths to memorialise this historic new chapter in their lives. Alas, he had been in the pub for several hours prior in deep discussion with friends, bar staff, or pretty much anyone who would listen, and he came to the conclusion that Bertram was a fine name. Bertram was a name that made people stop and think. Bertram possessed gravitas and, by God, Bertram was what his newborn son was going to be called.

Bertram was a name that had not even been on the radar during the discussions between himself and Mrs Duncan. Hence, the matter of the drunken foray to the registry office became the single biggest argument the two of them ever had up to that point. However, it paled at the side of future ones.

Tess, BD's mother, had sworn to head to the registry office the next day and get the certificate annulled or retracted or whatever one did with birth certificates. But a night's sleep found her warming to the name when she looked at the historic piece of paper the next day. And as the name Bertie left her lips, she couldn't help but smile a little.

She decided to give it a day to see how it fit. A little like getting a pair of boots from the catalogue and walking around in them for a while before deciding whether to return them and get the next size up.

A day ran into two, then three, and, finally, all thoughts of changing Bertie's name disappeared, and thus he was branded with it for life.

He didn't believe he was cursed or anything like that. He just believed bad luck had an eerie way of visiting him with regularity. Today, for example. His train didn't come, resulting in him having to run to catch the bus in the pouring rain, getting drenched, and finding the only seat on the double-decker left was next to an old man who smelled of turpentine. Unsurprisingly, he arrived at work late and was given sample duty as a punishment. Not only that but he had to take a trainee out as well. The rain had stopped within five minutes of him getting on the bus. If it had continued raining, sample duty would have been postponed to another day, but as it was, he would have to head out in his wet clothes with no hope of feeling comfort again until he was back at home.

Sample duty could be a gift of a job. When the sun was shining and the air was warm, wading into a cool, clear, slow-moving river with trout and perch swimming between your feet could put a smile on anyone's face, and given the events of the past few months, smiles were scarce at best.

On a cold day when there had been a downpour first thing, the heater in your works van was on the fritz and you were lumbered with the new girl who never stopped talking, they were not a gift. They were a…. *Curse. Nope. Nope. I am not cursed. I refuse to use that word.*

"D'you want me to carry one of those bags?" Taki asked. Arataki was of Māori heritage. She'd been a student on the day that changed the world forever. There was a big part of BD that felt sorry for her. He wondered if her endless yapping was a coping mechanism for the loss of her family. There was another part that was too selfish to care.

She'd been rabbiting pretty much since they'd left the office. His contribution to the conversation had been the occasional "Uh-huh," or "Hmm." But in truth, he couldn't even hazard a guess at what she'd been going on about for the last half hour. Now, though, she'd asked something relevant to the job at hand, which was an improvement.

"No, I'm good, thanks," he replied as they continued along the riverbank.

"You don't talk much, do you?"

How would you possibly know that? You haven't shut up since we got in the fucking van. You don't even seem to need air. I swear there are whales that can't hold their breath as long as you. "No."

"That's alright. I don't mind talking for the both of us."

Kind of figured that one out. "Heh!" A weak half laugh was all he could respond with.

"So, BD. What does that stand for anyway? I mean, I knew a girl called BJ once. Turned out the initials were nothing to do with her name, just her hobby." Silence. "That was a joke, by the way."

Please, please, please. Shut up. "Bert Duncan," he replied, trying his hardest to be civil. He was going to be with her for the rest of the day and the last thing he needed was an atmosphere or another complaint going in against him.

"Bert? That's a nice name."

"You're welcome to it if you want it."

Taki smiled. "I'm glad I was assigned to you. You're about the only one at the lab I've not hung out with so far."

"Yeah, well. They probably didn't see the point."

"What do you mean?"

"I mean that I'm a grunt, a dogsbody. I don't really do much."

"That's not what I've seen. You're the only lab tech who never stops."

"I do a good impression of being busy."

"So, as nice as this is, walking along the muddy bank on a cold day in May, why don't we just take our sample and head back to the cold but dry van?"

BD stopped and turned towards her. *Another question pertinent to the job.* "Well, the river's running way too fast and too high to take a sample where I'd normally look at taking one.

Above all else in this job, you've got to think health and safety first."

Taki looked towards the fast-flowing river. "I don't understand. Why can't we just head down the bank and fill the bottles?"

"I dare say there are some who'd do that. But y'see, to get a good sample with a minimal number of contaminants, you need to—"

"What the hell's that?"

BD's frustration at being interrupted dissipated in an instant as his eyes focused on the object up river that was heading in their direction fast. "Err…."

"That's a body. That's a freaking body, BD," she cried.

"Wait here." He immediately slipped his backpack and the sample bag off his shoulder and made his way down the slippery bank.

"Be careful," she called after him. "Remember what you just said to me about safety."

BD wasn't blind to the speed of the river. That's why they'd been heading to a section he knew to be far shallower and more agreeable to allowing sampling without risk. If he lost his footing here, there was a good chance he could get swept away, but at the same time, this was a body.

Wait a minute. Are their arms moving? It was impossible to tell if it was a man or a woman as they were face down in the water. The wild black mop of hair and the blue bubble jacket kept bobbing, but the face remained submerged. "I think they're still alive," he shouted over his shoulder as he took one step, then another into the surging current.

A wake formed around his waders as he continued out. "Be careful, BD," Taki cried again as she started down the bank too.

Need to get out further. With each step he took, he could feel the force of the water building, desperate to lift him up and take him. *Another step. One more. That's all.*

He was up to his thighs, the thick nylon waders doing nothing to block out the cold or the sense of dread that gripped him. He leaned forward, not daring to risk another step as the power of the current swept against him.

Four.

Three.

Two.

One.

BD reached and grabbed at the same time. His fingers closed around the padded bubble jacket. Water washed over the drowning woman. *It's a woman.* He could tell as leather boots appeared out of the turbulent wake for the first time.

He felt her hand claw at his thigh, desperate to get purchase, but tying him up in knots would do neither of them any favours. He pulled free as he yanked her up and across, heaving her back towards the shallows as still her head remained submerged.

One step. Two steps. Three steps and Taki's outstretched hand waited there for him. He took it with his left, piggybacking on her firmer footing and using the momentum and all the upper body strength he could muster to hoist the woman up so at least she could take a breath.

At that same instant, he caught sight and sound of something in the air further up river. *A helicopter. It's a helicopter.*

Military helicopters, in fact the military in general, had been a far more common sight than they once were since the prime minister's speech the previous autumn, but to see and hear one so close at that precise moment just seemed a little odd.

He grunted as he pulled one more time and the woman's feet finally caught on the riverbed. He could feel a sudden relaxation of the force he'd been exerting as her frame began to rise.

Taki kept a tight hold of his hand, tugging him towards the bank, but she suddenly released her grip, letting out a terrified scream as she fell back into the water. For a split second, BD thought she'd slipped, but then he caught sight of her wide-eyed stare as it fixed on the rescued woman.

He turned to see what Taki had seen and froze in horror and confusion. Horror because it was the first time he had ever witnessed one of the infected up close and not on a screen. Confusion because, although the world beyond UK and Irish shores had fallen to the reanimating virus, the few cases they'd been told about in the UK had been confined to Leeds and Portsmouth and those outbreaks were well and truly under control due to the special measures the government had taken.

To see one of these things—thing was the only word he could use—here in the flesh, the sickening, panic-inducing, deathly, pallid flesh, was bewildering. It straightened, raising its head, its black hair draping over much of its face but, alas, not its eyes. The ghostly grey marbles that sat within the sockets were punctuated by jagged, flaring pupils, blacker than any black he had witnessed, pulsing malevolence, hypnotising him, making it impossible to move, to run, to scream, even though he knew that's what he should do.

Barely two seconds had passed since this creature had birthed from the turbulent wash of water that continued to rumble. It was as if it was waking up, seeing everything for the first time, but the woman who it had been was probably in her thirties. She would have taken in a lifetime of sights, sounds and smells, but not this thing. This thing was a newborn.

A growl began in the back of its throat, not like any growl BD had ever heard. This wasn't a dog warning you to stay away from her bone or a tiger protecting her young. This was a growl of pure malevolence, of hatred, of utter feral malignance.

It lunged with alarming and surprising speed and, finally, BD's survival sense kicked in. He staggered back, one, two paces. The flow of the current was with him and he felt a little like Neil Armstrong on the moon, his legs and body moving further with less effort than he imagined as the water now worked on his behalf rather than against him.

The infected woman experienced the same thing, but the fast-moving waves did not work to her advantage. Her forward momentum caused her upper body to tip too far and her reaching, claw-like fingers grasped at nothingness as she fell flat into the water, disappearing just for a second before fighting the current and scrambling up. By which time, BD had taken another step back and to the side, to shallower depths.

The gurgling, guttural growl began again as the beast raised its head higher this time, trying hard to see through the even narrower gap in its thick raven hair as it curtained its face.

It had no reason. There was no instinctive movement to brush away the errant waves of black covering its eyes. It just knew one thing, had one goal, and that was to seize its prey. It attacked once more, this time managing to lay a hand on the thick material of BD's jacket.

Fresh terror surged through him, blocking out all other thoughts, sounds and sights as death took a step closer. Like a child throwing a tantrum, he flailed his arm wildly, trying his hardest to escape the creature's clutch as it used him to steady itself in the water.

It laid its second hand on BD's opposite shoulder as he desperately stumbled back, trying his hardest to escape its grasp, but it was impossible. This infection had spread so quickly for a reason. Its carriers were unrelenting, uncompromising, and all he could do was stare wide-eyed as inevitability came ever nearer.

The ghoulish monster's mouth opened wide. BD barely noticed the ugly pink-stained teeth, instead focusing on the gums, tongue and palate, all of which possessed an even darker grey hue than the beast's skin, sending a lightning strike of shivers and revulsion sparking through his entire frame. He tried to pull away once more, but his foot hit a submerged boulder. *Oh shit!*

He could feel tears welling in his eyes as he realised there was no escaping this demonic creature's hold. There was no escaping fate. A half-baked sob left his mouth as he understood his efforts were in vain, and for the first time since dragging this hellish thing out of the water, the vile stench of death extended tendrils up into his nasal cavities adding to the overwhelming horror that continued to assault his senses.

A blur of movement accompanied by a sound. "NAAGGHH!"

A jagged rock, maybe twice the size of a cricket ball, cracked against the monster's head causing it to release its grip and stagger back. BD dragged his eyes away from his assailant for one second to see Taki standing there with the granite chunk still in her hand, looking as surprised as he felt that she had managed to pause the attack for a moment at least.

Again, good sense overrode his fear and it was his turn to lurch forward, extending both his hands like a kid in the school playground in a pushing competition. He connected with the already stunned beast and it toppled into the water. Without pause he leapt away grabbing Taki's wrist and wading the last couple of metres to the bank.

They both looked over their shoulders to see the monster had no intention of giving up and it was back on its feet heading towards them.

"Run," BD ordered. "We need to get back to the van." They climbed the slippery slope, but before they'd reached the top, the creature was out of the water and in pursuit.

"I don't understand," was all Taki could say as they finally reached the footpath parallel to the river.

"No. Neither do I." Internet, radio, newspapers, TV were all controlled and strictly censored. Effectively, they were living in a kind of authoritarian, dystopian society, but it was one they were all grateful for. Freedom was a small price to pay for safety, for avoiding the fate that had befallen the rest of the world. But this encounter threw everything they had been told into question. Every broadcast by the PM, by Elizabeth Holt, the chief scientific advisor, by Elyse Kennedy, the transport secretary, by Theresa McCann, the foreign secretary, every soundbite, every word now had a question mark hanging over it.

"I thought the outbreaks were under control," Taki said as the pair tore along the path.

That was the narrative. Leeds and Portsmouth were under quarantine and the real danger had passed, but the government was continuing to monitor the situation closely, just to be on the safe side.

The pair glanced over their shoulders to see the beast tearing after them with a speed and focus that sent fresh waves of horror pulsing. It was only now that BD realised he was still holding on to Taki's wrist and he let go only for her to grab hold of his instead. He didn't try to shake free. He had never been more grateful for human contact in his life. They were both like petrified children. Fear, anxiety and hopelessness shrouded them as they sprinted faster than they had since childhood.

"GET DOWN!"

The shouted order boomed in the air as a soldier, then three, then five, then seven appeared from around the bend in the path. Neither BD nor Taki understood for a moment, but then, as the soldiers raised their rifles, comprehension dawned. They both dived and a volley of shots thundered.

The pair lay face down with their eyes closed for a moment, hoping the ordeal was over. Finally, they turned and looked behind to see the creature on the ground motionless.

"Shit! I honestly thought that was it," Taki said, still out of breath.

BD looked across at her. "Thank you. You saved my life."

She was about to reply when the sound of running feet jarred them both. They began to scramble to their knees but stopped on all fours as another order, "DON'T MOVE!" was shouted.

Briefly, they wondered if the infected woman had not been put down, but then, as the rifles were charged and they looked up to see them all pointing in their direction, they realised this was something else.

"What's happening?" BD asked.

"Did you come into contact with the hostile?" The soldier demanded.

"What's happening here?" BD asked again, his eyes fixing on the three stripes decorating the other man's sleeve.

The sergeant stepped forward, aiming his rifle straight towards BD. "This is the second and last time I'll ask. Did you come into contact with the hostile?"

Fresh fear reignited inside BD as he witnessed death in the sergeant's eyes. "Y-yes. I-I pulled her out of the water."

Furtive glances passed between the other soldiers as they kept their weapons trained on the two escapees. "Did the hostile attack you? Were either of you scratched or bitten?"

"N-no. No. There was a struggle, but Taki—"

The sergeant reached for the radio clipped to his belt. He brought it up to his mouth and hit the talk button. "Command, this is Unit One. The hostile has been neutralised. I have two civilians who came into contact, however. Awaiting instruction on how to proceed. Over."

"Why are you pointing your guns at us?" Taki asked. "What do—"

The radio crackled to life. "Unit One. This is Command. Police are on the way to cordon off the area while it's sanitised and the body is removed. We've received word that the field hospital at The Valley Stadium is now operational. Deliver the two subjects there and then return to base. Over."

"Roger that, Command." He reclipped the radio to his belt and breathed a long, deep sigh. "You are two lucky bastards." He shook his head and both BD and Taki could see the unbridled relief on the sergeant's face.

"Will you please tell us what's going on?" Taki asked.

"You're going to be taken to a field hospital for tests and an examination, and they'll—"

"Tests? Examination? I just want to go home," she said, starting to climb to her feet. All the soldiers aimed their weapons towards her and she let out a small whimper, throwing her hands into the air.

"That's not going to happen." The sergeant looked to two of his men. "Restrain them."

"Restrain us?" Taki cried. "We've got rights. You can't do this."

"Actually, ma'am, we can," he replied as one soldier forced Taki's hands behind her back and zip-tied them.

BD slowly climbed to his feet and willingly put his hands behind his back. The soldier dealing with him was subsequently gentler as he secured his wrists. BD looked into the sergeant's eyes and saw something resembling gratitude. BD was a spectacular underachiever, but he was bright. Many who knew him would say he was more than that. He understood what was going on. He'd read between the lines. *Awaiting instruction on how to proceed. You are two lucky bastards.* And then the expression of relief on the sergeant's face. BD understood how close to death he had just come for a second time that morning.

"The outbreak," he said quietly. "It's started, hasn't it?"

Again, the sergeant's face said everything he needed to know before he turned to the pair of soldiers who'd bound the two civilians. "Get them back to the chopper. Keep your eyes on them while we wait for the police. You get so much as a hint that something's off, you know what to do."

"Wait a minute," Taki said. "What does that—" Her words were cut off as a bag was placed over her head. It was a strange, thick material that she couldn't identify. There was a letterbox of gauze where her eyes were so she could see what was going on. She felt a wire tighten around her neck, sealing the bag. Understanding finally registered. This was in case she turned. This was in case, somehow, she had become infected. Suddenly, she couldn't speak even if she wanted to. *Is it enough just to be in the proximity of these things to become infected?* She thought about her family in New Zealand. She thought about how she had lost contact with them overnight and what fate had befallen them. Another whimper left her mouth and her head bowed with resignation and sadness as she and BD were led away.

1

Tess was always in a rush. Being a care worker was not the most leisurely of occupations and the industry seemed to have been terminally short staffed for as long as she could remember.

She staggered as she burst through the door of Derek's Blackheath one-bedroomed flat. No matter how many calls she'd put into the council on his behalf, they still hadn't been to repair it and it continued to stick in the jamb with more regularity than Winnie the Pooh's head got stuck in a honey pot.

"Sorry I'm late, Derek," she called out, locking the door behind her. Burglaries had gone through the roof since the prime minister's speech the previous autumn despite a vast number of special constables and auxiliary staff being conscripted. She picked up the mail and the morning paper then started to climb the stairs, manoeuvring her way around the chairlift when she reached the top. She flicked off her jacket and hung it up before entering the small living room.

She grabbed the glass from the coffee table, sniffing the thin film of alcoholic contents that coated it from the night before. *How that man's still got a functioning liver I will never know.* She collected the previous day's newspaper, which had been discarded untidily on the sofa, and noticed a small mountain of biscuit crumbs on the carpet before walking into the kitchen. She placed the morning's deliveries on the countertop, put yesterday's *Guardian* into the recycling bin and went across to the sink, shaking her head as she saw a plate sitting in the bowl with dried ketchup smeared over it from the day before. *Would it be asking too much for him to just run a bit of hot water over the bloody thing?*

She turned on the tap, squirting in a good measure of Fairy liquid. "HAVE YOU HAD BREAKFAST, DEREK?" she shouted over her shoulder as she plucked the handheld vacuum from the recharging unit and marched back out to the living room. There was no reply, which wasn't that unusual. Derek was by far and away her favourite client. He'd led a fascinating life, was always full of beans and stories, but sometimes, he was a little distant. His mind would wander, not in the same way a lot of older people's minds wandered, but in a thoughtful, solving all the world's problems kind of way.

Tess turned on the hand vac and noticed the biscuit crumbs were not just confined to the carpet but there were some on the sofa too. She quickly hoovered them up then headed back to the kitchen to turn the tap off. She returned the cleaner to its charger, checked the water level in the kettle, switched it on and then walked back out into the living room.

"DEREK?" she paused, waiting for a reply. Usually, by this time, he would have emerged grumpily from the bedroom or bathroom or wherever he was lurking when she'd first arrived, but only the distant sound of police sirens answered her call. "DEREK?"

Unease flashed on her face in the form of a small twitch. In the eleven years she'd been doing this job, she'd found half a dozen of her clients dead and the discovery of all of them had begun with unanswered calls to their names. She nervously retraced her steps out of the living room and into the hallway. The bathroom door was slightly ajar and it was plain to see that it was unoccupied. She walked up to the crack in the bedroom door.

The curtains were wide open letting the grey light from outside illuminate the room and she could clearly see the old man's head on the pillow and his eyes closed.

She knocked on the door. "Derek?"

Silence.

Oh God. Tess had once been the belle of the ball, but a

life full of disappointments and hard work had helped her gain over fifty pounds, made her pre-diabetic and resulted in her being put on blood pressure medication. Anxiety was not her friend, but at that moment, anxiety was exactly what she was experiencing.

She entered the bedroom, calling out the old man's name once more but gleaning no response. She walked over to the bed and moved in closer. "Derek? Derek? Oh no, Derek. Please, please, please." She whispered the last few words as she placed her fingers under his nose.

"About bloody time you showed up," he said loudly, breaking into a mischievous laugh.

Tess almost stumbled back, throwing her hand up to her chest. "Oh, you bastard, Derek," she cried. She'd been on the verge of tears and, despite her anger at him for pranking her in such a manner, a massive wave of relief swept over her.

"Hahaha. I got you, didn't I?" he cheered, clapping his hands together.

"I swear, you're going to put me in an early grave," she replied, still trying to catch her breath.

"I once had to spend half an hour on stage acting dead. It's actually much harder than you think, especially when you get an itch. Try lying still for half an hour when you've got crabs."

Tess shook her head. "I'll give that one a miss, I think."

"Yes, very wise. I would recommend neither crabs nor lying on stage pretending to be dead. But still, everything's a learning curve, isn't it?" He swung his legs out of bed with the energy of a teenager and sprang to his feet.

"You're chirpy this morning."

"Yes. I've already had two coffees."

"That's really not good for you."

"Yes, mother," he replied, plucking his robe from the chair in the corner. "Now, are you just going to stand there dilly-dallying or are you going to make me some breakfast?" he asked with a cheeky smile.

"I've got a good mind to make you some breakfast then wrap it around your bloody neck for what you just did. I can still feel my heart going."

"Well, correct me if I'm wrong, and I certainly don't have your medical experience and knowledge, but your heart going is a good thing, isn't it? I mean, it's when it stops that you encounter problems, right?" He winked and headed into the living room.

"You know I could just put a pillow over your face, don't you? Somebody your age and with everything that's going on at the moment, they probably wouldn't even do a post-mortem," she replied, following him out.

"I enjoy living life on the edge. Having a care worker with homicidal tendencies merely adds to the excitement."

"Yeah, well. You've been warned. You pull a trick like that again and you'll be experiencing my homicidal tendencies firsthand."

Derek chuckled. He waited for her to arrive in the living room and then grabbed her hand and pecked her on the cheek. "I'm sorry, darling," he said, still smiling. "Now, don't pout. Pouting doesn't suit you." He walked across to the sofa, plonked himself down and turned on the TV. "Toast and coffee, please."

"Y'know, there are some who'd say that you could actually manage pretty well without a care worker."

"Ah, yes. And to them I would say this. Fuck off and mind your own business."

Tess laughed. "And I'm not making you another coffee. Three coffees before ten o'clock in the morning is crazy. You'll get the jitters. You can have orange juice." She headed into the small kitchen dinette and got to work on breakfast.

The truth was, after his fall, he'd needed all sorts of help. He'd bounced back thanks to Tess, however, and now it was her companionship and the bond they had that he relished more than anything. Whenever assessment time came, he slowed right down, became remarkably forgetful, grunted and creased with pain. It was just one benefit of being an actor for so many years. Derek had lived an exciting life, a full life, but through bad investments, being scammed by his manager, who was also his much younger lover, and being ostracised by his family for his life choices, and, in fairness, some of his outrageous behaviour, he had ended up living his retirement alone in a one-bedroomed council flat. It was not how he had envisaged spending his latter days, but he was never one to feel sorry for himself.

"So, why were you late again?" he asked as he put on his glasses, picked up the morning's newspaper and started to read the headlines.

Tess put four slices of bread in the toaster and stepped

into the doorway to answer. "I was trying to get in touch with Bertie." She was the only person in the world who called him that. For all his protests, he would always be her little Bertie. "I'm a bit worried to be honest."

Derek stopped reading, lowered his glasses to the end of his nose and peeked over the top to look at her. "Oh. Why?"

"Well, he was meant to drop by last night and he didn't show up. I've been trying to reach him on his mobile, but he hasn't got back to me. I must have left a dozen messages. When I could get through, that is. The service is all over the place again."

"He's not even thirty, Tess. He's probably out having fun and sowing his oats."

"Fun and oat-sowing are not things you'd associate with my boy."

"Trust me. He'll be fine. When I was his age, I once went on a bender that lasted four days. Don't remember much of it at all, but by day five I was back home as if nothing had happened. Of course, that precipitated an acrimonious divorce and my outing in the papers, but the point is I'm still here, aren't I?"

Tess stared at him for a moment. "If that was your attempt to make me feel better it was really shit, Derek."

He shrugged and went back to his paper. "He'll be fine," he muttered as he started reading once more.

"Anyway. Why have you already had two coffees?"

"Ha! Bloody sirens. They started at about three o'clock and just kept on and on and on. I gave sleep up as a bad job at about five and got stuck into the latest Stephen King book." He thought for a moment. "Which is to say the last Stephen King book. It's rather sobering when you start thinking about it, isn't it? All the great and wonderful people who we've lost to this thing."

"What kind of siren?"

"Of course, there are plenty of utter bastards who probably got an end they deserved at the same time."

"What kind of sirens?"

"Oh, I don't know. Police, ambulance, fire engines. I can't really distinguish, especially at three o'clock in the bloody morning."

"Did you see the transport secretary in her speech last night?"

"Oh, dear God, no. D'you know how you can tell when a politician's lying? Their lips are moving."

"That may be so, but she was saying the hijacking and theft of supply trucks has become so serious that they're redesignating a hundred thousand conscripts in order to provide security."

"Oh, that'll help no end."

"What do you mean?"

He turned to her, lowering his glasses once more. "I mean, short of locking the country down like in the quarantine zones, there's no way to stop the criminal enterprises that are flourishing."

"Well, she says—"

"She can say what she wants," he said dismissively. "Think about it. The conscripts were drafted with minimal qualifying criteria. No background checks were done. Anybody could be working at the distribution depots; anybody could be driving the supply trucks. Believing the country would come together and we'd face this disaster as one with the famous British stiff upper lip was the pinnacle of naivety. You didn't need to possess a crystal ball to see what was going to happen, what is happening. Ever since Thatcher this country has fallen into—"

"Ohhh, God, Derek, don't go getting on your high horse about something that happened nearly forty years ago. It's 2017, for Christ's sake."

"Yes. It's 2017 and look where we are. The world is literally crumbling around us, and—"

"It's all Thatcher's fault? She's responsible for this reanimating virus that has wiped out most of the planet. Is that what you're telling me?"

He shrugged. "It's possible," he said with a smirk. "But that's not my point. The moral fabric of the average Brit began to spiral when that woman took—"

A sound came from the kitchen interrupting him. "Toast's ready."

*

Deano Duncan had been kept awake by the sirens and police helicopters as much as anyone. The difference between him and most people was that he knew the reason for much of the commotion.

He splashed some cold water on his face, picked up his freshly filled travel mug of hot, black coffee and stepped out of the caravan he called home. Of course, when his probation officer came around, it was not his home. It was just somewhere for him and his staff to take their breaks. For reasons that still baffled him, his son had agreed to include him on the electoral register so he would have a legitimate address when he was released. His mail went there and, from time to time, BD would pop around with it.

Their relationship was strained at best, and by Deano's own admission, BD made far more of an effort than he deserved. Whatever his son's reasons, though, it was a lifeline for Deano. It meant he was under less scrutiny than he would be if he was moving from doss house to doss house, and for this alone, he was grateful.

Deano had spent two stints inside. The last was a five-year stretch. He'd been out for the last eighteen months but hardly clean. He'd tried. He'd really, really tried. But some of the acquaintances he'd made over time were not the kinds you said no to.

He'd grown up alongside career criminals. He'd done lots of favours for career criminals, which had put him on the wrong side of the law, and now and again, he still did the odd favour, despite not wanting to. He was fifty-two. The world had pretty much come to an end beyond UK and Irish shores. If there was any time left, he wanted to spend it trying to make some kind of life, maybe repairing the fractured relationship he had with his son, maybe finding a lady friend to settle down with.

But as Vig, one of the most violent gang bosses in London, rolled into the yard in his chauffeur-driven Mercedes, he couldn't think about any of that. Deano knew what this was concerning and he looked across to his two staff, Aldo and Rocky, who were sons of his former cellmate and best friend who'd got shivved in Belmarsh. He did his best to look after the two boys as if they were his own, but at that moment, he wished he'd never laid eyes on them. *This could end badly.*

The driver got out and walked around the car opening the door for the passenger in the back seat. Vig climbed out, looking every bit the stereotype that he was, shades and all, despite it being an overcast day. He loved this life. He loved the notoriety, the fear he put into people.

"Deano." He said the word as a greeting.

"Alright, Vig."

"Shall we go inside?" he asked in his gravelly voice, nodding towards the Portakabin.

"Sure."

Two more men, the kind of men a bulldozer would struggle to topple, climbed out of the car too.

Oh fuck.

The four of them entered the office and Deano went to sit behind his desk. Vig sat opposite and the two brick walls stood behind him. Silence and menace hung in the air for a moment. "I understand you and Danny had somewhat of a fracas last night, or, more accurately, very early this morning."

Yep. I saw this coming. Deano let out a long breath. "Look, Vig. I don't mean you or your boy any disrespect, but—"

"He's got a name and he's not a boy anymore, Deano. I think that might be the problem. I think you might be remembering him as a kid. Well, he's the next in line. He'll be taking over from me. But regardless of that, with everything that's going on out there at the moment, his role is expanding on a daily basis and I need to make sure that all my little minions know that if he says something or asks something, it's as good as me saying it or asking it."

Deano looked at the two stoic figures behind Vig, who both fixed him with steely glares. *Fuck it. If the truth gets me killed, it gets me killed.* "I'm not looking to cause trouble or anything, Vig, but I think you'll agree; this place is a valuable resource. I mean, it's come in pretty useful over the years, hasn't it?"

Both men had lost count of how much evidence had been destroyed by the compactor. Nor could either of them estimate how much stolen merchandise had been stashed in one of the many hidey-holes around the property. "What's that got to do with anything?"

"Every street around here was lit up like a Christmas tree last night. Coppers were everywhere and he shows up at just after four in the morning with two meals-on-wheels trucks that him and his mates had just jacked. I mean, meals-on-wheels trucks, Vig. What the fuck's he going to do with those? Is there a black market for cellophane-wrapped scrambled eggs and hash browns that I've not heard about? It was a pure fucking miracle that he didn't lead plod right to my fucking door, and then that would have been it for this place. They'd tear it apart searching for anything and everything." Deano was about to go on but stopped himself. *Shit. I've gone too far. Shit.*

"Meals-on-wheels?" Vig said, taking off his sunglasses and removing a cleaning cloth from his inside pocket. "I was told they were pharmacy vehicles."

Deano shook his head. "No, Vig. They weren't. The centre at the back of the surgery on Peel Street does meals-on-wheels. The surgery has an in-house pharmacy and that part of the building doubles as a catering centre for the old folks. The pharmacy only delivers during office hours, not in the middle of the night. The trucks they boosted were full of food for the OAPs."

It was Vig's turn to let out a long sigh. "Where are these two trucks now?"

"They're scrap, Vig. I compacted them."

"Well. Danny obviously got some lousy information. I'll tell him to have a word with his sources."

The sound of three lorries pulling into the yard made Deano arch his neck and move to stand up. "What the hell—"

"Sit yourself down," Vig said. "I need to store something in a couple of your containers for a few days."

Shit.

"Okay, Vig."

"And I need you to look after this." He removed a handgun from his inside pocket and placed it on the desk.

Deano wasn't an expert, but he'd seen a CZ Shadow 2 before. The two goons behind Vig probably had the same model hidden on their persons somewhere. Deano had heard on the police scanner that someone had been shot and killed during the raid at the care centre. In all likelihood, it was Vig's idiot son who had wanted to play cowboy and shoot the place up. There were a hundred ways Vig could get rid of that gun, but this was another tax and another test. Holding on to something like this could get Deano put away for life. There was a difference between the stuff he normally did and being an accessory to murder. But if he said no, there would be immediate and irrevocable consequences.

"No problem, Vig," he replied weakly.

"That's my boy," the other man said, placing his shades on, beaming a toothy grin and climbing to his feet. "It's always nice to get misunderstandings with old friends ironed out, isn't it?"

"Course, Vig."

"Yeah." The gangster extended his hand over the desk.

Deano knew what was coming. It would be a bone-crushing squeeze to remind him that he could do whatever he wanted. He didn't disappoint and Deano grimaced as vice-like pressure was applied to his fingers.

"Well. I'll see you later, Deano."

"See you later, Vig."

The trio left the Portakabin and Deano watched from the window as they climbed back into the car and drove away. The sound of forklifts working in full vigour to unload whatever contraband the three lorries had brought in began to drone somewhere in the depths of the scrapyard and he was about to head out to try to find out what he'd been left on the hook for when he stopped and turned back to the desk.

Where the fuck am I going to put that?

He couldn't get rid of the weapon as much as he wanted to. He would have to store it somewhere, but where? He opened his bottom drawer, gloved his jacket cuff around his fingers and picked the gun up, placing it carefully beneath a couple of brown folders.

I'll figure out a proper home for it later.

The world's almost come to an end. It's just a matter of time before the infection spreads beyond Leeds and Portsmouth despite what we're being told. But it's still business as usual for pricks like Vig.

He started towards the door but stopped just as suddenly as the office phone rang. Mobile and internet services had been patchy for months, much like everything else in the country despite the government's guarantees. He walked across and picked it up.

"Duncan's."

There was a pause. "Deano. It's Tess."

He'd spoken to his ex-wife just a handful of times since getting out. Their marriage had never been made in heaven, and it ended acrimoniously, but he couldn't blame her for that. She'd been the apple of his eye once. A prize on his arm. But the world, or rather the underworld he inhabited, did not good bedfellows make with a girl like Tess.

"Y'alright, Tess. What's up?" There was no point making

small talk. When he'd tried before, he'd always been shot down in flames and his self-esteem was already at a low ebb after his confrontation with Vig.

"Have you heard from Bertie?"

He couldn't help but smile. He had agreed a long time ago never to call his son by that name, yet it was the only one Tess ever used. "No. Why?"

"He was meant to come around last night. He didn't show up. I've left messages on his phone, but—"

"I wouldn't worry about it, Tess. My service has been off and on for the last few days. He probably forgot. I saw him the day before yesterday and he was talking about how they were rolling out a new groundwater testing programme; sounded like they were going to be run off their feet down there."

Silence.

"I suppose I'm worrying over nothing."

"Do you want me to phone his office?"

"Umm. No. No. I'm being stupid. Like you say, he probably just forgot."

"I've told you. He'll be out sowing his oats. OATS!" Derek called out in the background.

"Who's that?" Deano asked.

"That's just Derek."

"Boyfriend?"

"Ha! That's a good one. No. I'm his care worker. I'd better get back to him."

"Look. If I hear from BD, I'll get him to call you."

"Okay. I'll—"

The line suddenly went dead and Deano looked at the receiver for a moment. "Tess? Tess, are you there?"

2

BD and Taki had spent the night in a glorified hut. There was a single reinforced plastic window with a grille over it making escape impossible. They had been stripped on arrival then examined thoroughly by doctors before having their dried clothes returned to them and being locked in the temporary accommodation without so much as a pillow to rest on.

Despite the fact that they were practically strangers in the grand scheme of things, the pair had spent the night huddled together, freezing cold, in a corner, wondering and fearing what would happen to them. During the night, they'd heard helicopters fly over and dozens of vehicles arrive and depart. Twice, they thought they'd heard the sound of distant gunfire, but neither could have sworn to it.

"They can't just keep us here," Taki said, placing her hands beneath her armpits for warmth.

"Well, I think they've proven they can, actually."

"Strewth! It's so cold."

"Yeah."

An echoing clunk filled the room and the door opened. A young nurse stepped inside with two cellophane-wrapped sandwiches and two bottles of water.

"How long are you intending to keep us here?" Taki demanded.

The nurse shook her head. "I'm sorry. I don't know."

"Well, I want to speak to someone who does."

"Umm. I'm sure someone will be in as soon as—"

"We haven't seen a soul since we were locked in here last night. We're not prisoners. We haven't done anything wrong. You can't treat us like this."

The nurse placed the food and water on the floor and backed towards the door. "Are we the only ones?" BD asked.

There was a long pause. "I … I really just wanted to fetch you something to eat. I don't get told anything."

"Please. This is a big stadium. Why have they set up a field hospital here? I understood the field hospitals were only to be established on the perimeter of quarantine zones. That's what it said on the news, anyway."

The nurse opened her mouth to say something but stopped just as quickly. "What aren't you telling us?" Taki demanded.

"I'm sorry. I'll have to get back to—"

"Can we have our phones back at least?"

"They'll be returned to you when you leave."

BD took a step forward and looked at the young woman's name tag. "Collette. I don't want to give you any grief. I don't want to get you into trouble by asking you stuff that you're not meant to answer, but we've been here for not far short of twenty-four hours." He pointed to the small, curtained cubicle in the corner. "Forced to share what's essentially a camping toilet and sleep on a hard floor. The doctors have examined us and I'm pretty certain they've ascertained that we don't present a risk to anyone, otherwise we wouldn't still be here. So, please, just tell us what's going on … please."

Collette exhaled deeply and took a step towards them. It was the first time the pair got to see her face properly and it wasn't hard to ascertain the fear present in the young woman. A single dried silver streak remained undisguised on her left cheek as a burst of shouted but unintelligible orders came from elsewhere in the stadium.

"I was transferred here from Maudsley Hospital yesterday. A few of us were. The only thing we were told was they were putting Catford into quarantine."

"Catford?"

"Yeah." She sniffed. "But they were too late. London's not like any other city. Every district, every borough just runs into another. It's not like Leeds or Portsmouth. You can't just ringfence part of it. London's a whole."

"What are you saying?" Taki asked.

The nurse sniffed and tears welled in her eyes. "By the time they finished setting this place up yesterday, it was already too late."

"What do you mean?"

"The infection's in the city. It's all going to hell."

"Then why are we being kept here?"

The nurse shook her head guiltily. "Things are changing by the minute. Yesterday, they were worried about word getting out. Today, they're just trying to put out the fires where they—"

"Collette!" They all turned sharply towards the door to see another nurse standing there. She was a little older but wore the same uniform and had the same telltale signs of fear, dread, and regret on her face. "We're pulling out," she announced as the sound of a helicopter taking off at the far end of the stadium reverberated.

"What do you mean?" Collette asked.

A shuddering breath left the other woman's lips. "All I know is they're setting up several more field hospitals on the other side of the river."

"The other side of the river?" DB asked.

The older nurse just looked at him before turning back to Collette. "We need to go."

"Wait a minute," DB said. "Are you saying they're quarantining the city south of the Thames?"

"It's the only hope they've got of containing it," she finally admitted. "It's spreading too quickly."

"What about us? What's going to happen to us?" he asked, gesturing towards Taki.

The other nurse shook her head. "It really doesn't matter now." And with those last words, she disappeared.

A sob left Collette's lips. "My family."

Dozens of bodies rushed by in both directions outside. The whole atmosphere was electric as a greater sense of chaos mushroomed. Shouts from elsewhere in the stadium were accompanied by cries of despair as news of this latest order spread.

The sense of foreboding and terror in the air was palpable to all, but for a moment, the trio in the temporary cell could only regard one another in horror at this latest news.

The sound of engines beginning to rev and an incoming helicopter drowned out some of the frenetic tumult for a moment. "We're leaving," BD announced, grabbing hold of Taki's wrist and dragging her to the door while Collette remained in a state of shell shock.

They walked past the young nurse not knowing what to expect on the other side, wondering if rifles would be pointed towards them by the guards they envisioned were outside their door all night, but as they exited, they understood that anarchy wasn't a big enough word to do justice to what was unfolding.

Soldiers were few and far between. Dozens, hundreds of conversations were going on as people rushed in all directions. The once green pitch had been churned and scuffed to muddy piles in places and the pair joined a line of people heading towards what they could only assume was the exit.

BD turned to look at Taki, whose wide eyes reflected his own fear. "Stay with me," he said, finally releasing her wrist.

She nodded. "You don't have to worry about that."

They were no longer concerned about being called out for escaping their cell. The whole city south of the Thames was one giant prison now. And whether they got out of the stadium in one piece or not, they were trapped.

*

Tess continued to stare at the receiver for a moment. "Deano? Deano?" Their relationship had always been complicated, and sometimes downright volatile, but the conversation hadn't been argumentative. There was no reason for her ex to hang up. "Deano?" She hit the end call button, waited for a few seconds, then pressed the green call button expecting to hear a dial tone.

Nothing.

"What the bloody hell's wrong with this thing now?" Derek grumbled from the other room.

Tess re-entered the living room and replaced the phone in the cradle. She looked across to see the old man fumbling with the TV remote in an attempt to get something other than a black screen.

"What is it, Derek?"

"It's the bloody Chinese, that's what it is."

"What are you talking about?"

"Nothing's built to last these days. My family had a Grundig when I was growing up. They still had it when I left home. You could fire cannonballs at that thing and it would still work. These days, they just fill them full of cheap plastic and you're lucky if you get a year out of them."

"Give me that," she said, taking the control as more police vehicles turned on their sirens somewhere nearby.

"And that's another thing," he continued, but on a slightly different rant now. "Since when did they start selling bloody fireworks in May?"

Tess's brow creased as she flicked from channel to channel, just finding one blank screen after another. "Hmm? What are you going on about now?"

"Fireworks. That was another thing that was keeping me awake last night. Boom, boom, boom. Bang, bang, bang. That's something else we've got to thank the bloody Chinese for."

"Fireworks?"

He shook his head irritably and picked up his newspaper and pencil once more. "Three across. An almost funny bone in the arm." His brow creased a little. "What sort of clue is that? An almost funny bone in the arm. Nonsense."

Tess had detuned to Derek's ramblings for the time being as she continued to try to get something … anything … on the TV. "I don't understand," she said to no one in particular.

"Yes. You and me both. An almost funny bone in the arm. Bloody ridiculous."

She put the remote down and went back out into the hallway to retrieve her mobile. The mobile and internet had been sketchy for a long time, but she hoped that this might just be one of the occasions when it was operating normally. *No signal.*

She went back into the living room and picked up the small radio that sat on the mantelpiece, immediately turning it on to the sound of static. She manoeuvred the dial slowly until a blaring continuous beep made her rush to turn the volume down. "What is that?" Derek asked, his curiosity piqued for a moment.

"I don't know. But it doesn't look like the TV's the only

thing that's out."

They both instinctively looked up to the ceiling as a low-flying helicopter passed overhead. Tess returned to the dial, edging it along slowly. A wave of relief gripped her as the sound of classical music burst through the small, tinny speaker. "Ah, this takes me back," Derek enthused, sinking a little further into the sofa. "*Adagio of Spartacus and Phyrgia* by Khachaturian. I once had a fling with the first violinist from the Yerevan Symphony Orchestra, you know. Dashing young man. Had a sister, Maral, or was it Marine? I forget. Anyway, hell of a cook. She used to make stuffed vine leaves, dolma they were called. God, it makes my mouth water just to think about them. And I'll tell you something else about—" He stopped as abruptly as the music and they both glared towards the small transistor radio before Tess frantically tried to find another channel.

✢

Deano exited the Portakabin, travel mug in hand, a little rattled by the fact that both the landline and mobile service were down. It wasn't that unusual for the internet and mobile to be out, but for the landline to go down as well was less common, although not unheard of in these past months.

He looked around for Aldo and Rocky, and when he couldn't see either of them, he started towards the sound of forklifts, stopping again just as quickly as he heard his name called by a familiar voice.

He spun around to see Poppy, a young woman who worked as a stripper and more besides, in Vig's club. As she approached him, he could see mascara had run down her face. She wore a long coat, the belt wrapped tightly around her middle, and as he walked up to meet her, there was fear in her eyes.

"Are they looking for me?" she asked.

"Is who looking for you?"

"Don't play dumb, Deano. Not you. Please."

"Poppy, I don't know who you're talking about."

"I saw Vig here. He's just left you. What did he want?"

"You're worried Vig's after you?"

She looked around nervously. "Can we go inside?"

This is all I fucking need. I'm already on his shit list and now this.

It was his turn to look around now. "Some of his men are still here, unloading in the back. Let's go into the caravan."

She sniffed. "Okay."

They entered the four-berth tourer and he closed the door behind them. Filthy lace curtains hung at all the windows. They weren't pretty to look at, but those and the encrusted dirt made it virtually impossible to see in. He'd once been given a private dance by Poppy on the instructions of Vig for a favour he'd done. Many would have relished the opportunity, but for all his failings, Deano wasn't like that. She was barely more than a kid. She was sweet, funny and kind. It broke his heart that she'd got mixed up with scum like Vig, and instead of making her put on a show and whatever else she would normally do to entertain one of the boss's special guests, they'd sat and talked for half an hour.

Ever since that day, she'd felt a bond with Deano, and in her hour of need, he was the only person she could think of running to. "What's wrong, Poppy?" he asked, pouring water from the still-hot kettle over the coffee granules in the bottom of the waiting mug.

"I've fucked up, Deano. I've really fucked up."

"What's happened?" he asked, handing her the mug, picking up his own and sitting down beside her.

She stared into the still-swirling liquid for a moment. "I tipped off the police about the pharmacy raid."

Deano paused in mid-sip, his eyes angling towards her. "And Vig knows?"

"I'm guessing. I phoned up 'cause it's not right, Deano. It's not right; there are old people who are relying on those meds, all sorts of people who are relying on them. It was one thing when they were dealing and getting their shipments from abroad, but they're heisting whatever they can now for a quick buck and it's not right. There are cancer patients and terminally ill people depending on those drugs.

"Danny was playing Mr Big, boasting about it in the club before him and his cronies set off, so I snuck into the back and put a call in."

"Tell me you didn't use the landline."

"I was going to. It was important enough. But then I saw I had a signal on my mobile. First time all day. But ten minutes later, Reeves walks in and marches straight to Vig's office."

Reeves was a detective, dirtier than any criminal Deano knew and he was on the hook for about fifteen grand's worth of gambling debts with Vig. Good information would go a long way to easing some of that burden.

"And you're sure it was about the call?"

"I didn't stop around to find out. I got out of there and I've been trying to figure out what the hell to do ever since. I daren't go home, Deano. I know he'll have people waiting for me."

"Jesus, Poppy."

"I'm sorry. I'm sorry I've shown up on your doorstep like this," she said, starting to cry, "but I've got nowhere else to go."

He put his arm around her as she leaned into him. "Right. If they didn't know before, they probably put two and two together when you went missing halfway through your shift. You're going to need to lie low for a little while until we can get you safely out of the city."

"Out of the city?" she asked, pulling away. "What are you talking about? I don't have anywhere else to go."

"Poppy. This isn't something that you can unfuck. There's only one solution as far as Vig or Danny are concerned and it's not a happy ending for you."

She started sobbing again. He took hold of her hand. *She's just a fucking kid.* "Look. Stay here. Get some kip. If you're hungry, I've got food in the fridge. Help yourself. Do not leave this caravan. When I close up tonight, we'll have a long chat and figure something out, okay?"

She sniffed loudly and wiped the tears from her eyes. "Okay, Deano. Thank you."

"Now, like I said, I've got some of Vig's men unloading fuck knows what into some of my containers. If I don't put in an appearance, it's going to look suspicious, so I'm going to have to show my face."

Poppy nodded. "Okay."

He leaned in and kissed her on the forehead. "I won't let anything happen to you."

For the first time since she'd arrived, a small smile bled onto her face. "Thank you. And again, I'm sorry."

He shook his head. "It was a brave thing you did, kid. You've got nothing to be sorry about. And for what it's worth, they didn't get the meds."

"They didn't?"

He didn't have the heart to tell her that Danny had killed

someone nonetheless. "No. Now, keep this door locked," he said, stepping out.

He heard the mechanism engage behind him and breathed out a long breath. *This fucking day.* He set off in the direction of the noise and finally reached its source. Vig's men were transferring the contents of each lorry into two cargo containers. Aldo and Rocky were standing back with their arms folded, watching.

The pallets were shrink wrapped and piled high with boxes. "Do we know what's in these?" Deano asked quietly as he joined the audience of two.

"I think they're rations," Aldo replied. "I managed to snag a delivery note off one of the pallets."

He surreptitiously handed it to his employer and Deano turned, stepping behind the two brothers for cover in case one of the workers glanced in his direction.

GBISW Logistic Solutions was emblazoned at the top of the dispatch note. The delivery address was the Headingley Sports and Recreational Centre in Leeds. He scanned the product lines:

Item	Weight/Vol	Qty
Brown Rice	1KG	800
Dried Penne Pasta	500g	2000
Dried Oats	1KG	1000
UHT Long-Life	1L	2000
White Flour	1KG	1000
Toothpaste	100ml	2000
Water	4L	1000

The list went on and, even though there was only one page, it clearly stated it was one of sixteen.

"Jesus. He's ripping off quarantine ration shipments now."

"We're nearly done here," called a voice and Deano quickly folded the note, placed it in his inside pocket and emerged from behind his two employees to see one of Vig's men pulling off his work gloves.

"I'm guessing you're wanting me to trash the trucks for you?" Deano said.

"Nah," he replied. "These are heading north."

"Empty?"

"Yeah."

"Okay," he replied, a little puzzled. "I won't ask."

The other man smiled. "Vig's idea. We're going to leave them at Watford Gap services. When they eventually find them, they'll think the heist went down there or thereabouts, and no one will even think about looking to us."

"Vig's thought of everything, hasn't he?"

"He usually does." The first truck engine roared back to life and the man turned and nodded to the driver. "We'll be back in a couple of days for this little lot. We'll be taking it down to Portsmouth."

"Portsmouth?" Deano asked. "Portsmouth's quarantined."

The other man laughed. "Yeah. But we've got contacts there and a way of getting in and out, and what you can get in the supermarket for a quid up here you can get ten times that for it on the black market down there."

"But aren't there curfews in place and—" He was cut off by the sound of two helicopters flying low nearby.

"Yeah. But if you know which palms to grease, it's not too hard to get around them."

"What about the infection?"

The other man laughed again and a couple of his cohorts earwigging the conversation did too. "It's a storm in a teacup. I heard they'll be lifting the quarantine in a week or so. But fingers crossed, we'll get this lot shifted before then."

"Right, chief. That's us." The call came from behind him and the de facto supervisor turned to look.

"Okay then. I'll see you in a couple of days." He turned and headed back to the cab of the first lorry.

Within a few seconds, both vehicles were gone, leaving Deano and his two employees standing there in front of the packed containers.

"If we get found with this stuff, it will be bad," Rocky said.

"Your dad had a gift for understatement too. If we get found with this stuff, we are totally fucked."

3

It was almost like a match day as they left the ground. Ambulances, army trucks and a host of other vehicles were lined up outside waiting to transport staff to the alternate sites, but many were no longer interested in doing their job. A surge of bodies flitted through the static traffic emptying into the side streets.

They weren't worried about what trouble they could get into for abandoning their positions, their careers. Doctors, nurses, auxiliary staff and more besides ran through the streets, heightening the sense of apprehension in the air.

This was it. This is what they had feared for so long. The infection had reached London, and whatever plans and good intentions were in place, they meant nothing.

"Where do you live?" BD asked as he pulled Taki from the fast-moving line of people on the pavement into a garden.

"Bloody Catford. That's where I live."

"You can't go back there."

"But everything I own—"

"You can't go back there. Look. My flat's on Belmont Hill in Lewisham. It's about three and a half miles, but my dad's scrapyard's only about a mile and a half away."

"Why would we want to go to a scrapyard?"

"Well. He'll be able to give us a car if nothing else." The yard was in a different direction to BD's home, but the value of getting a vehicle outweighed the detour.

"Shit. My phone. My life was in that phone."

They both looked out of the gate as people continued to run by. Two loud cracks suddenly made the air quake around them and a chorus of screams rose.

"Those were definitely rifle shots," BD said authoritatively.

"This is it, isn't it? It's really it. This is the end."

He wanted to say something that would make her feel better, but panic was thick in the air. "Look. Let's get to my dad's place. We can figure out our options from there. If nothing else, we'll be able to see the news, phone somebody."

"Okay."

*

"Ha!" Derek laughed excitedly. "Humerus."

"What?" Tess asked, looking at him quizzically as she desperately tried to tune in to another station.

"Humerus. An almost funny bone in the arm." He filled in the squares with his pencil.

"Am I the only one who's worried that the TV, the radio and the phones have all gone off at the same time?"

He shook his head irritably. "They'll be back on soon enough. The emergency broadcast system would be on if—"

An almost deafening blast of sound erupted from the speaker on the TV and a red triangle with a white exclamation mark appeared in the middle of it. EMERGENCY ALERT appeared all in caps underneath and Tess dropped the radio on the sofa and grabbed the remote to lower the volume.

She sat down next to Derek and both of them just stared at the screen in dreaded anticipation of what would come next.

"Attention! This is an emergency alert. Attention! This is an emergency alert. Attention! This is an emergency alert."

Goosebumps rippled up and down Tess's arm and she reached out, taking Derek's hand. He accepted gratefully, grasping hers tightly.

Incidents of infection have been identified in London south of the Thames. While military and civilian forces work in tandem to eradicate any further threat to the public, we ask that people stay in their homes.

All commercial and non-essential municipal premises should close with immediate effect. Public transport will stop running at four p.m. and the mandatory lockdown will stay in effect until further notice. If you normally reside north of the river, find alternative accommodation. You will be given priority when the situation is resolved and routes are reopened.

Updates will be given through further emergency alerts.

We thank you for your cooperation.

The message was repeated and another loud siren chimed and the emergency alert logo flashed on the screen once more.

"Oh, Jesus," Tess whispered.

Suddenly, their two mobile phones echoed the same siren, making them both almost jump out of their skin. She reached for them to find the same message that had been announced and written on the TV screen. The government had spent millions developing the mobile alert system since the outbreaks in Leeds and Portsmouth. Now, she was seeing it in all its glory.

"Dear God!" Derek said, turning a shade paler than she had ever seen him.

Tess stared at the screen for a moment. In the top right-hand corner it read Emergency Calls Only. "Oh, please, Bertie, please be okay."

She was almost in tears by the time she put the phone back down on the arm of the sofa.

"Trust me. He'll be fine," Derek said, trying his hardest to make her feel better despite the circumstances.

"He won't be fine, Derek. None of us will be fine. This is it. It's all gone to hell."

"Y-you can't think like that. They'll bring this under control. At the very worst, we might be quarantined for a while like Leeds and Portsmouth. I mean, good grief, it sounds like half the Royal Air Force is hovering over London at the moment."

"Yeah, and all the sirens. This started yesterday. They've been trying to bring this under control since yesterday." She gestured to the screen. "And clearly everything's gone to hell."

"Look. They're dealing with it. They're initiating a curfew. That's the first logical step to—"

"Don't talk to me about logic, Derek. My boy was meant to come round last night and he didn't show up. Today, we find out that the infection's reached London. I know something's happened to Bertie. I can feel it in my bones."

He squeezed her hand a little tighter. "You've been coming here for over four years. You've gone on endlessly about your Bertie, and although I've tried to tune out most of it out, there's one thing that's obvious. He's an intelligent and resourceful young man. He'll be alright."

*

This is just fucking brilliant. I've got two containers of stolen government supplies in my yard, a gun that was used in a murder, and a girl who every mobbed-up lowlife in South London's going to be looking for. What the fuck next?

The lorries had already gone, meaning he was solely on the hook for all the merch in the yard. But at least there was no longer any chance that one of Vig's men might see Poppy.

Deano walked around a row of four-high scrap vehicles to see exactly what was next. The door to his caravan was open and the young woman he was doing his best to protect was in front of it looking terrified.

"Deano," she cried, holding her mobile phone in her hand and running across to him.

"Jesus, Poppy. I told you to stay inside."

"Did you get the message?" she asked, almost in tears. "Did you see the message?"

He reached into his pocket for his mobile phone only to realise it was still on his desk. Instead, he took the phone from Poppy. A sinking feeling gripped him as it had gripped everyone who'd heard and seen the contents. He swiped down, reading the whole thing then re-reading it.

"Well, I was just wondering what else the day was going to throw at me. Now I fucking know, don't I?"

"What are we going to do?"

We? We? Deano didn't like we. Deano liked he. But he'd hate himself more than he already did if he turned his back on Poppy. "We're going to have to do what it says. We need to stay put."

Her eyes rose looking over his shoulder and he turned to see Rocky and Aldo heading around the corner. "Oh God!" Poppy whispered.

"It's alright," he said. "They won't say a word to anybody. They're good lads."

"You okay, Poppy?" Aldo asked.

"Poppy isn't here, boys. If anybody asks, you haven't seen her."

"Okay, Deano."

"You got this message on your phones?" he asked, handing it to one of the brothers before a symphony of emergency vehicle sirens erupted a few streets away. He turned towards the entrance of the yard as they got louder. *Fuck! Vig's set us up. He's fucking set us up.* It was almost too much to take in. The infection had reached London. Hell was literally breaking loose, but at the same time, some parts of life were still going on. He breathed out a sigh of relief as three, four, five police cars sped past the gates.

"What does it mean?" Rocky asked.

Deano loved the two brothers. In some ways, they were incredibly gifted, in others they were a little slow to catch on. Maybe that was one of the things he liked. Maybe because they were so dependent on him, it made him feel like a father figure, and he wasn't able to feel that way with his own son. "It means you need to go home to your mum, keep your heads down and look after her."

"What about you? What about this place?"

"Don't worry about me. I'll be fine right here. I've got everything I need. I'm going to shut those gates and wait until we get the all-clear. We're just going to have to sit this out like they're doing in Leeds and Portsmouth."

Rocky looked towards Poppy and then back to Deano. "What about—"

"Listen. Go home to your mum." He reached into his pocket and brought out a wad of bills rolled up in a thick rubber band. "There's two grand there. That should see you right until this is all over, although I doubt there'll be much to spend it on."

"No, Deano. You've paid us already."

"Take it," he insisted, shoving it into Aldo's hand.

"I don't like you being here by yourself with everything that's going on." It was obvious what the everything was. The fact that Poppy's appearance at the yard was meant to be kept quiet, the closed-door meeting with Vig and the arrival of two containers' worth of stolen goods was not just an average day. The emergency alert was just the icing on the cake.

"You don't worry about me. I've got two containers'

worth of food and a beautiful young woman to keep me company. People would kill for this," he said with a false smile on his face, trying hard to make them both feel better.

The brothers glanced at Poppy and then turned back to Deano. "You know where we are if you need us. Aldo and I can share. You and Poppy could have a room. You don't have to stay here."

"You're good boys. Give my love to your mum and stay safe."

The siblings each shook Deano's hand before walking across to the Audi parked by the side of the Portakabin. Aldo climbed into the driver's seat and started the engine. The vehicle idled for a moment before pulling away.

More sirens came into earshot and another helicopter passed nearby heading north.

"Are you sure it's alright for me to stay here?" Poppy asked. "I mean, we've got no idea how long this could go on for."

"You can't go back home and, by the looks of things, I'm not going to be able to get you out of the city for a while at least. So, yeah. You can stay."

"I don't have any clothes or toiletries or anything other than what's in my bag. I mean, I've got a spare pair of knickers and black tights. I've got a bit of perfume and makeup and a bottle of deodorant, but—"

"Look. We'll figure it all out. First things first; let's get these gates shut."

4

BD and Taki had managed to convince one of the fleeing medics to let them see the emergency alert on her phone before she snatched it back and disappeared into the ever-growing crowds running along the streets. They were heading through an industrial area that up until the announcement had been in full operation.

Although the world beyond UK and Irish shores had come to an end several months back, a massive, coordinated plan by the UK government to manage the disaster had resulted in repurposing of factories and warehouses, escalated manufacturing of the most-needed supplies and materials; in short, a countrywide effort to produce everything from toilet paper to packing crates to polycarbonate tunnels.

Conscription, along with a gigantic recruitment drive by some of the biggest manufacturers, had resulted in unemployment dropping to fractions of a percent.

Subsequently, most places of business were packed to the rafters with staff and the announcement to return home led to a mass exodus from all the surrounding buildings. Although the chances were that more buses would be put on, every one they'd seen so far had been jam-packed. It was a moot point, however, as neither of them had any money.

"Do you think this is what it was like in Leeds and Portsmouth when they were quarantined?" Taki asked. There was no reply as the pair continued to move forward. "I said do you think—"

"I heard what you said."

"Oh. So, you're just ignorant, not deaf."

"I was thinking."

"With all this hubbub, I wasn't able to hear the gears grinding. My mistake."

A small smile cracked on BD's face. *This girl is going to be a royal pain in my arse. But I'm stuck with her.* There was no real reason he had to be stuck with her, they were virtual strangers, but in good conscience he couldn't let her fend for herself. She'd saved his life. He owed her until the end of time, however soon that might be.

It was obvious that Catford was a no-go area and the second nurse had said how quickly it was spreading.

"I don't think this is like Leeds or Portsmouth."

There was a pause in her step and it took her a few seconds to get in rhythm with him again. "What do you mean?"

"London's geography's very different to anywhere else. The population is far more concentrated. There are over eight million people in this city. And like that nurse said, the towns, the boroughs, they just bleed into one another. Often there's no demarcation beyond a signpost. At a push, at an absolute push, they might be able to lock down south of the river, assuming the infection hasn't already spread beyond. But my gut's telling me this is it, Taki. What happened to the rest of the world is finally happening here."

They carried on through the streets for a moment. Taki looked around at the faces of the other people who'd been oblivious to the conversation. Everyone had fear in their eyes and uncertainty in their step.

"Some comfort you are."

*

The air felt different to Tess the moment she left Derek's flat. She hadn't really wanted to leave. She was worried about him. He was more able-bodied than some of her clients and certainly far more intelligent and resourceful, but he was in his early seventies and he was prone to bouts of depression. He had once told her that she was his lifeline, the moon shining over his dark and dreary moor.

She loved Derek like he was a favourite uncle or something. She liked a number of her other clients, but she actually loved him and it pained her to leave him alone with so much uncertainty in the air. She didn't know if this lockdown would last a day, a week, or a month. But as much as she loved him, she loved her son more and she needed to get home because there was a slim chance that he might show up there.

The phones were out of service, whether that was a short-term or a long-term thing it was impossible to tell, but her home was her home and there was a small flame of hope inside her that if he was okay, he would turn up at her door before four p.m. with a sports bag of belongings and they would get through this lockdown together.

The small cul-de-sac where Derek resided felt more like a private community than council-owned properties. The communal lawns were kept short, the pavements free of litter, and the road itself was quiet. Maybe that was another reason she liked coming here. Maybe it was the quiet and calm that contrasted so much with the other places she needed to visit.

She'd taken the bus to get there, first thing, but as she stepped onto the pavement bordering the main road and saw vehicle after vehicle already packed to the brim. She knew it would be foolhardy to try to get one back. She lived off Belmont Hill, about half a mile away from Bertie, and the one saving grace was that, from here, it was a downward trajectory.

The green across the road was awash with bodies rushing in every direction. Now she was out in the open, away from the confines of the relatively secluded cul-de-sac, the sound of sirens was omnipresent. Many in the distance, but some fairly nearby.

On the horizon she could see a black line of what she assumed were military helicopters heading north and even more butterflies began to flap in her stomach. She remembered the fear she'd experienced the night of the prime minister's speech the previous autumn. All that day rumours had been circulating and the odd clip of footage had surfaced online, but the service was so sporadic, as it had been for some time before, that she had only heard about it rather than seen it.

Then, when Prime Minister Beck had announced what

was effectively the end of the world beyond UK and Irish shores, it was as if every drop of blood in her veins had turned to ice. It was beyond apocalyptic. It was biblical. The end of mankind was surely just a few breaths away for them all.

But then his speech had continued. He'd laid out plans to secure the UK, to bolster food production and manufacturing, to conscript any and all able-bodied people not already employed to the army, to production lines, to councils and utility companies in order to keep everything running.

For months it had worked and then there were outbreaks in Leeds and Portsmouth and the country held its breath again; but a lockdown, strict curfews and a massive military presence meant the quarantine held, or so they were led to believe.

This was something else though. Despite the assurances given in the emergency alert, pandemonium was lording over the city. There was no sense of organisation, only chaos. And if this was just the beginning, what was it going to be like in an hour, two hours, a day?

She took a breath and started walking a little faster. She couldn't think about the things outside of her control. It was too terrifying, too bewildering. She could only think about her own little part of the equation, and even that was stressing her out.

Her next appointment was a bus ride away in Greenwich. There was no way she'd be able to make it in time on foot and the emergency alert was pretty explicit. Mrs Charlton would have to fend for herself. As would her later appointments, Mr Cleveland, Mr Delber and Miss Clunes. Hopefully, Mr Czurky's daughter would head straight to him from work, so that was one less to worry about. And Mrs Todd was doing much better after her fall and was probably going to lose assistance at her next assessment anyway, so she wouldn't need to fret about her either, but the others…. The others struggled.

It was no fun getting old and she just hoped there was still enough of an independent spirit within all of them to manage for a little while. Her mind drifted back to Derek and the look of sadness on his face as she departed. He'd remained upbeat all morning, almost like his old self, but when she'd left, she saw his eyes were heavy with the weight of sadness.

She was a few stones overweight and she was already starting to get out of breath as she walked along the pavement, trying her hardest not to get barged into the road by younger, fitter people undertaking and overtaking. The sound of screeching tyres followed by a thunderous metallic crunch made everyone stop and all eyes turned to the black cab at the junction up ahead, which had mounted the kerb and collided with a traffic light.

The driver's door flew open and he climbed out, staggering back as his eyes remained fixed on the back seat. The traffic behind and in front had all come to a standstill, too, as a result and now everyone was trying to understand what had caused the collision.

The roadside rear door burst open and a man in a business suit spilled out. Blood painted his neck, face and clothing as he desperately tried to crawl away from the vehicle.

"Help me. Help me!" His call was weak but just about audible to those nearby and at least half a dozen people ran forward to assist him, but all of them froze in a semicircle as their eyes drifted to the figure restrained by a seatbelt in the back.

From her position on the pavement, Tess couldn't see everything that was going on and she stepped onto the road. The nearby traffic remained static and she moved a little closer, then closer still, peering beyond the arc of figures between her and the vehicle.

The man's cries for help had fallen silent, and she couldn't see him for the moment, but she finally laid eyes on the other passenger in the back of the taxi and fear like nothing she had ever experienced before clutched her very soul. The woman, she didn't know if technically she could still be called that or not, writhed and strained against the seatbelt like some uncontrollable rabid beast.

Tess continued forward despite her terror, mesmerised by the scene. People remained unmoving on the pavement as hopelessness lay thick in the air. The traffic stood fast and horns from further back began to blare, but everyone was deaf to them. The taxi driver was frozen just a few metres from his vehicle, staring towards it in wide-eyed horror.

Tess came to a halt behind the handful of people who'd responded to the cries for help, but they were like her, transfixed by the hellish thing flailing in the rear of the cab. The now silent man who had begged for assistance lay forgotten at their feet as everyone bore witness to what was undoubtedly a turning point in the battle against the infection.

It was as if logic and reality were on hold. Everything they had been told, everything they had learned, all their instincts told them one thing. However, they couldn't help but do another.

Between the car horns, the sirens and the distant helicopters came pin pricks of another sound. Growls. The growls of something malevolent … ungodly.

"Oh fuck no. FUCK NO!" The cry came from one of the women in the semicircle surrounding the fallen figure and the car as she started to back away. "Look at his skin. LOOK AT HIS FUCKING SKIN!"

The heads of the others angled down as they finally dragged their eyes away from the thing in the back seat. They too began to retreat and Tess caught sight of the figure on the floor as it moved ever so slightly.

Then she understood what the woman was talking about. In the space of seconds, the man's skin had changed hue. She didn't have a great view from her position, but it was plain to see there was something unnatural about him.

Suddenly, he scrambled then sprang to his feet, charging towards the would-be helper nearest to him. The newly morphed creature leapt, a feverish, guttural growl leaving its open mouth as its clawed fingers seized the bewildered prey.

The victim staggered back, swiping, pushing, windmilling desperately only to collapse to the ground with the thing on top of him. A chilling, pained cry sliced through the morning air and Tess's eyes golfballed as she saw the monster's head jut back with a mouthful of flesh between its teeth.

The man on the floor writhed and cried, but no amount of tears or screams would change his fate. Then, like a child given a sack to fill in a sweet shop, the creature was back on its feet, lunging towards the next nearest living, breathing human.

It was as if people's disbelief suddenly became suspended and they finally understood what was happening. Shouts, screams, revving engines and drumming feet erupted in an atonal symphony as all hell broke loose around Tess.

She wanted to throw up. She wanted to cry. She wanted to go back fifteen years when she was a lot lighter and a lot fitter. She wanted to run. Run like she'd never run before. The turn for Belmont Hill was up ahead, but that would mean advancing further towards the utter mayhem that was unfolding.

She turned and started running, pushing her way back onto the pavement as barging and shoving bodies vied for position. Panic. Pure, unadulterated panic and fear washed over every man and woman like a tsunami.

Even those who had not witnessed the scene firsthand felt it and joined in the crazed rush to get out of the area. Tess was suddenly elbowed by a smaller but fitter woman who barged her out of the way. The pain made her clutch her rib cage and slow a little further, which resulted in another shove from someone else, edging her to the inside of the pavement and squeezing her against the garden wall of one of the aligning properties.

Another push and her hip caught, causing her to spin. The surge of bodies did not abate and Tess let out a cry as she fell in what seemed like slow motion. She flailed, trying her hardest to grab the wall or something, but instead she crashed onto the hard tarmac pavement.

"NAAAGGGHHH!" The sensation as someone's booted foot mashed her shin was agony. She had somehow ended up on her back and as she looked up at the grey sky, someone else's foot landed on her shoulder. She let out a stifled grunt this time and then, finally, she realised that if she didn't do something, there was a good possibility she would get trampled to death.

Screams, shouts, engines, sirens and helicopters all meant that any pleas would fall on, if not deaf, certainly overwhelmed ears and she reached up, grabbing the ridge of the wall as more bodies barged her.

She hoisted herself, refusing to let go despite several more shoves. Even when she was upright, she kept going, flipping over the wall and into a flowerbed. On the ground again, and this time face down, she paused on the damp earth for a moment just to catch her breath.

One.
Two.
Three.
Four.

She looked to the upper windows of the house to see an old man and woman peeking out from behind the curtains. Their eyes were transfixed firmly on the events at the junction. The same expression of horror she'd shared with every other witness was painted on their faces and, as she climbed back over the wall to rejoin the river of bodies, there was a split second when her head was above all others and she saw two grey figures pounce simultaneously as a third climbed to its feet.

Oh God! Oh God! Oh God!

She dropped to the pavement, this time abandoning the do unto others doctrine, which was how she had lived her life. She elbowed and pushed with the rest of them. It was everyone for themselves and at that moment Tess realised it always had been. Everything else was just a mirage.

She managed to stay upright, moving along, out of breath, pained, scared, until she finally reached the turn to take her back to Derek's. Only a couple of people veered off and she let out a small sigh of relief but did not slow; in fact, she started running faster as the sounds chased behind her.

She threw a glance over her shoulder as a line of bodies continued to cross the mouth of the street. Tears were streaming down her face as she reached the cul-de-sac, but still she did not slow.

She banged on the door, at the same time reaching into her pocket for the keys. It was instinctive, a warning, a cry for help, everything and nothing. She had never been so consumed by terror that she couldn't even think straight, but here she was.

She fumbled with the key, skirting the hole twice before finally managing to place it inside and disengage the lock. She burst through the door to see Derek at the top of the stairs, wondering what was going on. Telling him was the last thing on her mind at that moment and she slammed the door shut behind her, engaged the upper and lower bolts as well as the safety chain. It was the first time any of them had been used since she'd become his care worker, but they were used now.

She let out an exhausted breath and turned, leaning back against the door with tears still streaming down her face.

"Tess, you're bleeding. What the hell happened?"

"Just that, Derek. Hell happened."

*

Deano hadn't locked the gates as he'd intended. He was about to when he spotted a friend at the end of the street and, in all good conscience, he couldn't lock them out.

It was a Rottweiler named Petal. He wasn't sure who she

belonged to or if she even belonged to anyone, but every day she made a stop at the scrapyard. Sometimes, she'd even slept there overnight and helped him eat his breakfast the next morning.

She seemed loving and friendly but independent, too, and he wondered if she had a home or just lived on the streets. She had no tag and the only reason he knew her name was she'd once appeared at the newsagent's a couple of streets away while he'd been buying some gum and the owner had called her Petal.

Since then, he'd referred to her as such, and she seemed to respond to the name but on her own terms.

He stood behind the gate awaiting her arrival as she headed in his direction. Normally, she would drift from one side to the other, sniffing the lampposts and grass verges, getting the latest news on the canine grapevine. But today was different. Her solid figure just walked in the centre of the pavement, almost as if she was making a beeline towards the scrapyard.

"Whatever's happening out there, it sounds big," Poppy said, staying out of sight behind the gatepost. She understood that, now she had entrusted her life to Deano, it wasn't just herself who was at risk.

Deano let out a long breath. There was so much going on in his head that he wasn't quite sure what to concern himself with first. On any other morning, giving safe haven to a nark would be his biggest worry, but it seemed like a drop in the ocean compared to the news that the emergency alert had warned of.

"Yeah," he said eventually. "It is big. It's big, and it's bad, and something tells me that they're going to struggle to put a lid on this one."

"You really know how to make a girl feel safe, don't you?"

A small smile flashed on his face. "Sorry, Poppy. Tact isn't one of my strong points. I think—" His words cut off as three more military helicopters passed over a few streets away, the sound drowning him out for a moment. He looked across at the young woman and saw the desperation on her face. *Truth isn't always what people need to hear, Deano.* "We'll be alright in here though," he said, gesturing to the palisade gates. "Nothing's getting through these unless it's driving a tank."

"I hope you're right."

Two cars zoomed down the street. Thankfully, they were

in an almost forgotten part of town. The gigantic red brick factory opposite had remained empty for more than a decade. The place was full of asbestos and redevelopment came with no end of complications and expense. The expansive plot next to the yard had an incomplete office building, which had been stripped of anything valuable a long time since. Beyond were other industrial units, none of which housed substantial workforces. It had not taken long after the emergency message for these to be vacated, and so, despite the rumble of activity from the surrounding city, there were no children playing in the streets or elderly people trying to cross the road who could fall victim to the single-minded drivers as they travelled at breakneck speeds to get to their destinations.

Deano opened the gate a little wider as Petal reached them. "Fuck!" he exclaimed, seeing the bloody welt on her back.

"Oh God!" Poppy cried.

It was almost as if the dog understood she was with one of her own as she stepped through the gates and they slammed shut behind her. Deano pushed the heavy bolt into the brace and fixed the padlock around the chain before running to catch up with the Rottweiler, who instinctively headed up the steps and through the open door of the Portakabin.

Deano and Poppy raced to catch up with her and when they entered, she was lying down in front of the Calor gas fire, which was currently turned off but had many times warmed her in the more inclement weather.

As the pair studied Petal, they could see two streaks running from her eyes and, in addition to the welt across her back, there was some blood on her ear too.

"Jesus, girl," Deano hissed, heading across to his desk and pulling out a first aid box.

"Do you reckon a car hit her or something?" Poppy asked.

"No. Some bastard did this deliberately."

"Who? Who'd hurt an animal like this?"

He just stared at her for a moment. "You have far too high an opinion of people in general, Poppy. There are people who'd do this just for kicks."

"It's not right."

"I'm going to need your help."

"What do you mean?"

"I'm going to have to clean her wounds. Go to the caravan. There should still be plenty of hot water in the kettle. I need you to pour it into a bowl and bring it back here."

"Okay," she said, disappearing out of the door.

He knelt by the side of Petal as she stared at the fire. "You cold, girl? You want a bit of comfort?" He reached across, turning the dial. Gas hissed for several seconds before he pushed the ignition button; then a small wall of flames whooshed over the ceramic grid.

"I brought her a bowl to drink from as well," Poppy announced as she re-entered the Portakabin.

"Good."

She placed both bowls down and Deano opened a packet of gauze, immediately dipping it in the hot water. He squeezed to get rid of the excess liquid then started to dab at the lesser of the two wounds.

Petal's head shot up and he backed off for a moment. She sniffed at the gauze in his hand then placed her chin on the floor once more.

"You look like you've done that before."

"Never with a dog. I had to deal with a few wounds when I was away."

Poppy knew what away meant. She didn't know the ins and outs of everything that had led to Deano going to prison, but she knew enough. Petal let him clean both wounds despite the bigger one clearly causing her some discomfort.

"What do you want me to do?" Poppy asked.

"Get ready to dress my wounds when I use these on her," he said, retrieving a packet of antibacterial wipes from the first aid kit. "They're probably going to sting a bit and I dare say she's going to kick off, but without a vet and without antibiotics, this could get infected."

"Be careful."

He opened one of the packets and again dabbed the ear wound first then opened another and placed it on the back wound. Petal's head jutted upward for a moment and Deano thought it was a precursor to her snapping at him, but it was as if she understood he was trying to help her and she put her head down once more.

He took three wipes, overlapping them so they covered the entire wound. He pressed them gently and each turned a light shade of red. After a minute or so, he peeled them off then repeated the action with a second set of wipes. The Rottweiler seemingly remained untroubled.

"Good girl. Good girl, Petal," Deano said, gently stroking the dog's head. The fire was already throwing out a fair amount of heat and the canine's eyes began to drift.

"Do you think she's going to be okay?"

"Let's hope so."

Several shots suddenly cracked in the distance and Deano jumped to his feet, as did Poppy. Petal's eyes opened only momentarily before closing again and drifting back towards sleep.

The scrapyard owner led the way out of the Portakabin and lifted his head as another rifle report echoed.

"Where do you suppose that is?" Poppy asked.

"Hard to say. It's not a million miles away though."

"I'm really scared, Deano."

Again, those words reverberated in his head. *Truth isn't always what people need to hear.* "Don't worry, kid. You and me'll be alright."

5

BD seemed to know this area far better than Taki, but she couldn't help but question him as they headed onto a street lined by tall, dirty-red brick buildings. A single figure crossed the road about a hundred metres ahead and it was all a far cry from the packed streets they had been running down a couple of minutes before.

"Are you sure you know where we're going? I really don't like this."

He stopped for a moment and they both took the opportunity to grab their breath. "Those shots. They weren't a million miles away from here."

"Yeah, but haven't you heard of safety in numbers?"

"Safety in numbers doesn't apply out here. In fact, it's the exact opposite. There's a reason this spread so quickly. That last major street we were on. If one, two, three of those people were infected, how quickly do you think it would have been before six, twelve, twenty-four became infected? How quick before forty-eight or the whole street became infected? Staying away from people is the safest thing we can do in a situation like this."

"But … but what if…." She couldn't go on and she didn't need to go on.

"Look. We're not far away from my dad's place. When we're there, we can take a breath and figure out our next move. Everything I've heard, everything I've seen, everything I've read says that a critical blow to the head is how you stop these things. I mean, we saw that yesterday, didn't we? When you smashed that thing with the rock it was stunned. If we come across one before we reach my dad's, we'll just have to fight."

"That's easier said than done. I'm scared shitless, BD."

"Yeah. And I'll put money on the fact that you were scared shitless yesterday, too, but you still saved my life, didn't you?"

"I can't guarantee to repeat that performance if push came to shove. I've had time to think about it. I've got to know you better. No way would I take such a risk again."

BD laughed and Taki did too. "Thanks."

"I just want to be honest with you. Honesty's the foundation of any lasting relationship."

"Lasting relationship? I like your optimism."

"I'm speaking relatively of course. Lasting in relation to the length of time we've got left on this planet might be an hour, might be two."

"I don't think I'm the only one who needs to work on my motivational skills."

Taki shrugged. "I'm just a junior member of staff, remember."

Crack! Crack! Crack!

The sounds of a city in turmoil had become like white noise as they ran towards what they hoped would be relative safety, but this latest wrinkle, the gunshots, sent fresh pangs of dread and fear through them both.

"I think we should probably get on our way again."

"Yeah. I don't think that's a bad idea."

*

Tess sat at the kitchen table in tears. Her entire body was shaking and Derek did the only thing he knew how to help someone with shock. He poured her half a cup of brandy and a second one for himself before sitting down beside her in the small kitchen dinette.

"What on earth happened to you?" was all he could ask

as he reached out to take her hand. It was grazed and there was blood on the back of it. She had a small scuff on her face, too, but it wasn't bleeding too badly and the worst of it had already been washed away by her tears.

Silence dragged on for seconds, then a minute, before she finally answered. "I saw...." She didn't quite know how to continue and took a sip of the brandy. She squeezed her eyes shut tight. It was cold and it felt like it stripped the back of her throat as it went down, but after a few seconds, it warmed her insides a little and she took a breath and another drink. "I saw one of those things."

"What things?"

"One of the infected, Derek."

A huff of a laugh left his lips. "Nonsense. You've obviously had some kind of fright and—"

"I saw one, Derek," she insisted and went on to retell the story of what had happened. When she was done, he picked up his mug, drained it and poured himself another healthy measure.

"You're sure about this?" he asked. "You're sure it wasn't just—"

"I'm sure. It's not something I'm going to forget for the rest of my days, however many of them there are left."

"Dear God. That's practically on our doorstep." He paused for a moment. "Those shots. Those shots we heard were much further away."

"Yeah," she said, taking another drink. "This thing is spreading fast. You won't believe it until you see it, Derek. It's like.... I don't know what it's like. It's like some nightmare, some impossible nightmare. One minute, you're you. You're you with a past, a history, with all the things that make you you. And the next minute, you're ... God, I don't know what. A thing. A thing that can't be but is. A monster. A ghoul. A killing machine that's intent on nothing but finding its next victim.

"I so wanted to help. I left that pavement full of good intentions, much like those other people, but, like them, I stopped. I stopped when I saw that woman in the back of the cab. Only, she wasn't a woman anymore. Not really. She'd probably climbed into it as one. She'd probably been scratched or bitten or something. That man might have been her husband or her brother and he was trying to get her to the hospital maybe.

"That goes back to what I was saying about histories. We all have our own, don't we? There could have been a thousand reasons why they were in the back of that cab, and a thousand things might have led them to that one moment, but none of it really matters. Not in the end."

"You're rambling, dear. Have another drink," Derek said, pouring a little more into the mug.

"What I mean to say is when death comes for you, he treats everyone with an even hand, doesn't he? He doesn't care about your history. He doesn't care whether you were a good person or a bad person. He doesn't care whether you're married or single. He doesn't care about anything but his job."

Derek took another sip. "Well, regardless of what he does or doesn't do, there's not a tremendous amount *we* can do about whatever's going on out there other than to sit tight and hope things are brought under control."

The glazed expression finally left her face and she turned to look at him. "I don't think you understand what I'm saying. There is no bringing this under control. This is it, Derek. It's all over."

"Poppycock. Poppycock, poppycock, poppycock. I'm not denying you've had a fright, my dear, but they've got contingencies in place for just this kind of event happening. Within half an hour, there'll be soldiers flooding the streets and—"

"There won't be soldiers flooding the streets," she replied, pointing upwards as another helicopter went over. "At least, not this side of the Thames. That's what the emergency message was all about. They're quarantining us. We're like a gangrenous limb. They're lopping us off in the hope they can save the rest of the body."

Words stumbled on the older man's lips for a moment. "Th-they can't. They wouldn't. It-it's not right. It's not bloody British."

"Maybe not, but it's the truth." She started crying. She'd wanted to since first seeing the scene at that junction unfold, and now she let the tears flow freely. "My boy. My beautiful boy."

Derek exhaled deeply and squeezed her hand once more. "Come on now, Tess. We have no idea where he is or what's happened to him. For all we know, he might be under the covers with some luscious young maiden having the time of his life, oblivious to all this."

She shook her head, wiping away some of her tears. "I felt it. I felt in my bones that something was wrong. Last night, when he didn't show up and didn't call, I could feel it. I could feel something wasn't right."

"Rubbish. Nobody can feel anything in their bones other than rheumatism and arthritis. Mark my words. He'll be off fadoodling somewhere. Good grief, I mean, he's a good-looking boy. One of the posh girls from W1 might have taken a shine to him. He could be north of the river as we speak, joining giblets with some buxom wench, and all this worrying and boohooing on his behalf will have been for nothing."

Tess wiped more of the tears from her face and sniffed deeply, looking up at Derek as another burst of sirens sounded from across town. A half-hearted laugh left her lips as his hand remained tightly clenched around hers. "Fadoodling? Buxom wench? You do know it's 2017 and not 1617, don't you?"

A warm smile lit his face, if for no other reason than he'd managed to stop her crying for a moment. "A lifetime performing Shakespeare will equip a man with more euphemisms than he knows what to do with."

This time, her laugh was a little more sincere. "I've never known anybody like you."

"I am unique. One of a kind. Peerless. You shall never find the likes of me again."

She placed her free hand over his. "What are we going to do, Derek?"

"We shall do what every Brit worth their salt would do. Keep calm and carry on."

He said it with his traditional dramatic flair and raised chin. Tess desperately wanted to believe him, but she could see behind those old, grey-blue eyes that he was just as scared as she was.

*

BD and Taki turned another corner, not losing any of their pace as more sirens screamed not too far away. The shouts and fear-filled cries had become more distant as they'd fled further into a less built-up area, but as a gang of five men appeared on the road in front of them, they understood they were a world away from safety.

They both slowed down from a run to a walk, trying hard

not to show fear but at the same time knowing that the quintet ahead weren't out collecting for Oxfam. "Let me do the talking," BD whispered as they carried on.

"These people don't look like they're interested in talking."

A thought that amplified as two of them revealed the objects that had been hidden behind their backs until that moment.

"Shit!" BD hissed as the sword and cricket bat came into full view.

He felt a hand around his arm. "We should go back. Find another way."

"I think it's safe to say it's too late for that," he replied without even turning.

Taki glanced over her shoulder and wondered if BD had some kind of sixth sense as four more figures hung around about twenty metres back, blocking any hope of an exit from the street in the other direction.

"Oh, shiiit, BD. What do we do?"

"Like I said. Let me do the talking."

"This is our road. What are you doing on our fucking road?" the one carrying the bat called out as the five men spread across the lane and the pavements making it impossible to pass.

BD and Taki stopped about ten metres back. "We don't want any trouble. All hell's breaking loose. We just want to get by," BD replied.

"I don't have a problem with that. But y'see, this is a toll road. You can't use it without payin' a fee."

"Well, we're out of luck there. We don't have any money on us."

"In which case, we've got a problem then because, by my reckoning, you're already about two thirds of the way down, so you definitely owe us." He took a menacing stride forward and Taki, who still had her hand around BD's arm, squeezed a little tighter.

"Listen, I'm—"

"Oh, I'm listenin' alright," the man said, and the others laughed. Even the ones behind who were now only five metres or so away. A fact that had not escaped Taki as she continued to cast frightened looks over her shoulder.

"I'm sure if you come with us, my dad will sort out any

toll that you think you're due."

"Think? Think? We fuckin' know we're due."

"Okay," BD said, raising his one free hand placatingly. "Let's head to Duncan's and we can get this sorted."

There was a pause before the other man spoke again. "Duncan's? Why would we head to Duncan's?"

"Deano Duncan's my dad."

Another pause and, this time, one of the men from behind walked in a wide circle around to the front. "BD?" the man asked.

"Yeah."

"Jesus Christ. I haven't seen you in … it must be fifteen years."

It took a moment for BD to recall the other man's face from his memory. "Todd?"

"Yeah. That's right. Farkin' 'ell." He looked to the man with the bat and then the others. "This is Deano's boy."

There was an immediate change in the demeanour of all the men and the atmosphere mellowed in a heartbeat. "You shoulda said somethin'," replied the man with the bat.

"What you doin' down 'ere on foot?" Todd asked.

"You wouldn't believe me if I told you, Todd. But look, I really need to get to my dad's place."

"Yeah, well, we're not goin' to stop Deano Duncan's kid from goin' anywhere, are we?"

"Thanks. I appreciate it."

The men ahead moved apart, clearing any obstruction in the road. "You give your dad our best, won't you?"

"Course."

Taki and BD continued along. She still had hold of his arm and was now more bewildered than ever. The sirens, choppers and street sounds from elsewhere in the city played accompaniment, but she had been deaf and numb to everything as the scene unfolded.

She had felt certain that some unimaginable violence and grotesqueness awaited them both at the hands of the thugs. When they were out of earshot, and her heart rate had returned to something approaching normal, or at least as normal as it could be on a day like today, she managed to ask, "What the hell was all that about? Who's your dad?"

They carried on, not missing a step, but there was a short

delay before BD spoke. "He's the kind of guy who people like that respect."

"I don't understand. They were going to mug us or worse."

"This whole area's run by a bloke called Vig. If you operate in this area, you kick upstairs to him. Doesn't matter if you're dealing, jacking cars, or holding up people on the streets. If they'd have taken our wallets, Vig would have got a percentage of what was in them. That's how it works."

"How do you know all this?"

"I just know."

"So, your dad's friends with this Vig?"

"I wouldn't go that far. But Dad's useful to him, so he falls under his protection and everybody knows not to mess with him."

"So, is your dad…?" She didn't quite know how to continue.

"A lowlife criminal?" he asked with a smile on his face.

"I didn't mean that."

"To be honest with you, I haven't decided what my dad is. I hated him for a long time. I don't think all that's left me. But he's my dad and it's complicated."

"I dare say."

"No. You don't understand. I mean, when he was around, he was always alright with me. He never raised a hand, always tried to encourage me. But he wasn't around much. And my mum tried to keep him as far away from me as possible. Not due to him but the people he mixed with."

"That must have been hard."

"It was confusing for a kid."

"So, how are you now?"

"We're still a work in progress. Since he came out this time, he—"

"Prison?"

"Yeah. Since he came out, it's like he's been trying to make amends."

"With you?"

"With everyone. I don't hear about it from him, but I was in the area with work a couple of months back and I ran into someone not too dissimilar from those dicks we just met. He was going on about how my dad had gone around to his nan's house to fix the boiler when the council had no-showed twice. He told me about the previous Christmas when the unit that was being used for the food bank flooded and Dad let them operate out of a container in the yard until they could get sorted. It's like he's trying to do the best he can this time around."

"He sounds like a character."

"That's one word for him." Four more shots sounded in the distance and their conversation came to an abrupt halt before BD continued. "But you'll get to see for yourself soon enough."

*

"What is this place?" Poppy asked as she followed Deano into one of the shipping containers. He turned a light on, revealing shelving units stacked with all sorts lining the sides and a workbench at the far end.

There were twelve shipping containers in all spread across the property. Some were used to store Vig's ill-gotten gains. Some were used for legitimate storage and recycling purposes. But this one, this was Deano's.

He reached up to one of the shelves and pulled down a brand-new duvet still sealed in its bag.

"Take this," he said, handing it to Poppy; then he grabbed a bedding set, also still sealed, and a couple of pillows, still sealed too.

"You just had this stuff here?" She looked past him to the other things on the shelves. Kettle, toaster, coffee machine, microwave, curtains, towels, wallpaper and the list went on. She looked at the bedding. "John Lewis? This is proper nice. All this stuff nicked?"

"Nope. All bought and paid for."

"I don't get it. You live in a caravan."

"Yeah." He shrugged. "I don't suppose it matters now. I'd got myself a little place down in St Ives."

"Where's that?"

"Cornwall."

"Never been."

"It's nice down there. It's a world away from here."

"So, all this stuff is for there?"

"Eventually. Well. That was the idea before today anyway. I was doing it up. It was probably going to take me another year. It needs a new heating system, windows, internal doors. It needs pretty much everything. But it was a project and before the prime minister's speech my idea was that I was going to shut up shop and move down there. Live the rest of my days by the sea."

"Sounds nice."

"Yeah. It would have been." He gestured to the shelf. "I didn't want any knock-off stuff in there. It was all going to be bought and paid for. Nice, y'know, plush. But I suppose that's all gone to hell now and there's no point in me holding on to this bedding and shit when I've got a special guest staying with me, is there?"

"I-I don't need this. Just a blanket will do for me."

"It's not for you. It's for Petal."

Poppy laughed and play-punched Deano. Then she looked down at the bedding again. "I don't like this. This is like your dream or something. This is like saying it's all over."

"It was all over long before today. I just didn't admit it. I was going back and forth a couple of weekends a month before the PM's speech, but after that, I think I've only been there four or five times since. It's a shame. It was starting to come together too."

"I thought you were chained to this place. I can't imagine you anywhere else. Were you really going to live down there?"

"Yeah. You're right. I am chained to this place. It's like a millstone around my neck."

"But it's a good business, isn't it? You've got respect in this community."

"It comes with an awful lot of baggage, Poppy. And respect doesn't give you freedom."

"What about your son? You'd never see him if you moved all the way down there."

"Yeah. That was by design."

"I don't understand."

"I've fucked his life up plenty already. The best thing I can do as a father is stay the hell away from him."

Poppy reached out, taking hold of Deano's hand. "That's not true. You're a good man, Deano. There are plenty who'd kill to have someone like you as a dad. I know I would've."

He shuffled free. "Nah. I made plenty of mistakes straight off the bat when Tess had BD. Mistakes that can't be undone. I just wish—"

The sound of helicopters and sirens had been omnipresent while he'd been talking, but it was the harsh drilling ring of a bell that interrupted him.

"What's that?" Poppy asked, looking alarmed.

"There's somebody at the gate."

"Oh shit. Do you suppose it's Vig?"

It wasn't out of the realm of possibility. He might have had eyes on the place. Poppy might have peeked out of one of the curtains when the trucks were leaving. One of his grunts might have seen her. The different permutations of what might have happened began to flash in Deano's head like a strobe.

Up until this minute, he hadn't really thought about his options if he was found harbouring someone Vig wanted, but now adrenaline started to pump. *There's no one else it's going to be.*

"Stay here. Keep this door shut." He didn't say another word before exiting the container and closing the door behind him.

He started walking through the maze of scrap and containers and then another thought entered his head. *What if it isn't Vig? What if it's the coppers and they've had a mysterious tip-off about a weapon used in an armed robbery?*

Shit! Shit! Shit!

The bell rang again, suggesting whoever was waiting was in a hurry.

Think about this. Why would the coppers be coming around? They'll have more on their minds. Even if they are on Vig's payroll. No. It's going to be Vig. I should go get the gun. I should get the gun. This could be it. If he finds Poppy in here, I'm screwed.

He walked around the corner and his anxiety edged up a notch as he couldn't see anyone at the gate to begin with. Then two figures emerged from behind the brick entrance post.

"Dad."

Deano couldn't remember ever being happier to see his son but, sadly, not for the reasons a father should be happy to see his son.

"BD. What are you doing here?" he asked, rushing to the gate and releasing the padlock.

"It's a long story, but I need your help."

6

THEN

Andy Beck had assumed the office of prime minister with great pride in his heart. He had not gone into politics for self-serving reasons. He had done it to create genuine change and it was working. But the events of the past twenty-four hours had turned not just his plans but his understanding of reality upside down.

There was still a little piece of him that thought someone was going to jump out and shout, "Gotcha!" There was still a part of him that couldn't accept that this was real, that it was really happening, that he could conceivably be the last prime minister the country ever had.

He'd just come from a meeting and there would undoubtedly be at least a dozen more before the day was over. He was going to have to steer the country through the greatest disaster ever to hit. But first, before getting down to the very real work that would take, he was going to have to address the nation to tell the people what was happening. They'd already more or less shut down internet access. Comms were patchy at best and an embargo had been placed on what could and couldn't be reported on radio and TV channels as well as newspapers. Rumours were rife and panic could end up being a bigger enemy than the very real one they faced if it was not managed.

There was only so long they could hold off on telling the truth before it got out, so this was that. This was the truth getting out and he was the one to announce it. He would have to be the country's anchor now more than ever.

He looked into the camera as the director began his countdown, verbal at first, but then just fingers as airtime approached.

Two.

One.

Action.

My fellow citizens, these are grave times. Grave times demand grave measures and it is for this reason that I am addressing you this evening.

The deadliest virus our scientists have ever encountered is sweeping across the planet. It is unlike anything we have seen before. Something that was previously science fiction has become science fact. The dead are coming back to life.

This virus is not airborne. It is transmitted by bites, scratches or any other ingestion of bodily fluids from a carrier. It is for this reason that I am taking the unprecedented measure of closing our borders.

As of seventeen hundred hours, I have invoked a strict ban on international travel. All our airports will be closed to international flights. Our ports will close, and the navy, coast guard and air force will be patrolling our waters to guarantee our safety. I have been in close contact with the Irish premier and she has agreed the same. Britain and Ireland are two of the last places to have no cases of infection. I have recalled every serving member of the military back to our shores. Each one will be subject to a strict physical and medical examination and after a short period of quarantine will return to serving their country.

Every household in the country will receive an information pack about this virus in the next few days. In it there will be details on how to identify signs of the infection, what you should do if you suspect someone of being infected, and there will also be a list of emergency numbers.

Make no mistake, this is the greatest challenge this country has ever faced and it is more important than ever that we face it together. It is for this reason that I am invoking another set of measures. As every citizen of this country will be aware, the downturn in international commerce has seen unemployment skyrocket. While we have endeavoured to protect our social security system the best we can, the situation is now becoming untenable.

So, I am conscripting all unemployed people between the ages of sixteen and forty to serve in Her Majesty's Armed Forces and all the able-bodied aged between forty-one and sixty-five who are currently unemployed will be drafted into the food, textile, arms manufacturing and utilities industries. I am reopening all mothballed coal mines and renationalising all transport, communication companies and utility companies.

I realise online communications have been increasingly erratic over the past months and so, in an effort to facilitate the free flow of crucial information, internet service will now be free and available to everyone nationwide.

Our scientists are still receiving data from counterparts in several countries and, as ourselves and Ireland are the last remaining nations with a cohesive infrastructure, it has fallen to us to supply any state or country still trying to beat the outbreak with all the help we can. This is no time to be profiteering from the misfortunes of others, but the simple fact is we cannot afford to provide endless supplies of medicines, food and arms that we may very well end up needing ourselves. So, in return for our help, we have set up trade deals with the United States, Russia, Norway, France and a number of other nations still capable of operating on a basic logistical level. This will strengthen our own resilience in combatting this near-apocalyptic catastrophe and give these nations a fighting chance they would not have had before.

Although I am confident that we have and are taking every precaution to avoid the infection reaching us, I have asked our best scientists and military minds to coordinate with COBRA in developing a response plan should there be an outbreak.

I believe that as a nation we have the capacity to weather this greatest of storms. We have the strength to fight back and rebuild. Britain will prevail, it will survive this test, and it will become great again.

My fellow citizens, now is not the time to give up. Now is the time to stand tall; to be the best we can be. Your family needs you; your country needs you; your planet needs you.

Tomorrow is a new day. Tomorrow our war begins—and this is one I have no intention of losing.

Good night and may your God go with you.

Andy paused for a few seconds, continuing to stare into the camera before the director called, "Cut!"

*

Now

The speech seemed like a lifetime ago. It had been

September and now it was May. A hundred books ... a thousand books could have been written about what had happened in between. The weight of the remaining world had rested on Andy Beck's shoulders, but it felt like it was all coming to an end.

He had started this journey those few months ago wanting to be honest with the people, *his* people. But little by little, prudence and circumstance had got in the way of his lofty ideals. The official line was that the country had remained infection-free. The truth was minor outbreaks had been put down in multiple locations before the official and very public quarantines in Leeds and Portsmouth.

Stornoway, in the Outer Hebrides, became the site of the first outbreak on UK soil. It was quickly put down and a cover story was engineered by Xander Bright, the PM's old friend and spin doctor. Subsequent minor outbreaks also occurred in Scarborough, Dundee, Bristol, Belfast and Newport. Since the speech, the government had taken a tight control of the media as well as limiting internet and communication freedoms and access when they needed to. This had become more and more commonplace as time had gone on. Effectively, it had almost become like a police state. It was something that repulsed Andy Beck to his core. It was the last thing he ever wanted to be responsible for, but it was the only way to stop widespread panic.

It was all for nothing. He had become something he hated. For all the good he had tried to do, it was only delaying the inevitable, and as his wife, Trish, stood looking out of the Number 10 office window for what could conceivably be the last time, that simple fact was clearer than ever.

"You did everything you could. You cannot take the blame for this, Andy." It was as if she'd spent the last few minutes getting her thoughts together before speaking. This was the first time she'd been alone with her husband in forty-eight hours. Beck's bodyguards, Darren and Les, were on the other side of the door and at her desk would be Mel, a terrier of a personal assistant, come secretary, come therapist, come whatever Andy needed at the time, who would die before she let someone get into that office without the best of reasons.

"Did I?" Andy asked, turning from his desk to look at her. "Maybe if I'd been honest, I mean really honest. Maybe if the people knew about those other outbreaks this wouldn't have happened."

"You can second-guess from now until the end of time, but—"

Beck laughed. "The end of time? That shouldn't be too long."

"Stop it. Stop it, Andy. This isn't the end. Things are bad. We knew this was always a possibility; that's why we put contingencies in place. We hoped we'd never need them, but we knew we'd have to plan for them."

"But if—"

"No. What-ifs and buts won't do us any good now. The odds were stacked against us from the beginning. You'd think at a time of national need everyone would pull together, and for a while, most did. The conscription idea was working; everything was working, but then greed took over like it always has done. People saw an opportunity to profiteer, and you did everything you could to manage that too, but trying to keep our borders secure, trying to keep the country free from infection, trying to make sure people didn't go hungry, it left resources stretched to the absolute limit. It left you, our police, our military stretched to the absolute limit.

"You are the last person to blame for things turning bad out there, Andy, so don't you dare wear that crown of guilt that I know you're dying to put on."

There was a loud knock on the door and they both turned towards it. "Come in," Andy said.

It was Doug, the PM's special advisor and one of his closest friends. A solemn expression was painted on his face. "Everyone's assembled for the emergency COBRA meeting, Prime Minister. And there's a helicopter on its way for you and your family."

"A helicopter?" Trish and Andy asked in unison.

"Yes, Prime Minister." Doug was rarely emotional, but he had to gather himself for a moment before he continued. "You'll get a full brief in the COBRA meeting, but the defence secretary and I have just been in a conversation with the chief of defence staff." He paused again. "We've got the roads and train lines to the north, east and west secured for the time being, but the plans to re-establish control south of the river are no longer viable."

"What does that mean?"

"We can't save them, Andy." His words hung in the air for a moment.

"W-what are you talking about? We were talking about this less than an hour ago."

"Things are changing by the minute. It's spreading too quickly."

Andy laughed a disbelieving laugh and looked at his wife before continuing. "Then what the hell's this COBRA meeting for?"

Doug gulped again and took a long breath before continuing. "It's to buy a little more time for some of the people south of the river and to discuss the demolition of the bridges and tunnels."

"What?"

"There are currently no reported cases of infection north of the river, but that won't last. Luton, Milton Keynes, Durham, Swansea, Edinburgh, Derry, it's everywhere. We're getting new reports in all the time. Only about half of the military personnel who were called back to the capital have arrived. We don't have the manpower or the resources to save London. Our only hope is delaying things for as long as possible in order to evacuate essential personnel to the bunkers in Shoreham. This is it, Andy. This is the day we've been dreading."

The temperature in the room seemed to drop ten degrees in an instant and a sob left Trish's lips. The prime minister rose from his chair and had to hold on to his desk for a moment until he was confident his knees could take his weight.

"Okay. Let's get this over with."

7

It had taken BD about fifteen minutes to give his dad a potted account of everything that had happened to them. Fifteen minutes that he didn't have, but after giving Poppy the all-clear to come out of hiding, his father had insisted and he would need to remain in Deano's good graces to get a vehicle.

"You shouldn't go home," Deano said, surprising even himself. After hearing what his son and, to a lesser extent, Taki had reported, he became more convinced than ever that the events that were occurring were beyond management despite what the emergency alert had suggested.

"What are you talking about?" BD asked. He knew what his dad was. He knew he was pretty much a career criminal, but he also knew he was bright. He wasn't like the knuckle draggers they ran into on the way there. For all Deano's failings, he could see how things would pan out long before others, as a rule.

"They want people to get off the streets. That makes sense. But they're not going to be able to bring this under control. We've been hearing sirens and helicopters pretty much all morning. It's already out of hand. You can't put the toothpaste back in the tube."

"I realise that. But I'd rather have the comfort of my flat than be stuck in a Portakabin with you."

Deano laughed. "Yeah. I get that, BD. But how long before the power goes down and the water goes off? How long before the gas stops flowing?"

"I don't know. You don't know. Nobody knows."

"That's right. Nobody knows. How much food have you got in your cupboards?"

"I just went shopping the day before yesterday."

"Great. So how long will that last the pair of you?"

The belligerence from before was gone. Up until this moment, BD's only plan had been to get home. He hadn't even thought about the bigger issues. "Probably not that long. But I've seen how you eat, Dad. I don't think the takeaways are going to be delivering."

The corner of Deano's lips curled into a smile. "We've got supplies here, BD."

"Yeah. I don't think a twin pack of digestive biscuits counts as supplies."

"No. We've got supplies, BD."

The entire conversation had taken place in the courtyard outside the Portakabin, but now Deano gestured for them all to start walking.

"What are you talking about?"

"You'll see in a minute." They continued until they reached the shipping containers where the lorries had been unloaded. Deano unlatched the bolt and swung the heavy metal door open to reveal high-stacked and tightly packed pallets inside.

"What is all this?"

Deano stepped into the shadows beyond the doorway and pulled out a multi-tool from his pocket, selecting the knife attachment and slicing through the shrink wrap. He opened one of the boxes inside and pulled out a box of dehydrated potato flakes, throwing it to his son. "Supplies. Two containers full of them."

"Where did you get all this?" Taki asked, but the question remained unanswered as Deano continued.

"I've got a couple of full gas canisters for cooking and heating. I've got water and we'd have shelter here. If I'm wrong and they have got a plan to deal with this, we'll be able to stay safe, secure and fed until the streets are cleared. If they haven't got a plan, then we'll be able to stay safe, secure and fed until we figure out what to do next."

"You think Vig is just going to let you have all this as your personal stash?"

"Let me worry about Vig." It was the first time he'd said the words out loud, but the thought of what to do about the hard-as-nails gangster had pretty much been in his head ever since Poppy had shown up. These events were a prelude to the end of day-to-day life, the end of his responsibilities to everyone but himself.

"What's the news said on the TV?"

"The TV's gone off," Poppy replied. "There's just that emergency alert signal on screen."

Deano turned to Taki. "Regardless of what BD decides to do you're welcome to stay here. You saved my son. It's the least I can offer you."

Taki's mouth dropped open a little, as did BD's. "Thank you," she replied, a little taken aback by the offer.

"Can I talk to you?" BD asked his dad.

"Yeah," Deano replied, closing the container. "Poppy, why don't you take Taki and make her a cuppa or something?"

The two men waited until the pair disappeared before BD continued. "What is this, Dad?"

"What do you mean?"

"I mean you're offering me and Taki a place to stay. You've got this young woman here. What's going on? Are you starting a commune or something?"

Deano laughed. "I get why you'd be sceptical. Listen, I really do think there's no coming back from this." He looked around the scrapyard that, in some ways, defined him and his father before him. "And as much as there are times when I never want to see this place again, I honestly think it's our best bet of surviving through this."

"Our?"

"I've been a lousy dad. In fact, I'd probably have to do some serious work to reach lousy status." BD huffed a laugh and didn't disagree before Deano continued. "But I want you here with me."

"Why?"

It was Deano's turn to laugh. "Well, that's a good

question, isn't it? I suppose there are a few answers."

"Like what?"

"You're my son. And despite what you might think, I love you. You're also just about the smartest person I know."

"That doesn't say much, considering who you doss around with."

Deano laughed again. "True enough. I want to try to make amends."

"Right. Well, this is starting to make sense. So, you'd be doing this for yourself as much as me. You're wanting to clear your conscience, try to assuage your guilt for all the shit you've put me through."

Deano stared at BD for a moment. "Some of it's probably that. Like I said, you're a smart kid. You probably understand the reasons better than I do. I just know that I'd rather have you here than not. I think you'd be safer here. I think together our chances of survival go up."

"Chances of survival? You haven't seen these things up close. Just one of them put the fear of hell into me and nearly killed me. No one will stand a chance against a whole city of them."

"This place is out on a limb, BD. The nearest estate is almost half a mile from here. The fence around the yard is rock solid. It's a good stronghold."

BD scratched his head and didn't say anything for a moment. He thought about his flat and he thought about what his dad had said. The food in his cupboards would last no time at all, and being stuck within those four walls with a stranger was not appealing to someone who valued his own company so much. "We'd have to bring Mum here. We have to go get her while we still can."

Deano hadn't even considered Tess. In fairness, he hadn't considered much. He didn't know he'd be offering his son a place before the words were coming out of his mouth. "Your mum will never go for this."

"She will. If she knows I'm here, she will."

"We won't have much time to get her," he said, gesturing to the sounds in the distance and close by as the city continued to battle the rising stem of panic.

"Then let's not waste any more."

*

Tess and Derek had sat side by side in front of the TV with the volume on low, hoping something other than the emergency signal would finally be broadcast.

"Well," Derek finally said, breaking the morbid silence that had settled between them. "I always said that I never wanted to die alone and there is genuinely no one else I'd rather have at my side."

Tess just stared at him for a moment. "Seriously? That's all you've been thinking about?"

"There don't seem to be a lot of other options, do there?"

In her youth, Tess had plenty of fire in her belly. It's what had attracted Deano to her. He was handsome and dangerous and women swooned after him, but he chose her. And for a short time, she felt like the luckiest girl in the world. She didn't know about everything he got up to. She knew he was a bit of a wide boy and walked shoulder to shoulder with some pretty scary people, but that was part of the attraction.

Sometimes, she felt closer to him than she had ever thought possible. Other times, they went at each other hammer and nails. She remembered throwing a toaster at him once. He ducked and it made a dent in the wall, tearing through the paper. He straightened up, his eyes as wide as saucers, then they both burst out laughing and that was the end of the argument.

For all the battles, for all the conflict, he never raised his hand to her. The very thought of it was abhorrent to him. And despite his questionable ethical code in some respects, that was something that she always loved about him. He'd seen his mother get hit and he vowed he would never, ever do that.

I wonder where he is. I wonder what he's doing right now. She looked down at her stomach. If there was a fire in there, it was well hidden beneath the rolls of fat. *How did I let this happen?*

It was a fair question but one with a simple answer. Deano had broken her heart. BD had become the only good thing in her life. She had eaten for comfort, but the long hours and the hectic nature of her job had meant she had eaten what was convenient too. It was easier to grab junk food and wolf it down sitting in the back of the bus out of sight of the driver than it was to get home at seven or eight in the evening and make a healthy meal.

She was a carer, but she was pretty poor at taking care of

herself.

"Hello? Hello, is there anybody in there?" Derek asked as Tess seemed to be lost in her own little world for a few minutes.

"I don't know if he's alive or dead," she finally blurted.

"Err … there are roughly thirty-three million men in this country. You're going to have to be a little more specific."

"Bertie. I don't know if he's alive or dead."

"Well, as I said before, from everything you've told me about the lad and from that one time I met him, I dare say if anyone has the wherewithal to get themselves out of a scrape, then it's him. And I still stand by my thought that—"

"I swear to God, Derek, if you mention joining giblets or buxom strumpets again I'm going to wallop you." For the first time in a long time, half a smile appeared on her face.

"Wenches. I said a buxom wench. The lad's got far too much about him to go fadoodling with a strumpet."

Tess laughed a little and reached across, squeezing Derek's hand. "I'm not about to give up."

"What do you mean?"

"I mean my son might be out there in all of this, and while I've got breath in my lungs, I'm not going to give up. And at the very least, I've got you here with me."

"Please, my dear. You're making my head swell."

She giggled again. "I didn't mean that to come out the way it did. I mean … I mean I love you, Derek, you loud, grumpy, boozy old git," she said, leaning across and kissing him on the side of the face before standing up.

"Where are you going?"

"I'm going to check on Mrs Willow and the others."

"Well, that will be some trick. She's up in Sterling with her daughter. Roger's at Butlins in Minehead, and Maggie is … well, actually, Maggie should still be here."

From the outside, the four flats looked like two large semi-detached houses. They were fenced off with a garden surrounded by houses that in the main had been purchased through the right-to-buy scheme. They were all well looked after with maintained gardens and hedges and although people were friendly enough, they kept to themselves.

The residents of the four flats, however, were all of a similar age, all had more in common than the rest of the street's residents, and occasionally one would drop in on the other for a cup of tea or something more medicinal.

"Right then. I'll go see how she is."

"Do you want me to come?"

"Not unless you want to."

"I think I should stay here in case there's another message on the TV or something."

"Are you still sulking with her?"

"The woman wouldn't know a Dublin accent if it hit her in the face with a cricket bat. I performed in *The Plough and the Stars* in the West End and won plaudits for my Dublin accent."

"All she said was she thought it sounded a little—"

"I know what she bloody said and she's an idiot," he replied, grabbing the paper sulkily. "It's the last time I try to bring a little culture to these peasants."

"Okay. Well, I'm going to see if she needs anything, anyway. Y'know, it might be nice if we invited her in here. She's going to be all alone. She's going to be scared."

Derek muttered something unintelligible before clearing his throat. "Do what you must."

Tess left the living room with a smile on her face, but it disappeared the moment she was in the hallway. There was a reason she wanted to bring Maggie or one of the other residents around. As treacherous as it was out on the streets, she was going to head to Bertie's place. If he wasn't there, she would leave a note and head to hers in the hope that he might be there instead.

If that option failed as well, she would gather a few belongings and as much as she could from her larder and fridge while still being able to travel comfortably then head back here.

Bertie was her life, but she was someone who thrived on people needing her and in the absence of her son, Derek would need her, and that was enough to keep her going for the time being.

Bertie could have got stranded elsewhere in the city. It wasn't a stretch. Anything could have happened and now wasn't the time to think the worst and give up. Now was the time to fight, to outlast this first wave of terror.

Some of the fire that she lost all those years ago was starting to return as she entered the kitchen and withdrew a knife from the block. She placed it under her arm inside her jacket, feeling funny about heading out into the open carrying it in her hand. Feeling a little ridiculous too. The chances of coming across one of those things between Derek's door and Maggie's were astronomically small. Not just that, but what did she expect to do with a kitchen knife? She remembered hearing, back when all this started, that the only way to kill the infected was with significant brain trauma. Was she really going to stab one of these things in the head if it attacked her?

Still, there was something about having a weapon on her person that emboldened her a little.

"I'll be back in a minute," she called over her shoulder.

"Take as long as you bloody like," Derek chuntered. "You're not going to listen to anything I say anyway, so I don't even know why you bother telling me what you're doing."

She closed the door behind her and immediately felt less safe. Everything was clearer out there—the sirens, the screams, the shouts, the roaring engines, the sense of panic. The garden was enclosed by a hip-high picket fence. Beyond it lay a small stretch of woodland that teenagers occasionally frequented doing whatever it was that teenagers did. Beyond that was a large council estate. She couldn't see it through the trees, but she could hear it.

She turned and followed the building around the corner. Now, for the first time since she'd arrived back at Derek's, she felt the cold air on her face.

A figure sprinted across the junction up ahead and she froze. From this distance it was impossible to see if they were infected or not. It was a fleeting glimpse, but it was all that was needed to jolt fear through her. The unknown was enough to be scared of.

She started moving again, walking the few remaining feet to Maggie's door. She knocked on one of the frosted glass panels. Maggie was sweet. She'd have been mortified to know that her comments had caused Derek such offence, but Derek was always one to take offence at the slightest thing.

She knocked again and bent down, opening the letterbox. "Maggie! It's Tess. I'm just checking in on you, making sure that you're alright."

Silence.

Screeching tyres made her jolt upright and she looked to the end of the street once more as a vintage Golf sped by. A few seconds passed and then a chill shot down her spine as three figures chased after it. There was no question in her mind that they were infected. Their demeanour was foreign, alien, unnatural. A breath caught in her throat and the knife fell from underneath her arm, clanging like a bell on the concrete.

Fear seized her as the ringing echo seemed to fill the morning air. She looked back to the road terrified that the beasts would have heard and changed direction towards her, but they were already gone.

This is real. It's spreading. It's spreading fast. How many have turned already since that taxi crashed?

There was no way of knowing, but her mind started to go into overdrive and she imagined a gigantic crowd of infected milling around on the green.

"Maggie!" She called through the letterbox again, but still there was no response. She finally tried the door to find it open and her brow creased a little. Although this was a quiet cul-de-sac, it was not crime-free and the older people in particular usually locked their doors, but as the she gained entry, she found that even the safety chain hadn't been used.

"Maggie!" she called again, but still there was no response. She walked down the hallway and finally understood why she'd received no answer. The old woman was lying down on the sofa. Her eyes were closed and there was an expression of sadness on her face. Streaks of dried tears had traced silver paths down her cheeks and two blister packs of tablets sat empty on the small table by her side. There was a short handwritten note to her care worker and Tess read it.

Dear Jill,

After seeing the alert, I don't even know if you'll get to read this or if anyone will. I don't see the point in going on. I've spent every minute since the prime minister's speech frightened. My family barely have anything to do with me. I don't want to be around for what comes next.

I'm sorry.

Maggie

Tess let out a deep, shuddering breath and tears welled in her eyes for a moment as the sounds from outside played accompaniment to her sad thoughts. She could only guess that the noises had been a part of Maggie's decision to do what she did.

She wasn't close to the woman, but she always had a soft spot for older people, especially ones who'd been virtually forgotten by their family. She sat down in the armchair opposite for a moment and just stared towards her.

At least she's not scared anymore. She's not lonely. She's not in pain. She's nothing.

Tess looked down at the kitchen knife in her hand and wondered what Maggie would have made of her walking into her flat with a weapon in hand. *That would probably have given the old dear a heart attack.*

Finally, she climbed to her feet and exited the living room. She was about to retrace her steps to the front door when she stopped at the entrance to the kitchen. She entered and opened one of the cupboards, placing her knife down so she could rummage through the contents.

There were eight tins ranging from soup to baked beans in addition to some packet soups, an unopened bag of rice, and a box of crackers. She opened the adjoining cupboard to find a variety of biscuits and chocolate. *Maggie always did have a sweet tooth.*

She went across to the sink and snatched a bin liner from underneath. She was about to close the door again when she noticed an almost full bottle of disinfectant as well as an antibacterial cleaning spray. She took another bag and put those inside then paused and grabbed the rest of the roll before taking the washing up liquid from the window sill.

To her surprise, there was only the smallest part of her that felt ghoulish. *I'm stealing from a dead woman. I'm looting.*

The thought festered for a moment and she paused in the middle of the small kitchen.

"No, Tess. You're scavenging."

It was a stark admission. As much as she wanted to believe that this would be a lockdown like Leeds or Portsmouth, she couldn't. This was like what happened to France, Spain, Brazil, the USA, and every other country they lost contact with. And it was happening right here, right now.

Things had been bad before the prime minister's speech for a long, long time. International relations between multiple countries were strained and volatile. Britain and her allies had been hit with numerous cyber-attacks destabilising communications, utilities, the NHS, and more besides. The aftereffects were still being felt by the time the news of the infection broke and there were many who thought that the reanimating virus may have been some kind of bio-weapon. Whatever it was, there was little chance of finding out now, and as Tess flashed through the turmoil leading to this latest shitty milestone, she became more and more convinced that she was doing the right thing.

She emptied the cupboards of anything and everything she thought might be useful. There was an old carving knife in the cutlery drawer with a long blade. She wrapped a tea towel around it then placed that in one of the bags too. She picked up the heavy rolling pin that sat by the tray in the same drawer and felt the weight of it in her hand.

I bet smacking one of those things on the head with this would stop them. She put that in with the other supplies. She went from room to room taking everything useful. Toothpaste, toilet rolls, candles, a torch. Five minutes later, she was exiting the property once more with two almost full bags of swag.

She looked up to the end of the street and, although the scary sounds were ever present, for the time being there was nothing to see at least.

"Is that you, Tess?" Derek asked as she re-entered the flat.

"Who else is it going to be? If one of those things shows up, I don't think they'll be fumbling keys into the lock, do you?"

She closed the door behind her with her foot and turned to see the old man standing at the top of the stairs with a confused expression on his face.

"What the bloody hell have you got there?"

She put the bags down on the floor. "Maggie killed herself, Derek."

"What?"

"She took a load of pills and left a note for Jill."

"Oh. Well … I never really cared for the woman, but that's awful."

"Yes, it is."

"So, what's in the bags?"

"Everything useful that I could find in her flat."

"You burgled her flat?"

"Derek. Do you understand what's going on? Jill won't ever get to read that note. The funeral director will never enter Maggie's house. Her will won't ever be read out. There'll be no executor to divide up her estate. This is it. You and me. This is it. And we need to do everything we can to last this out." The trip to Maggie's had also ended any thoughts of Tess heading to DB's place. Those creatures in pursuit of the Golf had convinced her she wouldn't last two minutes out there.

"Well, we don't know—"

"Yes, we do. Or at least I do. I saw it out there more clearly than I've ever seen anything. It's everyone for themselves and that means taking every opportunity and grabbing every advantage we can."

8

Deano had access to a few vehicles at the yard, but he chose a Mercedes- Benz Citan. It was a small panel van and the body needed work, but it was spritely and speed would probably be needed at some stage.

Because BD had been face-to-face with one of these things, and it had been Taki who had saved him, he had hunted around the scrapyard for something to use as a weapon. In the end, he grabbed his dad's baseball bat. Deano had never played a single game of baseball in his life, but he'd broken it out on a number of occasions when someone had got belligerent with him at the yard.

Deano had thought long and hard about taking the gun from his drawer but, in the end, decided the risk outweighed the benefit. For one, it would be just his luck to get stopped and be found with a weapon that had murdered someone in his possession. Secondly, he'd only used firearms maybe three times in his life and he wasn't a great shot. And three, he was aiming for stealth, which was something a CZ Shadow 2 was unlikely to provide. So, in the end, he had opted for a long crowbar, although he hoped neither he nor his son would have to think about confronting anyone or anything.

"You said you spoke to her earlier?" BD asked as they pulled onto another quiet road on the outskirts of the estate.

"Yeah."

"But she wasn't at home."

"No. She was with one of her gimmers."

"Gimmers? Nice dad."

"Old people. Whatever the PC term is."

"She's sensible is Mum. As soon as that emergency alert went out, she'd have headed back home."

"Yep. Always one to do everything by the book was Tess."

"Yeah. It's baffling how you ever split up. You're so alike."

A smile cracked on Deano's face. "I know, right?"

At least half a dozen people sprinted across the intersection ahead as if they were running for their lives. Deano applied the brakes and the van idled in the middle of the road as the father and son watched on, expecting to see someone or something chasing them. Half a minute passed before he took the handbrake off and started to drive again.

"There'll be a lot of people trying to get home. We didn't see any infected on our way from the stadium. Hell, for all we know this whole area could be clear at the moment. I mean, those guns we heard could be crowd control or something."

"Yeah. They could have been a lot of things."

He was about to turn onto the next street when a figure went sprawling over the bonnet. Deano smashed on the brakes again as whoever it was disappeared out of view for a moment before they scrambled back up. Audible breaths of relief exhaled from both of them as they saw the terrified-looking woman. She splayed her hands on the bonnet for a second, staring at the driver as if she was in shock, then started running once more, seemingly uninjured by the collision.

They looked up and down the road to see dozens of men, women and children rushing in different directions. Panic was thick in the air as the foreboding sounds from elsewhere in the city continued.

Deano turned onto the street and started to accelerate once more but stopped again as a terrifying sound from childhood rose into the air. In the late seventies and early eighties, when tensions were high with the USSR and nuclear conflict looked like a real possibility, air raid sirens had been tested from time to time. It was a noise and a feeling he would never forget. The terror that welled in him back then surged now as the ominous wail made the very air around them vibrate.

"Oh fuck, Dad. What the hell's going on?"

*

Taki and Poppy had been told to stay out of sight. It was an instruction neither of them had any intention of disobeying. From the little Taki had heard of the events leading up to Poppy's arrival at the scrapyard, it sounded like she'd jumped out of a frying pan only to end up in a raging inferno. But it was still better than the alternative.

Rather than the cramped confines of the caravan, they'd closed the blinds in the Portakabin and watched over Petal, who, up until a few seconds before, had been fast asleep in front of the fire.

But as the howling siren screamed its warning, she was sitting on her haunches, her ears pricked a little, fret in her eyes. The two young women had sprung up from the couch and both looked through the slats in the blinds at the rear of the property as if, somehow, they would miraculously see the reason behind the frightening noise.

"That's an air raid siren," Taki said.

"But I don't understand. Are we under attack or something? I didn't think we had any enemies left."

"I don't understand either."

"I'm really scared," Poppy admitted.

"Me too."

"What should we do?"

"I don't know. There's not really much we can do. It's not like we've got a bunker or anything, is it?"

"Do you think we might be better in one of the containers? I mean, they're metal. They're pretty sturdy, aren't they?"

It was hard for Taki to think straight. So much had happened in such a short time, and now this. "I don't know. I really don't know." The siren carried on and the anxiety in all three of them continued to grow.

"I think we should," Poppy said, walking across to the door.

Petal let out a short, sharp bark as another sound erupted, and both women looked at each other with wide, fear-filled eyes. "We're too late."

*

Since the air raid siren had first fanfared, barely a word had passed between Tess and Derek. But as a second, even more ominous noise sped towards them in a wave of foreboding, they both let out frightened mutterings.

"It can't be. It can't bloody be," Derek cried as they rushed to the window.

They both stood side by side, looking up at the off-white sky, their hearts beating faster than was healthy. Tess reached out, taking the old man's hand like a frightened schoolgirl. He was more than happy for the contact. He couldn't remember a time in his life when he'd felt more petrified and he had never been so grateful to have Tess beside him.

"I love you, Derek."

"What?" he asked, breaking his vigil of the skies and turning towards her.

"I love you. You've become like family to me since I started this job. I just wanted you to know."

He wanted to tell her it was all going to be okay. He wanted ease her fear. But he couldn't. He was just as sure that this was the end. "Well. I love you too. You've become like a daughter to me." She squeezed his hand and a sob stifled in the back of her throat. "Not a favourite one, mind."

A sad laugh left her lips and she leaned in to peck him on the cheek. "You miserable old sod."

His face broke into a weak smile and he squeezed her hand even tighter. "Oh, dear God."

*

Trish had been to several prior COBRA meetings. She was a well-respected surgeon and had a knack for putting complicated medical jargon into layman's terms, so there wasn't a person around the table who wasn't grateful for her presence when they were briefed about the more scientific aspects of the virus.

However, this current COBRA meeting was nothing to do with science and, although she'd gained all necessary clearance to be present, it was for one reason and one reason only that she was there, and that was to provide support for her husband.

He'd just had to give the single worst order of his life and there wasn't a man or woman around the table who didn't feel for him. He held on to Trish's hand as they continued to watch the drone footage.

"Christ! There are thousands of them," Trish said in little more than a whisper.

"Our estimates are about three thousand," said Alistair Taylor, the chief of defence staff.

The video footage was of a giant square between several tower blocks, which had been more or less surrounded by infected. The camera closed in on a small group. The blood from their wounds still bright red. Their skin pallid, unnatural, chilling to look at. A few hours before, they would have been living, breathing, laughing, loving human beings. Now they were something else. They were beasts, ghouls, creatures that had no place on this earth but nonetheless had spread like a plague.

"And we honestly think this is going to help?" Andy asked, even though he knew it was too late to abort.

It was Will Ravenshaw, the defence secretary and an old friend of the PM's, who replied. "We've been putting down minor outbreaks for the past two days. This is by far and away the largest accumulation of infected we've seen. They're fast and they're easily distracted, and if this many were to disperse into the wider area, the speed of the subsequent spread would be exponential. We're wanting to get people in their homes and quarantine south of the river as quickly and safely as possible. There are going to be enough hurdles with that alone without having a giant horde of infected charging through the city."

Horde. A shiver ran down Beck's spine.

The drone pulled out a little and revealed the Chinook helicopters still hovering on the perimeter. Twenty minutes before, they'd dropped Special Forces onto the roofs of the blocks of flats and subsequently lost contact with each of them one by one.

There were still people alive in the buildings. That had been witnessed by every man and woman in the room as the drones had passed by some of the windows. But there were no options for getting them out. They were surrounded. An indeterminate and presumably ever-growing number of infected were in the flats, too, and the danger that the mass of infected filtering into the wider area presented meant there was only one logical option.

The camera image on screen split into four and all of them drew out, pulling back and higher. The Chinooks also banked and started to move away from the area as a rumbling sound began through the speakers.

Andy held on to Trish's hand even tighter as their eyes were glued to the screens. Nearly everyone in the room recoiled a little as the blinding flashes, followed by giant orange plumes of flames, exploded. The squadron of Typhoons never came into view, but their jets boomed, adding to the thunderous symphony as the massive horde disappeared in a sea of fire and smoke. Then further quaking sounds made the air in the room vibrate as first one, then two, and then all the tower blocks crumbled.

It wasn't the first time the prime minister's eyes had filled with tears in this job and he doubted it would be the last. But no one in the room thought less of him for it.

Giant black and orange pyres were all that were visible as the drones continued their retreat. It was a precision attack despite the impression being it was anything but. The camera panned wider and a square in the centre of Catford suddenly didn't exist any longer. The hundreds of families and thousands of people were just names in a history book that would never be written.

"Turn it off," Beck said.

"Sir?" asked the officer manning the laptop feeding the image to the display screen.

"Turn it off, please."

"Yes, Prime Minister."

The image on the monitor went black.

Beck stood up and looked around the table at all his advisors. "God help us for what we've just done."

9

It was as if the entire world had stopped rotating for a few seconds. The people speeding through the streets on foot had become statues. BD's mouth had dropped open as first the thunderous, quaking sound seemed to rip through the fabric of his reality and then an ever-expanding colossus of flames and smoke reached up towards the sky. He didn't even notice the siren stopping.

Deano couldn't believe his eyes either. They'd seen the Typhoons flying in formation overhead and disappearing out of view for a moment before the thunderous eruption. The van continued to tick over in the middle of the street as the shell-shocked driver stared in the same direction as his son.

Neither of them knew if this was the beginning of a bigger assault on the city or if it was all over for the time being, but fear gripped them both. This was London. It wasn't Beirut or Gaza. Bombs didn't just fall from the sky, decimating everything in their path.

"Dad." It was BD who broke the spell and Deano turned towards him.

"Yeah?"

"We need to go."

"Yeah." He checked his mirrors to see people still staring towards the giant towers of black; then he released the handbrake and pulled away.

*

Tess and Derek hadn't seen the planes, but they had seen the aftermath of their actions. It had only been a couple of minutes since they'd witnessed the single most terrifying sight of their lives, and neither could remain at the window. In fact, Tess closed the curtains.

She had started to guide the old man across to the sofa when she stopped once more and went back to open them.

"What are you doing?" Derek asked, puzzled.

Closing the curtains was a classic Tess of old move. Live in denial. That was how she'd navigated much of her life. *Deano will change. Things will be different when he gets out. He'll be the father Bertie needs, the husband I need.* Denial had been her coping mechanism but her worst enemy. Denial had been the reason she'd put on all the weight and become a shadow of the woman she had once been.

I'll go on a diet next week. I'm going to start swimming every morning before work. Promise after promise after promise. Well-meaning at the time, but all broken.

Closing the curtains, blocking out what had happened. *If we can't see it, we don't have to think about it. DENIAL!*

She stared in the direction of the rising smoke and then turned to look at Derek. "I'm going to see my son again."

"Okay. But what the bloody hell does that have to do with opening the curtains?"

"You wouldn't understand."

He looked at her for a moment. "No. I dare say I wouldn't. Never understood women."

"You do a good job of disguising it."

Derek smiled briefly before his eyes were drawn to the smoke once more. "That could be us. For all we know, there could be another squadron heading here right now to blast us to oblivion."

"Well, judging by that smoke. If they do, I doubt that we'll know much about it."

"Some bloody comfort you are."

*

Deano brought the car to a stop and this time pulled up by the pavement. It was obvious why. They'd found the roads getting busier as they'd travelled from the outskirts, the traffic on this street hadn't moved for the best part of two minutes and from what they could see of the main road up ahead, the same thing applied.

"It's still a good way to Mum's place from here."

"Yeah. I think on foot's going to be our only option though." BD reached for the door handle. "Wait a minute." Deano reversed until he was past the ever-lengthening line of traffic heading to the main road then performed a sharp, fast U-turn and parked next to the opposite pavement, pointing in the direction they'd come from.

"That's pretty good thinking."

"Something tells me that this line is going to be a hell of a lot longer by the time we get back here." Without further pause, the father and son exited the van.

BD hid the baseball bat as well as he could inside his coat and Deano did the same with the crowbar. No provision had been made for the free-wielding of offensive weapons in the streets and they could conceivably run into trouble if they were stopped. Especially considering Deano's past.

The moment they stepped out of the vehicle, it was like the air became different. The panic was like a fog, dense, menacing. They looked at the faces of others as they rushed to get where they needed to go.

Some had been crying. Some still were. Children were being dragged by parents as fearful howls left their mouths. It was mayhem. The selfish part of Deano, which was a big, big part, wanted to be anywhere but here.

Considering how he had been so ready to abandon his son before on many occasions, he wasn't quite sure what he was doing on these streets with him now. If this had been before the last stint he'd done inside, he probably wouldn't have been out here. But he'd changed more than he cared to admit. He'd changed even before he'd got out, but BD allowing him to register at his address was a favour and a level of loyalty that took him completely by surprise. It had knocked him off-kilter a little and it wasn't an obligation he felt he needed to reciprocate but a want. He wanted to help his son. He wanted to make amends for the shitty father he'd been.

"I can't remember the last time I saw so many vehicles," BD said as they walked along, occasionally parting as bodies hurried in the other direction.

Fuel duty for private vehicles had been hiked massively as part of Beck's measures to conserve resources. Public transport costs had been slashed and many more services laid on. But, seemingly, none of that mattered for the moment. Cars that might have been turned over only a handful of times since the speech just to keep them in working order now blocked the streets as people tried to reach loved ones.

The pair arrived at the junction but had no difficulty crossing. They stopped in the middle as a single cyclist sped by, but the lanes were gridlocked as far as the eye could see. The sound of horns up and down the road joined in with that of the sirens from elsewhere, but in the last few minutes, the rhythmical chug of helicopters passing over the city had dissipated. Neither of them thought that was good news.

They reached the other side of the road and battled their way through the milling bodies to another street that was far less congested. They carried on and then cut down an alley. At the far end, they could see more people frantically trying to get to safety, but for the moment, it was just the two of them.

They joined the flow of bodies heading in the general direction of Belmont Hill when, suddenly, a sound ripped into the air, silencing the frightened conversations, bringing the drumming feet to a standstill.

It was a scream, but not like any they'd heard before. It was a scream of desperation, abject horror, and agony all weaved together. Heads darted around, trying to get a bearing on where it had come from, and then the father and son began to move forward in unison, manoeuvring and barging through the static bodies. Somehow, they understood what it was and their shared survival instinct kicked in.

A chorus of terror erupted before they reached a small circle of gawping figures, all too terrified to act for a moment, lost in the unreality of the very real scene that was playing out in front of them.

A man, or at least that's what he had been not so long back, was on top of a woman. His head jutted back and a wedge of crimson, spongy flesh protruded from his lips, dripping horror over the screaming, pleading victim who flailed on the ground, desperate to escape the straddling monster.

BD and Deano became entranced like the others for a beat, then two, before a pulse of electricity shuddered through the younger man's head. This could have been him. He was seconds away from this very fate when Taki had acted, fending his attacker off. He lunged forward, leaving his father statuesque, leaving the rest of the audience frozen in bewildered terror.

He slid the baseball bat out from under his jacket and swung with every ounce of strength he could muster. The sound was a loud, echoing clop, which managed to drown out all other noises. The creature had just begun to rise, doubtless getting ready to attack someone else, but, instead, it collapsed to one side.

BD stood there in shock as he saw the woman's wound for the first time. Blood gushed from the jagged oval in her neck, and tears washed her eyes as they struggled to stay open.

From the scream to this, just seconds had passed, and most were still desperately trying to process what they were witnessing, but the events unfolding in this new world waited for no one. Another scream sounded nearby, then another, and several heads turned. Across the lake of bodies, it was possible to see the mouth of an alleyway as a pallid-skinned beast dived towards a teenager whose friend had just been dragged down by one of the other monsters.

"Oh shit!" Deano cried. He rushed towards his son, grabbing the younger man's arm as bodies began to move again, now with a fresh horror to fuel their pace. "We've got to go."

BD didn't move as a new level of chaos erupted around them. He stood looking down at the woman whose eyes had closed seconds before. It was like watching a time-lapsed image, the kind he'd seen in nature programmes to show the decay of a body or plant. The colour drained from her face with a speed that left him cold. Even when his father's hand closed around his arm, he could not drag his gaze away. Then, almost as if they were spring loaded, the woman's eyes shot open.

"Fuck!" BD's word was drowned out by the pounding feet, the screams, the car horns, the panic as the rest of his senses came back to life. Gone were the almost sapphire-blue marbles that had glimpsed the horror show ending this woman's existence on this earth. They had been replaced by ghoulish, grey, otherworldly orbs, so foreign, so unnatural that it was hard to believe that this wasn't some trick of light or mind.

Bodies barged and he and his father staggered a little, but he continued to stare until the newborn creature jolted, first sitting up then springing to its feet. Its fingers splayed, ready to claw, grasp, tear. It focused on BD. The broken ebony shards of pupils danced in the centre of its eyes, hypnotising, mesmerising, terrifying. It pounced, reaching out as a gurgling growl rumbled from the back of its throat.

BD started to bring his bat up again, but he realised he was too late. He had been quicker than everyone to act originally, but he had been drawn into the horror just like them. No. Not just like them. Everyone else had moved on, fleeing for their own safety. He had stayed back. He had tried to help and he had been caught up in the tragedy, the hopelessness, the confusion. He had struck and then faltered and now it would cost him everything.

This is it.

An arc of movement blurred to his right as the beast's talon-like fingers stretched towards him.

Clank!

It dropped like a stone face down on the ground and he managed to jump back a little so it didn't come into contact with him. He turned to see his father standing there with the crowbar in his hand. There was an expression of surprise on his face matching what BD was feeling and, as anarchy continued to melee all around them, they both just stood for a second, looming over the creature's body.

Suddenly, it began to stir and breaths caught in their throats. The force of the strike from Deano should have been enough to bring a rhino down, but this thing wasn't dead yet.

It was BD who rallied now, bringing his baseball bat up and hammering it down with brutal force. The crack echoed in the small circle of space around them and the beast fell flat once more.

"Come on, BD. We need to get the hell out of here," Deano cried, grabbing his son's arm once more.

Further screams echoed from a few metres away near the entrance to the alley their attention had been drawn to earlier and it was obvious what was happening. A lot of things became obvious in those few seconds, like how this infection had managed to spread so quickly, so relentlessly. Both men would have said it was impossible if they hadn't seen it with their own eyes. Even though they'd witnessed it, it was still hard to comprehend.

They ran out onto the road, escaping the pavement and instead weaving through the stationary traffic as drivers and passengers stared towards the unfolding horror.

"We've got to get to Mum," BD called out over his shoulder as they both glanced towards the pavement. There were at least five attacks taking place at the same time. And while the odd loved one tried to intervene, the father and son knew it would only be seconds before five became ten, ten became twenty and, before long, the street would be swimming with infected.

"Where do you suppose they came from?" Deano asked, catching up to his son as they charged along the centre white lines. They ducked into a gap to let two cyclists by before continuing.

"All it takes is one, Dad. That's all it takes."

His words sent a chill down the older man's back. Never had truer words been spoken. "BD," he replied, slowing a little and placing a hand on his son's shoulder. "Y'know, there's nothing to say your Mum's at home. I mean, she was with one of her clients when I spoke to her earlier. She could be anywhere."

"I knew you'd try to get out of this. You go back. Go back to your yard, Dad. Look after yourself; that's what you're good at." He turned and started to run even faster.

"I didn't mean that," Deano replied, catching up. "I just mean that this might not be straightforward."

"I think the days of straightforward are over for everybody now. Don't you?"

"I suppose they are."

10

Derek looked towards the window as Tess opened it a little. "What are you doing? It's already like the bloody Arctic in here."

She turned to look at him. "I want to hear the sounds of the street."

Sirens, car horns, shouts and screams all came in waves as she stood peering through the net curtains.

"Oh, well, that's alright then. I'll just sit here freezing my todger off while you listen to the sounds of the street. Don't you worry about me."

She disappeared out of the room for a moment and came back in with a woollen blanket, dropping it next to him. "Here. Your todger can stay nice and warm under that."

He muttered something unintelligible under his breath and grumpily grabbed the blanket, placing it over his knees before picking up the paper once more. He hadn't read a word since the jets had flown over, but it was there like a child's favourite toy to give him comfort. "I don't know why you want to hear what's going on out there. It's pretty obvious, isn't it?"

"All I know is that we're not getting any news from the TV or the radio. The only information we're going to get is what we gather ourselves, so I just want to hear what I can."

"And what are you expecting to hear?"

"I don't know, Derek. Maybe something, maybe nothing, but there's no harm in listening, is there?"

Right on cue, a shout squeezed through the gap and raced towards them through the lace curtains. "H-ELP MEEE!"

"Bloody morbid if you ask me."

"Yes, well, I wasn't asking you, was I?"

"The last time I checked this was still my flat, you know."

"You want me to go home? Is that what you're saying?"

He frowned and brought down his newspaper once more. "I'm sorry," he said. "I…. No. I'm glad you're here."

"I'm going to fill the kettle and make a flask," she said, starting into the kitchen.

"What? Why?"

She stopped. "Because we don't know what's happening, Derek."

"And filling a flask will tell us? Let me guess, you've taken up tasseography and you're going to—"

"What's tasseography?"

"Reading tea leaves," he replied, irritated that his joke had been wasted.

"Well. Sorry for not being as well educated as you, Derek."

"No apologies necessary."

She picked up a pair of woollen socks she'd been threatening to darn from the bureau and flung them at him. They landed squarely on the side of his face and they both laughed. "I don't know what's going to happen, Derek. I don't know if the power's going to stay on. I don't know if the gas is going to keep flowing. Hell, I don't even know if the water will stay on.

"I read that in the first couple of days after the lockdowns in Leeds and Portsmouth everything went to hell until they got organised. There were no repairs to lines, pipes or anything. It's not a stretch to think that the same will happen here."

Derek turned back towards the pyres of smoke in the distance. "I don't think you can equate what's happening here to

Leeds or Portsmouth, Tess."

"Exactly. Don't you think we should be doing everything we can to improve our situation while we can?"

Derek shuffled forward and slowly stood up. "You're right."

"Two words I never thought I'd hear coming out of your mouth."

"Very funny. What can I do?"

"Go fill the bath. I'll grab every container I can find from the cupboards and fill those. It might all be unnecessary, but there's no harm in being prepared."

*

Staying out of sight had been all but forgotten after the first of the bombs was dropped. Poppy and Taki had drifted outside. They had heard the rumble in the distance and could only guess as to what it was until a minute later when giant black spires had reached up towards the sky.

Petal had ventured out, too, a little nervous at first but adjusting to the sights, sounds, and smells quicker than her two companions. She left the pair of them standing in the middle of the yard almost shoulder to shoulder. Up until this morning, they had been strangers, but now they felt like two sisters lost in the woods, each dependent on the other.

Only muttered exclamations of horror and disbelief had passed between them over the course of the minutes since the explosions. The street beyond the gated entrance was deserted and if it wasn't for the distant sound of sirens, they could have been forgiven for believing they were the last two people alive.

"D-do you think Deano and BD got caught up in that?" Poppy asked, her voice shaking.

Taki shook her head. "No."

"Are you saying that just to make me feel better?"

"No."

"Oh. Okay then."

"That's Catford."

"How can you tell?"

"Direction. Distance. BD and his dad will have been nowhere near that when it happened."

"So, you think they'll be alright?"

"I didn't say that, did I?"

"What do you mean?"

"Poppy, the RAF has just bombed part of the city. Do you understand how fucked up things would have to be for that to happen?"

Tears welled in the other woman's eyes. "What are we going to do?"

"What do you mean?"

"I mean what are we going to do?"

"There's nothing we can do. We stay here and hope BD gets back with his mum and dad."

"And if they don't?"

"Then we'll have to figure something else out, won't we? Right now, we're in a miniature fortress with a truckload of supplies, so we're in a much better position than any of the poor bastards out there."

"We can't live in a scrapyard."

"It beats dying in the streets, doesn't it?"

*

Trish had tried her hardest not to cry in front of the children. It had been virtually impossible, but somehow she'd found the strength from within to manage. Now, as she flung a few final belongings in her sports bag, she couldn't help but succumb to tears. She flopped down on the bed with a small toiletries bag in her hand.

The four full suitcases had already been forwarded to what was going to be her new home in Shoreham. Nobody knew how temporary or permanent that particular residence would be, but it was obvious that their stay at Number 10 had come to an end. She had attempted to remain stoic for Andy, too, holding his hand as they'd watched the bombs drop on the tower blocks in Catford, and she'd managed to an extent, but now it was all bubbling up from the depths.

Sob after sob left her lips. The pain was immeasurable. The suffering, the loss, the heartache balled up inside her like a tumour threatening to burst. The bedroom door opened quietly and she looked up to see her husband standing there.

She did nothing to wipe away the tears or hide her pain. It would be pointless. He knew her better than anyone and such a subterfuge would be spotted in an instant.

He closed the door behind him and went to sit down by her side, taking her hand in his. "We will get through this."

Trish shook her head. "We don't know that, Andy. We

don't know anything."

"We do. The compounds in Shoreham are secure. The bunkers are impenetrable. We can catch our breath there, form a plan and start the fightback."

A shuddering breath left her mouth and she raised her teary gaze towards him. "There is no coming back from this. Don't you get it? This is our asteroid. This is our extinction. Humankind had its chance and now it's time for us to bow out just like the dinosaurs did."

"I think this is a first."

"What do you mean?"

"I mean, in all the years we've been married, I think this is the first time you've been wrong."

A weak and brief smile twinged on her face before stinging tears made her look away once more. "I'm not wrong, Andy."

"You are. I'm not going to stop fighting, Trish. I can't stop fighting. Even if it's just for those people who died today. Even if it's just to keep their memory alive and make sure they didn't die for nothing. This virus has the upper hand at the moment. It's going to get an awful lot worse before it gets better. Hell, Doug showed me some more drone footage before I headed up here to see you.

"It's spreading through the streets like wildfire despite what I did. All we can do is try to keep it from jumping the river for as long as we can. They've been preparing the Shoreham base since all this started. It might seem like the end but it's not."

"How can you say that, Andy? How can you believe that?"

"Because I know my people."

"Your people? I don't think the cabinet is—"

"I'm not talking about the cabinet, Trish. I'm talking about my people. I'm talking about the men and women who we met on the campaign trail. I'm talking about the ones who've kept this country going in the midst of an international disaster like no other. After my speech, the spirit of the Blitz came back. Yes, there were some who took advantage of it. There will always be people who are only out for themselves, only out to feather their own nests. But there are a whole lot of decent people out there too. People who fought to make things better for their families, their friends, their communities and their country. Those people won't give up."

"They won't have a choice, Andy."

"They will. They might not have an army at their disposal and state-of-the-art bunkers, but the sensible ones will find ways out of the towns and cities. They'll find their own little safe havens and keep that spirit flourishing." He clenched his fist tight. "I know my people, Trish. I know that they're capable of the most amazing things when the most amazing things are asked of them. That's why I'm going to keep fighting. Because, when we get to the other side of this, when we figure a way out, then I want to be there to unite the country again. I want to be there to make sure this isn't an extinction-level event."

The pair sat in silence for a moment just holding hands until Trish wiped away her tears using her sleeve. "You really believe that, don't you?"

"I do. But with one proviso."

"What proviso?"

"That you're by my side."

Trish let out a huff of a laugh. "I really don't know what good I'm going to be to you from here on in."

"You're the key to everything. You're the person who makes me want to do this. You're the one who gives me the self-belief that I can. With you by my side, everything's possible."

She let out a long sigh, pulled Andy's hand up to her lips and kissed it. "For everybody's sake, I hope you're right."

*

Few words had passed between Deano and BD since their confrontation with the infected. They had slipped onto a side street, then another and another, running all the way, their fatigue ignored as fear fuelled their steps. Finally, Deano reached out and squeezed his son's arm, signalling the need to stop.

They were in a narrow ginnel in between the brick wall lining a terrace of modern houses and a waist-high black one lined with hedges surrounding a small park and children's play area. Unsurprisingly, it was empty, and for the time being, the ginnel was empty of everyone but them. The upheaval continued to ring out in the surrounding streets. Horns and sirens were starting to diminish now, however, as people began to realise the gridlock was not going to clear and their only hope of getting anywhere would be on foot.

"We're not going to be able to get back to the van,"

Deano said, almost doubled over as he rested his hands on his knees.

"Yeah. I figured that," BD replied. "So, maybe Mum will forgive you under the circumstances and let you stay with us."

Deano smiled, straightening up. "That's funny."

"Yeah."

"We're going to have to figure out a way to get back to the yard. The yard is the only way we survive this."

"You're talking about the three of us heading there on foot? You saw what happened on that street. We'll be lucky if every street isn't like that by the time we get to Mum."

"Then what's the plan, BD? We just stick it out in Tess's flat and wait until the cream crackers and Hobnobs run out?"

A pained cry, louder, nearer than those that had played an accompaniment to the conversation made them both turn their heads in the direction they had come from. When they were sure nothing was heading their way, BD continued. "This is a nightmare."

"Yeah. It is. But getting back to the yard gives us an advantage that very few people will have. I know I seem to have made it my life's mission to let you down, kid, but I'm not going to let you down this time. If we can get back to the yard, we can last there for weeks ... months even. And by that time, the boffins and the air force and whoever else is still around might have figured out a way to bring all this under control."

BD gestured towards the continuing noise. "You can't really believe that. You can't really believe that this can be brought under control."

"Maybe it will. Maybe it won't. But the yard gives us a chance."

"Jesus Christ," BD said, shaking his head. "I really can't believe it's come to this. I hoped I'd be able to get through the rest of my life without ever laying eyes on that fucking place again, and now, if we survive through this morning, it's all that's going to give us a chance."

"I get what you mean, but—"

"No. You don't, Dad. You don't get what I mean. All those times when I came to you for weekend visits as a kid and you promised the world. You promised we'd go see the Eagles at home, or we'd go to the cinema or whatever, and we always wound up at that fucking yard dancing to whatever tune Vig and his pals wanted."

"It was my living. It was how I put food on the table."

"Put food on the table? None of it ever got onto our fucking table."

"Your mum didn't want it. She didn't want anything I—"

"You have no idea how much of a struggle it was for her. She pulled every shift she could get to make sure I didn't go without."

"I tried to give her money. She'd never take it."

"Mum didn't want to raise me on blood money."

"It was hardly blood money."

BD leaned his baseball bat up against the wall and turned towards his father. "Can you honestly stand there and tell me that all Vig's dealings never wound up with people getting hurt? Fuck me. Half the estate was into him for bad debt. He was the biggest loan shark going and are you saying that if people couldn't pay they just got off with a stern warning? Are you saying that all the heists and hold-ups and smash and grabs and all the rest of his shady-as-fuck dealings never wound up with people getting hospitalised or worse? And are you honestly standing there and telling me that you didn't help and launder money and hide stuff in the yard for him? Are you telling me Mum wasn't right to question where the fuck that money came from, how many families it broke, how many kids wound up as junkies on the back of it, how many people bled out in gutters?"

"I never got involved in any of that stuff."

"You go on believing that. You go on believing that because you never sold the drugs, because you never held a jeweller at gunpoint, because you never turned some young mother who couldn't make ends meet into a prozzie you had nothing to do with it. You covered for that prick every step of the way. You served fucking time for him without a second thought for us and—"

"There were no second thoughts to have. Your mum had well and truly washed her hands of me by then, hadn't she?"

"I wonder why."

"Okay. This isn't getting us anywhere and it's not a conversation that we should be having with the fucking world crumbling around us."

BD exhaled deeply. He'd waited a long time to get some of this off his chest, but Deano was right. This wasn't the place.

He picked up his bat once more. "Why are you really doing this?"

"Doing what?"

"Coming with me to get Mum. I mean, you never gave a fuck about her before. Why now?"

"You don't know what you're talking about."

"What do you mean?"

"I always loved Tess. I still love her. It's true what they say about there being someone out there for everyone. She was my someone."

"Ha! That's priceless, that is, Dad."

"Believe me, don't believe me." He shrugged. "Just 'cause I fucked everything up, it doesn't mean it's not true." He gestured back in the direction of the street. "And this, giving you and her a chance when everything is turning to shit, might be the one thing I can do to say I'm sorry."

"Are you serious?"

"I know it's going to take a lot more than one thing, but it's a start, isn't it?"

"I really don't understand you."

"I get that a lot."

"Yeah. I bet you do." They began to move again. "So, have you got any thoughts about how we're going to make it back across town once we've got Mum?"

"I'm working on it."

"Oh, well, that's a fucking relief."

11

Poppy and Taki had gone back into the Portakabin. Despite the chill, they left the door slightly ajar so Petal, who had still not returned from her wander, could join them when she chose to.

The two young women perched side by side on the couch, each cradling a cup of coffee as they sat in quiet contemplation.

"I feel like I should be doing something," Poppy said.

"Like what?"

"I don't know. Just … something. I mean, Christ. Half the city's up in flames and we're just sitting here drinking coffee."

Taki took another sip and considered the other woman's words for a moment. "You're right. Maybe we should check the fence or something like that."

"Check it for what?"

"Check that it's all intact. Check there are no weak points for any of those things to get through."

"Do you think there might be weak points?" the other

woman asked with genuine concern in her voice.

"I've got no idea. The first time I ever laid eyes on this place was today, and now it looks like it's going to be my home for the foreseeable future, so maybe it wouldn't be a bad idea to make sure it's safe."

"Yeah. Yeah, you're right," Poppy said, climbing to her feet. "We could do that. You and me."

"Yeah." Taki got up, too, and headed over to the desk. She opened a drawer and took out a pad of paper.

"What are you doing?"

"I figured we could make a plan of the place. We'll survey it then mark any points that we're worried about."

"That's a good idea."

Taki opened another drawer looking for something to write with. "Strewth, hasn't he got a pen at least?" She opened another drawer and froze, her eyes widening as she stared at the contents.

"What is it?" Poppy asked, seeing the concern on the other woman's face.

"Um … I'm no expert, but I'm pretty certain it's a gun."

Poppy walked around the desk to join her. "Can't really say I'm an expert either," she replied, picking it up. "But I've seen enough of these to know you're right. Vig's men carry them."

"Great."

"Didn't BD tell you about Vig and Danny?"

"BD and me don't really know each other that well. Until yesterday, I'd probably said about five sentences to him."

"I thought you were a thing."

"Ha! No."

"He seems nice does BD. Don't say it like that."

"I don't mean it that way. I just think I'm the last person he'd be interested in."

"Why?"

Taki shrugged. "Because in all the time I've worked in the same building, he hasn't so much as looked in my direction."

"He's probably just shy," she replied, placing the CZ Shadow back in the drawer.

"If you say so. Why is this Vig bloke after you anyway?"

"That's a long story."

"This is a big yard. It's going to take us a while to check it out properly. We've got time for a long story."

Poppy looked at the other woman and a small smile lit her face. There were very few people in her life who she could tell things to and trust other than Deano. Probably all but one of her friends at the strip club would buckle in a second under questioning. Her enemies would run to Vig and Danny to lay out the full story of what she'd done and why, but Taki was like a shrink. She was completely separate from her day-to-day life. Telling her had no downside for Poppy and it might actually help get her own thoughts straight. In addition, she actually liked the other woman. She liked how she was direct, and funny, and open. "Yeah. I suppose it will take us a while at that, won't it? Just promise me that you don't breathe a word of what I tell you to Deano."

Taki's brow creased. "I thought you trusted him. I thought you were here because he'd have your back."

"I do trust him, and he does have my back, but he's old-school. He'd go spare if he thought I'd spilt my guts to someone I barely even know. But the way I see it is you and me are going to be stuck here for a long while together, so if we don't make ourselves friends, then the time's really going to drag, isn't it?"

Taki smiled. She liked Poppy. She liked her simplicity and practicality. Becoming friends was as easy as just deciding to do it as far as she was concerned. In truth, it really was that straightforward, but people always put up fences making it much harder. "Don't worry, Poppy. I won't say a word."

*

"Tess! Tess! I've got something."

Tess was in the kitchen, about to get the sewing kit. She needed to fill her time doing something, something useful, but she rushed into the living room to see Derek with the small transistor radio held up to his ear.

"What is it?"

"It sounds like it's underwater, for Christ's sake," he chuntered. He handed it over to his carer and she raised it up, adjusting the dial in micro movements in the hope that the signal would become clearer, but more than half a turn in either direction and the sound turned to static. In the end, she got it as clear as she could, raised the volume and sat down.

"….Garber Street to Waring Terrace. Morley View to Eddingham Place. These are all no-go areas." It was a man. A scared man at that. He sounded unsure of himself, but both of them were equally grateful just to hear another voice.

"Who do you suppose it is?" Tess asked.

"How the bloody hell should I know? Let's never mind who it is and just listen to what he's got to say, shall we?"

They both squinted a little in concentration as the broadcast continued. "We've established a temporary shelter at Dunston Primary School for anyone who can't get home. Repeat. We've established a temporary shelter at Dunston Primary School for anyone who can't get home. The approach from Olive View is currently clear but we don't know for how much longer."

There was a pause in the transmission for a few seconds as other voices could be heard in the background. "Do you think we should try to get there?" Derek asked. "I mean, it's only a few streets away."

"I think we're better off here."

"Haven't you heard of safety in numbers?"

"Course I have, but you heard what he was saying about Garber Street and the surrounding area and it's only going to get worse second by second. Minute by minute. We've got food. We've got water and, right now, we're safe."

"Safe? You call this safe?"

"We're safer here than we are on the streets. Look. I've seen those things up close, and I don't mean to be unkind, but if we were attacked out there, you wouldn't stand a chance and I wouldn't fare much better. And that's if there was just one of them."

"Well, speak for yourself. You'd be surprised how fast I can move when I need to."

"We're not talking about a trip to the offy for a bottle of brandy that's on sale, Derek. We're talking about a dash for life and how would we be any better off there than here?"

"There'd be people. A school would have supplies. I mean, have you seen the size of those kitchens? They'd probably have enough to last for weeks."

"We'll go careful with what we've got. We'll make it last."

"Until when? What happens when it runs out?"

"Well, by that time, hopefully, the government will have sorted something out. I mean, Leeds and Portsmouth got rations, didn't they?" *Denial.*

"Good God almighty, Tess," he replied, standing up and pointing in the direction of the black plumes that continued to rise. "Does this look like Leeds or Portsmouth to you? This is the end times. It's every man and woman for themselves and how long do you think we're going to last in here?"

She was about to answer when the voice began to broadcast once more. "Avoidance is the best tactic when it comes to the infected. But if you have no other choice, arm yourself with something sharp or a blunt, heavy instrument. Critical damage to the brain is the only way to stop these things. They're fast and they don't get tired."

The transmission went quiet once again.

"See. I told you," Tess said.

"And I told you," he said, raising his fists and pacing up to the window. "I'm not as useless as you make out. I got into plenty of scrapes in my youth. I could still look after myself if push came to shove."

"Oh, give over, Derek. I have to check the shower for spiders before you go in there. A lot of protection you'd offer if we went out onto the streets."

The bravado drained away from him as quickly as it had arrived and he sank down into the chair by the window, staring out once more towards the smoke plumes.

"It's a thing to get old."

Tess looked at the radio. It remained quiet for the moment and she turned to her ward who continued to gaze into the distance.

"What?"

"I said it's a thing to get old. It's a thing nothing can prepare you for. Day by day, a few more pieces of you fall away. A pain in the knuckle here, a twinge in the hip there. They're sporadic at first, once in a blue moon. Then they start to happen more often. Then they're constant and one week's inconsistency becomes the norm and it's not just the physical things that nag at you any longer. You start to doubt yourself. You start to doubt what you might be able to do, so you don't even bother trying it in the first place. You start to question memories. Did that really happen? Did I really manage to do that?" He paused in quiet contemplation as he continued to stare out. "Yes. It's a thing is getting old."

Tess climbed to her feet and walked across to join him,

taking a tight hold of his hand. He turned to look up at her. Getting lost in his words, he'd never felt so alone, but now she reminded him that he wasn't. "Well, you might be old, but I'm not. And I've got enough fight for the both of us, so you don't have to worry about anything."

The sadness that had painted his expression bled away and a warm smile lit his face before he brought her hand up to his lips and kissed it. "You're a good girl, Tess. I knew it from the first time you set foot in this place."

"We both know that's not true. The first time I came here, you complained to my manager that I was too bossy."

The smile stretched his mouth further. "You are."

"Your problem is you don't know the difference between bossy and organised."

"Well, your problem is—" A loud click of static burst through the speaker of the small radio. The telephone beeped loudly and started flashing and the red light on the four gang behind the TV went off all at the same time.

"Oh crap!" Tess exclaimed, immediately letting go of the old man's hand and walking over to the phone. The battery light flashed on and off for several seconds before the display dimmed. She placed the handset back in the receiver then walked over to the wall and flicked the light switch. *Nothing.* She rushed out of the room and into the kitchen to see the display on the microwave was blank. "I'm going to check the fuse box!" she called out, heading down the short hallway to the small utility cupboard. She opened it up and switched on her mobile phone torch. None of the switches had tripped and her heart sank a little. *This is it. This is where it all starts to fall apart.*

*

BD and Deano had managed to keep moving and avoid any more confrontations since that initial one. That wasn't to say they hadn't come close a number of times. It seemed like they were always just a street or so away from trouble.

The landscape was changing by the second and the air had become more charged. The whole city pulsed with panic, made worse by road after road of gridlocked traffic.

The extra public transport that had been put on to get people home in time for the curfew was useless. So many had abandoned their vehicles and fled on foot, making entire carriageways impassable. The occasional police, fire and ambulance siren blared, but they were becoming fewer in number as the operators of those vehicles started to comprehend the futility of it all.

They were on Tess's estate now. It was quiet in comparison to the main streets, but there were plenty of people still running for home. Deano's yard on the outskirts of town seemed like a world away from where they were, and as much as BD didn't want to admit it, he longed to get back there.

Nothing about the built-up areas was safe. He had witnessed this with his own eyes. One after another falling to the infection like dominoes. They had left that street behind, but he wondered if there was a living, breathing human left on it now or whether it was the domain of the dead. Had it become an infected zone? Would the street itself spread into others like a virus?

The two men opened a tall wooden gate and ducked into the compact courtyard, closing it again behind them. The council flats in the small complex were bordering on luxurious compared to most. A narrow, shared garden with a rockery bordered the line of recycling bins for each of the apartments. Although none of the tenants owned their properties, they treated them as if they did. They painted their doors, kept up with minor repairs, and tended the grass and the flowers. It was a small slice of heaven in the midst of an estate that could often be anything but.

None of the flats had been broken into either—another miracle considering the high crime rate in the area. But BD knew it wasn't a miracle at all. He knew that Deano had put the word out long ago that these flats were off-limits. Anyone choosing to go against his warning would face the full wrath of not just him but, in all likelihood, Vig as well and that was just about as good as a death sentence.

The thing was, though, and this really irked BD, Deano didn't need wrath. People liked him. Lots of people liked him, and if he said somewhere was off-limits, they didn't obey because they were scared, although, if they thought about it long enough, they probably would be. They obeyed because they respected him. Deano had been there for a lot of people. Granted, he'd rarely been there for his family when they needed him, but from loser junkies all the way up to made guys he'd had their backs in times of need. Subsequently, when he'd said these flats were off-limits, and Tess was off-limits, a virtual iron dome of protection had fortified the place.

BD tried the door then knocked loudly. The two men waited a moment before he crouched and opened the letterbox. "Mum! It's me." He paused a few more seconds then attempted to open the door again.

"Don't you have a key or something?" Deano asked.

"I told you. They took everything from us when we were at the ground." He stood back from the entrance and squinted through the strip of frosted safety glass then raised his bat.

"Whoa. Whoa, Trigger," his father said. "Give me a minute. I've got a way with locks."

"Course you have," BD replied, standing a little further back and allowing his father access. In the confines of the small courtyard, the sounds of chaos were a little more muffled. The occasional drum of running feet reminded them that they weren't alone, but it was all a far cry from the main roads.

There was a loud click as the lock disengaged and Deano returned the small toolset to his inside pocket as he opened the door. "Tess?" he called out as he and his son entered. The two men walked down the hallway, peeking into each room as they went. "Well. She's not here."

"You figured that out all by yourself?"

"Look, Son. I'm no happier about this than you, but we can't just go searching the streets. If your mum—"

"When you spoke to her earlier, where was she?"

"I told you. She was working."

"Yeah. But where? Who was she with?"

Deano was about to shake his head when he stopped and the memory of the conversation suddenly became a little clearer in his mind. "David … Denis … Derek! She said the guy's name was Derek."

A small smile lit BD's face. "I know Derek."

"Oh yeah?"

"It's nothing like that."

"That's what your mum said."

"Trust me. It's nothing like that."

"Well. Whatever it is, we don't know if she's still there. It could be another wild goose chase. I mean, the instruction was for people to get back home before curfew. Your Mum's always been one for following the rules, BD. If that's what she was told to do that's what she'll have tried to do."

"Maybe. But Mum's pretty smart. She might have figured out it was safer to stay put."

"Might. A thousand things might be the case, BD. She might have stayed there. She might have tried to make it back here and got…." He didn't want to say the words, but it was obvious what he meant.

"You came this far and you didn't need to. I can make it the rest of the way and you can get back to the yard."

Irritability flashed on the older man's face. "I'm not about to leave you now, am I?"

"Those are words I've never heard coming out of your mouth before."

Deano smirked. *I deserved that. I deserve everything he throws at me.* "So, where does this Derek live?"

"Blackheath."

"Fuck's sake!"

"It's not that far."

"No, but it's all uphill, isn't it?"

"You don't want to go 'cause you're worried about it being uphill?"

"Listen, BD. From everything I've heard about the infected, they don't get tired like us. All I'm saying is if we run into a few of those things and have to try to escape, it's going to be tough if we're heading uphill."

"Yeah, well. Like I say, you don't have to come." He started walking away, but Deano caught hold of his arm.

"Say we get to this Derek bloke's house and your mum's not there. What then?"

"Then I'll have tried, won't I? I'll have tried to find her rather than sitting on my arse back at the yard doing nothing."

Deano closed his eyes and inhaled a deep breath. "Okay. Okay, BD. We'll do this, but we need to be smart about it."

"What do you mean?"

"I mean that getting to Blackheath is one thing. Making it back to the yard is another. You and I could probably do it, but Tess wouldn't be able to keep up with us."

"So, what are you saying?"

"I'm saying that we need a better plan."

*

"Sir," Les, one of the PM's bodyguards, said as he stood

in the entrance to the office.

"Yes, Les. What is it?"

"We've just had notification that the car park's been cleared at the FCD building and the chopper's ready when you are."

Beck stared at the other man for a few seconds almost as if he was speaking a different language. All this had been discussed previously, but now it was happening, now it was real, it seemingly felt far less real.

"Okay, Les. Thanks."

The bodyguard nodded and retraced his steps back out of the door. "Well, this is it," Doug said from across the desk. "The end of an era."

"It's the end of more than that."

"True enough."

"Have we heard where the hell Ashford is?"

A bitter smile flitted across Doug's face. "Well, your home secretary certainly isn't at home if that's what you're asking. Right now, he's incommunicado."

"Incommunicado? In the middle of the single biggest catastrophe ever to face us the bastard's disappeared?"

"Oh, I doubt very much that we're that lucky. He'll be cloistered in some little corner somewhere plotting away."

"That's what worries me."

"You don't need to worry, Andy. He's got his supporters, but people understand that you're the only one who's up to the job."

"I think you have entirely too much faith in people." Doug laughed. "What's so funny?"

"A few months ago, our roles were reversed. I'd be the one saying that."

"I suppose you're right. I should have a little more faith."

"You should. What you've done is nothing short of a miracle. Those who matter aren't going to forget any of that in a hurry."

"I hope you're right."

"When have you ever known me to be wrong?"

"Didn't you hear what Les said? The helicopter's going to be here in five minutes. We don't have that sort of time."

"Funny."

Beck walked across to the window. "I'll see their faces

until the day I die."

Doug didn't need to ask whose faces he was talking about and it wasn't a time to come up with off-the-cuff humorous remarks to try to cheer his friend up. The same doubts and regrets plagued him, too, even though he'd never admit it. "We'll never know, Andy."

Beck turned around from the window and looked at the other man. "What won't we know?"

"We won't know if our actions saved people. Logic tells me they would."

"Logic tells me we bombed citizens who were depending on us."

"We sent soldiers in to try to help them. Sending more in would only have resulted in further deaths. The people trapped in those buildings were living but they were already dead too. Bombing that square wiped out thousands of infected and it might have made the difference between life and death for a lot more people."

"Might. Ha."

"Might is the best we can hope for right now. There are no absolutes, Andy. Might is something. Might is hope."

Beck let out a sigh. "Christ knows we need that by the skip load right now."

The door opened suddenly and both men turned to see Trish standing there with her jacket on. "We're packed. The girls are ready to go." The telltale silver streaks were no longer present, but her eyes looked uncharacteristically heavy.

"I'll be up in a minute."

She nodded and disappeared as quickly as she'd arrived. "And on that note," Doug said, "I'd better make tracks as well. I'll see you later this afternoon."

"I'll need briefing on—"

"I know what you'll need briefing on, Andy. I'll see you later." He headed out of the door as well, leaving the PM alone.

Beck folded his arms, leaned against the windowsill and surveyed the office. For so long, he'd dreamed of holding this position. He shook his head and started towards the door, pausing for just a second by the side of his desk. He trailed his fingers across the surface and a verse entered his head from a book he'd read many years before.

"Together, we will toast our loss. Then we'll be reborn."

A sad smile crept onto his face. He brought his fingers up to his mouth, kissed them and then pushed them against the mahogany surface once more. "I really hope we get to do both of those things."

12

Taki hadn't made a single note on the pad. The palisade fences and their barbed wire crowns barely had a dent in them. "I should have known Deano would have kept this place like a fortress," Poppy said.

"It certainly seems to be that and more besides," her companion replied, pushing against a section of fencing just to make sure it was as secure as it looked.

"Considering whose merchandise he sometimes looks after here, I don't suppose it would make sense taking any risks."

"From the bits I've pieced together, I'm guessing this place is not quite legit."

"I don't ask questions. But I've seen plenty."

Taki surveyed the other woman's face for a moment. "Yeah, well. Let's just be thankful for whatever made BD's dad this paranoid, shall we?"

Poppy giggled. "I like you. You've got a way of finding positives in things that are anything but."

"There are always positives if you look for them." She suddenly considered her words and looked in the direction of the pyres, which, for the time being, were hidden by a tall row of piled vehicles. "Well. Maybe not always."

They were about to continue their inspection of the fence when a loud bell reverberated through the air. "That's the gate," Poppy said excitedly. "Deano must be back." She started towards it and Taki reached out to stop her.

"Aren't you meant to stay out of sight?"

"Who else is it going to be?"

"I dunno. But don't you think I should go look before you show your face?"

Poppy opened her mouth to say something else and the excited expression finally disappeared. "Well … I suppose." The bell rang again and this time was followed by a clattering sound as someone banged against the gates.

Taki's brow creased. "Whoever that is, they're an arse wipe. There could be infected in the area for all we know and they're making a noise that could wake the dead." She started marching in the direction of the courtyard.

"Be careful," Poppy called after her.

Taki's irritation turned to uncertainty as she arrived at the gate to see three men standing there. A lorry idled behind them. The youngest looking stood with his arms folded, not saying a word but watching her as she approached.

"Can I help you?" Taki asked as she arrived at the gate.

"Who the fuck are you?" the young man asked.

"My name's Taki. Why, who the fuck are you?"

The man turned to look at the other figures on either side of him and let out a small chuckle as he turned back to the woman. "You Deano's tart or something?"

"I'm nobody's tart. Now, I'll ask again. Who are you?"

"My name's Danny. Danny O'Dell."

Taki shrugged. "Is that meant to mean something to me?"

"It should mean something to you. It means something to everybody around here."

"Yeah, well. I'm not from around here."

"I can tell."

"What do you want?"

"I want to get in there is what I fucking want."

"Yeah, well. Mr Duncan's not here and I've been given instructions not to open these gates for anyone."

"Mr Duncan." Danny laughed and the two thugs flanking

him sniggered too. "What are you, his lawyer or something?"

"Look. I don't know when he'll be back. And I wouldn't suggest loitering around here."

"Oh, you wouldn't suggest it? Well, it's a good job I don't give a fuck what you suggest or not. Now, let me through these fucking gates or we're going to have a problem."

Taki's skin bristled. These weren't people to mess with, but, equally, they weren't people she wanted to let into the yard either. "These gates aren't opening until Mr Duncan's back here."

Danny grabbed the chain in his hand and squeezed it. "Listen to me, you Paki bitch. If you don't open these fucking gates in the next ten seconds, a world of trouble is going to come down on you. Do you get me?"

A switch suddenly flicked in Taki. "First off, I'm a Maori, you learning-challenged, racist sack of shit. Secondly, maybe you need to head to the ENT department because you seem to be having a real problem hearing me. These gates are staying shut until Mr Duncan's back here."

Fury burned in his eyes and he let go of the chain kicking the gate at the same time. "You're making a big mistake, girl. When I get in there, you're going to wish you'd never laid eyes on me."

"Way ahead of you on that one."

One of the other men placed a hand on Danny's shoulder and whispered something in his ear, causing a grunt of irritation to issue from his lips. "The only reason I'm not ploughing through these gates in that lorry is out of respect for Deano. But we'll be back here in a while, and whether he's here or not, we're coming in. This chain will either be coming off with a key or an angle grinder. You fucking understand that, bitch?"

Taki shook her head despairingly. "You understand what's going on out there, don't you?" she asked, pointing in the direction of the smoke plumes. "This could be it. This could be the end times. If ever people should be pulling together it's now, and yet you're here acting like a prize dick. What's wrong with you?"

Danny stepped closer to the gates. "Oh, I understand what's going on. That's why I want in there. Deano's holding on to something for us and we need it. We've got merch in there that just shot through the roof in value, girl. Supply and demand. We're the new fucking Tesco and people are going to be begging us to take their money."

"Jesus Christ. You're as horrific as you are stupid. Money's not going to mean much after today."

"Money's always going to mean something."

"I'd argue the toss, but I can feel myself getting stupider the longer I talk to you. It must be catching."

His arm suddenly shot through the gap in the palisade barrier, but Taki jumped back before he could grab her. His snarl disappeared as quickly as it had formed and he pulled away once more with a bitter smile on his face. "I'm really looking forward to getting in there. You and I are going to have a proper chat about women knowing their place."

"Screw you!"

"Danny!" one of the thugs said and the younger man looked at him irritably then turned to see where he was pointing. At the far end of the road two figures were sprinting towards them. Even at this distance, it was clear that there was something not quite right about them. They had all seen images of these things and the odd little piece of footage here and there, but this was the first time any of the men had fixed eyes on the infected.

All the cocksureness and belligerence from before vanished in a heartbeat. "Come on," Danny said, heading back to the lorry. "We'll tool up and get some more hands for when we come back here." He cast a glance towards Taki. "We'll be back in a while, bitch. Something tells me you're going to be happy to see us."

"I doubt there's anyone who's ever happy to see you, so I wouldn't build your hopes up," she called after him, but he was already in the cab of the truck by the time the last of her words were out.

From her position, she couldn't see what the others had seen. At the front of the property, the compound was shielded by a tall, dirty red brick wall topped off with razor wire. She stayed put as she watched the truck drive away. Despite the words that had come out of her mouth, the confrontation terrified her, but it was only now that her entire body began to quiver. The engine finally faded away to nothing and Taki nearly jumped out of her skin when she felt a hand on her back.

"I'm sorry," Poppy said.

"Strewth. I swear I'm going to have a heart attack before this day's out."

"You were really brave standing up to him like that."

"Piece of shit."

"He's the one who's looking for me."

"I figured. I'm guessing you heard all the conversation?"

"Only bits."

"He's coming back with more men."

"I'm dead if he finds me. I mean … eventually. I don't even want to think about what they'll do to me first."

"Well, I don't see things going too well for me if he gets on this side of the gates either."

"I hope Deano's back soon."

"Somehow, I don't think Deano will be able to do much. He said he was—AGGHH!"

The pair of figures that the other men had seen suddenly came into view and turned on a penny, charging towards the two women as they stood behind the gates. The entire frame vibrated as they smashed against it and the women jumped back.

Taki had been up close and personal with one of these things before, but that did not reduce the panic she felt. A frightened whimper repeated in the back of Poppy's mouth as she desperately reached out, taking Taki's hand like a little girl lost in a fairground. "Oh, God. Oh God, Taki!"

The creatures were freshly turned. It was probably just minutes ago that they had been going about their business trying to get home. One of them had been a policewoman in her previous life. The other wore an expensive business suit, the kind that suggested he made million-pound deals before breakfast. But he wouldn't be making any more deals and she wouldn't be arresting any more perps. They were no longer interested in money or protecting and serving. They were only interested in the supple, warm flesh of the women standing on the other side of the gates.

Their pallid skin chilled the marrow in the two women's bones, but their animalistic growls and the mesmerising, soulless gazes that beamed from their eyes were enough to send terror-filled tears streaming down Taki's and Poppy's faces. The seconds ticked by and all they could do was watch as the relentless beasts reached and flung themselves against the gates, time and time again.

A shuddering breath left Taki's lips. *Get a grip. You need to get a grip, girl.* She wiped the tears from her eyes and stepped back. Another growl started behind them and both women turned on their heels to see Petal there on her haunches, baring her teeth towards the two monsters. She started barking, jumping forward in a threatening manner. If these had been living, breathing, thinking humans, they would have undoubtedly felt threatened. But they weren't. Even when Petal lunged and clamped her jaws around one of the creature's arms as it squeezed through the gap in the pales, the beast's resolve did not falter.

"Petal, no!" Poppy ordered. It was almost as if the two had been companions for life. The Rottweiler immediately relinquished her grip but continued to growl and snarl at the creatures. A few more seconds passed and, suddenly, a third beast appeared.

"Christ!" Taki hissed. "We need to do something. Otherwise there's going to be a whole bloody herd of these things."

"Do what exactly?" Poppy asked, crouching down and taking hold of Petal's collar to pull her back.

"I don't know," she admitted before turning and running towards the Portakabin. She skidded as she entered but steadied herself. *Get a grip. Get a grip, Taki.* She started towards the desk. Although she'd never used a gun in her life, she was pretty sure she could figure it out, and then she stopped again just as quickly. *If I turn this place into the O.K. Corral, every one of those things within a half-mile radius is going to know we're in here.*

She glanced around, looking for something, anything, that might help as the growls and rattling gate persisted outside. She headed behind the desk and opened a small cupboard door. There were various cleaning materials inside, but at the back was a cylinder vacuum cleaner with a metal extension pipe. She reached in, grabbing it and unhooking it from the hose. She stood on the cleaning head and yanked it free. Her fingers closed around the cold brushed steel and she jabbed at the air a few times as if she were a medieval pikeman.

This is crazy. You've gone crazy, girl. She looked at her makeshift weapon for a moment and a sad breath left her lips. *This won't do. I need a spear, not a fucking pipe.* Then she had a light bulb moment. There was a large stone that was used to prop the door open and she ran across to feel its weight. *Holy shit! This might work.*

She went back outside and laid the pipe down on the top paving slab step then smashed the weighty stone down at an angle.

"What are you doing? What the hell are you doing?" Poppy obviously thought she'd gone mad as the New Zealander hammered the stone down time and time again until part of the end section of the pipe was virtually flat.

She stood once more, jammed the door shut against the flattened section of pipe then seesawed until it finally broke. A smile lit her face as she raised the point of her homemade spear. If she'd had the right equipment, she could probably have done a neater job, and she was concerned about the noise she'd made creating her weapon, but as she looked towards the gate, she saw that no more infected had joined the first three and so, for the time being at least, it had not cost them anything.

"What the hell are you doing?" Poppy cried again as Taki marched towards the entrance.

"Giving us a chance." She stood for a few seconds surveying the infected trio as the malevolence raped the air around her. Despite her weapon, her resolve and her good intentions, her stomach still churned with fear as she hovered just beyond their grasp, but then she raised the tubular, tapered spear up to shoulder height, grasping it firmly in both hands, and lunged. The first strike went astray, inadvertently parried by a reaching arm. But the second drove true.

She could hear a breath catch in her companion's throat as the sharp, jagged spearhead disappeared through the eye of one of their would-be assailants. Time seemed to halt for a moment as the creature remained upright, its arms continuing to reach towards her. But as she withdrew the weapon, it collapsed back, and some of the nerves and fear fell away a little. She lurched forward once more, desperate to ride on the wave of her first victory. This time, the razor-sharp weapon crumbled the cartilage of her victim's nose, rising up into the brain. There was no pause on this occasion, and the monster's eyes flicked shut as it dropped.

"Two down," Taki said to herself more than anyone. The third beast was taller, its arms longer. They flailed wildly as Taki tried to find a good striking position and she could feel her hesitation beginning to cast doubt in her mind. *Screw this!* She took one big stride, ducking down then rising up sharply and bringing the spear with her. It vanished through the palate of the creature, cracking through the top of its skull in a crimson explosion of brain, bone and tissue. Taki remained in position for a moment.

There was far less blood than there would have been if this had been a living person. She'd read somewhere that these things bled far less. She remembered reading the scientific explanation for it, too, but had long since forgotten that. But now she was witnessing it for herself.

Her breathing continued to be erratic and she could feel her heart pounding in her chest like a bass drum. But for the time being, at least, the imminent danger was over.

"Taki!" Poppy's exclamation suddenly brought her back to the real world. "You did it."

Taki turned to her new friend then finally withdrew the spear and they both looked as the final beast fell to the ground.

"I really need the loo."

Poppy laughed. "Yeah. I get that."

"And then we need to get rid of these bodies before any of their friends appear."

"Okay. I'll wait here for you. Just in case any others come."

Taki nodded and handed the other woman the spear. "We're going to be okay you and me. I promise."

Even though Poppy knew it was a promise that was out of the other woman's control, especially with the threat of Danny's return hanging over them, she smiled. If nothing else, she wasn't alone, and that was something to be grateful for.

*

BD had filled a backpack at Tess's. He'd thrown in underwear, a couple of T-shirts and a pair of jeans. Nothing major, but if she was still alive, he could guarantee she'd be grateful for it as much as he'd be grateful for a rucksack of his own belongings.

He didn't live that far away, but heading to his flat would be an unnecessary waste of time. He would have to share his father's wardrobe back at the yard and there were no personal possessions he owned that would benefit him beyond feeling a little better about himself, so it was a sacrifice he was willing to make.

Where they were going, however, was still a little puzzling to the junior Duncan. "So, what are we doing again?" BD asked as they paused at the corner of another alley. He had his baseball bat clenched in his fists, no longer worried about being spotted by the police and pulled up. Hell had literally broken loose. One only needed to use their ears to understand that as shouts, screams, and a diminishing number of horns bore testament.

"We're going to see Benny the Brum."

"Why?"

"He owes me a favour."

"Okay," BD said, seeing the coast was clear and leading the pair of them out onto the narrow street. Curtains twitched as they walked down the centre of the narrow tarmac road lined with red brick terraced houses on one side and garages on the other. "And is this favour going to help us get to Mum somehow?"

"Hopefully."

"Well, don't give too much away, will you?"

"Look. Let's just get to Benny the Brum's place and we'll see if he can help us or not. He doesn't live too far from here."

They carried on walking down the centre of the street. They were on the outskirts of the estate and, subsequently, unless they were lost, fewer people had reason to be this far afield. "Why do you call him Benny the Brum?"

"'Cause he's a Brum."

"Okay. But why not just call him Benny?"

"Well … we used to."

"Okay. So, what happened?"

"Benny the Scouser got out of the clink."

"And it was too confusing for people to discern between them?"

"Yeah, quite frankly. Somebody would get an order to go pick up Benny or use Benny for this job or that job and they'd end up getting the wrong Benny. So, we started to call them Benny the Brum and Benny the Scouser to avoid any mix-ups."

"Um … okay. Didn't they have surnames?"

"Well, course they had surnames, but people just found it easier this way."

"Jesus Christ, Dad. What kind of fuckwits do you hang around with?"

"Only the best London has to offer, Son," Deano replied with a smirk.

They came to a stop at a junction and looked left down the road that led further into the estate. A shrill cry echoed from somewhere beyond their field of vision and the two men cast each other concerned glances. They'd avoided further confrontations, but they knew it would probably be only a matter of hours before all the streets were swimming with infected.

They continued across the junction and carried on walking for less than a minute before Deano slowed down.

"What is it?" BD asked.

"I can never remember which house it is," Deano replied, surveying the identical white uPVC doors.

"Great. That's great, Dad. We'll just knock on all of them, shall we?"

"I think it's this one," Deano continued, ignoring his son.

He led the way up the short garden path to the door and rang the bell. A few seconds passed before a man answered. "Deano?"

"Benny? What are you doing here?"

"I thought this was who we'd come to see," BD said, a little confused.

"No. This is Benny the Scouser."

"You're here to see Benny the Brum?" their greeter asked.

"Well, yeah. This is his house, isn't it?" Deano replied.

"Yeah. He's in the khazi."

"What are you doing here?"

"Benny the Brum's helping me out with some merch."

"Wait a minute," BD said. "You call him Benny the Brum even though you're Benny the Scouser?"

"Who's this?" the man asked, looking at Deano.

"This is my boy."

"Oh. Alright." He turned back to BD. "Course I call him Benny the Brum. Why wouldn't I? That's his name."

"But why?"

"Well. It'd just be too confusing otherwise, wouldn't it? Nobody would know who was talking to who." He turned back to Deano. "No offence, Deano, but he's not very bright your boy, is he?"

"What can I tell you? It's the schools I blame."

BD was about to speak when another figure appeared in the doorway behind Benny the Scouser. "Sorry about that," the man said. "I needed a wicked shit."

BD's mouth dropped open a little but Deano continued without missing a beat. "I need a favour."

A smile crept onto the new arrival's face. He turned to his companion in the doorway. "Why don't you bang a kettle on the stove? I'll be with you in a minute."

"You be careful out there, Deano. It's getting a bit hairy," Benny the Scouser said before disappearing down the hallway.

"Is this a favour or repayment of a debt?" Benny the Brum asked.

"There's no debt between us, Benny."

The other man turned to BD. "They broke the mould when they made your dad."

"Have we met?" BD asked.

"You probably won't remember. You were little more than a babby. But it's not like there's no family resemblance. You can tell a mile off that you're father and son."

"Thanks. I didn't think my day could get any worse, but you've just proved me wrong."

"Kid's got some lip on him," Benny the Brum said with a smile as he turned back to Deano. "Something else you've got in common."

"I need a ride. Actually, I need two rides."

The man at the door shrugged. "Sure thing. I've got a Yaris and Focus parked in two of the garages. They're yours."

"No. The roads are fucked. Nobody's getting anywhere on the roads."

"I'm all out of helicopters, Deano."

"You got any bikes?"

"What, you mean like mountain bikes?" the other man asked with a smile.

"You see any fucking mountains around here?"

Benny the Brum stepped out and pulled the door closed behind him. "Come with me," he said, leading them back down the path as he pulled a set of keys from his pocket.

"That's a lot of keys," BD said.

"No flies on this one."

"I thought you were only allowed one garage per council

house."

"You are."

"Um. So, are all those spare keys or something?"

"Inquisitive, your kid, isn't he?" Benny said, looking at Deano before turning back to BD. "Let's just say that they're all sublet. Everyone on this row has a garage, but they all let me rent them for a little taste, so everybody's happy, and if plod ever comes around and wants to look in mine, all he'll find is my wife's Corolla."

"Oh."

"Happy now?"

"Yeah."

"Good." He walked up to one of the doors and inserted a key, twisting it and lifting the handle at the same time. "Okay. Take your pick."

There were several motorbikes and at least five helmets on a shelf at the back. One of the bikes still had a food delivery box on the back of it. "You own all these?" BD asked and the other two men laughed before Benny replied.

"Yeah. You want to see the vehicle reg docs?" He turned to Deano. "Take whichever two you want. The keys are in them."

"Which would you recommend, Benny?"

He walked up to the two nearest the entrance. One was a Honda VFR 1200 X, the other a Triumph Street Twin. "Me and Benny the Scouser were out on these two just the other day. All I'll say is avoid The Squirrels and the surrounding streets. You might get some unwanted attention."

Deano walked up to the Triumph. "Takes me back."

"I know, right? When the two of us used to have a couple of 900 Thunderbirds? Happy days."

Deano raised his eyes towards his friend. "I think happy days might be behind us all."

"Yeah. Something tells me the power's not going to come back on either. God knows how long it'll be before the gas and water goes off and then just like that we'll be living in the dark ages."

"The power's off?" BD asked.

"Yeah. Went down a while ago."

"What's your plan, Benny?" Deano asked.

"You give me too much credit. Other than staying here

with the missus and kids and keeping a watch over the place, I haven't got one."

"Well, we're going to try to find Tess then we're heading to the yard. I figure it's well protected and we can stay there until either this blows over or we figure out another move. We've got room, y'know, Benny. Shipping containers and stuff. You can join us if you want."

The other man looked back towards the house on the other side of the road. "Give up a warm bed and all our belongings so we can live rough in a big metal box. Tempting, but I'll give it a miss, I think."

Deano laughed. "The offer's there if it gets too hot here."

"Cheers, Deano," he said, extending his hand.

Deano took it and the pair shook. "Okay, BD. Grab a helmet. We're off to Blackheath."

∗

"I've been thinking," Derek said.

"I've told you before, nothing good can come of that," Tess replied, threading a needle as she did her best to stay busy, repairing a pair of the old man's trousers.

"You're such a wag. No, seriously, maybe we should put something in the window."

She fed the cotton through then raised her eyes towards him. "Like what?"

"Like a sign."

"What kind of sign?"

"To let people know we're in here, that we're alive and we need help."

"I don't think that's one of your better ideas."

"Oh. Why not?"

"Because most people will be doing whatever they can just to keep their own heads above water. The chances are if we put a sign like that on show, we'd attract entirely the wrong kind of people."

"What do you mean?"

"I mean this isn't the 1950s anymore. Neighbours don't look after neighbours. Kids can't play out in the streets until midnight without you having to worry about them. The world is a shitty place now, and as nice as Blackheath is, Derek, our best bet is to keep our heads down and our ears and eyes open."

He let out a quiet grunt before climbing to his feet.

"More than a day in here without being able to grab a breath of fresh air is going to send me insane."

"I think the boat may have already sailed on that one."

"You are on form today. This whole end of the world thing suits you."

"Don't say that."

"Don't say what?"

"That. That it's the end of the world."

He gestured towards the towers of smoke. "I think all evidence points to it, don't you?"

"We're still here, aren't we? There are obviously people still at the primary school. Ergo, it can't be the end of the world."

Derek walked across to the window. "Have you heard the traffic?"

So much had been happening, Tess had been so lost in her thoughts and worrying about her son that the white noise of the traffic had dropped into the deep background, but now that she was paying attention, a feeling of dread came over her.

"No," she said, rising from her chair and walking across to the window to join him.

"No more tooting horns, no more revving engines, no more, no more, no more." He turned to look at her. "Whichever way you look at it, it's not good news."

"Maybe the wind's changed direction and we can't hear it." *Denial.*

"Wind?" He pointed to the hedge of one of the houses further up the street. "What bloody wind, Tess?"

She closed her eyes for a moment to concentrate. It really had gone quiet. It had been a lot quieter than normal ever since the prime minister's speech. More and more people had been forced to use public transport due to the spiralling cost of fuel, which had been earmarked for key workers and government business, but there would still be some noise. The loud whoosh of air brakes or the squeaking wheels of a double decker, something. *There'd be something.*

"So, either the traffic's become gridlocked and people have left their vehicles or it's all moving again and—"

"Nothing's moving, Tess."

It was true. A sudden scream from a few streets away convinced them both that they were not alone on this planet, but they maintained their vigil at the window, hoping, silently praying that things had not got so bad so quickly.

Then a figure emerged from a narrow ginnel further up. "That's Mr Morton from number thirteen. You can tell him a mile off with that ridiculous hat he wears," Tess said.

"There's nothing ridiculous about it. I think I've still got a fedora somewhere. I used to look quite dapper in it, actually."

"What's he doing?"

"It looks like he's looking for something."

Morton got closer. There was something unnatural about his movements, something alien. "What's wrong with him?"

"Probably three sheets to the wind. There are a lot of lightweights out there who can't take their drink."

"Being an alky isn't something to wear as a badge of pride, Derek."

"Excuse me. I am not an alky. I'm just a proficient social drinker."

"You drink indoors by yourself. How is that social drinking?"

"I enjoy my own company, so I choose to socialise with myself."

"I don't even know what to say to that."

"Another first on a day full of them."

"Very funny, you old fart."

They turned back to look at Morton. "He's just standing there."

"Oh no."

"Oh no, what?"

"That's not Mr Morton."

"What the hell are you talking about? Of course it's Morton."

"Not anymore it isn't, Derek."

The old man squinted. "What do you mean?"

"His skin. Wait until his head turns again."

They remained at the window, peering towards the lone figure in the street. "Hells bells. You mean he's one of those things now?"

"Yeah." She grabbed hold of Derek's arm. "Come on. Nothing good can come of us seeing this."

"Wait. I want to watch for a while."

"That's pretty morbid even for you, Derek."

"I want to see how they move, how they react. You've already seen these things up close. I haven't."

"Yeah, I have seen them up close and I got a bellyful. I'd really like never to see them again if I had a choice."

"Well, get back to your sewing then."

Another distant scream rang out from somewhere and the Morton creature turned on its heels and began to sprint faster than either Derek or Tess thought it possible. The pair stayed in the window a moment longer before finally drifting away.

Tess went across to the table and picked up her thread. There were tears in her eyes as she sat down. "What are you crying for? I didn't think you were that close to Morton."

"I'm not."

"Then why the tears?" She dropped the needle and slammed her hand on the table, turning away and folding her arms. Derek was about to sit down on the sofa when, instead, he walked across to her. "What is it, Tess?"

"He's gone, hasn't he?" Her chin was almost on her chest as the old man arrived by her side. Tears poured down her cheeks as her frame shook with heartache.

He didn't need to ask who she was talking about. It was obvious. "You can't think like that."

"I promised myself I wasn't going to live in denial anymore, but I don't know who I'm kidding. If I think somehow Bertie is still out there, then I'm telling myself the biggest lie I ever have. He's not out there. He's probably one of those things." She wiped her tears on her sleeve, desperately trying to regain control of her emotions but failing.

"No. We don't know that."

"Oh, Derek," she said, taking the older man's hand as it rested on her shoulder. "I know you're trying to be nice, but we really do."

"No. We don't. Your boy is something special, Tess. He has to be if he came from you. He's got nouse and vigour and vim. So, he might not have been able to get a message to you. That doesn't mean he's not out there somewhere. For all we know, he might have gone to your place. He might be at Dunston Primary helping people, organising them. Like I said, he's a smart cookie. Don't give up on him."

She squeezed his hand a little tighter. "When you chip

away all the stippled brickwork, you're actually very sweet inside. Y'know that?" she said, wiping her tears once more.

"Now don't get all emotional on me."

"You're right."

"Of course I'm bloody right. I'm always right."

13

A lot had happened in the fifteen minutes or so since Danny and his thugs had left. Taki had killed three infected. They had opened the gates for the first time since Deano and BD had departed, dragged the bodies inside, and now both women and Petal were back in the Portakabin.

"You need to hide," Taki said.

Poppy had been thinking about nothing else since Danny had threatened to return. She wasn't the brightest bulb in the pack and she knew it. But that had no bearing on the person she was. And the person she was wouldn't let Taki confront Danny alone.

"No. I won't let you face him by yourself."

"You need to think about this, Poppy. I might be able to keep him on the other side of the gates one way or another. But if he sees you, then from what you've told me, wild horses won't keep him from getting in."

"When he comes back, he'll get in. There's no doubt in my mind. He'll come back armed. He'll come back with more men. There's no way it's going to end well for us, so I'm not going to cower hidden away in some cargo container deep in the depths of this yard while you deal with him."

"That's sweet of you. But I can look after myself."

"No. You can't." She slumped down on the couch and Petal immediately walked up to her. Poppy stroked the Rottweiler for a moment before she continued. "You don't know what these people are capable of. I know stuff about them that would turn your hair white. And Vig's got a lot of power. Danny comes across as a two-bit thug, and I suppose that's all he really is, but his dad is something else. And any slight on his son is a slight on him."

"A lot of power? You mean like manpower?"

"A lot of power, full stop. He's got fingers in so many businesses, legit and not so legit. A lot of people owe him favours. Coppers, celebs, even some politicians. You can't cross the O'Dells. And if you do, you can't expect to get away with it."

"It sounds like you crossed them," Taki said, sitting down beside her.

"It was one of those moments."

"What do you mean?"

"It was one of those moments when you just have to decide to do something. There are certain lines you don't cross and ripping off meds meant for people who've given their all to this country is well out of order. I just wanted him to be stopped. I wasn't thinking about anything else."

"You did the right thing from what you told me."

"And now I'm going to have to pay the price."

"No. Fuck that," Taki said, standing up.

"What do you mean?"

"I mean the world is literally falling apart out there." She clicked her fingers. "Just like that, it could all come crashing down due to circumstances outside of our control and yet there are wankers like this Danny and Vig, who are trying to profit off the back of it. No. I won't allow it. I don't want to live in a world like that."

"None of us want to live in a world like that, but we do. It's how it is. It's how it's always been. There will always be people like Danny and Vig. It's just the way things are."

"Yeah, well, not anymore."

"What are you talking about?"

"If this is all coming to an end, then I'm going to hold

my head up high. I'm not going to be beaten down by some crooked, racist little piece of shit like that."

The bell rang once more and both women stared at each other for a moment. "He's back."

"Yeah, well. Fuck him." It was clear there was fear in Taki's voice, but she said the words anyway then walked to the desk.

"What are you going to do?" Poppy asked.

"I'm going to fight fire with fire."

*

Deano and BD had made good progress. They had avoided main roads and streets almost completely. They'd traversed paths, children's playgrounds, a park and even a village green, witnessing several infected along the way but managing to dodge and outpace them up until now.

They pulled around a corner into a narrow alleyway. Walls lined both sides. Beyond one were gardens to houses and flats. Beyond the other was a steep bank leading down to a river. There were only two ways out, forward or back.

Ahead, however, were three beasts charging towards them. From what they had seen of the infected so far, it was clear that they were uninhibited. They did not seem to possess any reasoning power. All they were interested in was the next kill.

If Deano and BD were in a car or a truck then they could probably have risked heading at the trio straight on, but from everything they knew about these creatures, all it would take was one scratch and they would be goners and it wasn't out of the realms of possibility that an extended arm, or a grabbing hand as they tried to get past on their bikes, could end up with a fingernail inadvertently sinking into their exposed flesh.

"You okay, Son?" Deano asked.

It was a strange thing. The two had bonded more, been more open with each other in the course of one morning than they had in the past thirty years. And as Deano said the word son now, it actually felt right. There was still a mountain of conflicts and animosities piled up between the pair of them, but out here on the streets, facing danger beyond any they'd known, the two of them actually felt like family. Real family.

"You mean other than three flesh-eating monsters charging towards me?" BD asked, holding his bat tight in his hands.

"Well … yeah."

"Spot on, thanks, Dad."

"Good."

The two men waited. It was a long alleyway, but the bikes were loud, and the second they had entered, the hope of remaining undetected was blown. Now the vehicles stood behind them with their kickstands down ready to be ridden away once more provided the new owners weren't brutally ripped to pieces beforehand.

The three creatures charged in a slightly off-centre arrowhead formation, and with each pace they took, the fear both men felt edged up a notch. Deano avoided fighting whenever possible, but he'd been in more affrays than most men on this side of the prison wall. BD was much more out of his element. This was all about survival though. This was about getting to his mother and saving her, if she was still alive to be saved that was. As such, he was the first to move when the creatures came into striking distance.

He jumped forward, swinging the bat over and down. It made a whooshing sound in the split second it was travelling towards its target before an echoing, thunderous crack filled the entire alleyway like a gunshot. The beast crumpled mid step. Everything happened so quickly, and BD couldn't swear to it, but he felt sure he felt his victim's skull give beneath the weight of the bat.

*

Deano was barely half a step behind his son as he ran forward, ducking in low, parrying the reaching hands of the second creature then whipping the crowbar around with lightning speed against the side of his attacker's knee. The monster dropped, crashing down on the pavement as Deano, not missing a beat, rose up and swung the crowbar in the other direction, connecting with the chin of the third beast.

Its head jolted to one side, dislocating its jaw as it stumbled into the wall.

*

Barely a couple of seconds had passed since the confrontation had begun and his father's speed had taken BD by surprise. He wasn't quite sure how this would go down, but he had expected to play the lead role.

He spun around as the first creature his father had kneecapped scrambled to climb to its feet. At that same moment, he caught movement out of the corner of his eye and glanced towards the entrance of the alley from the direction they had initially arrived to see five more creatures heading towards them.

"SHIT!"

He pushed his foot down hard on the back of the flailing beast and forced it flat on the ground then raised his bat.

Strike!

Strike!

Strike!

His victim fell still and BD whipped around once more.

*

Being in a brawl always meant you needed to rely on your co-brawlers to have your back. Deano had been in plenty with Vig, Benny the Brum, Tutti Frutti, Beef Stu and more besides. He knew they would always give as good as they got. But being in a tight spot with BD as his backup was a first, up until this morning. His only option was to fight like he'd never fought before.

He lunged forward as his target almost bounced off the alley wall, spinning a little before finding its centre and tearing towards him. Deano ducked sideways, avoiding the creature's grasp. As he came back up, he spun around with the crowbar fully extended and smashed it against the back of the beast's skull. Its front foot hit the ground and the rest of its body followed.

Deano turned on his heels, ready to strike one of the other attackers, only to see his son standing over the fallen body of his second victim. The two cast each other a fleeting glance before focusing on the approaching creatures further down the alleyway.

"Come on, BD. Let's get the hell out of here."

The pair ran back to the bikes and, without another word passing between them, the engines roared and their journey resumed.

*

The seconds dragged on as the echoes of the ringing bell chimed in the ears of the two women. Petal stood to attention, too, responding to the heightened anxiety in the room.

"Stay here," Taki said, placing the gun in the back of her jeans like she'd seen so many people do on TV. It felt uncomfortable, cold against her skin and like one intake of breath might cause it to slip below her waistline and down one of her legs.

"I told you," Poppy said, climbing to her feet. "I'm not letting you do this alone."

The bell rang again. *Oh God.* Doing the right thing was always important to Taki, but invariably it came with a cost, and this time, the cost could be everything.

She took a deep breath, but it shuddered a little as it left her lips, revealing the fear she was feeling deep inside. She picked up the homemade spear leaning by the side of the door and stepped out, not looking towards the gate for a moment, instead taking in the carefully built alleys and throughways of this scrapyard city that Deano had built.

Maybe we could run and hide. This place is huge. By the time they find us, BD might be back and maybe he and his dad can smooth this whole thing over.

The truth was, though, the longer Deano and BD were out there the less hope she had of them returning at all. The soundscape of the city had changed. The helicopters were no longer in earshot. The horns and sirens had faded away to virtual silence. There was still some time to go before curfew, so that could only mean one thing, and it wasn't good. She felt Poppy join her on the top step of the Portakabin.

No going back now. This is going to get nasty.

She finally turned and looked towards the gate to see an Audi pulled up outside and two young men looking towards them.

"Who the hell are these clowns?" Taki asked under her breath.

"It's alright," Poppy said excitedly. "It's Aldo and Rocky."

"Who the hell are Aldo and Rocky? They sound like chipmunks."

Poppy giggled. "They work for Deano. They're practically like sons to him."

"So, they're friendlies?" Taki asked, turning towards the other woman.

"Yeah. They're definitely friendlies."

"Thank Christ for that." The two women almost ran to the gate with Petal in pursuit, wagging her tail enthusiastically.

The brothers looked more than a little confused when they saw the stranger standing next to Poppy.

"It's alright," she said, wanting to alleviate their concerns. "She's BD's friend."

"Where's Deano?" Rocky asked.

"He's gone to try to find BD's mum."

"What, out there?" Aldo asked, sharing a concerned glance with his brother.

"Yeah. They've gone into Lewisham."

"Shit."

"They'll be okay. This is Deano we're talking about."

"Nobody's okay out there. Everything's turning to shit fast. We tried to get to my uncle's place. The main roads are gridlocked. They're all like one big car park. Buses, cars, police vehicles. Nothing's moving."

"How've you got here?"

"The outlying roads are okay, but if you head into town, you're screwed."

"Not that we're not happy to see you, but what are you doing here?"

"Deano said if we needed anything we should come and see him."

"What is it you need?" Taki asked, taking over.

"We want to stay here with Deano."

"But you've got a nice house," Poppy said. "Why the hell would you want to come and stay in a scrapyard?"

"It's not safe out there," Rocky replied this time. "Nowhere is safe. We didn't see any infected on the estate. But we heard screams. We know it's just a matter of time. The whole city's going to shit."

"What makes you think here is going to be any safer?"

"This place is like a mini fortress. It's got walls and fencing all around. It's off the beaten track too. You don't just happen by this place. And…."

"And what?"

"Deano's like a dad to us. He thinks he's invincible, thinks he's the one who's always got to look after everyone, but if ever there was a time when we all need someone to look out for us, it's now."

"Danny's coming back here."

"What do you mean coming back?"

"He came earlier, trying to get in. I think he wanted the supplies. Taki wouldn't let him through the gates, but he said he's going to come back with more men."

The two brothers looked at each other once again. Deano had done his best to keep them out of the nuts, bolts and grime of the operation. But they'd had to get their hands dirty plenty of times.

"Who's that?" Taki asked, looking beyond the two brothers for the first time to the back seat of the Audi.

"That's our mum," Rocky replied.

Suddenly, the strangers seemed far more human to Taki and she reached into her pocket and grabbed the key for the thick, weighty padlock. "Get in here, quick. We've already had to deal with a couple of infected."

"What?" Rocky asked as the gates swung open.

Taki pointed to three figures draped in a tarpaulin. "You killed them?" Aldo asked.

"Yeah," Poppy replied. "She was like some kind of warrior princess." She gestured to the homemade spear leant against the wall.

"You made this?" Aldo asked.

"Made's a bit of a strong word. Fashioned is probably more accurate."

The two brothers walked over to the tarpaulin. They'd never seen one of these creatures in the flesh before. Aldo lifted a corner of the sheet and stepped back, doing his best to hide a gasp.

There was a universe of difference between seeing a grainy image on a mobile phone screen and seeing one in real life; the pasty hue of the flesh made goosebumps charge up and down the two men's arms. The creature's jaw was locked open in an eternal grimace and the gaping hole where its eye had once been only made them focus more on the ghoulish grey orb in the other socket. It was something that belonged at the workstation of a movie special effects artist, not under a tarpaulin in a London scrapyard.

"Aldo, Rocky?" Their mother's voice made them quickly cover the chilling figure once more. Despite them having been born and bred in London and having no trace of Italian in their accent, their mother still had a hint of a Tuscan lilt in times of stress or excitement. "What is going on?"

"Nothing. I'll bring the car in," Rocky said, guiding his mother, who had walked past the two strangers at the gate to look for her sons, back to join Poppy and Taki.

He stepped out onto the street then looked left and right. Yes, it was a scrapyard, hardly the place he would choose to live given a choice, but this place could give them safety for a short time at least.

He thought back to the three infected under the tarpaulin. In all likelihood, they had followed the truck Danny had brought or been drawn by the noise of the bell. *The bell.* It was something Deano had installed so they would be alerted to customers even if they were in the far depths of the yard. He looked up and down the street. There was no sign of anyone or anything, but one of the first orders of business would be to disconnect that bell and make sure it never rang again. He climbed into the car and drove it through the gates. Poppy immediately closed them and he glanced in the rearview to see that Taki replaced the padlock almost straight away.

Smart.

By the time he got out of the car, Aldo was already leading their mother into the Portakabin.

In the space of just a few minutes, the idea of returning to the yard thinking it may be the answer to their problems had turned into one giant, confusing ball of wool with no seeming end. *If Danny finds out Deano's hiding Poppy, the infected are the last thing we need to be worry about.*

14

BD had been brought up with his mother's values and work ethic. This area of Blackheath was familiar to him because, in high school, he'd subsidised himself by doing an early morning milk round in the holidays and on a few days during term time when he could get away with it.

He and Deano had cut the engines and climbed off the bikes at least five minutes before. There was a small wooded area at the end of the large council estate they had navigated and this led straight to the rear of Derek's back garden.

It was quiet in that small strip of woodland. It was as if the world was just turning as normal and they would get to the other side and find that all of the morning's horror had just been a nightmare.

"So, how come Benny the Scouser owed you a favour big enough to give us these bikes?" BD asked.

"He didn't. It was Benny the Brum who gave us the bikes."

"Okay. Forgive me for not being up on all the gangland Bennys. Why did he give you the bikes?"

"He just owed me one. That's all."

"It's a pretty big favour."

Deano stopped and let out a breath. "They offered me a reduced sentence for spilling my guts about him."

"And you didn't take it."

"No."

"So, you served time for him, basically."

"It's not that straightforward. People in our line of work don't grass."

"How much time?"

"Doesn't matter. It's done, isn't it?"

"How much time?"

"Two years."

"Ha. Priceless."

"What's that supposed to mean?"

"It doesn't matter that you left me without a father and mum without a husband as long as you looked after some lowlife gangster."

"Tess and I were finished long before then and it's not as if I played any big part in your life, is it? If anything, I was doing you a favour being away from you. Hell, BD, if you'd have stayed around me, you'd never have wound up a scientist. You'd have probably ended up inside whether I tried to keep you straight or not."

"Firstly, I'm not a scientist; I'm a lab tech. Secondly, is that really your excuse? You thought you'd be a failure of a dad, so you didn't even bother trying."

Deano opened his mouth to reply but then closed it again. When it was verbalised like that it sounded weak, pathetic even, but it was true. Every word of it was true. "Yeah. It is."

"Nice. Thanks. Great to know I was worth all that effort."

"It's not like that."

"Oh no? What's it like then?"

Deano thought for a moment before answering. "I'm a fuck-up. I've always been a fuck-up. My dad was a fuck-up before me. He got me into this life and if I'd have stayed around, you'd be learning the family business."

"You don't know that."

"It's the way it works, Son. It's the way it's always worked."

"That's bollocks. What about Aldo and Rocky?"

"Aldo and Rocky are good boys, but they're not squeaky. If some plod with a beef wanted to go after them, they could. I didn't want that for you. I didn't want you to get any dirt under your nails if for no other reason than I knew Tess would need you. She's somebody who doesn't do well alone. Me leaving the picture was one thing, but if you disappeared, that'd kill her. I couldn't let that happen."

"So, it was all for her?"

"And you."

"I got it all wrong. You're a fucking martyr. Saint Deano of Lewisham. I'm surprised they haven't put up a statue of you."

"I'm not going to bite back, BD. Every piece of shit you want to fling at me I probably deserve and more besides. But do you think we can put a pin in it until we're back at the yard, at least?"

BD stared at his father for a moment and let out a laugh. "Yeah. Sure."

"What's funny?"

"Just that the yard is the place you're blaming for ruining your life, ruining my life, ruining Mum's life, and yet that's the place where we're miraculously going to find sanctuary. It doesn't bode too well for us, does it?"

Deano chuckled too. "And they laughed the laugh of the damned."

*

"Nothing. Not a bloody thing," Derek grumbled as he turned the dial on the radio once more.

"And you've checked the frequency where you picked up the Dunston broadcast?"

"Of course I bloody have."

"There's no need to snap."

"Well, I'm not likely to miss that out, am I?"

"I was only asking."

"If our power's down, their power will be down as well. It's all dead. Dead, dead, dead. We're cut off from the world, Tess. It's just you and me."

She put down the sewing, which she really hadn't managed to muster any enthusiasm for, and walked back to the side window. The black smoke in the distance continued to rise. She walked across to the front window and cast her eyes up the street to where she had seen Morton appear then disappear. "It really does feel like that, doesn't it?"

"It can't stay like this forever."

"What do you mean?" she asked, turning around to look at him.

"I mean the government are going to have to do something. This is London, for God's sake. It's the heart of the country. They can't just let it fall. They'll be putting a plan into place. Mark my words. It all seems grim right now, but we won't be left to fend for ourselves long. Mark my words."

"I hope you're right."

"Of course I'm right. I remember the Blitz. It was—"

"You don't remember the bloody Blitz, Derek. You weren't even born during the Blitz."

"Well, I remember my parents talking about it. I remember them telling me what it was like, what they had to go through, how they had to adapt. This is just like that. We're going to have to muddle through however we can until a bit of order returns."

The doorbell suddenly rang and both of them shot concerned glances towards each other. "I ... I don't understand," Tess said. "I've been standing at this window for a while. There was no one to be seen out front."

"Maybe you missed them when you were interrupting me."

"I'm telling you, Derek. There was nobody out front."

"Well, who the bloody hell is it going to be then?"

"How the hell do you expect me to know? I'm not a psychic."

"Maybe we should ignore it."

"What if it's somebody who needs help?"

"What if it's somebody who wants to rob us?"

"I don't suppose we'll know until we answer it."

Seconds ticked by, but neither of them moved. The bell rang again and Tess started towards the staircase.

"No. Don't," Derek said fearfully.

"It's alright. I won't open the door." She stepped into the hallway and ducked into the kitchen to grab the rolling pin she'd liberated from Maggie's kitchen then slowly made her way down the steps. She clutched the bannister as she descended. Her heart started drumming faster. *There was nobody there. There was nobody on the street.* If she'd have seen someone, stranger or not, at least she'd have been able to mentally prepare herself, but there had been no one. So, whoever it was must have come from the back and climbed over the fence.

Why the fuck would somebody do that? Tess didn't swear often, but now her mind was filled with expletives. *Fuck! Fuck! Fuck! Fuck! Fuck!*

She was the first and last line of defence for Derek as well as herself. She froze on the middle step as the letterbox opened letting in a small strip of white light that became shadowy again just as quickly as someone stepped in front of it.

"Mr Murtaugh," came the voice. "It's Tess Duncan's son. Mr Murtaugh?"

Tess's mouth dropped open in shock and then she put her hand up to cover it.

"Tess? Tess? Did you hear a voice?" Derek called out.

"Mr Murtaugh? Mr Murtaugh?"

Tess finally broke her statuesque pose and ran down the remaining stairs, removing the safety chain, unlocking the door and flinging it open. For a second, she was sure she was dreaming as she saw her son and ex-husband standing there, but then she dropped the rolling pin and rushed forward, throwing her arms around her boy and squeezing him tightly. Tears flooded her eyes and a sob left BD's lips, too, as he reciprocated the embrace.

"Bertie!"

As much as he hated that name, this was one occasion he relished hearing it. He felt her tears against the side of his face and they warmed his soul. He hadn't dared to admit it up until this point, but there was a big part of him that had thought this was a fool's errand. He thought he was never going to see his mother again, but it was the only thing he could latch on to. It was the only thing that could give him some means of looking forward, looking beyond the disaster that was unfolding.

The two remained hugging in the doorway for seconds, and then a minute, then more. And it wasn't until they heard shuffling feet on the landing and a grumpy, "What the bloody hell's going on down there?" that their embrace finally broke.

"It's Bertie," Tess announced, raising her head to look at Derek. "He's here!"

There was a pause before he replied. "See. See. I told

you. Smart cookie, that one. Well, don't just stand there letting in all the cold air. Bring him up."

"Go up," Tess said to BD and then remained at the entrance. It had been a long time since she'd seen Deano and, especially with the events of the morning, a swirl of emotions engulfed her. She had tried hard to hate him all these years, but she could never find real hate in her heart. Annoyance, disappointment, anger, he had stirred them all inside her. Sadness, humiliation, loss. Her self-worth had begun to ebb from the early days of being with him and the foundation had remained weak and cracked ever since.

"Come up," she said, gesturing for her ex to enter the flat.

If this was any other day, if this was a day when he had simply given a lift to his son to drop him off here, he would have been out of there in a heartbeat. But this was no normal day. There would never be a normal day again.

"It's good to see you, Tess," he said, entering the flat and heading up the stairs.

She closed the door behind him, turning the key and sliding the safety chain across.

"Come in, come in, come in," Derek said, leading the younger man down the short hallway and into the living room. "Your mother's been worried sick."

"Yeah, well, she wasn't the only one, Derek."

"Will you have some tea?"

"No. I'm good, thanks."

"Tess. Make some tea," Derek called out, ignoring him.

"I think we've got more important things to think about than tea. Don't you?" Tess said.

"You're absolutely right. This is a celebration. Bring out the gin."

"I'm not bringing out the gin," she replied irritably. "Can I get you anything?" she asked, looking first at BD then Deano.

"Actually," Deano replied. "I could murder a cuppa."

"In truth, I could too, Mum."

"Okay. So, we are having tea then."

"I'll give you a hand," BD said.

"No, you sit down."

"No. I want to give you a hand."

The two left Derek and Deano in the living room.

"So, you're the career criminal who ruined Tess's life, I'm guessing?"

Tess's shoulders sagged as the words followed her into the kitchen, but a smile lit BD's face as it came back to him just how loud and unfiltered Derek was.

Deano sat there for a moment just staring towards the old man. "Things were complicated for me and Tess."

"No doubt," he said, sitting back in his chair. "I'm sure running a gangland operation presented no end of complexities."

"So, let me guess. You were a school teacher or something?"

"I was an actor, my boy. An actor." He cleared his throat dramatically. "All the world's a stage, and all the men and women merely players."

"*As You Like It*."

Derek's head shot towards the other man. "You know Shakespeare?"

"Some."

"I'm impressed."

Deano shrugged. "There've been occasions when I've had more time on my hands than I knew what to do with."

"I dare say."

*

"I hope your father can hold his temper for a few minutes at least." Tess put the full kettle on the stove and lit the ring. "Oh, I was so worried about you." She turned and threw her arms around her son once more.

Normally, he'd have tired of her neediness by now, but not today. "Listen, Mum," he said, eventually pulling away. "We need to talk."

"Okay." Everything had happened so quickly. Her mind was still a maelstrom. "About what?"

"Take a guess."

A huffed laugh left her lips. "Sorry. Stupid question, I suppose. My head's still all over the place. I've gone through the full gamut of emotions today and then when we saw those bombs drop—"

"Listen. It's worse than you think out there."

"I was out there, Bertie."

"What do you mean?"

"I mean when the alert came. I started back to my flat

and then I saw something. I saw one of the infected. Only there wasn't just one of them for long."

BD nodded slowly. "Okay. So you know what we're dealing with. A lot's happened since that alert and things have got much worse. By this time tomorrow, the streets are probably going to be heaving with infected."

"Probably," she agreed. "But they'll have to send the army in at some point, won't they? I mean that's why the curfew, right? They want people in their homes so they can mop up the streets."

"In an ideal world. But I don't think we should count on that happening."

"What do you mean?"

"I think we should try to be more self-reliant."

"And do what exactly?"

"You're not going to like this, Mum."

"Just those words make me know I'm not going to like it."

"We need to head back to the yard with Dad."

Tess burst out laughing. "That's a good one, Bertie. Even at a time like this you can make me laugh."

"I'm not joking, Mum."

Tess had started to lay four mugs out, but she stopped again. "Why would I do that?"

"Because it's secure. There's a big, sturdy fence around the place. It's out on a limb. There are supplies there and it's where I'm going."

"But ... I thought...."

"You thought what, Mum? You thought that we'd all just sit around drinking tea and playing Monopoly and waiting for the all-clear to sound?"

"Well, I didn't really think about it. I just wanted to know you were safe."

"Yeah. And I wanted to know you were safe, and I want you to be safe, and this is how we do it."

She turned and gazed out of the window. "When you didn't show up last night, when I couldn't get in touch with you, I thought—"

"I was arrested."

"Arrested?"

"Kind of. Me and Taki came into contact—"

"Taki?"

"She's a friend ... a colleague. She's back at the yard. We ran into one of those things yesterday, and before we knew what was happening, we'd been escorted to a facility by soldiers and we were in some sort of forced quarantine. When everything started kicking off this morning, we managed to escape. It started bad out there and it's getting worse by the minute. Loads of roads are gridlocked and I don't even want to think about the people who are trapped with nowhere to go."

The conversation paused for a moment and they both started listening to the sound of the water beginning to bubble in the kettle as it heated up.

*

"So, you're both here now," Derek said. "I don't suppose Tess would turf even *you* out on the street given the circumstances, so here are the house rules. Keep your hands off my gin and brandy unless I give you express permission." He thought for a moment. "Well ... those are pretty much all the rules that matter come to think of it."

A smile curled up the corner of Deano's lips. Derek was brash, loud and devoid of subtlety, but somehow that had endeared him to Deano in just the few minutes he'd spent at the flat.

"Good to know. But we won't be staying."

"We who?"

"Me, BD, Tess."

"Oh? And where are you going exactly?"

"To my yard."

"Oh yes. It's a mystery how she let you get away. Why offer her a life of luxury when she can live out the end of days in a rat-infested scrapyard?"

"I don't think you understand what's going on out there."

"Oh, please enlighten me. I'm sure I've completely misunderstood what the jets bombing half the bloody city to oblivion meant."

*

"I can't," Tess said.

"You can't what?" BD asked.

"I can't live with your dad again, BD. I'll end up killing him."

"You won't be living with him, Mum. I'm not asking you to renew your vows. This is like being in a warzone. If we're going to survive this, everybody's going to have to band together. Not everybody's going to like one another, but we've got one common enemy and that's what we need to focus on."

"Okay. Is that your dad or the infected?"

BD laughed. "I'm being serious, Mum. We can last a good while there. Yeah, it's not going to be that comfortable, but it will be liveable, and living is all that matters right now. What do you say?"

"I need a minute to process this, Bertie."

*

"You should come with us." The words were out of Deano's mouth before he'd even thought about them. Inside, he had been forced to band together with his own kind to survive. It was a different kind of war being waged in there, but the rules were the same, and now Derek, as unlikely as it would ever seem up until today, was his own kind. *What the fuck am I doing? Why did I say that?*

"What?"

The incredulity on Derek's face as he asked the question was apparent and it was one that Deano shared. *Why did I say that?* he asked himself again. Yes, he liked Derek, as grumpy and caustic as he was, but Deano had always measured the value of a relationship in what he could get out of it. Apart from Derek providing mild amusement, there was no value in having him around. In fact, considering his age and the fact that he had a carer, it was obvious that he would be a drain on resources, if anything.

"I said you should come with us." His words lingered in the air and, suddenly, Deano understood the reason behind his invitation. If he could persuade Derek to go, Tess would have to go, have to rely on him, have to depend on him. She had always been selfless. That's why he'd asked. It was subconscious problem solving. It was his devious, plotting, calculating brain doing a cost-benefit analysis. He desperately wanted BD to stay with him and, by extension, he needed Tess for that. Inviting Derek would tie the little bundle of dependency up nicely. Yes, all these were for selfish ends, but there was something else as well, something he hadn't quite fathomed yet, but the abacus beads were flicking fast as he awaited the old man's reply.

"Why would you possibly want a relic like me to tag along?"

Deano thought for a moment. "Well, the way I see it there are a few miles to cover between here and the yard. If we get into a tight spot, we could push you off the bike and that would occupy the infected for a little while so we could escape."

Derek stared at the other man for a moment; then a raucous bellowing laugh left his mouth and he clapped his hands together. "Bravo. Bravo. An excellent answer."

*

BD and Tess glanced towards the door as booming laughter and applause rose from the other room.

"Well, they sound like they're getting on, anyway," BD said.

"Your dad can be quite funny and charming when he wants to be."

"He hides it well most of the time."

"Tell me about it."

"So?"

"So, what? You've only just sprung this on me, Bertie. I'm processing."

"TESS! TESS! FIND MY HOSPITAL BAG," shouted Derek. "WE'RE OFF TO GO LIVE IN A SCRAPYARD!"

15

"You are worried," Liliana, Rocky and Aldo's mother, said, walking up to Taki as she stood at the gate.

"You could say that."

"This man, Danny, who came. He scared you?"

The initial impression Taki had got of Liliana, or Lili as she preferred to be known, was that of some shrinking violet. The two boys were very protective of her, steering her away from the covered bodies of the infected, but within a couple of minutes of arriving, she had taken a look for herself. It was clear she was a huge personality and seemed like someone who needed no protection. Brief introductions were made and both sides had revealed their own accounts of the events leading up to that moment. Lili was probably in her mid to late fifties but looked younger. She wore makeup, eyeliner, and lipstick, which were expertly applied. Her skinny 501s and leather jacket portrayed casual but classy at the same time and there was a friendliness and approachability to her that betrayed that first impression.

"You could say that," Taki eventually replied.

"I have not met him. I have met his father. Vig is what

my papa would call a segaiolo."

"What's that?"

"Wanker."

Taki burst out laughing and Lili smiled too. "You're funny."

"No. It's true. He would only have himself to play with if he did not pay for it." Taki laughed again. "He is also a bastard."

"You're not friends then?"

"My husband, Matteo. It was because of Vig he went to prison. It was because of him that my boys grew up without a father for many years. It was Deano who looked after them, looked after us when we needed help. It should have been Vig. That is how it's meant to work, but he is not a good man. He has no honour, and from everything I've heard his son is worse."

"Well, up until this morning, I wouldn't have an opinion on the matter, but the guy who came here was bad news. I know that much."

"You were brave to stand up to him. I don't know you long, but already I like you."

"Well, thanks, Lili. I like you too."

She threw her hands up in the air. "Well, sure. What is there not to like?"

Taki laughed again. "BD and his dad have been gone a long time."

The smile on Lili's face faded. "It's bad out there. The boys think they protect me from knowing what is going on, but I have eyes and ears."

"That's what I mean."

"I've known Deano a long time. He's a smart man. He will be back."

"Even smart men aren't immune to this, Lili."

"This is true. But Deano will be back. Trust me. And in the meantime, we will protect this place and get organised."

"What made you come here? What made you leave your house to come to a scrapyard?"

"Like I said. It's bad out there."

"Yeah. But something tells me you're pretty resourceful, Lili. I'm sure if anyone could get by you could, especially with your two boys."

Lili exhaled deeply. "My boys told me about the shipment that was brought in."

"Shipment?"

"Food and supplies. Three lorries' worth. This place is like a small fortress with its walls and fences. Some are thinking about what happens tomorrow. I am thinking about what happens next week, next month."

"Yeah. Like I said. You're pretty resourceful."

Lili shrugged and a smirk appeared on her face as the two women continued to stare out through the gates. "There was another reason."

"Oh?"

"Deano has been like a father to Aldo and Rocky since Matteo passed. It was not right for him to be here alone."

"Well, he was hardly alone."

"Now I know this, but all I knew before was that there was an on-the-run stripper with him and that would not end well."

"You think it's going to end well now?"

"Whether it does or it doesn't, he will not be left to face things alone. Matteo would not have liked that."

"They were good friends?"

"They were like family. Deano never got close to anyone again after Matteo. He was the one who held him as he bled out. He was the one who sent me money, made sure I was always okay."

"He sounds like a good bloke."

Lili shrugged again. "He was to me. He was to my boys. I'm sure Tess will tell you a different story."

"BD's mum?"

"Uh-huh. I always liked Tess. She was warm. She had a big heart. Too big. It got hurt badly. I love Deano, but he could have played things differently with Tess … and their son for that matter."

"Sounds complicated."

"Love is never simple."

"I wouldn't know."

Lili turned towards the younger woman. "I can tell you have a big heart, too, like Tess. This is why BD likes you, I'm guessing."

"Oh, no. You've got the wrong idea. Me and BD aren't a thing. We work together … worked together anyway. We don't know each other that well."

"Meh!" Lili replied, shrugging once more. "If they both make it back, you will have plenty of time to get to know each other."

Taki let out another small laugh and shook her head. "You're unbelievable, you are."

"Why? What have I done?"

"We're in the midst of the biggest disaster ever to face humankind and you're trying to play matchmaker."

"Meh! What is wrong in finding happiness if it is out there waiting to be found?"

Taki smiled again. Despite everything that was going on, she'd met two people in the course of a morning who she liked more than anybody she'd met in the previous six months. And if it wasn't for this particular set of circumstances, the chances were she would never have encountered either of them.

"I don't really have an answer for that."

"See. I make sense. You stick with me. I'll teach you plenty."

*

Even though they had a generator at the yard, Aldo and Rocky decided not to use it. Instead, they opened the doors of the cargo container that doubled as the yard workshop wide and dragged the hefty wooden bench to the entrance so they could work in natural light.

Poppy, was grateful to be with them in the depths of the labyrinthine scrapyard, if for no other reason than here she was well out of sight of the main gates. Petal had attached herself to Poppy. Two lost souls in a chaotic world. Both were grateful for the companionship and the sense of comfort and warmth the other offered.

The two brothers had already disconnected the bell as the first order of business and now they were getting to work on what came next. Neither of them were shirkers and both understood the value of giving their all to a job. There was a vast array of items for scrap in the yard. Among them were several sections of wrought-iron fencing that had once bordered an old school. When the school was demolished, the fencing had appeared in the back of an open-backed truck. No questions were asked about how it had got from one place to the other and what permissions were sought, but for several months it had remained in one corner of the yard stacked.

Today, however, one section of it would get a new lease of life. Both brothers had been impressed with the handmade spear that Taki had constructed. It was something they hadn't even considered until laying eyes on it. Yes, the yard was like a mini fortress, but a fortress still needed defending and what better way to put down any attacking infected than by spearing them through the fences?

The salvaged, sturdy, black wrought-iron pickets already had spikes attached to the end making them look like medieval spears, so why not put them to good use? The brothers hoisted one of the weighty sections of fencing onto the bench and angled it around. Aldo pressed down hard on one end while Rocky fired up the angle grinder and began to cut through the horizontal rails, holding the spear-like vertical tines in position. They'd laid down several thick blankets on the metal floor of the container to avoid the Big Ben like clang as each picket came free, but they could do nothing about the noise of the grinder cutting through the thick metal. Both agreed, however, it was better to do it now than later. Later there could be hordes of infected within earshot. For the time being, at least, that was not the case.

One after another after another, the freshly cut spears were born as sparks flew, lighting up the inside of the container and bouncing off the protective goggles both brothers wore.

They stopped at eight. Then, one after the other, they finished the spikes off with a quick flurry, sharpening them and turning them into lethal killing implements. When they were done, they removed their goggles, removed the welding gauntlets they'd been wearing, and leaned one after another up along the wall. Some of the spikes still glowed red a little from the friction and heat. They would cool down soon enough, but they had plenty more to do than just stand around and wait for that to happen.

"I feel like a bit of a spare part," Poppy said. "Is there anything I can be doing?"

The brothers were a good team. Often, Deano would join them. They had an understanding, a way of working together to complement one another's skills, to get the job done quickly and efficiently. Nobody gave orders; there was just a knowing of what needed to be done. It was this knowing that was driving Aldo and Rocky now.

In Deano's absence, it fell on them to get done what needed to get done. They had to make this place secure, defendable. They'd disabled the bell, made a handful of weapons. They already had supplies taken care of for the foreseeable future, but next came shelter. As it stood, there were five of them. Poppy and Taki had relayed that Deano and BD had gone in search of Tess. That would be eight assuming they returned safely.

The Portakabin and the caravan could house eight people comfortably, but they would require a little adaptation. The windows would need light-proofing, not from light getting in but light getting out. On a night, they did not want to become beacons for the infected. Both the Portakabin and the caravan had toilets and Calor gas heaters, so, again, the occupants would be … comfortable might be a stretch, but certainly they wouldn't be living like savages.

"The bus," Aldo said.

"What about it?" replied Rocky.

"It might be comfortable."

"What are you talking about?" Poppy asked.

"Nothing. I'm thinking out loud."

"Is there a bus here?"

"Yeah. It's a vintage thing. Nice nick too. Deano was talking about doing it up and selling it. The engine would need a complete overhaul, but it's pretty pristine inside like it's out of a museum or something."

"Okay. No offence, but what does that have to do with anything?"

"Like I said. I was just thinking out loud. Someone could live in that at a push."

"A bus?"

"Yeah. It's going to be a lucky girl who marries you, Aldo."

All three of them laughed and Petal's tail wagged happily as the friends enjoyed a moment of normality. "All I'm thinking is … it doesn't matter."

"You're thinking what if it ends up being not just us."

"Yeah. I mean, we've got shipping containers, we've got vehicles big and small, we've got all sorts here."

"Maybe we shouldn't plan too far ahead. Maybe we should just think about dealing with what we know we have to deal with right now."

"Yeah. You're probably right."

"So, with that in mind, is there anything I can be doing?"

"Yeah, actually, there is."

"Okay. What?"

"Car mats."

"Car mats?"

"Yeah. The mats that go in the footwells."

"I know what they fucking are, Aldo. What do you want me to do with them?"

"If we can find a way of knitting a few of them together, they'd be perfect for blocking out the light from the windows on a night."

"Isn't that what curtains and blinds are for?"

"Yeah. But we're talking about all light, Poppy. We can't let so much as a twinkle show through those windows."

She thought for a moment. "Actually, that's a good point. Okay. I'll go look for car mats."

"Cool."

"What are you going to do?"

"We're going to get these to the gates," he said, nodding towards the spears, "and then we're going to start transferring some of the stuff those lorries brought in this morning to another container."

"Why?"

"When Danny comes back, it'll be for the supplies. He'll be coming back heavy and there won't be much we can do but let him take them. There's nothing to stop us taking a few weeks' worth for ourselves though. They brought in tonnes of the stuff this morning. They're not going to miss a box here and there."

"You'll tell me when he shows up, won't you?"

"You don't need to worry, Poppy. We won't let that prick anywhere near you."

*

"I thought you'd have put up more of a fight about leaving your home," Tess said as she helped Derek gather a few last belongings from his bedroom. A muted conversation was going on between Deano and BD in the other room as they considered the next step of the mission.

"What the hell is there for me to stay here for?"

"All your things. Your comforts."

"Things. Things. Things. Things mean nothing."

"I never thought I'd hear those words come out of your mouth."

"See this, Tess," he said, pointing to the watch on his wrist.

"Well, of course I see it. I'm not blind."

"Well, it's a vintage Patek Philippe. It was given to me in 1980 by a man who I ended up utterly loathing. Do you know why I keep it?"

"Because it's worth thousands?"

"No. Because it tells the time well."

"Um … okay. I don't really see what your point is."

"You see this?" he said, pointing to his face.

"You mean your cheek?"

"Yes, my cheek. That's where David Armitage kissed me and told me he'd love me forever. We'd been to a party in Malibu and in the early hours, before the sun had risen, we walked along the beach hand in hand while everyone else crashed. It was one of the most wonderful nights of my life, and if he hadn't died three years later, I dare say we'd still be together now. Some people will never get to experience that happiness, that feeling of joy, that feeling of belonging."

"You've never told me that story before. But I still don't understand what it has to do with leaving your flat."

"The point is," he said, gesturing towards the watch, "this"—he pointed to the lamp on his bedside cabinet—"this, this, this, this, this,"—he aimed his finger at other things around the room—"they're all just things, Tess. Things aren't important. Things can be replaced … or not, for that matter." He raised his index and middle fingers to his temple and gently tapped on it. "It's what's in here that counts. It's what's in here that can help you get through the worst days."

Tess reached out and grabbed his hand tightly. "That's beautiful, Derek."

"The older you get the more you realise it's the truth."

She leaned in and kissed him on the cheek. "Am I interrupting something?" Deano asked, appearing in the doorway.

"Good God, man, yes, can't you see? I was just about to give your ex-missus a damn good rogering before we set off and now you've spoilt the moment completely."

Tess slapped Derek on the arm and shook her head. "I swear this man will be the death of me."

"You used to say that about me," Deano replied.

"Yeah. I divorced you. I don't think I can get out of my contract with him."

"Too right," Derek said, standing up. "Now, let's get off to this scrapyard and witness firsthand the life of luxury you could have lived."

16

Taki and Lili remained at the gate in comfortable silence. A thousand thoughts were flashing through each of their heads, but they were at ease with each other when normally Taki would have been putting her mouth into overdrive in an attempt to make someone like or at least accept her. Lili had a way of making people feel relaxed quickly and this is what she'd done.

There was a noise behind them and they both jerked around to see Poppy struggling with a tall pile of car mats in her arms while Petal sauntered by her side.

No sooner had the two gate guards laid eyes on her than she lost her grip and the entire collection fell to the ground with a thump.

"Shit!"

Taki and Lili hurried over to help her pick them up. They had been at the gate for several minutes without seeing a soul and something told them that was how it would remain for a while at least.

"Okay," Taki said. "I've known people who collected stamps, coins and even porcelain frogs, but I don't think I've ever met someone who collected car mats before."

"It was Rocky and Aldo who asked me to do it."

"Um … why?"

"They want to make them into a kind of thick curtain for the windows. Y'know, so on a night no light can get out just in case any of the infected pass by."

"Okay, but there are like a million tarpaulins around here. Wouldn't it just be easier to use them?"

Poppy shrugged. "I'm just doing what they said."

A barely perceptible smile passed between Lili and Taki. This idea would work, but it was a little labour intensive, and the two women both came to the same conclusion in an instant. The idea was practical, resourceful, but at the same time, it gave Poppy something to occupy her mind and it made her feel useful.

"My boys are always full of ideas," Lili said, picking up the last of the mats. "No doubt they have plans for the tarpaulins if they chose not to use them."

"They're smart are Aldo and Rocky."

"Course they're smart," Lili replied. "They are my boys. But don't tell them I said they're smart. It will go to their heads. Always leave them trying to impress rather than impressing. That's how you get the best out of men."

The other two women laughed. "I can tell I'm going to learn a lot from you," Poppy replied.

"Lili's university welcomes all."

The three women climbed the steps and entered the Portakabin with Petal behind them, her tail wagging enthusiastically. Since her arrival, her spirits had brightened no end. Her wound was clearly causing her less discomfort and being around people who had genuine affection for her was a better medicine than any other. She nudged each of the women for a fuss and they all reciprocated once they'd placed the mats down on the desk.

"Okay," Taki said. "So, what do we do with them now?"

Lili grabbed a large pair of scissors from the pen holder on the desk and proceeded to drill two holes in the upper corners of one of the thick, rubber-backed, rectangular mats. "Well, what we need to do is string them together in a line, then another, then another, and have them overlapping vertically and horizontally, so any joins are covered. But first, we need to find some kind of pole to suspend them from. It's going to have to be sturdy to take the weight." A smile lit Lili's face. Her sons were right. There was something about even the most mundane tasks to occupy the mind that was a little therapeutic. *Smart boys.*

*

Rocky and Aldo had always understood the world Deano and their father had lived in. They hadn't been blind to it, and, in some cases, they had participated in it, albeit reluctantly. They had no interest in gaining insurmountable wealth or power. When they had been given jobs at the scrapyard, they were both pretty sure it was just so Deano could keep an eye on them while their mother went out to work.

They never thought they would end up loving the place. But they did. They really did. They enjoyed being busy and there was always something to do there. They enjoyed being resourceful. Deano was old-school. He'd been taught by his father that a penny saved was a penny earned, and yet he was by no means tight-fisted, quite the opposite in fact, but he was one to adapt, mould and use what was around. He had instilled the same ethic in Lili's two boys and now their minds were working overtime as they continued the barrowing of supplies from one shipping container to another.

"What are we going to do if Danny comes back before Deano?" Aldo asked.

"What do you mean?"

"I mean, it goes without saying that we keep Poppy out of sight, but what about BD's girl?"

"I don't think she's his girl."

"Whatever. I mean, by the sound of it, she tore a few strips off him. He's not going to let that go."

"So, what are you thinking?"

"I'm not. That's why I'm asking you."

Rocky stopped outside the second container and opened the door. They'd already transported a good forty boxes of various supplies, which would keep them going for some time, but they wanted to gather as much as they possibly could without it being obvious that they were ripping Vig off.

"Well," Rocky said after some thought. "If we don't let him in, then we've got a war on our hands, 'cause there's no way he's not coming back here armed and with a crew."

"I figured that much out myself."

"So, we keep her out of sight."

"Keep her out of sight?"

"Yeah." He began to unload his barrow, stacking the boxes against a wall. "We'll finish up here, get them hidden, and you and me will deal with Danny. We'll tell him that she decided to head home before the curfew hit. It's not like he's going to tear this place apart looking for her, is it?"

"You realise that if we get caught out in a lie with that prick, we'll be on Vig's shit list as well?"

"Then we make sure we don't get caught out." He gestured around. "Jesus, there are like a million places to stash someone in here."

"Yeah."

Rocky stopped for a moment. "Do you think Deano's going to make it back?"

Aldo stared at his brother. "Yeah. I do. But if he doesn't, it's going to come down to us to make sure that we all stay safe in here."

"Yeah."

*

"Well, it's a bloody good job we said we were coming with you, isn't it? Otherwise, we could have a bloody swarm of infected coming at us from behind and we wouldn't even know about it," Derek said as the quartet, adorned with various bags and satchels, entered the back garden and observed the steamrolled wooden fence that had allowed the father and son to wheel the bikes in.

"Roads weren't really an option on the way here," BD replied. "Most of the time, we used pavements and we even went through a couple of gardens."

"We can't go anywhere near the roundabout," Tess said. "It was bad when I was there and things have only got quieter in the last half hour."

"What do you reckon?" BD asked, turning to Deano, who was rubbing his chin in contemplation.

"Well, we could retrace our steps for a bit, turn right at the Taste of India and then drop onto Peddler's Lane."

"You don't think we'll run into another car park?"

Deano shrugged. "It's possible, but there's not a lot around there other than big posh houses. Then we should be able to get onto Holt Park Estate, which should take us to

Cannon Way and we'll be on the back streets all the way to the yard."

"Good God. Have you swallowed an A to Z, man?" Derek asked. "Let's just get on the bloody bikes and get on with it, shall we?"

"Don't mind Derek," Tess said. "He's just grumpy because … well … he's never needed a reason actually."

"Ha, ha, bloody ha. I just don't want be standing out in the open all day risking life and limb while your ex gives us a recitation of the knowledge that he no doubt decided to learn during one of his various spells banged up at her majesty's pleasure."

Tess closed her eyes and shook her head. Deano smiled. Even though the barb was directed at him, Derek was funny and this amused him. "What's the knowledge?" BD asked.

"Good God, Tess. You never told me your boy had learning deficiencies. How long have you lived in London?" Derek asked, turning to the youngest member of the group.

"All my life. Why?"

"The knowledge, my lad, is the test that black cab drivers must take to show they know every name and location and the quickest route there."

"Oh."

"Now," he said, turning to Deano once more. "Can we please get on our way?"

Deano nodded. He and BD wheeled the bikes back over the demolished wooden fence and into the small wooded area before he turned to Tess and Derek. When he spoke, it was in a hushed tone. "Okay. Out here, noise isn't our friend. When the motors of the bikes aren't running, we need to be as quiet as possible. You get me?"

"Not at all. Could you break it down to make it a bit simpler?"

"Derek," BD said. "You're a nice man, and my mum thinks the world of you, but you need to start taking this a bit more seriously." He gestured to the baseball bat in his hand. "This isn't some OAPs' outing. If we screw up, we could very easily die out here."

The start of a reply began in Derek's throat, but Tess's fingers closed around his arm, stopping him. She looked at the rolling pin she carried in her other hand and the hairs on the back of her neck shimmered a little as she thought about what might transpire in order for her to use it.

The four of them continued along the footpath in the small wooded area, finally emerging on a deserted street at the edge of the large council estate. The odd car was parked here and there, but there was no sign of life as they continued down the centre of the road.

Then, as they went past one house, an upstairs blind twitched.

"It's like everybody's in hiding," BD said.

It was a world away from what they had experienced earlier. The pyres of smoke in the distance were just about visible and were a painful reminder of the fear confusion and mayhem that had exploded around them. The sounds of pain, sadness and horror had seemed to play a constant accompaniment up until them arriving at Derek's house.

In truth, the soundscape had shifted subtly minute by minute before then as people had found refuge, fled or become one of the growing legion of infected that was no doubt lurking somewhere. They could be around any corner, down any alley, behind any skip or parked vehicle. They could be anywhere. And to say the streets were silent would not be accurate. There were still sounds. The odd distant and pained scream still travelled on the breeze, but it was different from what it had been, and that ignited more unease in BD and Deano, not less.

"Everybody *is* in hiding," Deano finally replied. "Everybody with any sense, anyway."

They turned right onto another long street lined with more houses. Again, there was a distinct lack of human life. A blur of black made them all stop for a beat and each let out a small snigger as a well-fed cat leapt from the roof of a shed at the end of someone's garden and shot across the road, disappearing down a ginnel.

"Are we taking these bikes for a walk or are we going to get on them at some stage?" Derek chuntered.

"Like I said," BD replied. "Noise isn't our friend out here. The longer we can go without firing up the motors the better because, trust me, when these things start roaring, every infected in the—" He fell silent, coming to an immediate standstill, and his father did the same. Tess and Derek didn't understand for a moment, but then they saw the two figures that had emerged from the crossroads up ahead.

"Oh, God," Tess whispered as BD and Deano lowered the kickstands and moved forward.

They spread out, left and right, casting a single glance back to see pure, unadulterated fear sully the complexions of their two companions. For once, even Derek was lost for words. All he could do was focus on the strange, unnatural, godless creatures that were tearing towards them.

He felt Tess's fingers tighten more and he placed his hand over hers, grateful for the warmth. "Dear Christ," was all he could whisper as the malevolent intent of the beasts became ever clearer and their guttural growls travelled towards them like some song of death.

"When we make it back to the yard, we're going to have to figure out better weapons than a baseball bat and a crowbar," Deano said.

"I like the way you say when. That's an optimism I didn't have you pegged for."

The two beasts had been running almost shoulder to shoulder as they made their approach but now they split up, each targeting one of the two succulent bags of flesh standing in front of the bikes.

*

"Stay behind me," Tess said, letting go of Derek's arm and striding forward with her rolling pin held up in front of her as if it was Excalibur.

"Like buggery I will," Derek replied, pulling out the knife he'd grabbed from the block in the kitchen and placed in the side pocket of his rucksack. He'd been in plenty of fights in his life, mainly as a result of making a pass at the wrong man, but never had weapons been involved, and never had he faced an opponent capable of putting the fear of hell and damnation into him before.

"Be careful, Bertie," Tess's words barely came out as a whisper, but she felt compelled to say them. She was his mother. She would always be his mother. He was the best thing she had ever done with her life and she was more scared for him than she was for herself.

*

BD and Deano had faced these things before, but their skin still bristled as the beasts neared them, as they laid eyes on the pallid flesh, as they heard the duet of fearsome growls and saw the bloody wounds that had no doubt turned them into these abominations.

BD leapt forward letting out a grunt as again he chose to windmill the bat down rather that pitch hit. His timing was perfect. The barrel of the makeshift weapon smashed down on his attacker's head and a loud crack reverberated up and down the street as Deano fended off the grasping hands of the second creature and side swiped with the crowbar.

This sound was more of a wet thud as the sturdy strip of metal disappeared into the thick mop of curly hair. The creature fell to the side at the same moment BD's attacker dropped like a sack of stones.

One

Two

Three

Four

The father and son stood still, catching their breath before the beast Deano had struck began to rally. BD didn't waste a second; he leapt across, raising his bat and bringing it down with the might of Thor's hammer again and again and again until the creature's skull caved and the polished wood became coated in a thick residue of globulous tissue.

Both men watched as the gory concoction dripped from the bat onto the tarmac, staining it deep crimson. BD wiped his weapon off on the clothing of his second victim and finally straightened up. The two men looked back to Tess and Derek who were both frozen in slack-jawed horror at the sight. It was clear they were petrified, sickened and bewildered all at the same time. Tears threatened to flood from Tess's eyes for a second, but she managed to get a grip on herself. Tears wouldn't help them.

Curtains rippled on the upper floors of a couple of the houses. Although it was only early afternoon, people had seemingly gone into night mode, desperate to block out the world and hope they could wake up to a new day tomorrow and find out everything was okay again. It was a natural reaction, a normal reaction, but it was also one that would leave them ill-prepared for the reality of what was unfolding.

Deano wiped his crowbar clean and both men returned to the bikes. "Come on," he said. "When we get to the end of this road, we'll fire these up and, hopefully, we won't have to stop again until we reach the yard."

The four of them proceeded along the street in virtual silence. All their hearts were still beating way faster than normal, but they had survived their encounter and that was something.

"We've been lucky so far," BD said quietly to his father as Tess whispered words of comfort to Derek.

"It doesn't feel like we've been lucky. It feels like we've managed to get out of a couple of really shitty situations through quick thinking and sheer brute force."

"No. I mean we've been lucky that we've only come across twos and threes of these things. What happens when we run into fives and sixes? What happens when we run into a crowd of them?"

"Let's just hope we get back to the yard without that happening."

"I don't just mean today, Dad. We won't be able to stay at the yard forever without heading out again. I don't care how well supplied you think it is at the moment; at some stage, we're going to run out of stuff, need medical supplies or something. This situation is only going to get worse." He gestured to the houses around them as a couple more curtains and blinds moved. "Everybody was told to get to safety before curfew and that's probably as far as a lot of them have thought. When they get down to their last tin of beans in the cupboard or their last drop of water from the tap, what then?"

"You think the water will go off?"

"Course it will. It's just a matter of time. The power's already gone off. When the backup generators that power the pumps run dry, what do you think will happen? People in the First World aren't equipped to deal with these kinds of problems. Kids in Burundi and Somalia have to walk half a day to collect water. What the fuck does someone from London know about doing anything for themselves? All these houses have gas central heating. There probably isn't a single one with a real fireplace anymore. How are they going to stay warm?"

"I get it. It's bad. What's your point?"

"My point is people are going to figure out that they're rats caught in a trap pretty quickly. They're going to realise that they need more than what they've got in their house to survive, and they're going to head out looking for it, and that is seriously going to compound this already shitty situation. In a few days, this estate will probably be crawling with infected. Maybe not even in a few days. Maybe sooner than that, and that's my point. Two, three, four of these things might seem scary, but they're nothing compared to what's coming."

The pair carried on walking for a moment before Deano replied. "Real fucking bundle of lightness and joy you turned out to be, didn't you?"

BD laughed. "Come on. You must have thought about this."

Deano hadn't managed to think about much up until that moment, but everything his son said made perfect sense. There had been no more jets; there had been no massive influx of military personnel into the area. Everything pointed to the people south of the river being left to their own devices and, as BD said, it would only be a matter of time before things got completely out of hand.

"Let's get back to the yard and then we'll figure it all out." He turned to the others. "Okay. It's time to mount up."

"You're not the Lone Ranger, Deano," Tess said as the quartet came to a halt once more.

"I'm guessing you'll want to go with BD?"

"Too right I want to go with BD," she replied, placing the long strap of the bag she was carrying around her shoulder.

"Come on then, Derek. You're with me." He climbed onto the bike and angled it a little so that the old man could position himself on the bench seat.

"It's a long time since I've felt the power of a throbbing motor between my legs," he replied with a smile in his voice, the first since the confrontation with the creatures.

"You're not going to make this weird, are you?"

"Not at all. Now, should I wrap arms around your chest or should I grab a tight hold of your hips?"

"Yeah. This isn't going to be weird at all."

"You okay, Mum?" BD asked as Tess placed the rolling pin in the bag and put her helmet on.

When she was done, she pulled up the visor. "Yep. All ready to go."

"Okay. Next stop, Hell."

17

The sound of multiple large vehicles travelled along the road to the entrance of Duncan's scrapyard. It was loud enough for the three women in the Portakabin to hear. It was loud enough for Aldo and Rocky to hear and they had set off at a sprint, but not before padlocking the door of their new makeshift larder.

They burst through the entrance of the cabin and a startled yap left Petal's mouth. The three women on the other side of the desk looked alarmed, too, but the two brothers didn't have time for apologies or placating words. Instead, they rushed to the opposite side of the room, pulled the vertical blinds across and opened the window.

"You two need to go," Aldo said, turning to Poppy. "That bus we talked about earlier. It's just a bit further on from the workshop. Head there; go upstairs; duck down behind the seats and don't raise your heads again until we come and get you."

"You want me to go too?" Taki asked, surprised.

"Yeah. Danny's not a guy who takes nicely to someone

mouthing off at him."

"I wasn't mouthing off. I was—"

"Look. It doesn't matter. That's how he'll see it. Now go."

Taki opened her mouth to protest but closed it again just as quickly. Poppy climbed through the opening and dropped to the ground on the other side then helped her friend do the same before Rocky closed the window and the blinds once more.

The two brothers looked at each other and then at their mother. "You stay here, Mum," Aldo said.

Lili laughed. "Since when do you give me orders?"

"I don't want you having to deal with this guy. He's a scumbag."

She shrugged. "I've dealt with plenty of scumbags before now. My guess is this one's a chip off the old block."

"Well, at least don't say anything to try to deliberately piss him off. It wouldn't be good for Deano."

"What is it with you? Are you saying I'm an embarrassment to you?"

"No, I'm—"

"I'm winding you up, Aldo," she said as a warm smile crept onto her face. "I wouldn't do anything to make life difficult for you or Deano."

She headed out of the door and both brothers looked at each other nervously, both thinking the same thing. *If only that were true.*

Petal followed the trio but then split to the left in search of her other new friends.

The first of the three lorries pulled up at the gate. Rocky and Aldo could see the driver who had come earlier in the day to drop off all the stolen supplies.

Rocky undid the chain and he and his brother pulled the gates wide open. The driver's window lowered and the man who had seemed aloof if not arrogant earlier on in the day looked far less sure of himself.

"Get these gates closed again as soon as we're through. I think we've picked up a few tails."

"What, police?" Rocky asked.

"I wish it was." He drove through quickly followed by the second and third trucks. When the last vehicle had crossed the threshold, Rocky and Aldo poked their heads out to look up and down the street and, about two hundred metres away, they could see multiple figures in the middle of the road charging in their direction.

"Well, don't just fucking stand there," Danny shouted, jumping down from the passenger seat in the cab. "Shut the fucking gates."

The two brothers did as they were told and fixed the chains and padlock in place once more. "What is it? What did you see?" Lili asked.

"Um. Some people are heading in this direction," Rocky replied.

"People?" Danny said. "They're not fucking people. I mean, they might have been once, but not now. We hit one. Bounced like a fucking beach ball then just got up and carried on after us. They're not fucking people," he repeated.

They didn't have to wait long to get a look for themselves. One, two, three, four, five. Within another couple of seconds, all fourteen were lined up at the gates, thrusting, smashing their bodies against them, making the chains rattle and clack as their audience watched on in slack-jawed horror. Several tried to reach their arms through the gaps in the pales. Their fingers grasped the air, desperately trying to lay a finger on one of the living, breathing entities on the other side.

"Jesus, Mary, Joseph," Lili said, crossing herself.

"Let's take care of these then do what we came here to do," Danny ordered, looking around at the other five men who had come with him. They all pulled handguns, what types exactly the two brothers had no clue, but Rocky ran in front of them, putting his hands up.

"No!" he said.

"The fuck do you mean no? I'm not having those things here when we drive out."

"Noise will bring more."

"So what do you suggest? Reading them a fucking bedtime story and hoping they'll fall asleep?"

He pointed to the bodies covered with a tarpaulin and then to the home-fashioned spears leaning against the wall. "We use those."

"You want to skewer them?"

"Using those won't run the risk of bringing more to the area."

"He's got a point, Danny," the driver of the first vehicle replied.

"Did I ask for your fucking opinion?" Something approaching a snarl appeared on Danny's face as he looked at the other man then towards Lili and finally the two brothers. "Have at it. If you want to play cowboys and Indians chucking spears at these things, that's up to you. We've got work to do."

"You're not going to help us?" Aldo asked, glancing towards the creatures once more as their excitement rose to feverish levels.

Danny put his gun away and smirked. "Nah." He turned to Lili. "I'm guessing these are your boys. They look like you. Be sure to give us a shout if they get snagged by those things. We'll put them down gently for you."

"My boys will handle things just fine. They don't need some segarsi to help them."

"Some what?" Danny asked.

"Segarsi."

"The fuck's that?"

A bitter smirk appeared on Lili's face as her two sons lowered their heads. "It means rich boy."

The two brothers looked up again. They both knew it didn't mean rich boy. It was a term Lili used on a regular basis for people she didn't like. She'd told them a long time back it was Italian for jerk off and it applied to everyone from people who barged her in the supermarket to members of parliament. That was the thing with Lili. She didn't discriminate.

"Well. I can't dispute that. I'm fucking rolling in it, I am. And I'm about to be rolling in more of it when we get this shipment out of here."

"You really think money means anything now?" Lili asked.

"Look, darling, you get back to making pizza and pasta and whatever else you Wop birds do. Let the men worry about their own business."

Lili's mouth fell open a little and she took a stride forward, ready to tear a strip off Vig's son, but she felt Aldo's hand on her shoulder. "Go inside, Mum. We'll be there soon."

Fire burned behind Lili's eyes, but she knew if she said what she wanted to it would only make things bad for her sons, so she headed towards the Portakabin. They all watched her go, but Danny was the only one with a smile on his face. It was obvious from the body language alone that he was not liked by the others, but due to who his father was, they had to obey him.

"Now, before me and the lads get loaded up, I want a little chat with that bitch who was guarding the gate the last time I was here."

"She's gone," Rocky said without hesitation.

"What do you mean she's gone?"

"She set off to town on foot."

Danny stared at the other man for a moment then sniggered. "Oh well. She'll be dead before she gets halfway there. Bitch wouldn't have lasted long anyway with a mouth like that on her." He looked to the gates once more and the fourteen rabid creatures beyond. "Time's wasting, boys. You better get to work."

※

It had been anything but a smooth ride thus far. Deano and BD had been forced to think fast as they'd run into multiple situations that would have led to the bikes being engulfed by swarms of infected unless they performed one-eighties.

They rode side by side; neither of the men wore helmets, instead giving those to their passengers. They'd developed crude but effective hand signals to communicate while travelling but had cut their engines a minute before and now they were all on foot again heading through the grounds of an old school that had been on the cusp of redevelopment before the prime minister's speech.

"We heard a broadcast," Tess said quietly. The journey up to this point had shown them time and time again how noise was a trigger for the infected, so even though the school and its grounds appeared abandoned, she didn't want to take any risks.

They all stopped for a moment. The towers of smoke were still visible in the distance and as they surveyed the horizon, they could make out other smaller streams of grey and black too. They could have been from anything, but one thing was for sure; there would be no fire engines or rescue personnel to help. There would be no nine, nine, nine calls connecting. There would be no emergency operators to take the details.

In the space of just a few hours, their worlds had fallen apart. They were by themselves, despite the promises made in the emergency alert. They each wondered how many had made it home so far, how many more would before the curfew, and what would come after the curfew. In all likelihood, nothing. Nothing good anyway. It would probably be more of the same. The infected were taking over. Gradually in some places, much more quickly in denser population centres. They were unrelenting, taking the streets by storm; taking the population by surprise. There was no negotiation with these things. They were an unstoppable force.

It had been inconceivable to many how the world beyond the UK and Ireland had fallen so quickly. Sure, there were likely to be pockets of survivors here and there, but the life, the existence that was taken for granted in this modern world had been upended in little more than a heartbeat. But now everyone got it.

It seemed like an age ago since Tess had uttered the sentence, but finally Deano responded. "A broadcast?"

"Yeah. From Dunston Primary School. People had set up a camp there for those who couldn't get home in time for the curfew or lived on the other side of the river."

"Sensible. There'll be supplies at a school. Vehicles, equipment."

"Yeah. But my point is there'll probably be a few places like that, won't there?"

"Yeah. So?"

"I'm just saying. It won't just be us."

"Probably not."

"What are you getting at, Mum?" BD asked.

"I … I don't know. I'm just thinking out loud, I suppose. It's just a shame that we can't connect with them, tell them they're not alone. Help them maybe."

"Help them?" Deano replied. "We're the ones who are out on the streets. They're all tucked up safe and sound with supplies."

"Hardly safe and sound. The power went out before we got the full picture of what was going on."

"Look. All I'm interested in right now is getting the four of us to the yard. That's it. That's all that matters. Because if we don't get there, then nothing else means a thing."

"Like I said. I was just thinking out loud. You don't need to make a thing about it."

"I'm not. I'm just saying—"

"Oh, you are. Just like you always did, always do."

"It's baffling why the two of you got divorced," Derek chipped in.

Silence reigned for a moment before Deano and Tess both chuckled. They had argued over nothing countless times in the past. Their default setting when they were married seemed to be conflict and now they were at it again.

Deano put his hands up. "You always had a big heart, Tess. It's you all over to be thinking about other people, but right now, I'm thinking about our son and you and me."

"Oh, don't worry about me. I'm not bloody here, clearly," Derek said grumpily, forcing a smile onto Deano's face again.

"Oh, stop sulking, you grumpy old codger," Tess replied, looping her arm through his.

They carried on walking, the father and son leading the way as they wheeled the bikes. "Y'know, it's something worth thinking about," BD said.

"What do you mean?"

"I mean the longer we're out here the more I'm sure that it's just us. This isn't like what happened in Leeds and Portsmouth. This isn't an organised lockdown. This is a mad scramble, every man and woman for themselves thing. This is it, Dad. I mean, think about it. The TV was pretty much reporting news in a loop over the last week or so. The internet and phones have been patchier than ever. It's like everything's been falling apart a little more each day. Sure, we've all gone about our routines and the daily briefings say that things are all heading in the right direction, but I don't buy it. I think things have been getting more and more fucked and they've just spun a story to avoid panic and now I genuinely believe we're on our own."

"You haven't said anything I disagree with, BD."

"Yeah. Well, what Mum said. Maybe banding people together wouldn't be such a bad idea. Maybe they've got it right at Dunston's. Maybe getting as many people under one roof as they can is the right way to go."

Deano carried on for a moment, mulling it over. "It's a surefire way to use up resources faster."

"Spoken like a true capitalist."

Deano laughed. "Look, BD. I can't really think about anything beyond getting us back safely. I mean, don't get me wrong, there's a lot we're going to have to talk about and plan for. But I can't plan out here."

"Okay. I get that. I'm just saying that it's something we need to keep in mind."

"Duly noted."

They continued in silence until they reached the gates at the far end of the school grounds. Beyond was another council estate. For the time being, at least, it was quiet.

"Weird, isn't it?" BD began. "You get big build-ups of them and then you get to areas where there aren't any."

"From everything I've seen, they respond to sound and movement. They'll follow sounds, they'll follow people. If an area's quiet, there's no reason for them to stay there."

"I suppose."

"So, I say we stay on foot for the time being. We can't see any, so we make the most of the quiet." He turned to look at Derek and Tess. "You two okay with that?"

"Makes sense," Derek replied.

"Are you alright walking?"

"Why the bloody hell wouldn't I be? Just because I'm in my seventies it doesn't mean I'm ready for the knacker's yard, you know."

"I was just asking, Derek. I mean, you do have a carer."

"Yes, well. She helps me with other things, but my legs are perfectly fine." It was only a small fib. He'd been wincing for the last hundred metres or so and getting sharp pains in his knee, but he wasn't about to let on.

"Okay then."

18

Aldo and Rocky had put all but six of the creatures hammering at the gate down. It had taken a while to both get into some kind of rhythm and deal with the horror of what they were seeing.

It was like something out of a childhood nightmare. These things were relentless; their growls were enough to send Arctic chills through all that heard them, but the skin, the eyes, the teeth, some still stained red by the blood and flesh of their last kill, made the brothers' stomachs churn and their hands and bodies quake a little. But they couldn't give in to the fear. They had to defend the yard, protect it for their mother, for Taki and Poppy, for Deano when he got back. This was their responsibility and one they did not take lightly.

They suddenly felt a presence behind them and turned to see Lili had re-emerged from the Portakabin. She walked across to the wall where the remainder of the makeshift spears were leaning and picked one up, gauging the weight of it in her hands before joining her two sons.

"You should go back inside," Aldo said.

"These things are going to be a big part of our lives from

now on. I need to know how to deal with them." She looked at the bodies already fallen. Each one possessed head wounds. A couple had other injuries as well, no doubt slight miscues.

"Hold the spear as close to the butt as you can without feeling off balance with it," Rocky said. "You want to keep as much distance between you and these things as possible. When you feel comfortable with the weight distribution, step forward, strike and pull back straight away. Like this."

He demonstrated, gripping the spear firmly and slightly above shoulder height. He lunged forward, cracking the spiked tip through the head of one of the beasts. He withdrew his weapon again just as quickly, almost skipping back.

"Okay," Lili said. "Let me try." She mimicked her son's action, holding the spear in both hands above shoulder height. It was a little heavier than she had first anticipated and she adjusted her grip to get a better distribution then took one, two, three breaths and lurched forward, stabbing the tip of her weapon through the gap at her nearest target. There was a clatter as the spear clacked against one of the pales and merely skimmed the side of the beast's head. "Merda!" she hissed angrily, retreating quickly as her son had demonstrated.

"It's okay. That was good for a first attempt."

"Don't patronise me, Rocky. You know I get pissed when you patronise me."

It was true. Lili had a legendary temper and patronising her was one of the worst things you could do to get onto her shit list. "I'm sorry. You're right. That was lousy."

Lili glared at him for a moment then laughed. "If this was any other time, you'd get such a slap for that." She had tried to acclimatise herself to seeing and hearing the infected. She'd watched her sons at work putting these creatures out of their misery before joining them. But for all her efforts, being so close had freaked her out more than she had let on and that's why her aim had gone astray.

The sight, the sound, the smell. Everything about them was terrifying. The eyes. *Those fucking eyes.* Now she was close up, the eyes were more of a focus than ever. Cloudy grey with wild, dancing ebony pupils, seemingly flaring with fevered anticipation as they fixed on their prey.

The growls emanating from the backs of their throats as if they were rabid animals set to pounce were impossible to ignore and, even though she knew they could not reach her, they could not stretch beyond the bounds of their own physiology, there was something that stirred up untold fear as she made that step forward.

She took a breath, still determined not to show weakness in front of her boys as she got into position again.

"Okay," Rocky said. "Maybe hold the spear a little further up the shaft. It will mean you get closer to them, but it will give you better balance. I think you missed because you overreached a bit."

She shuffled her fingers along a little as her son suggested, took another deep breath and then struck again. This time, the spike shot through the gap unencumbered and spiked its target straight through the bridge of its nose. The ghoulish monster fell back. "AGGHH!" A frightened scream left Lili's mouth as the spear disappeared through the aperture with him.

She had followed it for a split second before her two sons reached out, grabbing her shoulders and stopping her from nearing the gate.

"It's okay," Aldo said. "We've got plenty of spears. You got one. That's the most important thing. You got one."

Lili looked between the other jostling figures to see the creature she had put down lying still with the spear still sticking out of its head, albeit at an angle now that some of the bone fragments around it had disintegrated. She tried to control her breathing, but for a moment it bordered on hyperventilation, and then she forced herself to bring it under control once more. When she did, she marched over to the wall and grabbed another spear in both hands. "You boys stand back. I clearly need to practice."

*

"I don't understand this," Splodge said as the others began to reload the wagons that had only been unloaded that very morning. "I mean, we only just dropped this stuff off. Why are we picking it all up again?"

"You questioning my dad?" Danny asked. Splodge had always done his job, always done what Vig and, by extension, Danny had asked him, but with everything that was going on outside the fences, this seemed like a dangerous waste of time. All he wanted to do was go home like the others. But Vig and Danny weren't people to say no to.

"Course not. I just don't understand."

"The sheer weight of what you don't understand would sink an aircraft carrier."

"Just saying," he replied almost apologetically. "Your dad only had us deliver this stuff here this morning."

Danny stared at the other man for a moment. "Well, things have changed a bit since this morning, haven't they?"

"I suppose."

"We stashed this stuff here until we knew there wouldn't be any heat on it. Well, I don't know if you've noticed, but plod's got other things on his mind right now, and when people realise that they can't just go down to the local corner shop to get a can of beef casserole, they're going to pay whatever we're asking so they can keep their families fed. Before, this stuff was just going to be a nice little side hustle. After this morning, it's going to be a fucking goldmine, and the way things are going out there, we don't want to be getting in a lorry and coming out here every time we want to fulfil a fucking order. We're going to have everything nice and central at the club."

The club had changed hands numerous times before Vig took over. It had been a working men's club, a social club and the previous owner had even tried to run it as a small concert hall.

Before all that, it had been a mill, but over the years, it had been adapted. Surrounded by a tall brick wall, it gave Vig and the patrons no small amount of privacy, which was just as well considering what went on there. It consisted of a sizeable main hall and bar with a network of private rooms at the back. An annex had been built and Vig was in the process of applying for an operating licence to turn it into a casino before the prime minister's speech. He called it the Pleasure Palace, although the grimy nature of the outer structure and the even grimier nature of the goings on made the name bitterly ironic.

It was famous in the area and beyond and everyone knew where the Pleasure Palace was. They knew who owned it. They knew what went on there. They knew who frequented it and they knew that if they needed anything from a high-risk loan to drugs to a weapon to a short-term vehicle rental, no questions asked, then that was the place to go. They also knew that if they wanted to just kick back and enjoy a show, private or public, with or without extra service, then their needs would be catered for too.

It was positioned on the edge of one of the biggest council estates in the area and Danny had questioned the wisdom of them staying there considering what was happening, but Vig was all about the numbers. He'd seen all the angles, seen the potential for how he could turn this disaster to his advantage.

Yes, the danger of the infected was a concern, but the place was already like a castle. After the gang war of 2005, he'd spent the best part of half a million fortifying it. That had been like something straight out of a Mario Puzo novel. It had been a crazy and dangerous time. But they had come out the other side. This was something very different, however, but Vig believed those same security measures would be the things to keep them safe now.

Danny wasn't so sure, but Danny did what his father said. "I was thinking," Splodge began as the others continued to unload the containers.

"That's a fucking scary thought right there." There was a pause. "Okay. Go on then. What were you thinking?"

"I was thinking that maybe me and the lads could head off after we've got this stuff to the club."

"Oh, is that what you were thinking?"

"Yeah."

"Listen. Who pays your wages?"

"Well … Vig."

"Yeah. Exactly. He pays your wages and he tells you when to jump. He tells you where to jump and he tells you how high to fucking jump. He's also the one to tell you when it's knocking-off time."

"Yeah. Course. Sorry, Danny. It's just that the boys are nervous. They're worried about their families and stuff."

Danny looked at the other man with irritation for a moment before his expression mellowed a little. "Listen. Whatever this thing is, one way or another, we'll get to the other side of it. Since all this began, it's been like a licence to print money and this'll be no different. After today, things'll settle down a bit. There'll be relief trucks, and supply trucks, and weapons trucks flooding the streets. We're going to be rolling in so much lolly we won't know what to do. So, I get that you want to see your families, but everything we do today sets us up for whatever's happening next, yeah?"

Splodge nodded reluctantly. "Yeah."

"Right. Now. You be a good boy and make sure these trucks get loaded. I'm going to have a little shufty around to see if there's anything else worth taking back to the club."

"Okay, boss."

Danny smiled. He liked it when they called him boss, or chief, or guv. Usually, these terms were reserved for his father, but when someone referred to him as such it was a nod as if to say that he'd be next.

"Good boy."

It took Splodge everything he had not to lay Danny out there and then. He seethed as he watched the other man walk away. *Good boy? Does he think I'm a fucking dog? I'm a year older than that little cunt.*

The moment Danny disappeared out of sight, one of the other men, Tank, so-called because he was built like one, walked up to him. "Did you ask him?"

Splodge exhaled deeply. "Yeah. I asked him."

"And what did he say?"

"Well, the gist was shut your fucking mouth and do what I tell you."

Despite his size and his ability to evoke fear in some of the most stolid figures in the London underworld, Tank was quite soft underneath. He lived with his girlfriend, his mum, and his dad in a small semi that his parents had worked all their lives to pay for. He'd do anything for his family and they were what he was thinking about more than anything.

He wanted to be there with them to protect them. Tank hadn't really been out in the streets. He'd pretty much spent most of the day loading, unloading and driving. The first time he or any of the others had seen infected was on the journey to the scrapyard, but that didn't mean they hadn't heard the rumours that had been circulating all morning with growing foreboding. It didn't mean he didn't understand what the sirens, the helicopters, and the bombing raid meant. They all did. They all just wanted to get back to their loved ones, and if this was anything else, if they were working for anyone else, then they all probably would have done without a second thought.

But they weren't shop assistants or librarians or bus conductors or office clerks. They couldn't simply stop what they were doing and walk out. If any of them did that to Vig, no matter what the situation was, there would be ramifications not just for them but their families too. So, that was why they were all still there, loading the wagons that had been unloaded just a few hours before rather than being at home.

"It's getting really bad out there," Tank eventually replied.

"Forget getting. It *is* really bad out there."

"I want to be with my girl. I want to be with my mum and dad."

"Now don't go getting any crazy thoughts in your head," Splodge said, laying a comforting hand on the big man's arm. "Look. Let's get this done. Hopefully, by the time we get it dropped off at the club, Vig might have had a change of heart."

"Do you think so?"

"Yeah. Sure. Why not?"

*

Vig stood in what was once the floor manager's office at the old mill but was now his management suite. He wasn't like a lot of the other bosses who'd had the family business handed down to them. He'd worked his way up, grifting, grafting, and, when the time had come, taking. He'd seized power in a grand coup d'etat in the early nineties and never looked back.

He was hard edged, uncompromising, and his single greatest talent was being able to see the angles long before others. This latest kink in the chain was just another, as far as he was concerned. Whether it was a lockdown like Leeds and Portsmouth or something more widespread, something more permanent, it didn't matter for the moment. Being on top was all about taking advantage of situations and that's what he was doing.

While most of his peers would be running for cover, keeping their heads down until the all-clear sounded, or at least until they had a better idea of what was going on, he was taking full advantage of the situation. It was obvious that the police were going to be occupied. Organised crime wouldn't even be on their radar on a day like today or tomorrow or the day after for that matter.

Since the prime minister's speech, his business had flourished like never before. *Angles. Angles is what it's all about.*

He had seen angles everywhere. The mass conscription programme had involved anyone who was out of work and even those who were retired but able bodied. He had deliberately taken a number of names off his books so they could become moles in the various organisations to which the conscripts were recruited. Textile factories, utilities, the NHS, the army, the special constabulary—the latter always brought him particular amusement.

All his moles gave him access to information that he would have had to go hunting for otherwise. He found out about shipments, stores, depots and more besides. Hence the fact that if you went down to the beer cellar at the Pleasure Palace, you'd find a newly constructed underground warehouse, the building of which had been expedited soon after the PM's speech, full of everything from underwear, jeans, clothes and uniforms to vehicle supplies, stolen shipments of materials for the construction of polytunnels and greenhouses to weapons and everything in between.

The club was the club. Booze, strippers, it was a good-time place and, to many punters, that's all it was. But those who knew could ask one of the bar staff for a meet with a trader; that's what Vig called them. A few minutes later, they would be escorted by a dancer, seemingly with a view to getting a private show but instead being given a few minutes in one of the negotiation rooms behind the main hall.

He'd got it all down to a fine art, but this latest development was going to require a little more finessing. Like many of those he had working for him, he hadn't even laid eyes on one of the infected until the three lorries had set off back to Deano's yard. Then several creatures had appeared from somewhere within the estate, presumably drawn by the sounds of the engines.

His men had managed to close the chain link gates before any got inside. After some discussion, they had then gone about neutralising them. Up until that point, it had all been theory, but today, the theory was put to the test and the four would-be attackers were put down quietly with snapped mop and sweeping brush handles; quite ironic given some of the munitions supplies that were available to them.

No more creatures had appeared, but their sudden rallying at the slightest noise made the cogs in Vig's head begin to whir. He had envisaged the Pleasure Palace becoming a hub of sorts for the local community, the last supermarket standing, albeit a supermarket that gouged its customers. But it was clear that there was no way they could have the gates open as if it was any other day.

So, the moment the attacking creatures were put down, he got his staff on the job of building a service window. Two of the men laughed at his suggestion, believing it to be a joke until his glare silenced them. Built into the wall next to the gate was a post box. Before everything had changed, one of Vig's daily rituals had been to collect the mail. He could have got any one of his many minions to do it, but he loved collecting the mail. Before the internet became decidedly patchy, some of the rooms behind the main hall were for the Pleasure Palace camgirls. They were open 24/7. And just like the girls inside the club itself, punters could pay the camgirls for private sessions. They could also purchase photos, videos, items of personal clothing, the list went on.

Vig paid the girls well and so they were happy to accommodate him when he suggested a side hustle, which, until the whole online bubble burst thanks to a deteriorating internet connection, had been incredibly lucrative. During the private sessions, the girls convinced many a punter that they were hard up, struggling even, and what they got paid for their work barely covered the bills. They told them that when they were out of the financial jams they found themselves in they would visit, maybe even go on vacation together.

Vig had found it amazing how many desperate men would blindly send cheques and even cash to a P.O. Box. He had set up business bank accounts in all of the camgirls' screen names. The girls themselves would get a thirty-three percent cut of any income from the venture, which was only fair. After all, they were doing the hard work. Every morning, when Vig had gone to collect the mail, his face had lit up. There were often dozens of envelopes. Some of the men sent photos and long letters with the payments. Others sent cards. It was what set him apart from the other gangsters. He was always thinking outside the box what next. There was always another rock to turn over with a tonne of cash underneath it.

And so, as he stood at the window breathing in the smoke of what was probably one of the last few real Cuban cigars in existence, a mix of emotions ran through him. He was sad to see the post box removed from the wall and replaced by what was essentially a small metal door with a viewing grille and drawer, which had been hastily constructed by his people. That post box had brought him many a happy memory. But times changed and businesses had to change with them. It had never been his ambition to run a post-apocalyptic cash and carry, but here he was and he knew it was going to be a goldmine.

It was why he'd sent more of his men out to roll over whatever shops, stores and suppliers they could before the curfew. No one really knew what would happen after four p.m. The streets could be teaming with soldiers, police or both and, even with his contacts, he probably wouldn't be able to arrange favourable terms for his people. You could grease local wheels pretty easily, but when it came to government mandates that was something else. He didn't mix in the right circles to pay off MPs and the military, even though there were those within the ranks of both who owed him.

He sucked in another mouthful of smoke and froze as a single grey creature began its charge from the top of the street towards the men who were working where the post box had been removed. He couldn't see the two on the outside, but the ones on the inside were safe for the moment as they slid the newly constructed hatch into position.

After witnessing the first attempted attack when the trucks had left earlier, it was easy to understand how these things had multiplied so quickly and even though, for the time being, there was just one of them, it didn't mean it was nothing to worry about. One could become two, four, eight, sixteen in a heartbeat.

He looked towards his men. The ones working on the hatch were oblivious to the charging beast. He turned towards the two guards on the gate. Both were smoking and in conversation with each other as if this was just any other day.

Fucking idiots.

He finally breathed out and a cloud of blue smoke blurred the image momentarily before he strode forward and pulled the window open. He did not shout, instead clapping his hands loudly like some irritable school master and pointing in the direction of the approaching danger.

Everyone turned towards him, including the ones hard at work on the hatch. It was the two guards he was focused on, however. He cast a steely glare towards them and they immediately dropped their cigarettes. They had firearms, but they were a last resort. Instead, they pulled machetes, the go-to weapons of every wannabe gangster kid, and they ran forward, stopping about ten metres in front of the gate, making sure they were the focus of attention and not the workers.

The creature pounced before either man had truly readied themselves. It grasped the guard to the right and both fell to the ground. The second man was glued to the spot in terror for a moment. Finally, he burst into action, grabbing the beast by the scruff of its collar and pulling it off his friend.

It toppled back and the second guard hacked down with his weapon, slicing through the monster's head and rendering it still on the ground. He remained standing over it for just a moment before turning to his compatriot, who lay motionless. He got down on his hands and knees, placing his fingers up to the other man's neck to find a pulse, but before he could, the creature's victim, now one of the risen himself, lunged.

It had been just seconds since the initial confrontation, but it was easy to see how everything could fall apart if this wasn't dealt with. The gates were slightly ajar and for the first time in a long, long time, fear and uncertainty shuddered through Vig.

He put the cigar in the corner of his mouth, gently gripping it between his teeth, and ran across to his desk, pulling open the bottom drawer. There, beneath an old lever arch file, was the sawn-off shotgun he'd confiscated from Danny's pal who had been on the nighttime raid with him.

He had thought about taking this to Deano as well, but as it hadn't even been discharged, there was little point. He broke it, checking it was loaded, and then ran out of the room and down the stairs. It was dark near the bottom as the small landing window provided the only light in the absence of electricity. He ran along the even darker corridor past the doors of all the private rooms and out into the main hall where the bar and stage were. Lanterns lit the place and at least a dozen men sat around waiting to be released so they could go home to their families.

He pulled the cigar from his mouth. "Everyone outside, now. Make sure you're fucking carrying," he cried without missing a step. He tore towards the entrance as everyone scrambled after him and the cool air chilled a little more as a piercing scream rose from somewhere out of sight.

He looked beyond the gates to see no sign of either of his guards. He turned towards the hatch and the two men who had been hard at work a moment before were retreating, as if the hatch itself was about to spring at them.

But it was the sound beyond that which filled them with fear, the sound of the other two workers in agony as they were attacked by their former comrades.

"Where do you want us, Vig?" one of his lieutenants piling out of the club doors asked.

"The gates. Lock the fucking gates," he ordered, placing the cigar in the corner of his mouth once more and marching forward with the shotgun braced against his shoulder ready.

"No worries, boss."

He glanced to his right to see another group of men who, up until a moment before, had been unloading two more vans of food and supplies into the cellar in preparation for this new venture but now were charging towards the entrance to the grounds.

"We can't let one of those things get in here. Y'hear me?"

"Don't worry, Vig. We're on it," someone shouted back.

The screams of the two victims continued for several seconds more before falling silent. At that same instant, the first of Vig's soldiers reached the gate. It rang like a bell as it clanged shut and the lock engaged. Another couple of seconds passed and the two original guards, now turned, threw themselves at the chain links.

Most of those present had been there when the three trucks had departed and infected had stormed towards the entrance, but this was the first time they had witnessed some of their own people turning. They were all taken aback, slowly gathering around like gawkers at a freak show. A little more time passed and the pair were joined by their victims, the two men who had been working on the outside of the wall.

Still no one acted, they all just watched on in horror. These were men they had done jobs with, shared drinks and good times with, and now they could no longer accurately be described as men at all. They were things. Undead things. Monsters, for all intents and purposes.

Even Vig froze for a moment as he reached the crowd. The cigar still hung from the corner of his mouth as he watched the four beasts continue to throw themselves at the chain link gate, making it rattle each time.

"That's Calum. That's Calum," one of the men cried incredulously as he watched his one-time friend.

Vig took the cigar out of his mouth and cleared his throat. "Right. This is shit. There's no two ways about it. These were our boys, but we can all see they're not our fucking boys anymore." His words were given greater emphasis as one of the creatures pressed its face hard against the metal links, creating a blooded grid on its skin. "This is what we have to do. We have to put these things down. Finish up that hatch and get the rest of the stuff from those vans into the cellar. I want everybody out here until that's done. Everybody understand?"

Muted acknowledgements circulated throughout the small crowd and Vig stayed in position for a moment longer before turning and heading back to the club.

19

Deano and BD had been forced to take a few detours. They had run into a couple of packs here and there, which meant travelling faster and louder than they were happy with, but they had avoided confrontation with them. They had to stop on a few occasions to take out the odd one or two infected that were blocking their way, but in the past five minutes, they had returned to wheeling the bikes rather than riding them and they hadn't seen a soul, living human or other.

The distribution of the infected was sporadic, but it was clear it would only get worse as time went on. "At least we're in the closing strait now. It won't be long before we're at the yard," Deano said.

"Then why the bloody hell aren't we riding there rather than walking there?" Derek demanded.

"Because I don't want to lead a load of these bastards right up to my front door, that's why."

"Well … I suppose you know what you're doing."

"Thanks for the vote of confidence. That means the world to me."

"The mystery of why Tess ran away from her vows of holy matrimony only deepens by the second." He turned to his carer. "How could you possibly let this one get away?"

"Oh, fuck," Deano blurted and slowed down to a stop as a small shop on the corner came into view. It was a combined newsagent and grocer. There were grilles over the windows, but the door had caved inward and the once heaving shelves beyond were virtually empty.

"What's wrong?" BD asked.

"I know the owners of this place."

They all stared in the direction of the dark interior. It was devoid of life like the rest of the street.

"You think it was looted?"

"That would be my guess."

"Doesn't this place belong to Hagop and Nune?" Tess asked, stepping forward to join Deano.

"Who are Hagop and Nune?" BD replied.

"Garo the Armenian's mum and dad," Deano answered.

"What is it with you? How come virtually every Christian name that comes out of your mouth is followed by 'the' and then some place name or geographical stereotype?"

Deano shrugged. "That's just what he's known as."

"I'm guessing he belongs to the seemingly bottomless well of underworld inhabitants with no surnames."

"I think a lot of people called him that so they know to stay clear."

"Why?"

"Because you don't wanna fucking mess with the Armenians."

"Looks like someone missed the newsflash, Dad," BD said, gesturing towards the open door and empty shop beyond.

"Yeah," Deano replied, drifting towards the entrance.

"It's obvious that whatever went on here is over and done with. Don't you think we should be on our way?" Derek asked.

"In a minute." Deano looked up and down the street to make sure it was still clear then turned back to his son. "You see anything, you shout."

"I don't want to sound insensitive, Dad, but I think Derek's right."

"Ring out them bells," Derek chuntered. "The senile old

man's making sense."

Deano ignored him and carried on. He crossed the threshold to the small shop and examined the frame and the door. The glass behind the grille had shattered. It looked like the door itself had been struck by some kind of battering ram as a good portion of the frame had splintered too.

"Hagop? Nune?" he called out, stepping a little further inside. The door behind the counter had suffered a similar fate to the entrance and as he looked around the store, there were only hints as to what it had been before the raid. It was like fifty contestants had played *Supermarket Sweep* and piled everything into trolleys, leaving the shelves empty. The odd piece of stock littered the floor, a bottle of baby oil here, a cheap pair of sunglasses there, but most everything else was gone. "Hagop? Nune?" he called out again.

There was a shriek as the buckled door behind the counter separated from the frame and a man with a dressed wound on his head stepped out carrying a kitchen knife. A woman stood behind him with a similar weapon. When they saw who the caller was, they both relaxed.

"Deano," Hagop said.

"What the hell happened?"

"It was Vig's men."

"Vig did this?"

"They took everything. They demanded the money from the safe too. They took Nune's jewellery. They took everything."

"But ... I don't understand. You've always had an arrangement."

Most businesses in the area paid protection to Vig. However, Hagop and Nune's place was protected under the wing of an Armenian gang and so no one ever interfered with their business, especially as their son, Garo, was one of the gang's most notorious enforcers.

"It looks like the arrangement is off."

"They took the money from the till. They took the stock in the back. They took everything, Deano," Nune said, stepping out a little further into the shop. "They even took food from our cupboards."

Deano ran his fingers through his hair. "I'm guessing you haven't seen anything of Garo."

"The phone is dead. We cannot reach him."

"What are you going to do?"

Hagop shook his head. He was just a little older than Deano. "I don't know. I think maybe we will try to get to Garo's flat. We have a key."

"I wouldn't do that," Deano replied. "It's bad out there. I mean really bad. We went to Belmont Hill to get Tess and we barely got out alive. The streets are filling up with infected."

"I think this is why Vig has done this," Nune said. "It is not just punishment for not paying him off for all these years, but he realises there will be no retribution." Her eyes were heavy and it was clear that her mascara had run due to tears, but she had done her best to hide it and she was doing her best to stay strong now.

"You come with us," Tess said from the doorway and everyone turned around to look at her, although no one knew how long she'd been standing there.

"What?"

"You come with us," she repeated. "We're heading to the yard."

"What is at the yard?"

"Not a lot. I'll grant you that. There's not going to be much in the way of comfort and when Deano and BD first spoke about the idea, I probably had the same look of horror on my face that you've got now."

"Thanks," Deano said under his breath.

"But I've been out on those streets and they're terrifying and only going to get worse. Don't even think about trying to undertake a journey like the one you're suggesting. Many of the roads are gridlocked. If you set off in a car to a built-up area, you'll be forced to abandon it." She turned to look at Nune specifically. "I get what you're feeling. Up until a little while ago, I didn't know if my Bertie was alive or not. I know what it's like for a mother to have that not knowing in your heart. But heading out there will do nothing but get you killed."

"But—"

"Tess is right," Deano said, taking over. "If anyone can look after himself, it's Garo. He's a bright boy." *Scary as fuck, too.* He turned to look at Hagop. "You need to do what's best for you right now. You can't stay here. You've got no protection, no food."

"We have the flat upstairs. If we barricade this door," he

said, pointing to the one behind the counter, "we will be safe."

"You'll be safe with no food, no supplies, and no electricity. You can't eat thin air, Hagop. Come with us. Yeah, it's not going to be the Ritz, but we've got shelter and food. We've got heat."

The other man looked towards his wife. They had been part of an Armenian community in Egypt before moving to the UK. They had known each other since childhood. She was the love of his life and vice versa. It was his mission to look after her, keep her safe, provide for her, and this shop had done that for so many years, but now the dream was over. "I cannot expect my wife to live in a scrapyard, Deano."

"Listen. It's not my intention to stay there until the end of time. Y'know how in the war people used to flood into the underground or duck into bomb shelters when the German planes flew over? Well, this is that, Hagop. The planes are flying over. Earlier this morning, they were literally flying over. We just need somewhere safe to sit out the storm. That's all this is, sitting out the storm. It might be for a few days or a few weeks, but at least we'll be safe there."

"Deano's right," Tess said. "I mean, look what they've done to this place. They've left you with nothing."

"The shed," Nune said suddenly. "They didn't take what was in the shed."

"What's in the shed?" Deano asked.

"The things that are not kept out all year around. Bags of compost in the spring and summer, Charcoal and disposable barbecues, bags of logs for the winter."

"Well, that's not really anything that will come in useful for us right now, but I'm glad they didn't clean you out completely."

The momentary excitement that lit Nune's face was gone again and she turned to her husband. "We will leave a message here for Garo."

"You're serious? You want to go?"

"To stay is to die."

"No. I will find a way."

"Hagop," Deano began. "I've lost count of the number of times you've helped me. Don't let pride stop you from coming with us. There's no defeat in this. Defeat would be dying and letting Nune die too."

Hagop closed his eyes and shook his head. "When we came here, I never thought for a moment that I would end up a pauper depending on charity."

"That is the opposite of what this is. This is payback for everything you've done for me in the past. And nothing has ended. There's a next, Hagop. Something will come after this; we just don't know what yet. And whatever happens, I want people around me who I know and can trust and will work and do whatever needs doing to keep their family and my family safe. This isn't charity; this is a trade. This is a proposition made for mutual benefit."

The other man studied Deano's face and Nune sidled up to her husband, taking his hand in hers and squeezing it tightly. "Please, Hagop," she whispered.

"Very well. We will come."

Deano's face broke into a genuine smile. "Good. That's good. Now, go throw a couple of bags together. I know there's not too far to go, but we're better doing it as one convoy and as quickly as we can."

"I should bring the van?"

"We might be pushing it to get two passengers with luggage on each of the bikes."

"You never lived in Egypt. Whole families used to travel on a single bike," Hagop replied with a smile.

"I think it would be better with the van. Bring whatever you think might be useful, but be quick about it. Things are getting worse out there all the time."

The man and wife disappeared through the door behind the counter and Deano and Tess listened as they heard them running up the stairs.

"That was nice of you to say those things," Tess said when she was sure there was no way she'd be heard.

"Nice nothing. I was serious. I've lost count of the number of times the two of them helped me out."

"They're good people."

"They are."

"There are a lot of good people out there who aren't going to make it."

"Yeah. There are."

"Y'know, you were pretty quick to dismiss what Nune said about the stuff in the shed."

"What do you mean?"

"I mean wood, the barbecues, compost. If we're stuck in that yard for a few days and then get evacuated, then yeah, it's all probably a bit redundant. But if this is it, Deano. If this is the end of everything, then don't you think those things might be useful?"

"Well—"

"I mean, yeah, we're in May, but it's been pretty chilly. Hopefully summer will be better, but it will go quick. I don't know how many bottles of Calor gas you've got back at the yard, but they're not going to last forever, and—"

"Okay, okay. Point made. When they come back down, we'll get everything loaded onto his van."

"Is everything okay in here?" BD asked.

They both turned to the doorway." "Yeah. They're just getting a couple of bags and then we're going to get all the stuff they've got in their shed."

"Oh yeah. I wouldn't want to be facing the apocalypse without some garden chairs and a lawnmower."

"They've got logs and compost," Tess replied.

DB raised his left eyebrow. "Actually, that might be pretty useful."

"What's happening out there?" Deano asked.

"It's quiet. We wheeled the bikes into the alley so we can't be seen from the road, but it's deserted for the moment."

"Small mercies, I suppose."

"There is something though."

"What?" his mum and dad replied in unison.

"It's hard to describe. You can't hear it all the time, but it's like there's a weird sound on the breeze. I can't quite figure out what it is."

"What do you mean a weird sound?"

"Well, come and listen for yourself."

All three of them headed back outside and stood in the street. As BD had said, it was empty.

"There you bloody are. I thought you might have been taking forty winks in there or something," Derek said, joining them from around the corner of the alley where he had been keeping an eye on the street.

"I can't hear anything," Tess said.

"I told you. It comes in fits and starts on the breeze."

"I don't know what he's talking about," Derek replied. "I can't hear a bloody thing."

"Well, that's no surprise. You're half deaf," Tess replied. "The volume you have that radio on sometimes is—"

"Shush!" BD ordered, holding his finger up.

Tess stopped in mid-sentence and concentrated hard, trying to hear what her son had heard. She and Deano screwed their faces up in concentration. "I don't hear anything," Tess said.

"Seriously?"

"I'm sorry, Bertie. I don't hear a thing."

"Yeah. Me neither, BD," Deano added.

"Listen. Really concentrate."

"I am. I don't—" The words stalled in his father's mouth as he heard a sound.

"You heard it?"

"I heard something."

"I still can't hear a th—" Now it was Tess's turn as the noise drifted towards her. "Oh. Yes. I do hear something. What is it?"

"That's what I'm trying to figure out," BD replied.

"You're all barking mad if you ask me. There's not a thing to be heard beyond our own voices."

"Be quiet, Derek," Tess snapped.

"Oh yes, be quiet, Derek," he grumbled. "Nobody listen to the voice of reason. He's just an old man. Well, I tell you what," he said, speaking louder to no one in particular, "this old man's still got all his faculties, you know. I'm not to be admonished like some petulant child."

"Derek, please!"

"There it is again," Deano said, just about managing to ignore the tête-à-tête between the grumpy old actor and Tess. "It's like a drone."

"No," BD replied. "Even big drones don't make that kind of sound."

Deano looked confused for a minute. "No. I don't mean a flying drone. I mean like a droning sound."

"Oh. Right. Yeah. I suppose it is. Do you think it's like some big engine or a load of engines or something?"

"Like plane engines?" Deano asked, looking up at the skies.

"I dunno. Maybe. It just sounds … weird."

"Whatever it is, it sounds like it's a long way from here."

"Yeah."

"I.…"

"What is it, Mum?"

"Nothing."

"What is it, Tess?" Deano asked.

"I think … no. It doesn't matter. My head's fried. My mind's playing tricks."

"Finally," Derek said. "Someone's beginning to see sense."

"What is it, Tess?" Deano persisted.

"I think it's them."

"Them?"

"The infected."

The sound was gone again as they all listened. "It'd have to be a hell of a lot of them, Tess. I mean, that's a wall of sound we're talking about."

The breeze wisped around them once more and, this time, even Derek heard the noise they'd all been discussing. "Good God. Is that what you're all blethering on about?"

"Yes," Tess replied.

Any remaining colour drained from the old man's cheeks as the noise repeated. "She's right. That's not the sound of bloody engines. That's a dirge if ever I've heard one."

Not for the first time that day, the air suddenly seemed colder around them in the space of a few seconds.

"Okay. Now the shits are well and truly up me. Thanks, Tess," Deano said.

"Nice."

"You can't plant a thought like that and not expect people to react."

"I just told you what I was hearing, that's all."

"We need to get out of here. I'm going to go get Hagop's keys for the van so we can get loaded up."

20

The sound of the forklifts played a steady hum somewhere in the centre of the scrapyard. All Taki and Poppy knew was that they were far enough away not to cause them any concern. Petal had gone off for a wander a moment before leaving the two young women sitting shoulder to shoulder with their backs to the body of the big double-decker bus.

They'd thought about going in, but if they were discovered, they'd be trapped, whereas this way there were a few options if they needed to make a run for it.

"Deano's been forever," Poppy said sadly.

There were a hundred markers in Taki's head for each time this thought had passed through her mind too. "Well, at least Aldo and Rocky got that food put to one side, so when he and BD do get back, that'll be one less headache."

"Yeah. Yeah, I suppose you're right." It was obvious the other woman was just trying to make her feel better, but Poppy was more than happy to buy into the lie for the moment.

"It's funny, isn't it?" Poppy began. "You work hard to get money to buy things you think are important. Y'know, makeup, nice shoes, a bit of bling. But when it all comes down to it, none of that stuff is important. I mean, y'know, look at us. I'd trade all my handbags for one of those SAS survival books or something now. That might actually help in a situation like this. What's a five-hundred-quid handbag going to do?"

"I was never really one for glam, but I'm in the same boat. I put my money into a savings account for a rainy day, but what was the point? What was I thinking? I just put all my faith in the government and the system and thought if we stand, we stand together; if we fall, we fall together. I didn't think there was ever going to be an in between. I thought when the end came, it would be all at once like it was in the other countries, but I suppose there was a part of me that kind of shut all that out."

"What do you mean?"

"I mean I lost contact with my family pretty much overnight. I didn't know what happened and there was a part of me that hoped they'd clung on despite what everyone was saying. Then there was another part that didn't really want to think about that possibility. I mean, imagine my gran being in a position like we are in now. I think I just got it into my head that it happened, and it happened quick, and that was the end of it. There was no suffering, no pain, no fear. That's how I coped. If I'd have thought about it a little more, if I'd have given in to the possibility that there were other options then maybe I'd be a bit more prepared for this, but I just blocked it all out and—"

The sound of gravel crunching underfoot silenced Taki in a single breath. Poppy reached out, grabbing her new friend's hand and they both sat there on the ground like children playing a deathly game of hide and seek. Fear filled both of them. They hoped it might be Rocky or Aldo, but they couldn't take the risk to break cover and peek.

Whoever it was climbed onto the bus and both women scrunched their legs up tightly in the hope that the lone passenger did not catch sight of them out of the side window.

They held their breath as the footsteps walked up and down then began to ascend the staircase.

"What should we do?" Poppy whispered.

"Stay put. If it's Rocky or Aldo, they'll probably call out."

"What if it's not and they find us?"

"Let's not think about that, eh?"

The feet started moving again, this time down the stairs.

Crunch. Whoever it was hit the gravel once more and continued their journey. The two women remained frozen, fingers intertwined, just waiting as the seconds ticked on and on. Gradually, the footsteps began to move away, fading into the distance.

They both exhaled loud, deep breaths and finally released their grips. "That was close."

"You can say that again." Taki was about to continue the conversation they'd been having when she heard the sound of churning gravel once more. "Oh shit!" she hissed and Poppy grabbed her hand for comfort again.

Seconds later, Petal appeared around the corner with her tongue lolling out of the side of her mouth and her tail wagging wildly. Both women laughed as the happy Rottweiler bounded up to them. Firstly, she stopped by the side of Taki, who stroked her and ruffled her collar, before stepping over their extended legs, walking around twice in a circle and nestling down beside Poppy, who placed a hand on the canine's back and slowly began to tease her hair as much for her own comfort as that of Petal.

"So. You were saying about your family," Poppy said.

"Yeah. So—"

"Well, well, fucking well." A voice shattered the calm that Petal's arrival had brought and both women's heads shot around to see Danny standing there. The hatred he harboured for the pair was evident on his face.

Poppy and Taki used the bus to slide up to their feet. They still weren't sure what was coming next or what they were going to do, but they had more options standing than sitting. "Look. We don't want any trouble," Taki said. "Just get what you came for and leave us alone."

The vicious snarl that had been ever present on Danny's face since laying eyes on the two women turned to a wicked grin. "You might not want any trouble, but that boat sailed when you didn't let me in here, bitch. I gave you plenty of opportunities, but you thought it would be a better use of your time to mouth off." He turned to Poppy. "And you." His eyes flared. "You think you can fucking try to dob me in without any consequences? You've been listening to the fairy stories your punters have been feeding you for too long, you fucking slag." He took a step towards them and they both retreated.

Petal was standing as well now and Poppy's leg nudged

her a little as she shuffled away.

"I don't know who you think you are that you can talk to people like this, you prick," Taki said, her anger getting the better of her.

The nerve of the woman, any woman, daring to speak to him in such a manner sent a wave of fury through Danny. He leapt forward, grabbing Taki by her thick, black curly hair. "Let's see how fucking brave you stay when there isn't a gate between us, you little—"

"GRRRAAA!" It was a cross between a growl and a bark but rooted with hatred from the very pit of Petal's stomach. Her entire forty-five-kilogram frame launched at Danny like a guided missile.

Before he knew what had hit him, his body smashed back against the side of the bus, his head bouncing, the pain forcing him to let go of Taki's hair. This was just the first wave of the attack, though, and Petal pounced again, this time, knocking him over and down onto the ground. She grabbed hold of his upper right arm, her teeth closing around it like a vice. Crimson fountains immediately began to gush as a childlike scream of agony made the air around them quake.

There were already tears in his eyes as he started reaching into his jacket. The events unfolded so quickly that neither Poppy nor Taki could process them. Until they spotted the gun in Danny's hand that was. Then time seemed to stand still.

"NOOO!" Poppy screamed.

"NOOO!" Taki echoed. She'd always loved animals, dogs in particular, and the thought of one getting hurt caused her physical pain in her heart, especially one that had sacrificed its own safety to protect her. Red mist engulfed her and she suddenly remembered the cause of the discomfort in the back of her jeans. She reached around, withdrawing the weapon and aiming it towards the man on the ground as he tried to gather himself while the Rottweiler continued to tear at his arm. *He's really going to shoot her.* Taki pulled the trigger but nothing happened. She dropped the gun, instead diving on top of Danny and grabbing his arm.

She managed to pin it down as he writhed, flailed and screamed. "GET IT! GET HIS GUN!" she ordered as the battle continued. "GET HIS FUCKING GUN, POPPY!" she cried again, using all her weight and force to hold Danny's left hand down on the ground as he continued to try to buck her.

Poppy ran around the scrapping trio, stamping down hard on Danny's wrist. His fingers splayed, letting go of the weapon, and she swooped down, picking it up. She was as angry as Taki for what he had tried to do, angrier in fact. She hated this man with a passion long before today. He had taken so much from her in the past and to see him struggling and weak perked her soul a little. She brought her foot up and then plunged it down hard on his face. The sound of his nose breaking trumped the growls and screams for a split second. There was an eruption of blood beneath her boot and she brought it up, hammering it down again. This time, Danny fell still and his head dipped to one side.

Petal did not stop, however. She continued to tear and pull and more blood jetted like geysers from the various wounds.

"Enough, Petal!" Poppy said, but the determined Rottweiler carried on. "Enough," she said again, taking hold of her collar and pulling her back. The canine finally relented. She sat, staring at her victim with blood tinting her teeth crimson.

Taki continued to straddle Danny's body. Her eyes were wide and she struggled to believe the sequence of events that had led to this moment. "We need a tourniquet," she said.

"What?" Poppy replied.

"We need a tourniquet. He's going to bleed out."

"You were going to shoot him a minute ago."

It was true, but the heat of battle had chilled and she was returning to her normal self a little. Anger and hatred had flared. In that split second, she had wanted him dead. She lifted his still motionless body, surprising Poppy with her strength, then removed his jacket as the blood continued to spurt. She tore the left arm from his Savile Row shirt and proceeded to wrap and tie it around his right upper arm, stemming the flow. "That should tide him over until we can get him seen to."

"Seen to?"

"Maybe one of his thugs can get him to the hospital or something."

"You think the hospital's still open?"

"I … I don't know. It would have to be, wouldn't it? I mean, there'll be all those patients. They couldn't just lock them all in or turf them out, could they?"

"I don't know."

"No. Me neither now I come to think about it."

"I really shouldn't have done that," Poppy said, looking at the deformed and bloody nose spread over much more of Danny's face than it used to be.

"He had it coming."

"Yeah, but this won't end well."

"What do you mean?"

"I mean he's a psycho, his dad's an even bigger psycho, and neither of them are going to forget about this."

"You really know how to put a girl's mind at ease, don't you?"

"What are we going to do, Taki?"

"I don't know."

*

"That's the last of it," BD said, slapping down the final bag of compost in the back of the open van.

"Oh, really?" Derek replied. "That's such a shame. I was having a bloody ball standing out here keeping watch for you all while there are a million bloody extras from some Bela Lugosi film lurking in the shadows nearby. Are you sure there's nothing else? Maybe we could take up the carpet from the living room or the lino from the kitchen. I know. Why don't you go and grab the bloody washing machine and put that in the back of the van too?"

"He's something, isn't he?" Deano asked, looking at Tess.

"He's something alright."

"Talk about me while I'm standing right here, why don't you?" Derek muttered.

"I got these from the loft," Nune said, throwing in three black plastic bags.

"What are they?"

"Sleeping bags. We tried to go camping once."

"Tried?" Tess asked.

"It was not for us."

"Too right," Derek agreed. "A mini bar and room service. That's how you spend a holiday. Not freezing cold with nothing separating you and the night sky but a piece of bloody canvas."

"You don't have the tent to go with it?" Deano asked.

"Moths. There were more holes than material. But the

bags are okay."

"Alright." He looked towards Hagop. "When we—"

"What is that sound?" Nune asked, interrupting him.

"You don't want to know."

"I do. What is it?"

"It's the infected," BD answered.

"But…."

"Don't think about it," Deano said. "There's obviously a build-up of them not too far away. The one saving grace is that if noise attracts these things, they're going to be drawn to that sound and not us." He turned back to Hagop. "So, like I said, noise draws these things. When we set off from here, I don't want to stop until we're at the yard. I don't care what you see and, trust me, you might see all sorts. You just keep going. You put your foot down and you stay behind us. Okay?"

"Yes, Deano."

"Good." He looked around at the assembled faces. He was grateful for the fact that they'd managed to load the van without seeing any infected, but he was not under the illusion that it was anything beyond a piece of good luck. They were not out of danger. There was little doubt that when the engines began they would attract any beasts within earshot. His one hope was that they wouldn't lead too many back to the yard. "Let's go."

21

Poppy and Taki were still in shock, still staring down at Danny's unconscious body, when their worst fear came true.

"Danny? Danny? Where are you?"

The words made their blood turn to ice. Here behind the bus they had some cover, but if Danny wasn't found, they'd have everyone looking for him within five minutes.

"What are we going to do?" Poppy whispered.

"One way or another, they're going to find him. One way or another, this is going to come out," the other woman replied.

"I'm scared."

"Yeah. You're not the only one."

"Danny? Danny? The boys reckon there's stuff missing. They want to know what to do. Danny?"

"Shit, shit, shit," Taki hissed.

"Danny?"

The voice was getting closer with each call and both women's stomachs were churning. Petal letting out a short, sharp bark did nothing to relieve the tension.

"Quiet girl," Poppy pleaded, crouching down by her side, desperately trying to comfort her in an attempt to prevent any further noise.

The seconds ticked on and they were convinced the danger had passed for the moment when a plodding, overweight figure emerged from around the corner of the bus. "Danny?" His eyes widened as he saw his boss's bloodied frame on the ground.

"It's not what it looks like, Splodge," Poppy said, standing once more.

The other man just continued to gawp. "He was going to shoot the dog," Taki said, not knowing Splodge but hoping it would incense him as much as it had incensed the pair of them.

Splodge finally broke his gaze and looked towards the two women. "He'll kill you for this," was all he could say before a groan dragged all their eyes back down to Danny's slowly rousing body.

Taki didn't know what to do. This was a nightmare to end all nightmares. "Shit!"

*

The echo of the motors combined with the van engine seemed way louder than they had done at any time before that day. It was as if some magic spell had amplified them to make sure that their sound rang out over the entire city.

In truth, it was because so many other places had fallen silent. The white noise that usually played accompaniment to daily life was absent. There was no traffic, no ambulance sirens, no radios and TVs blaring through open windows, no children playing in the streets, no drunks shouting at pigeons from park benches, no planes flying overhead, no squeaky washing carousels turning in the wind, no gates slamming shut and mothers calling after their children. The familiar life, the life from before, was gone. And at that moment in time, it felt like it was just them and the infected.

The one light on the horizon was that the rising sounds of the infected from somewhere not too far away was drowned by the noise they were creating, but the flip side was they were moving targets for any creatures still in the area.

"SHIT!" Deano cried as if this realisation had actually manifested the three beasts that came out of a side street just as they were passing. He swerved, as did BD on the bike behind, but this was the first time the two former shop owners had witnessed these monsters close up.

*

"HAGOP!" Nune's desperate, fear-filled cry was accompanied by her pointing as if somehow her husband had managed to miss the sight of the swerving bikes and the things that had made them deviate from course.

His fingers were wrapped tightly around the wheel and, subsequently, his own swerve was sharper. The tyres screeched and multiple deafening thuds boomed against the side of the van as the three beasts collided with it.

"Jesus Christ!" he hissed, squeezing the wheel even tighter as he stared in the wing mirror to witness the trio bouncing off the body of the van and collapsing back onto the road before, one by one, rallying, jumping to their feet and beginning their pursuit.

"Oh, my God, Haggy. We should go back. We should go back home. It isn't safe to be out here."

"It's too late for that." His heart felt like it was going to jump out of his chest. This was a bad day, a horrible day, for so many reasons. Not least of which, he felt like he was failing his wife. He had not been able to protect their business, their home, their livelihood, and now that he was out here on the streets, he felt even further out of his element, more of a failure, as the fear ratcheted up inside him. On top of all of that, he had no idea where their son was or even if he was safe. "I'm sorry, Nune," he said, reaching out apologetically and taking her hand.

She grasped it and brought it up to her lips as he pushed down on the accelerator even harder.

*

"FUUUCCCKKK!" Deano blurted as five more infected stormed out of a side street up ahead. He and BD, who were riding side by side, cast fleeting looks towards each other before veering left onto the pavement and speeding up in the hope that the creatures would follow and preoccupy themselves with them so as not to encumber the van's passage.

"WHAT THE BLOODY HELL ARE YOU PLAYING AT?" Deano could just about hear Derek's screamed words from below his visor as the bike sped up.

The creatures followed the bait heading to the pavement rather than running down the centre of the street. Deano and BD accelerated even more and a scream pierced the sound of the roaring motors as one of the creature's fingers brushed Tess's jacket as the bike powered by.

It was over in an instant and the speed the bikes were going ensured there was no hope of the pursuers catching them, but all their hearts sank as they glanced in the mirrors and saw the rabid monsters pivot, halting their chase as quickly as it had started and storming through the gap in two parked cars back out onto the street.

*

"WAAAHHH!" Hagop's cry was laced with surprise as much as terror. It had seemed as though the small pack was steadfast in its pursuit of the bikes, but, just like that, they had veered.

BOOM!
THUD!
CRASH!

"HAGOP!" His wife's horror-filled scream magnified the tension even further as the windscreen shattered into bloody spiderwebs. The van shook as it went over at least one body and the force tore the wheel out of the driver's hands.

The van veered wildly, and another crash, this time much louder, threw the two occupants forward, their bodies straining against the seatbelts. Despite not having a clear view, it was obvious they'd collided with one of the parked cars by the side of the road before rolling into the middle of the street.

The engine had been rendered silent, but the sounds of the creatures filled the void it left. They feverishly began to smash and hammer against the body and windows.

"Oh, God! Oh, Christ," Hagop whispered, turning the key in the ignition in a desperate attempt to restart the vehicle.

The engine coughed and spluttered like an eighty-year-old chain smoker, but it didn't start.

"Hagop!"

It was amazing how one word could mean so many things. *I'm scared. What are we going to do? We're finished. Our son.* Those thoughts and more were encapsulated in the speaking of his name, and at that moment, he didn't have a response.

*

BD and Deano had manoeuvred back off the pavement and both bikes were pointing in the direction they'd come from, but for the moment, neither moved. The riders just watched as two more infected emerged from around a corner to join the pair still left standing after the collision.

"They're going to get in there. They're going to break the glass at some point," BD said.

A door to a nearby house opened and a woman emerged, staring down the street towards the disaster that was about to happen. "Somebody's got to do something," she said as a man came up behind her.

"There's no hope for them," he said, about to pull the door shut then turning to look at the bikers. "If you've got somewhere to go, you should get there. Things are only going to get worse."

"Get off the bike," Deano ordered.

"Wh-what the hell are you talking about?" Derek asked.

"Get off the bike." He looked across at Tess. "Get off the bike and get inside."

"Deano. What are you—"

"Just do as I say, now!" he ordered, cutting Tess off.

"Wait a minute," the man said. "We don't want any part of—"

Deano's head shot towards him and his eyes stopped him before his words needed to. "You'll let them inside. Or we're going to have a fucking problem."

"Billy. That's Deano Duncan," the woman who had originally opened the door suddenly whispered.

The man looked towards the figure who had given him the command; then he turned to Derek and Tess, beckoning them as he spoke.

"Come on, quick. Get in."

*

A shuddering breath left Nune's lips as the four creatures continued to hammer and pound against the van. Beyond the beast hammering at the driver-side window, another came into view, charging across the road towards them. "We will be surrounded soon."

Hagop turned looking into the back of the van for anything he could use to defend them. They had been forced to escape so quickly that they hadn't thought of anything beyond getting from A to B and they certainly hadn't considered a confrontation with these things, but now it seemed as though the lack of planning would be the end for them.

BANG!

The fifth creature finally reached them, throwing its weight at the door. Its pallid face pressed up against the glass. Its mouth opened and closed revealing red-tinged teeth contrasting wildly against the grey gums.

Another loud thud and an even louder scream from Nune as one of the macabre quintet smashed against the passenger window. The growls seemed to surround the van, blocking out any other noise.

Hagop tried to start the engine again, but it was no good. Then, suddenly, the sound that they had each dreaded began to fill the van. It was that of the windscreen beginning to cave as two beasts smashed and pressed against it.

"We're finished!" Nune sobbed.

*

Neither man was the hero type. Neither wanted to be there. Neither wanted to be heading back into the fray, but neither would be able to live with the guilt of doing nothing.

They accelerated towards the vehicle with no real plan. *This is crazy. This is seriously fucking crazy,* BD thought as he drew level with his father on the Triumph. They were already making considerable noise, but the creatures were unrelenting in their hunt. They continued to bang and pound, trying to break into the van as if it were a giant Easter egg.

The windscreen collapsed beneath the smashing hands of the two attackers at the front of the vehicle and they began to scramble, desperately trying to gain access to the living, breathing, screaming, crying prey within.

Oh shit!

*

Neither Hagop nor Nune were sure why they still had their seatbelts on, but both hurried to disengage them as the windscreen was stoved inwards.

"Get into the back. Get into the back," Hagop ordered and they both frantically slid over the seats, trying their hardest to avoid the determined reaching, grasping fingers of the invading hands.

They flopped into the cargo compartment, thankfully onto sacks of compost rather than logs, but pain and discomfort were the last of their considerations for the time being. They gathered themselves, kneeling and peeking over the headrests as first two creatures, then the other three, vied for position to climb into the van.

The beasts dug their claw-like fingers into the dashboard desperate to gain purchase so they could get access into the van as their growls reverberated beyond the cab and into the cargo area.

Hagop and Nune could see the advancing bikes, but both were resigned to the fact that there was nothing Deano and BD could do but become victims themselves.

Hagop suddenly shuffled a little further into the van but returned in a matter of seconds with one of the net sacks of chopped logs. He tore into it, grabbing a hefty clump of wood. He hurled it towards the creature who had managed to grasp hold of part of the steering column. It clomped against the beast's head, and it slumped back, disappearing out of the van once more while the others continued to jostle.

Hagop grabbed another piece of wood as did his wife and they both readied themselves for the next would-be assailant. Sadness rivalled their fear as they knelt side by side. Their life together had been filled with happiness and so many adventures, so much love, but now it was about to come to an end at the hands of monsters that belonged in horror stories.

*

The father and son lowered their kickstands in virtual synchronicity. Despite the sound their bikes had made roaring back to the van, the five creatures seemed mesmerised by Hagop and Nune, unable to drag their eyes away for just a moment. If they had, they'd have seen that two far more easily accessible targets were creeping up behind them.

Deano and BD paused about fifteen metres back. The infected were relentless, clawing and scrambling and desperately trying to gain access. The occasional log would fly out from the gap where the windscreen had been, but nothing was stopping them.

"Dad," BD whispered, glancing to his left. About half a dozen more creatures were heading up the street. Presumably, their attention had been won by the sound of the bikes and now they were coming to find the source. "Whatever we're going to do, we'd better do it fast."

Deano took a breath and shook his head. "What the fuck is wrong with me?" He ran forward with the crowbar raised high. The fast and sudden action took his son by surprise, but he followed suit, grasping the baseball bat with both hands as he caught up with his father.

Deano grabbed one of the creatures by the collar, dragging it back from the van. He brought his weapon down with a speed and strength he didn't know himself capable of. The heavy metal implement vibrated in his hand as the beast dropped to the ground. Already congealed blood and skull fragments dripped from the crowbar as another creature turned towards him.

It was about to pounce when BD performed a pinch hit against the side of the monster's head. Its whole body smashed into the front of the van, slithering down as two more of the creatures leapt, one at each of the living assailants.

The father and son jumped back, causing the beasts to overstretch, giving the pair a moment's respite to prepare themselves for the next round.

The fifth creature was well on the way to gaining access into the van despite the barrage of chopped logs that continued to fly.

BD swung again. This time, his target shifted and the bat slapped loudly against the side of its neck. It was enough to knock the monster off balance, however, and it went flailing to the ground.

Deano jumped back once more, giving himself the extra second he needed to hammer down the crowbar. It juddered in his hand and up his arm while his victim crumpled to the tarmac. BD's attacker began to rally again and now Deano was in a better position to deal with it than his son.

"I've got this. Get the one in the van." He raised his weapon, glimpsing the approaching pack from the other street. *Shit! Shit! Shit!*

BD heard the metallic thud as his father sprang into action and he was about to grab the final creature's jacket when a missile from the interior of the van shot towards him like a cannonball.

He ducked and it whistled over his head. He tried again, this time grasping the monster's clothing and yanking it out of the van. BD brought his leg around quickly, knocking the creature's legs from beneath it. Then he stamped down, pinning its neck to the tarmac as it writhed and struggled. He brought the bat up high then down hard and fast. The echoing crack should have been a prelude to silence, but the drumming feet of the approaching pack was getting louder by the second.

"Come on. MOVE!" Deano ordered, gesturing to the two occupants of the vehicle.

They both dove over the seats, adrenaline still coursing through their veins. They each grabbed a bag of belongings understanding that any hopes they had of driving to the yard in the van were well and truly over.

They barged open the van doors and followed the two men to their bikes as the pack, which had now swelled to at least a dozen, finally reached the junction. There were already bags carefully straddled over the seats and it was obvious the journey to the scrapyard was going to be anything but comfortable, but just making it to the end of the road would be a victory for the moment.

BD and Deano leapt onto the bikes and made the engines growl. The second they felt the bodies of their passengers press against them they raised the kickstands and set off in a haze of burning rubber as they did one-eighties and powered back up the street.

They mounted the pavement once more and it was obvious that Tess, Derek and the others had been watching the events unfold from a crack in the door. The old man and his carer rushed from the entrance and the solid uPVC barrier slammed shut.

Neither Deano nor BD needed to look in their mirrors to understand how close the creatures were. They could hear their pounding soles against the pavement, but more than that, they could see the petrified gazes of Derek and Tess as they looked beyond the bikes.

"Get on. Get on the bikes for fuck's sake!" It was BD this time whose panic got the better of him. Hagop and Nune shuffled back on the bench seats as far as they could, allowing Tess and Derek, backpacks and all, to slot in the middle.

"GO! GOOO!" Tess screamed the second she was on. A shiver of guilt ran through her realising her fear had caused her to shout the order without even knowing whether Derek was in position or not, but as she turned her head, she found she needn't have worried. The old man was more than spritely when his life depended on it.

The pack of creatures loomed like giants in the mirrors as

BD and Deano cast them a final glance before revving their engines once more. Everyone held their breath for a second as the pause between intention and action seemed to drag on for a lifetime. There were mere centimetres between the first beasts' outstretched fingers and the jackets of Hagop and Nune as the bikes finally started moving.

The increasing wind against those whose faces were uncovered on the bikes felt like they were being brushed by the hand of freedom. The more wind the faster they travelled and the further they were from those hellish things. Deano looked in the mirror again to see that even more infected had joined the pack and now they were all chasing them down. But there was still some way to go and the only hope was that, somewhere in between, their attention would be diverted again.

BD felt his mother's arms tighten around him. He felt her head press against his back. When he'd set off from the yard that morning, he'd had no idea what awaited him and his father. Now he understood. This was the end of all things. This was the dawning of a new age. Curfew or not. There was no coming back from this.

22

Taki and Poppy had done the only thing they could think of doing when Danny had begun to rouse and Splodge warned them of what was likely to happen. They ran. Of course, before they set off at a sprint leaving a bewildered henchman and the battered and bleeding body of his boss behind, Taki had swooped down and grabbed Danny's gun and the one she had been carrying for all the good it had done. But she thought it might work well as a bluff when they got into another tight spot.

Something is better than nothing.

Petal remained with them stride for stride. They'd known the dog for just one day, but she'd already become their protector. That's the thing with dogs. They have a sense of people. They know their own. Taki and Poppy were lost souls, two strangers thrown together at the end of the world. Petal understood that. She understood that they were now part of her pack too. They were no longer lost. They had one another.

"We can't run around here forever, Poppy. They're going to find us."

"Maybe we can find a good place to lie low until Deano gets back."

"What difference is that going to make?"

"Deano won't let him hurt us."

"There are six of them and they're probably all armed. What is he going to do?"

"He's got a way has Deano. People listen to him."

"That might be so. But we don't even know if he's coming back. They've been hours. Expecting some knight in shining armour to save us isn't a viable plan. We need to figure something out for ourselves."

"Like what?"

"I don't know. I'm working on it."

*

When Danny had begun to come around, his senses returned quickly. He heard the muted conversation. He heard the sound of running feet. And then he felt the presence of Splodge kneeling by his side.

"Get me up," he ordered as pain surged through him. He coughed, clearing some of the blood that had gathered in the back of his throat. Then, when he was on his feet, he looked at his arm. "Fuck!"

"We need to get you seen to, Danny."

"Yeah. But we need to find those two bitches and that fucking mutt first."

"Um … I dunno, Danny. Your arm looks pretty bad."

"I'll live. Can't say the same for them." He looked around the ground. "Did they take my fucking piece? You let them run off with my gun?"

"It all happened so quick, Danny. I wanted to get you some help, but before I knew what was going on, they were out of here."

"Fuck me. If you had half a brain in that head of yours, you'd be dangerous. You couldn't do both things at once?"

"I'm sorry."

He shook his head angrily. "Give us your piece."

The big man handed over his Glock 17. Vig had scored a small consignment of weapons and ammo that were heading to Portsmouth a couple of weeks before. The Glock 17s were among them and many of the gang were equipped with them.

Splodge did as he was asked, a little concerned that the weapon might be pointed at him. Danny had a notorious temper. He also liked to show off. It wasn't out of the realm of possibility that he'd put one in Splodge's head just for the sake of a good anecdote to finish the story about the time two women got the upper hand.

"I'm sorry, Danny."

"You've already said." Danny was a mess. It hurt to move the fingers on his hand and he wondered if the dog had done some nerve damage as it attempted to shred his upper arm. "Fuck!"

"Is it painful?"

"What the fuck do you think, you fucking … full-on fucking fucktard?"

Splodge shrank back a little. It wasn't unusual for Danny and others to put him down, but the venom in the other man's words was far greater than usual.

"What do you want me to do?"

Danny thought for a moment. "Get everyone to the entrance. I want to make sure they don't leave here."

"Are … are you going to kill them?"

"What business is it of yours what I'm going to do?"

Splodge shook his head. "None, boss. I was just asking," he said, starting to walk away.

"Yeah. I'll kill them. Eventually." He watched the rotund figure disappear around the corner then winced and took a closer look at his arm. "Fuck!"

*

"Maybe we can hide in one of the vehicles or something," Poppy said as they continued through the yard.

"What is it you don't understand? They will find us eventually." Taki had placed Danny's weapon in the back of her jeans and now looked at the one she had tried to use earlier. "This thing," she said, using her thumb to flick the safety. "This is probably one of those things. Y'know. Like what you see on TV. The safety switch or something. I bet that's why it didn't fire."

"I don't know. I don't know anything about guns."

"It's time to start learning," Taki replied, pulling the other one from the back of her jeans and handing it to Poppy.

"What do you expect me to do with this?" she asked, looking at it with horror on her face.

"What do you think?"

"I couldn't shoot anyone."

"Listen to me." They had been up and down several of the rows looking for some clue as to what to do next, but it was words that were important for the moment. "This is real, Poppy. This is happening. I mean, forget what's going on outside those gates. That's a nightmare for later. Those guys are going to come looking for us and it's going to be bad."

Poppy stared at the gun again and started to cry. "I should never have opened my mouth. I should have just stayed quiet and none of this would be happening."

"Yeah, well. There's always a price to pay for doing the right thing."

*

"You've finished? Where are the vehicles? What's going on?" Lili was more than a little confused when five of the six men who had arrived in the lorries appeared in the courtyard outside the Portakabin. Aldo and Rocky, who had been guarding the entrance with their mother, cast each other concerned glances. There was no logical explanation as to why the men would be leaving a job half done.

Splodge looked almost apologetic as he spoke. "Danny's orders."

"What's Danny's orders?" Lili demanded. "What the hell's happening?"

"I'll tell you what's going on." The voice came before the man and Danny appeared from around a corner. All eyes widened other than Splodge's as they saw his wounds and the paleness of his skin. It was obvious he'd lost a lot of blood, but that did nothing to quell the hatred welling within him. "You're all on my shit list is what's going on." He turned to Aldo and Rocky. "You think it's okay to hide a fucking grass? What planet are you living on? You are all in a world of fucking trouble."

"What are you talking about?" Lili asked.

"I'll tell you what I'm fucking talking about. That Poppy bitch squealed. She seriously tried to screw with me and we're taking her and that other one back to the club." He turned to Aldo and Rocky. "The pair of you are coming too. There's no place for narcs or their fucking helpers in this organisation."

"I don't know anything about narcs. I don't know anything about much but what's going on out there." She looked towards the other men. "The world is coming to an end and all you're interested in is some childish vendetta. What is wrong with you?"

"Childish vendetta? LOOK!" he ordered, gesturing to his upper arm. "Look what they did to me."

Lili shrugged. "I'll admit I didn't think either of them had teeth that sharp."

Another flare of fury lit Danny's face and he almost ran towards her. At the same time, Aldo and Rocky stepped forward, protecting their mother on both sides. It didn't matter what happened to them, but if Danny laid a finger on her, that would be a whole new ball game. The other men just stood watching the scene play out.

"I don't know who you think you are, but nobody makes fun of me."

Lili shrugged. "Maybe not to your face, but I bet they have a ball behind your back."

He clenched his left hand into a fist and Aldo took another step forward as the sound of roaring motors sliced through the mounting tension. It was the first significant noise any of them had heard from the streets outside for some time and it was impossible to ignore.

It got louder until screeching tyres announced the arrival of the two bikes at the gate.

"GET THESE THINGS OPEN!" Deano yelled and, almost forgetting what was unfolding between Danny and his mother, Aldo ran to the gates, fumbling in his pocket for the keys. He opened them wide and immediately noticed a single creature that had been drawn to the sound charging towards the yard as the bikes drove through.

No sooner had he shut the gates and clicked the padlock than the beast flung itself at the sturdy barrier.

"Jesus!" one of the men cried out. It was clear from the expressions on the others' faces that they all shared the same horror.

Aldo jumped back as the thing tried to reach for him then remembered himself and ran to grab one of the spears leaning against the wall. He watched for a moment, acclimatising himself to the fear once more, before plunging the point through the creature's eye. He withdrew the weapon just as quickly and the beast dropped.

"You may as well stay there," Deano said, climbing off the bike. "There was a small army of those things trailing us not so long back. It wouldn't surprise me if they showed up here."

"Nice of you to fucking join us," Danny said, oblivious to the other man's words, oblivious to the danger they were all in.

Deano threw a look towards the bikes to see the rest of the new arrivals dismounting, but BD was already by his side. It was obvious something was going on and the heightened sense of danger awareness that they'd both shared since setting out earlier that day was still in full flow. "What's happening?" Deano asked, turning back to the other man and glaring at the wound on his upper right arm before glimpsing the gun and then finally staring him straight in the eyes.

"Oh, I think you know what's happening. You've been hiding a grass. And that's like being a grass yourself."

Deano's gaze turned to a glare. "I think you'd better watch your fucking mouth, Danny. Don't you?"

Tick.

Tick.

Tick.

"Tell me you haven't been keeping her here and me finding her round the back of that old bus was all just a coincidence."

"I don't think you understand the gravity of what's happening outside."

"Oh, I understand. I understand plenty."

Deano's eyes drifted to the other men then back to Vig's son. "What are you doing here, anyway?"

"We came for the merch that was dropped off this morning."

Deano's right eye twitched a little. "Already?"

"Change of plan. Dad's decided to open a cash and carry, hasn't he? Not that it's any concern of yours." There was a condescending tone behind the words and an arrogant smile bled onto the younger man's face.

"Never one to miss an opportunity to make money, your dad, is he?"

"Oh, I'm sorry. I must have missed the registered charity sign at the gates when I came in here."

Deano's brain was running at a hundred miles an hour. *The supplies.* He'd been counting on those. They were the things that were going to get them through in the short to medium term. They were the thing that was going to give them some small chance of riding out this initial storm.

"Hey, look. I don't deny I've made plenty of cash over the years and not all of it was squeaky, but I never bled my own kind. I never took from those who didn't have enough."

"Oh yeah. Saint Deano. You're famous far and wide. I think they've put up a plaque for you in the local orphanage."

Despite Deano's past, he had started to make recompense since getting out. There weren't any plaques up, nor would there ever be, but he'd become a silent benefactor to many causes in the area. After all, the measure of a person was what they did when no one was looking and he'd done plenty since getting out. But sainthood would never be something he'd have to think about. If there was a god in Heaven and a devil in Hell, he'd be burning with Vig and the others despite everything he'd done in recent times. But he was trying to make up for the past.

Deano turned towards the other men. "It's getting worse out there minute by minute. There's—"

"Don't fucking talk to them. We're having a conversation, you and me. Now, this is how it's going to play out. You, your little Wop helpers here and those two bitches that are in hiding somewhere in this yard are all going to take a trip to see my dad. I don't think he's going to be too happy when he knows what you've done."

"Don't take this the wrong way," BD said, cutting Deano off before his father could respond. "But have you suffered some kind of brain damage? Have you any grasp of what's happening? It's—"

Danny shot a look towards the younger man, facing off as his eyes burned holes into his head. "You'd better watch your mouth, son. You might be a civvy, but that don't mean you can go shooting your—"

"Back off!" BD growled, pushing hard against the other man's chest and making him stumble.

"Don't ever lay your fucking hands on me," Danny hissed, raising the Glock 17 and pointing it square at BD's head.

"No! Please!" Tess cried. Ever since climbing off the bike, she, like everyone else present, had been mesmerised by the unfolding drama, but now that her son was actually in harm's way and the gravity of the situation became painfully clear, she moved forward too.

"You don't move. Nobody move," Danny said, pointing the gun from one person to the next.

Tick.

Tick.

Tick.

"Look," Deano said, putting his hands up placatingly. "Everybody needs to just take a breath." He had tucked the crowbar into his belt next to his hip for easy access on the journey to the yard and now the cold metal dug into him, reminding him how useless it was against a gun.

"You're not the one giving orders around here. I'm the one giving orders and this has gone on long enough. What's going to happen next is you're going to call those slags, get them here, and we're all going to go for a little ride to see my dad and this'll get cleared up once and for all."

"It's a war zone out there," BD protested, taking over again.

"You're not paying attention. It's a war zone in here, boy." He turned to Splodge. "Go get some zip ties from the lorry."

Tick.

Tick.

Tick.

A sudden crash made them all turn towards the gates to see one, three, six, ten creatures then more hammer and smash at the barrier causing gasps of fear and consternation to circulate through most of those present, but not Deano, BD or Danny. They were in a different place for the time being.

"They probably heard you shouting. You might want to work on that," Deano said.

"I'm not about to take survival tips from a dead man."

"Don't you think we should do something about those things?" Splodge asked, staring beyond his boss to the gate.

"They're not getting in here any time soon. Now, do as I fucking say and go get those ties."

Tick.

Tick.

Tick.

"Please," Tess begged. "Please don't do this. Just take whatever it is you've come for and leave us."

"Shut it!"

"Drop your gun!"

All heads turned once more. Taki was at the corner of the Portakabin. Half her body was shielded but her weapon was there for all to see clearly, pointing in the direction of Danny.

He reached out, grabbing Tess, wrapping his left arm around her neck and using her as a shield. He swivelled towards the Portakabin and started shooting, oblivious to the danger that put them all in.

Tick.

Tick.

Tick.

BOOM!

Even after all this time, and despite the rivers of hurt that had flowed between them, Deano's instinct was always to look after Tess. He'd been a shitty father and an even worse husband, but when it came to anyone threatening the people who had been closest to him in this life, a switch flicked.

There was no thought process between Danny grabbing Deano's ex-wife and his fingers seizing the crowbar. There was no thought process between him raising said crowbar over his head and swinging it down with a speed that made the makeshift weapon blur. There was only instinct.

The shots ended as quickly as they began. Danny's left arm dropped, immediately releasing Tess, who rushed away, desperate not to be grabbed again. His right hand, still with the gun in it, fell to his side and Danny staggered back one, two, three paces before finally dropping the Glock.

He remained upright as a crimson stream emerged from his thick black hair and ran down the centre of his forehead. Despite the growing rabid army of creatures at the gates, nobody could do anything but stare at the spectacle unfolding before them.

Finally, Danny collapsed face down like a cut tree. There was a loud thud as his body smashed against the ground, but still nobody moved.

It was Deano who broke the spell. He dropped the crowbar and stooped down to pick up the Glock.

"Listen to me," he said, turning to Splodge and the other five men without missing a beat. "I don't have a beef with you, but those supplies are staying here. Any of you want to make something of that then have at it. Any of you want to spill your guts to Vig about what went down here then feel free." He pointed to the creatures at the gate. "Today is just the start. It's only going to get worse from here on in. All Vig is worried about is Vig. He's still thinking in pounds and pence. You think the Bank of fucking England will be open for business tomorrow? 'Cause I don't. The only currencies that count now are food, water, shelter, heat, and watching one another's backs." He held up the gun. "These are more of a liability than a help. If there's one thing I learnt out there, it's that noise is not our friend. You stay out of sight and out of earshot of these things and you stand a chance."

"B-but what do we say to Vig?" Splodge asked, still unable to comprehend that his old life, the life from before today, was gone.

"Who says you say anything to Vig, Splodge? Who says you even go back there?" He turned to the other men. "Listen to me. None of us know how the next few days are going to play out. What I do know is that there's strength in numbers. You saw that emergency alert. We're by ourselves. We need to get organised. I'm opening this place up. Yeah, it's not going to be the lap of luxury, but I'll make sure there's shelter, food and warmth if you want to bring your families or loved ones here."

"Vig won't be happy," one of the other men said.

"I really couldn't give a fuck. Every man for himself doesn't work in a situation like this."

"Could I bring my dad, Deano?" Splodge asked, almost apologetically.

"Yeah. Course you can."

"You know he's gone a bit … funny, don't you?"

"I know, Splodge. I only hope that when I go that way I have someone like you to look after me."

"No, but I mean he won't be able to do much. He won't be able to help out or anything."

"I realise that, Splodge. But I've known you long enough to understand that you'll work twice as hard to make up for it."

"I can't see my missus agreeing to come and stay in a pissing scrapyard," one of the other men said.

A clang chimed and they all turned towards the gate to see Aldo and Rocky, who had started to put down the massing creatures one by one using the spears they'd fashioned from the fence.

"I get that," Deano said, turning back to the man who'd spoken. "I can't say Tess was really made up when I told her. But the offer's there. I strongly suggest you try to convince them. This compound is pretty secure. But if you don't want to, then take some food with you, and you know where to come for more when you run out. If you can get to us, that is."

"What do you mean?"

It was BD who took over. He didn't know these men, but his dad was right. There was strength in numbers and although these were people he'd have stayed clear of in the time before, he understood that if they worked for Vig they knew how to fight and they were a resource not to be sniffed at. "He means that on our way here we heard something. We didn't know what it was at first, but then we figured it out. It was those things. There might have been hundreds. Hell, there might have been thousands for all we know. We couldn't see them, but we could hear them. Wherever they were, there was no hope for any people in that area.

"Time is running out to get our ducks in a row. You don't want to stay here; I get that. You don't want to bring your families here; I get that too. But whatever you decide to do, make it quick."

"Deano. The trucks are already half loaded," Splodge said.

"I can give you vehicles. If there's one thing we're not short of here, it's vehicles."

"Deano!"

He turned quickly and a set of Audi keys were already flying towards him. His hand rushed up to catch them. "You sure?" he asked Rocky.

"We've got no plans to head out again," he replied before turning back to the gate and spearing another of the potential invaders.

Deano tossed the keys to Splodge. "The keys are already in the Connect," he said, nodding in the direction of the maroon Ford van.

"You serious about us coming here, Deano?" Tank asked.

"Yeah, I'm serious. If any of you have been at odds with me before today because of Vig, it's forgotten. I know what it is to be on the payroll. This is bigger than any of that shit." The five men started towards the vehicles. "One last thing," he continued and they all turned back towards him. "We're going to keep those gates clear. That's going to be our job. But I can't tell you what the rest of the city's going to be like. Keep your eyes peeled and your ears open. I hope some of you choose to come back. If you do, there'll be no more slave and master. There's only one thing we have to worry about anymore. It's not plod. It's not the tax man. It's not Vig and it's not even some crew from the top of Old Kent Road. It's the infected." Each of the men nodded slowly as if finally latching on to what was happening.

Deano turned back to the gates to see Lili had joined her two boys and all three of them were putting down the remainder of the pack that had formed. When the last body fell, Aldo removed the padlock and he, Rocky and Lili were joined by BD, Hagop and Nune as they all cleared a path for the two vehicles.

The Audi and the van both turned right onto the main road and Deano stood there for a moment wondering if the occupants had taken heed of anything he'd said or if they were heading back to Vig.

"What do you think they'll do?"

Deano's head shot around to see Poppy standing there. She wasn't watching the vehicles leave; she was staring down at Danny's lifeless corpse.

"I honestly don't know," he replied. "But if they go back to Vig, I'm guessing we've got a war coming."

"That's reassuring." It was Tess's voice that joined the conversation now.

He shook his head. "Don't pay any attention to me. They won't go back to Vig. We're going to be fine."

"We're not going to be fine. We're going to be a long way from fine," she replied as the gates closed once more. "But we'll manage. We'll find a way to manage."

"Well, if it isn't Annie Oakley," Deano said as Taki and Petal gathered around too.

"I suppose I've made life difficult for everyone, haven't I?" Poppy said.

"You haven't made life difficult. Life was difficult long before today. Things just came to a head. That's all."

"What does that mean?" Tess asked.

"Poppy called the bill when she found out Danny was about to roll over a truck full of meds. True to form, a bent copper spilt to Vig and five minutes later, her name goes up in lights."

"You did the right thing," Tess said, placing her finger under Poppy's chin and raising the younger woman's face to look at her. "It took a lot of bravery did that."

She shook her head. "I don't know about that. I just…. A lot of old people depend on those drugs."

"You don't have to tell me, sweetheart. I'm a carer. I know how important they are."

"Nonsense," a voice piped up from behind. "Drugs are just a way for pharmaceutical companies to get wealthy and doctors to receive nice spivs. Brandy. That's what you need. The stuff's a bloody cure-all."

"Oh yes, Derek," Tess replied. "It's a cure-all. Shall we ask your liver how much of a cure-all it is?"

"There's nothing wrong with my liver."

"I'm not going to have this argument. Not now."

"Well. I suppose out of respect for the dead and so on," he replied, looking down at the body they were all standing around. "Although…."

"Although what?"

"Well, he did possess the air of a complete twat who had it coming."

Deano started laughing.

"It's not funny," Tess protested. "I mean, I didn't like the man, but he's dead."

"He used you as a human shield and he was trying to shoot at the young woman there. Good riddance to bad rubbish, I say."

"Too right," Lili agreed, walking up to them and spitting on Danny's corpse. "Piece of shit."

"Long time, no see, Lili," Tess said, smiling.

"Long time, no see," Lili replied and the two women embraced.

"Can I make a suggestion?" said BD, coming up behind the small gathering.

"What, Son?" Deano asked.

"I know we've got a tonne to talk about and plan for, but before we do anything else, I think we should get rid of the dead mafioso's body that's lying out here in the open for all to see. I think we should try to find some sidings or something that will block anyone or anything on the outside looking in and I think anybody who's not doing either of those things should head inside because those gunshots from a few minutes ago are going to have any infected in the area hunting their origin."

"Top-notch thinking, young man," Derek said, clapping his hands. "If anybody wants me, I'll be in that hut over there looking for anything that has the appearance or odour of booze."

"Okay," Deano said. "Let's get to work."

EPILOGUE

It had been a long day. The longest day. But everyone had worked like Trojans. Tess, Lili and Nune had done their best to make the temporary accommodation they were sharing somewhere nearing liveable. Derek had tried his hardest not to get in the way and keep his criticisms to a minimum while the rest of them had gone about the tasks of disposing of bodies and fortifying the front gates as best they could.

Aldo and Rocky had operated the mechanical digger somewhere near the centre of the site to create a mass grave where Danny, along with all the infected they'd killed, were buried.

During the course of the day, more creatures had shown up, but not the horde they'd all been dreading.

Splodge had arrived with his father and as many supplies as he could load into the Connect. These included food, a heater, two Calor gas bottles, bedding and one tomato plant in a pot. Most of the small fruits on the vine were still green and it wasn't as if it would bear any significant crop for any of them to consume, but it was a living thing in a wilderness of gravel, dirt, concrete and scrap metal, and that was something.

"I can take over," BD said, pulling up a chair beside his father as he kept a vigil at the gate.

"No. I'm okay. But you can sit a while if you want."

It had been an age since BD had wanted to sit with his father, but the day had been full of surprises and this was the latest one. He found that he did. He did want to sit with him. He glanced back towards the Portakabin and beyond it to the caravan. He knew for a fact there were lights on inside. He knew there were people talking and comforting one another, but there was no sign that was the case. "Yeah," he said eventually. "I'll sit a while."

"Your mum okay?"

"Considering the world's been taken over by a legion of reanimated corpses, I'd say she's positively chipper."

Deano laughed. "She always was a glass-half-full kind of girl was Tess." The sky was overcast and there was very little natural light to see the gates, but even if there was, there wouldn't have been much to see. They had been covered on the inside using a host of materials, from vehicle sidings to tarpaulins. Nobody could see in or out, but that didn't mean that Deano was about to leave the place without a sentry just in case something happened.

"Thanks for today, Dad."

"What do you mean?"

"I mean coming with me to find Mum. I wouldn't have managed it by myself."

Deano thought for a moment. "I don't think you give yourself enough credit, BD. I think you'd have managed just fine."

"I doubt it, but it's nice of you to say."

"I know I've been lousy at showing it, but you and your mum mean more to me than any two people on the planet."

"Well, sure, you can say that now most of them are dead."

Deano chuckled again. "Good point."

They sat in silence for a while before BD continued. "Do you think Vig's going to show up here tomorrow?"

There was a pause before he answered. "I'd be surprised if he didn't. I'm pretty certain none of the boys who were here today went back there. Even if they had an axe to grind with me, they all love Splodge. They'd never do or say anything that might hurt him or his dad. That being said, Vig's nose is going to be itching. He knows Danny would never run out on him and he's got all that merch tied up here. He's going to want that."

"Why do you think he hasn't shown up?"

"Well, the Pleasure Palace is pretty secure, but the area's well built up compared to this place. I mean, half of the buildings around here were set for demolition and redevelopment before the PM's speech. Hell, I'd accepted a bid for the yard."

"What?"

"Yeah. I mean, there's a lot of land. Sure, the drainage is shit and there's a bit of a subsidence issue at the north end, but they gave us a pretty tasty offer. Course, when everything kicked off, that went to shit. But who knows, maybe my old man knew what he was doing when he bought this place all those years ago."

"What were you going to do if you sold?"

"Hang around until my P.O. didn't want to see me any longer and then head to St Ives."

"Cambridge?"

"Cornwall. I bought a little place."

"What, seriously?"

"Yeah."

"You were going to retire?"

"Kind of. I figured I'd done such a bang-up job looking after my wife and kid here, I should probably spread my gift around a little, see who else's life I could fuck up."

BD laughed. "You do have a real talent for that."

"Let's hope it's not hereditary."

"Anyway, you were saying about the Pleasure Palace."

"Yeah. There's a good chance they could be penned in. There could be infected swarming from the estate for all we know. That's the only reason I can think of why he hasn't shown already."

"He could be dead."

"I'm not that fucking lucky, Son."

"You were close once."

"Once."

"What happened?"

"I realised he was only ever concerned about himself. I'm

a piece of shit, BD, but he takes that to a whole different level."

"You're not a piece of shit, Dad. You're infuriating, and you've disappointed me and broken my heart more times than I can count, but you're not a piece of shit. When I heard you talking to Splodge and the others today, I don't think I've ever been prouder of you."

"Proud? Why?"

"Because you've figured this out. While everybody else is flailing around for answers and trying to figure out what to do next, you've got it sussed."

"I'm not following you."

"You said there's strength in numbers and you're right. There is strength in numbers and we need to build on what we started here today."

"What do you mean?"

"I mean we need to build an army because it sure as hell looks like there's no one else coming to save us."

"I don't get you."

"Curfew started at four o'clock out there. I've heard a few explosions in the distance, but I haven't heard tanks moving through the streets or the sound of marching boots. There's nobody coming to save us, so we need to save ourselves. We need to get as many people as we can inside these gates. We need to prepare for what comes next."

Deano shook his head. "The more people we get in here the less time we have. We've got a lot of supplies, but they'll only last so long."

"So, we get more. We get more supplies, more weapons, more ammo, more people. Strength in numbers, Dad. That's the only way we're going to get through this."

"Fucking hell."

"What?"

"When you sat down, I thought we were going to have a nice little chat about the good old days or something."

"Face it, Dad. There weren't many of them."

"No. I suppose not."

"But there's no reason why there can't still be some good days ahead of us. We have the chance to do something here, to save people, to fight back against these things."

Even though his son didn't see it through the dark, a smile lit Deano's face. BD reminded him of his young self. "That sounds like it's going to require a lot of planning, BD."

"Yeah. Some fathers and sons make Airfix models or go fishing. This can be our project."

Deano laughed. "I think we need to talk it over with the others. Your mum used to get pissed if I decided to go to the pub without telling her. This is a little bigger than that."

"I can guarantee you Mum will be on board with it. As long as you promise to do something to get rid of those bloody rats at the far end of the yard, she'll be good."

Deano stood up. "Right then. I suppose I'd better go and get some kip."

"I thought you said you were okay."

"That was before you decided that two of us were single-handedly going to save mankind. Give me a shout if anything happens. I'll make sure Aldo or Rocky take over from you in a couple of hours."

BD laughed. "Okay."

Deano carried on walking away for a moment but then turned back. "BD."

"What?"

"You weren't the only one who felt proud today."

Silence lingered in the air for a moment before a reply came. "Thanks, Dad. Goodnight."

"Goodnight, Son."

The End

UNSAFE: BOOK 1

A NOTE FROM THE AUTHOR

I hope you enjoyed this book and would be very grateful if you took a minute to leave a review on Amazon.

If you would like to stay informed about what I'm doing, including current writing projects, and all the latest news and release information; these are the places to go:

Join the fan club on Facebook
https://www.facebook.com/groups/127693634504226

Like the Christopher Artinian author page
https://www.facebook.com/safehaventrilogy/

Buy exclusive and signed books and merchandise, subscribe to the newsletter and follow the blog:
https://www.christopherartinian.com/

Follow me on Youtube:
https://www.youtube.com/channel/UCfJymx31VvzttB_Q-x5otYg

Follow me on Amazon
https://amzn.to/2I1llU6

Follow me on Goodreads
https://bit.ly/2P7iDzX

Other books by Christopher Artinian:

Safe Haven: Rise of the RAMs
Safe Haven: Realm of the Raiders
Safe Haven: Reap of the Righteous
Safe Haven: Ice
Safe Haven: Vengeance
Safe Haven: Is This the End of Everything?
Safe Haven: Neverland (Part 1)
Safe Haven: Neverland (Part 2)
Safe Haven: Doomsday
Safe Haven: Raining Blood (Part 1)
Safe Haven: Hope Street
Safe Haven: No Hope in Hell
Safe Haven: War Zone
Safe Haven: Raining Blood (Part 2)
Before Safe Haven: Lucy
Before Safe Haven: Alex
Before Safe Haven: Mike
Before Safe Haven: Jules

The End of Everything: Book 1
The End of Everything: Book 2
The End of Everything: Book 3
The End of Everything: Book 4
The End of Everything: Book 5
The End of Everything: Book 6
The End of Everything: Book 7
The End of Everything: Book 8
The End of Everything: Book 9
The End of Everything: Book 10
The End of Everything: Book 11
The End of Everything: Book 12
The End of Everything: Book 13
The End of Everything: Book 14
Relentless
Relentless 2
Relentless 3
The Burning Tree: Book 1 – Salvation
The Burning Tree: Book 2 – Rebirth
The Burning Tree: Book 3 – Infinity
The Burning Tree: Book 4 – Anarchy
The Burning Tree: Book 5 – Redemption
The Burning Tree: Book 6 – Power (Part 1)
The Burning Tree: Book 7 – Power (Part 2)
Night of the Demons
The Devil's Face
Madhouse

CHRISTOPHER ARTINIAN

Christopher Artinian was born and raised in Leeds, West Yorkshire. Wanting to escape life in a big city and concentrate more on working to live than living to work, he and his family moved to the Outer Hebrides in the north-west of Scotland in 2004, where he now works as a full-time author.

Chris is a huge music fan, a cinephile, an avid reader and a supporter of Yorkshire County Cricket Club. When he's not sitting in front of his laptop living out his next post-apocalyptic/dystopian/horror adventure, he will be passionately immersed in one of his other interests.

Printed in Great Britain
by Amazon